Dedalus Europe
General Editor: Timothy Lane

BE AS CHILDREN

Praise for *Before & During*

'One of the most fascinating books in post-Soviet literature… even twenty years after its publication and translated into English, Sharov's *Before & During* reads as if it were completed yesterday.' Mark Lipovetsky in *The Russian Review*

'If Russian history is indeed a commentary to the Bible, then *Before & During* is an audacious attempt to shine a mystical light on (Russian history), an unusual take on the 20th century's apocalypse that leaves the reader to look for their own explications.' Anna Aslanyan in *The Independent*

'A Menippean satire in which historical reality, in all its irreversible awfulness, is for a moment scrambled, eroticized… and illuminated by hilarious monologues of the dead.'
Caryl Emerson in *The Times Literary Supplement*

'Translation should not strive for perfection, but for excellence. Perfection is impossible, whereas excellence is only nearly impossible. And excellence is what Oliver Ready achieves in his rendering of *Before & During* by Vladimir Sharov. He captures the clear voice and confused mentality of the narrator who is able to love both Christ and Lenin, who prays for the sinner Ivan the Terrible and who tries to unravel the legacy of the Bolsheviks.' Jury of the 2015 *Read Russia Prize*

'*Before & During* is a darkly brilliant book which sometimes ironizes, sometimes genuinely challenges conceits woven through modern Russian history and culture: fleshly resurrection, holy foolishness, erotic utopia and the sexualization of terror.' Muireann Maguire in *Russian Dinosaur*

'Since the late Alexander Solzhenitsyn, no Russian novels have penetrated Western consciousness, and we have had to wait a long time for this one: Vladimir Sharov is 62, and this was first published in Moscow in 1993. Superbly translated by Oliver Ready it is worth the wait, and is the only one of his eight novels to have appeared in English. We should know more of him.'

Canon Michael Bourdeaux in *The Church Times*

'*Before & During* is very much a novel from and of and about Russia, highly allusive and steeped in Russian history and literature. The real-life figures can serve as reassuring touchstones for foreign readers, but there's clearly (and/ or unclearly) much more to it; nevertheless, even just superficially – without closer familiarity with Orthodox and Bolshevik history and creeds, for example – *Before & During* is rewarding, a rare work of fiction that is, on several levels (including literarily and philosophically), provocative as well as simply exhilarating. An impressive achievement.'

M. A. Orthofer in *The Complete Review*

'*Before & During* remains a disorienting read. The novel invokes real historical events and people (Tolstoy, Madame de Staël, Saint John of Kronstadt, Alexander Scriabin and Stalin, among others), swirling them into a phantasmagoric alternative chronology. Stories germinate within other stories, unfolding in astonishing variations.'

Rachel Polonsky in *The New York Review of Books*

'*Before & During* justifies Sharov's place as one of contemporary Russia's most significant literary voices, and Oliver Ready is most deserving as the winner of the 2015 Read Russia Prize for his remarkable English translation of it. The novel's theme that a life is nothing more than others' memories of it may feel bleak, but memories, as witness to our past, also offer hope: that humanity can avoid repeating history's mistakes, that we can free ourselves from committing the same unpardonable crimes against our fellow man.'

Lori Feathers in *Rain Taxi Review*

'Whatever your views on religion, you cannot fail to be impressed by Sharov's undertaking. He has given us a radical view of Russian history, from the early nineteenth century to the present day. He has completely changed the historical facts about major historical figures: Stalin, Mme de Staël, Scriabin, Lenin, Fyodorov, not to mention a bit of Tolstoy and used them to make his point about a Christian Utopia. But this is not a simplistic view of the matter. He sees that it is complicated and he and his characters struggle with it. Reading it as a novel, and not as a religious and political tract, which, of course, you should, it is an outstanding work.'

John Alvey in *The Modern Novel*

'When you put down Vladimir Sharov's books you feel as if you have woken up from a strange but captivating dream. As in all dreams, you visit a reality that has been turned upside down. Oliver Ready's thoughtful translation of *Before & During* and *The Rehearsals* guides us through the Russian past which at times is comically absurd, at times dark and poignant – but always personal.'

Elena Malysheva in *The Forum Magazine*

Praise for *The Rehearsals*

'Sharov, whose historical fantasies allow us to confront not just the facts but also the emotional realities and hidden logic of a tortured past, will not be forgotten.'

Boris Dralyuk in *The Literary Review*

'A good read for fans of Tolstoy, Dostoyevsky and Solzhenitsyn.'

Book Blasts Top Ten Reads for Independent Minds

'Nikon is a compelling mixture of piety, ambition and apocalyptic fervour, and at first it seems as if the novel will centre on his contradictory character. But Sharov, a trained historian, is also ambitious, and skilled at painting the bigger picture. So he leaves Nikon behind to follow the peasant-actors and their descendants right up to the twentieth century as, exiled in Siberia, they remain steadfast in their commitment to the play and its role in catalysing the return of the Messiah. This expanded scale, in conjunction with Sharov's deft handling of allusion and Oliver Ready's nuanced translation, allows the allegorical significance of the narrative to become apparent. As time passes, the peasants' ascribed identity as "apostles", "Jews" or "Romans" becomes their primary allegiance, trapping the community within centuries-long cycles of violence and recrimination that mirror the brutal patterns of Russian and European history.'

Jamie Rann in *The Times Literary Supplement*

'This is a most original novel, and in particular, in the period when they are exiled to Siberia. It is clearly, at least to some degree, an allegory of the situation in the wider world. It is about Russian history, particularly the mid-sixteenth century and the time of the religious reforms in Russia, but also about the Russian Revolution (there cannot be many novels that feature Patriarch Nikon and Beria). It is about Russian character and the nature(s) of the Russian people. I judge novels in many ways but one of the ways that I judge them is whether I think long and hard about them after I have read them and whether I discuss the ideas that they raise with my significant other. This novel passed both those tests with flying colours. It clearly is a first-class novel and rather a pity that it has taken twenty-five years to appear in English but we must be thankful to Dedalus that it finally has.'

John Alvey in *The Modern Novel*

'The backdrop is Russian history and its continually revived messianic themes of God's chosen people and the Promised Land. With the advent of the Soviet period and the horrors of the Gulag, the village community, where the rehearsals had continued, turns into a labour camp, with the Apostle Peter as camp boss and the Apostle James as the secret-police chief. The novel's end satisfyingly connects with its beginning when the identity of Kobylin, the mystery man, is revealed: as a small child, he alone survived a massacre in the labour camp, and was adopted by Maria Trifonovna Kobylina. The Russian word for a rehearsal is *repetitsia*: Sharov in this novel conveys the endless repetition of human folly and cruelty.'

Xenia Dennen in *The Church Times*

'Rarely does one get this feeling when reading a translated book. *The Rehearsals* appears to be first and foremost a book about Russian history, but transpires to be more of a journey into an abstract few hundred years of Russian history. Written by Vladimir Sharov, who won the Russian Booker Prize in 2014 for *Return to Egypt*, this book is easily worthy of the same award. The basic synopsis itself is bizarre: it tells you that *The Rehearsals* is about a theatre production where the actors are untrained, illiterate Russian peasants, and nobody is allowed to play Christ. They are persecuted, arrested, displaced, and ultimately replaced by their own children. Yet the rehearsals continue, onwards and upwards.'

Carl Marsh in *Buzz Magazine*

'Sharov's structuring and tone are unique in world literature, with some parallels to the anonymous narrators of Julian Barnes, the nation-narrative allegory of Salman Rushdie, and the historical mastery of Umberto Eco... Sharov packs more content into one novel than most writers can dream of in a lifetime.' *The Historical Novel Review*

'Vladimir Sharov and Oliver Ready introduce us to a captivating and unsettling prose where the characters share an ability to see something hidden from the rest of us. They are devoted to memory and passionate about historiography in their endless effort to understand. To understand power, to capture the image of the epoch, to explain the changes in national character and identity, to understand history. After all history is theatrical and what is life but a rehearsal of an eternal play?' Elena Malysheva in *The Forum Magazine*

'Indeed, what is perhaps most surprising about this truly extraordinary novel is that a full thirty years after it was written, it remains as fresh and relevant – if not more so – than when it was first published.'

Bradley Gorski in *The Russian Review*

'Vladimir Sharov plays with history, and the narrative is even compared by critics to both Tolstoy's realism and Kafka's absurd. Sharov looks philosophically at the Gospel and Russia's past.' *Russia Beyond*

'Grand in its scale, epic in the telling, and clinical in the presentation this is an interesting thought-provoking book.'

The Messenger Booker

'*The Rehearsals* pulls readers along to some strange places, not so much at a slow pace but in a roundabout fashion, but it's worth the unusual ride.'

M.A. Orthofer in *The Complete Review*

'…it's phenomenal, a strangely riveting story of a group of peasants putting on a Miracle Play… this novel reads like the great metaphysical works of nineteenth-century Russian writing.' Kasia Bartoszynska in *Three Percent Review*

'Oliver Ready hears and renders into English many stylistic registers, reminding us that Sharov began creative life as a poet. If it is true – and I believe it is – that translation requires the most intimate dialogue possible with another's consciousness, then Sharov's rebirth into English in such staggeringly fine prose is the perfect tribute to commemorate the departure of his mortal body.'

Caryl Emerson in *The Los Angeles Review of Books*

Vladimir Sharov

Be as Children

Translated with a Foreword and Notes
by Oliver Ready

Afterword by Caryl Emerson

Dedalus

This publication was effected under the auspices of the Mikhail Prokhorov Foundation TRANSCRIPT Programme to support Translations of Russian Literature and with the support of The Russian Translation Institute.

Published in the UK by Dedalus Limited
24-26, St Judith's Lane, Sawtry, Cambs, PE28 5XE
email: info@dedalusbooks.com
www.dedalusbooks.com

ISBN printed book 978 1 912868 34 6
ISBN ebook 978 1 912868 79 7

Dedalus is distributed in the USA & Canada by SCB Distributors
15608 South New Century Drive, Gardena, CA 90248
email: info@scbdistributors.com   web: www.scbdistributors.com

Dedalus is distributed in Australia by Peribo Pty Ltd
58, Beaumont Road, Mount Kuring-gai, N.S.W. 2080
email: info@peribo.com.au   web: www.peribo.com.au

First published in Russia in 2008
First published by Dedalus in 2021

Be as Children copyright © Vladimir Sharov
Agreement by Wiedling Literary Agency
Translation and Foreword copyright Oliver Ready 2021
Afterword copyright Caryl Emerson

The right of Vladimir Sharov to be identified as the author & Oliver Ready as the translator of this work has been asserted by them in accordance with the Copyright, Designs and Patents Act, 1988.

Printed and bound in the UK by Clays, Elcograf S.p.A
Typeset by Marie Lane

This book is sold subject to the condition that it shall not, by way of trade or otherwise, be lent, resold, hired out or otherwise circulated without the publisher's prior consent in any form of binding or cover other than that in which it is published and without a similar condition including this condition being imposed on the subsequent purchaser.

The Author

A historian of late-medieval Russia by training, Vladimir Sharov (born 1952) began his literary career as a poet before turning to fiction in the early 1980s. When his unusually imaginative and daring novels reached the wider public in the 1990s, they caused acrimony and controversy, yet by the end of his life he was widely recognised as one of Russia's most distinguished recent writers. In the words of the new *History of Russian Literature* (OUP), 'Sharov invented a new form of writing about the past', and 'his constant theme is the indivisibility of Russia's spiritual quest'.

In his later years Sharov received several major awards, including the Russian Booker Prize and the Big Book Prize in 2014. *Be as Children* was named Book of the Year on publication in 2008. Sharov completed his ninth and final novel, *The Kingdom of Agamemnon*, shortly before his death in Moscow in 2018.

Disputing the characterisation of his fiction as 'alternative history', Sharov told *Moskovskie novosti* in 2002: 'God judges us not only for our actions, but also for our intentions. I write the entirely real history of thoughts, intentions and beliefs. This is the country that existed. This is our own madness, our own absurd.'

The Translator

Oliver Ready is a Research Fellow of St Antony's College at the University of Oxford, where he has taught Russian for a number of years. His translations include five books for Dedalus: *The Zero Train* and *The Prussian Bride* by Yuri Buida, and *Before & During*, *The Rehearsals* and *Be as Children* by Vladimir Sharov, as well as Dostoevsky's *Crime and Punishment*, and stories by Nikolai Gogol under the title *And the Earth Will Sit on the Moon*.

Ready was awarded the inaugural Rossica Translation Prize in 2005 for *The Prussian Bride*. In 2015, he and Dedalus won the Read Russia Prize for *Before & During*, while in 2018 they received the international version of the same award for *The Rehearsals* (for the best translation of contemporary Russian literature into any language).

He is the author of *Persisting in Folly: Russian Writers in Search of Wisdom, 1963-2013*.

Foreword

by Oliver Ready

Of the three novels by Vladimir Sharov now available in English, *Be as Children* is the first to be published posthumously. Sharov died from cancer in Moscow in August 2018, at the age of sixty-six. It is some consolation to know that in Washington D.C. in February of that year – his last public appearance – we were able to celebrate together the belated arrival in English of *The Rehearsals* (1986-88), a book towards which, as with *Be as Children* (2001-2007), Sharov expressed especially tender feelings. Then, just a month before his death, he witnessed the publication in Russia of his ninth and longest novel, *The Kingdom of Agamemnon*, written in and out of hospital and completed, as he put it, 'under almost extreme conditions'.

The response from the literary community to Sharov's

Foreword

passing was unusual both for its warmth and for the urgent sense that his death was also a beginning, that much, almost everything remained to be done: not by the author, who had been single-mindedly composing one substantial novel every three to six years for several decades, each as if it were his last, but by his readers. Eugene Vodolazkin, who in his own acclaimed novels has, like Sharov, brought the eye of a medievalist to bear on the modern period, described the late author as 'the most undervalued writer of his time', adding that 'in a certain sense the epoch of Sharov will begin only after his death'.[1] As if in response to such calls, Mark Lipovetsky and Anastasia de la Fortelle put together, at un-academic speed, a 700-page collection of essays and memoirs by authors, scholars, critics, translators, artists and friends. This remarkable volume, entitled *On the Far Side of History* (*Po tu storonu istorii*, NLO, 2020), opens with the sentence: 'Vladimir Sharov (1952-2018) was a writer whose every book changed the notion of what Russian history is and of what kind of literature can assimilate it.'

There is little reason to doubt that Sharov's work will live on among Russian readers, to be discovered by generations that have no personal memory of the traumatic history that Sharov experienced within his own family and described and refracted in his every book. This history, many feel, continues to play out in Russia today according to the scenarios his novels 'rehearse', issuing from the same unhealed schisms

---

[1] See https://iz.ru/779185/evgenii-vodolazkin/pamiati-sharova; and https://gorky.media/context/horoshij-chelovek (both in Russian). For my own tribute, see: https://www.themoscowtimes.com/2018/08/21/remembering-writer-vladimir-sharov-a62594.

Foreword

and wounds. Precisely because of this immersion in the Russian past, however, it is less clear when his novels will find the global audience they deserve. How 'translatable' is Sharov?

One contribution to *On the Far Side of History*, from a major living author to his departed friend, touches on this very issue. In his forty-five-page letter *to* the far side, entitled 'The Runner and the Ship', Mikhail Shishkin writes:

'With your novels you managed to create your Russian reader – your translator must manage to create your reader, too. Become both a runner and a ship. The monstrous Russian twentieth century is, of course, untranslatable. What can be translated is family, and love, and death, and faith.'

These concise comments express both the problem and the remedy. The challenge is real, for translators and readers alike, and in some ways it is a deeper one than Shishkin suggests, since at the root of Sharov's understanding of the Russian twentieth century lies his expertise, as a trained historian, in the country's late-medieval period, the Time of Troubles in particular, the violent interlude between the Rurik and Romanov dynasties. Because of this historical density, coupled with a unique, spiralling method of composition, entering a Sharov novel is not unlike entering Dante's Hell, with its factionalism, its saturation in complex local resentments and relationships, its foregrounding of convoluted local events against the backdrop of Empire and Church, of individual lives against collective history. The analogy holds in a topographical sense as well. Dante's Florence is cramped; the damned just can't get away from each other. Paradoxically, the boundless space of Sharov's Russian and then Soviet empire is equally cramped, with 'coincidental meetings' engineered over thousands of kilometres by the dark workings of power. Sharov did not want footnotes to his novels, with good reason, but I have come to believe that, as with the *Divine Comedy* (which was much in Sharov's mind in his later years), they are necessary, especially since Sharov supplies no Virgil-figure to guide us. I hope that they will save the non-Russian and non-Russianist reader pointless confusion and distracting internet searches, the better to plunge them into the more profitable disorientation that Sharov actively sought as an artist and which his Russian readers feel no less than those now coming to him in other languages.

As Shishkin also intimates, in Sharov's art the local, the national, enfolds the universal. Peeling back the layers of Russian history in his novels, we reach a bedrock of myth that is genuinely global. Sharov himself described Russian history as a commentary on Scripture – one he explores from a non-confessional perspective. So it is that at the centre of the 'Russian' doll of his novels we find Biblical myths of the chosen people, Job and Jonah, New Testament parables and even apocrypha, all of which have been more central to modern Russian literature (from Dostoevsky to Bulgakov to Venedikt Yerofeyev) than they have to its anglophone counterparts of the same period. This is one way in which Sharov's fiction opens out, from its very kernel, to parallels with other histories both collective and individual; thus, the ghost of the Children's Crusade of 1212, said to have been led by the twelve-year-old shepherd boy Stephen of Cloyes, haunts the various strands of *Be as Children*. Another route is supplied by the direct transnational encounters that structure Sharov's novels: the three lives of Madame de Staël among

FOREWORD

the Russian revolutionaries in *Before and During*, a Breton director teaching Russian peasants how to act out the Gospels in *The Rehearsals*, the friendships between Russians and the indigenous peoples of northern Siberia in *Be as Children*.

Finally, in Sharov the local enfolds the universal on a human as well as historical level: not only 'family and love and death and faith' but creativity, language (verbal and nonverbal) and sexuality, illness, aging and disability, earth and water, smell, touch and food. I was delighted to learn from Olga Dunaevskaya, Sharov's widow, that her husband, who was no glutton, hated restaurants because you could consume only as much as you were given. Like their author, Sharov's novels, and the characters within them, are free of limits and borders.

***

Bud'te kak deti – *Be as Children* – was published in Moscow by Vagrius in 2008. In 2017, it was reissued by AST with many small authorial amendments – chiefly aimed at eliminating any descriptive redundancy or literariness. My translation is based on that edition.

Complex as Sharov's novels are in construction, their language is direct and unpretentious, and in their initial form virtually unpunctuated (anybody who ever heard Sharov read – a mesmerising, quasi-liturgical flow of language – will understand how this could be so). For the commas and full stops, as for so much else, I and Sharov's readers have Olga Dunaevskaya, his wife of forty-four years, to thank. Sharov did not use email, so during work on my previous translations I would send questions to Olga to pass on to the author, if I could not see him in person. Now the answers come directly from Olga; the voice may be different, but the comments are just as clear and enlightening as if they came from her husband.

I have also been helped, in every paragraph and in every way, by Caryl Emerson, who read the translation tranche by tranche. It is a particular joy that our collaborative endeavour led to her afterword, the first serious appreciation of this novel I know. I would also like to express my gratitude to the Mikhail Prokhorov Foundation, the Institute of Translation in Moscow and St Antony's College, Oxford, for supporting my work, and to Eric Lane at Dedalus for his steadfast commitment to the task of bringing Sharov into English. Thank you finally to Ania, mother of three young children of our own, for making it possible for me to complete this translation during the long months of lockdown.

VLADIMIR SHAROV

BE AS CHILDREN

In memory of my father

In September 1914, when our offensive in Eastern Prussia hit the buffers, the GHQ of the Supreme Commander immediately sent in the reserves. Three counterattacks were launched. The main blow was struck in Petrograd, Moscow and regional cities, where mobs smashed the shop windows of hundreds of 'Fritzes', 'Hanses' and 'Ludwigs', and celebrated their triumph – proprietors hung signs out everywhere saying *Sorry No German Spoken Here* in big Cyrillic letters. Two auxiliary strikes were undertaken by the Imperial Mariinsky Theatre: in 1915, Wagner's operas, those paeans to the national spirit, suddenly vanished from the stage, while in a gesture of solidarity with German-occupied Warsaw the management of the same theatre introduced alterations to the end of Glinka's *Ivan Susanin*: to avoid any awkward questions, nobody was now remotely responsible for the plight of the wretched Poles – they just died from cold.[1]

---

[1] Mikhail Glinka's opera of 1836, *Ivan Susanin*, also known by the title *A Life for the Tsar*, is set in 1612-13, at the end of the 'Time of Troubles' that followed the death of the last Rurikid Tsar. It tells of the sacrifice of the peasant Ivan Susanin, who deceives invading Poles intent on killing the newly elected Tsar, Mikhail Romanov, by leading them into a remote, snowbound forest. The Poles kill Susanin, but the Tsar is saved. (For discussion of all three operas mentioned here, see Afterword.)

Wagner was replaced by the works of Rimsky-Korsakov: first *Sadko*, then, a little later, *The Tale of the Invisible City of Kitezh*. The former was given a rapturous reception. The theatre was packed and Davydov, in the title role, earned a standing ovation lasting more than half an hour. Still more important was the fact that the merchants and industrialists favoured by our supreme authorities managed to double their production of howitzers by the end of 1915, while the quantity of shells supplied to the army quadrupled. As a result, by the spring of 1916 the front line had stabilized and the conflict took on a protracted, positional character.

The Mariinsky's *Kitezh* is harder to evaluate. Perhaps it was just a poor production, or perhaps the mournful pealing of the bells of the churches that had sunk to the bottom of Lake Svetloyar were simply incapable of rousing the infantry against the enemy. Whatever the reason, on hearing that only the righteous are granted sight of the Holy City and that directly before the coming of Our Saviour the waters will part and it will float up from the depths in all its former splendour, the soldiers repented of their sins, and according to reports sent by front-line commanders in spring-summer 1917, entire armies began deserting their positions to go off in search of Kitezh.

Following the evacuation of Crimea some five years later, thousands upon thousands of refugees – mostly military men: officers and Cossacks – began arriving in Paris via Gallipoli. They already knew that hundreds of their comrades had been drowned alive by the Reds in the Caucasus, near Tuapse, and in Crimea, a little north of Sudak. It was in memory of these comrades, it seems, that Diaghilev put on a new production of *The City of Kitezh* as part of the *Saisons russes* under way at that time in Paris, with scenery by the late Mikalojus Čiurlionis, who became famous overnight. The backdrop consisted of his usual greenish canvases with seaweeds and rushes, and above them, from end to end, alternating strips and ripples of a somewhat lighter shade. In the distance, through that same murky-green shroud, one could see fortified walls surmounted by the golden domes and towers of the beautiful city.

The illusion that all the action takes place under water is total. Against this backdrop, stage right, is a long, long column of officers. The feet of each man are tethered with rope to large stones or lumps of iron. This deadly weight lies still and level on the lake floor but the officers themselves, supported by the water, stand bolt upright, just as they are supposed to. The figures are alive. Their bodies sway gently in the current, which tousles their hair like wind. It is almost as if, after seven years of war, they are still marching in file, marching towards the walls of the city that slumbers in the deep.

***

On 25th January 1970 we lost Sashenka. The death of this four-year-old girl and everything linked to it shocked all who knew her family. Her parents, Vanya Zvyagintsev and Irina Chusovaya, had been my friends since childhood. They married when they were still students and Irina was barely eighteen; Vanya was two years older, but they had always known, it seems to me, that they would live together when they grew up. The marriage turned out well. The husband and wife, as it says in the Bible, shall become one flesh. And that's how it was with Vanya and Irina. Seen from the outside, theirs was a relationship without any great ecstasies or even passion, they just needed each other day in, day out, and they were always in each other's thoughts.

They lived modestly enough, making do at first with student grants and the occasional bit of help from their parents, and later with university stipends as junior researchers, but Vanya would still bring home flowers every evening. The kind of love, in other words, that you only find in a romance novel. And, as in those books, there was only one sadness: for almost five years Irina was unable to have a child. She conceived easily but always ended up miscarrying, even though she would take herself off to the maternity hospital at the first sign of pregnancy. At the age of twenty-three, following a pilgrimage to the Kiev Monastery of the Caves, she finally gave birth and the child, a girl, was a true miracle.

At three months, when babies are still scared of strangers, Sashenka was already smiling at everyone and holding out her hands to them. There really was something radiant about her, and all who found themselves near her immediately began to smile and fill with joy, as if no other response were even possible. At the funeral nobody could remember ever seeing her cross; she might occasionally have felt sad, of course, but she was never angry with anyone. A month before she died, Sasha caught measles, and complications followed. Her temperature hovered around 40 for four days running, and the two doctors – both close friends of ours – said that the child was so weak there was no guarantee she would recover. The fourth night was especially bad: she didn't respond to any medicines or injections and she was unconscious for hours. Her pulse was just a thread, her breathing almost inaudible. On two occasions they even brought a little mirror to her lips: they thought she had died.

The previous evening, when the situation did not yet seem hopeless, Dusya, a holy fool famous throughout Moscow,[2] mentioned to the doctors in passing: 'Stop all this pointless fussing, I've already begged her death.' Then, to Irina: 'Now she's a pure angel, if she dies she'll see Heaven, but let her grow and there'll be so much sin that no prayers will help.' Dusya's words, however, were ignored amid the general hysteria. When the doctors said there was nothing more they could do, Irina took her daughter into her arms, pressed her close, started stroking her, kissing her, and Sashenka began to breathe once more. Towards morning her temperature suddenly dropped and it became clear that the crisis had passed. Now, God willing, she would start to pick up.

After that night, with her mother never letting go of her for even a minute, Sashenka was visibly on the mend. But two days later her temperature suddenly shot up again. Nobody had been expecting a relapse, and by the time anyone reacted it was too late. The sickness spread instantly to her brain and the little girl was dead within twenty-four hours. It was all so terrifying, so unjust that even now, a quarter of a century later, the pain has barely lessened.

Then came the funeral. They buried her at Vostryakovo

---

[2] Russian holy fools, or 'fools for Christ's sake', have long been distinguished by their provocative, theatrical behaviour, often aimed at exposing sinfulness or complacency in the self-righteous. Usually but not always male, they are traditionally homeless, indigent wanderers, often protected and revered by God-fearing folk, frequently canonised after their deaths, but also persecuted by Church and State at various times since their first flourishing in medieval Russia.

Cemetery, where the Zvyagintsevs had their own plot. Sashenka's father, Vanya, was still holding himself together, but her mother was black and puffy with tears. She couldn't walk on her own: two friends took an arm each and more or less carried her. When it was time to lower the coffin into the grave, Irina asked, against the usual custom, for the lid to be removed one last time. She was obeyed. Nearly a hundred people had come to say goodbye. The girl lying before them on a satin pillow was, beyond all doubt, an angel, but an angel that, contrary to nature, was dead. It seems to me that all those present were simply afraid of placing Sashenka in the earth, and not knowing how to put a stop to everything, began talking about her as if she were alive.

The workmen with their ropes and spades were keeping a distance, but they soon got fed up waiting and moved in closer, to hurry things up a bit. Perhaps it was just a coincidence, but there, walking in front of them, was Dusya. A woman of saintly life, Dusya loved to pray, and I thought she would find the words to reconcile us, at least in part, to Sashenka's death. The Zvyagintsevs needed this desperately, as did everyone else. Instead we were told that there was nothing to cry about: she, Dusya, had sung for the little girl's repose four days earlier, which was when Sashenka should have given up her soul to God.[3] But at first her mother had managed to pray it back, beg it back from the Lord. She shouldn't have done so. If the good Lord had let her live, the girl would have become the

---

[3] The Orthodox rite of *otpevanie* (literally, a 'singing-off' of the dead to the other world) takes place, usually in church, on the day of burial (the third after the person's death) and consists of a long series of litanies, hymns, psalms, readings and prayers.

Devil's own spawn, would have been the ruin of many, lured them into sin and temptation. Which was why she, Dusya, had intervened. For as long as Sashenka had not yet committed her first reprehensible deed, salvation and eternal life awaited her; beyond that point she could expect only the flames of Hell. Then Dusya mentioned to Irina, as if throwing her a bone, that the mothers of innocent children abide with them in the same place after their own deaths.

What was said at the cemetery shocked everybody, but I was no less astonished by the fact that Vanya and Irina, the parents of the little girl whom Dusya had essentially killed, did not break off contact with this holy fool; instead they drew even closer to her. Dusya was at their home day and night for almost a year. The Zvyagintsevs had treated her reverentially even before this but now they fawned on her, almost grovelled, as if they thought that just because Dusya had once succeeded in begging Sashenka's death from the Lord, she would also be able to beg her resurrection. People said that they even prayed together, and following the holy fool's cue, thanked the Lord for taking back their only daughter, for not allowing her to grow up and become a tool in the hands of the Devil. I don't know whether that was true or not, but the day came when I realised that I could no longer bear to watch them kissing her hands and to hear their endless keening: Dusyenka, sweet Dusyenka. My parents also carried on seeing her, and whenever I knew she was due to visit I would make sure I was out. Then I got a room of my own near the Arbat and some seven years must have passed before I so much as saw her. We only started having anything to do with each other again after the death of her son Seryozha, whom I had loved deeply since childhood and to whom I owed a great deal.

After her daughter's death, Irina took to drinking. Every now and again she appeared to come to her senses, said she had to have another child, as simple as that, or else she would never get over it, but then she went off the rails again. I'm not sure though, whether she could have had any more children – her last experience of labour had been very tough – or whether she even wanted any. I once heard a friend of hers tell her own mother that ever since Sashenka's funeral Irina hadn't let her husband near her.

The strange triangle of Dusya and the Zvyagintsevs lasted just over a year. Then Vanya went off to Zarechny, on the other side of the Urals, where we were still building one of our first nuclear power plants (he was a good experimental physicist). By that point Irina was already out of control. Nobody, it seems, was especially surprised. After Vanya left, Dusya also stopped visiting.

The terrifying thing about Irina's debauchery was that it brought her no pleasure; she didn't even manage to lose herself in it. She was chaste by nature, and once she became Vanya's wife she was no longer capable of taking an interest in anyone else. Irina was pretty, but her indifference to other men was so strong that before Sashenka died nobody had even tried to flirt with her. Her whoring, it seems to me, had a purpose. She reckoned that this was how she would prove to the Lord, at the cost of her own salvation, that He had been wrong to take Sashenka from her. That the world had not become better without her daughter, in fact there was more evil now than before.

And so, in the space of three years and for no obvious

reason, she destroyed some fifteen families. Shuffling her lovers, she would live a week with one, six months with another, but sooner or later she dumped them all. Later, when her drinking was totally out of hand, she liked to say that the first thing she did in the morning, instead of brushing her teeth, was to check whom she had spent the night with. And yet, however much Irina tried to play the field and act the slut, she didn't learn anything from anybody. After ten years of whoring, she was still the same woman at heart: a Christian wife for whom sex could only be justified if there was a child at the end of it.

I don't know what it was about her that made us desire her so much. Some, I expect, hoped to awaken her senses, to be her first come what may, others were pulled in by her beauty, but we all failed equally. And we all suffered just as badly when she left us. I'm not the only one to have gone through life in the knowledge that the main woman in it was Irina, and this woman never loved you, she just used you in her quarrel with God. For Dusya's son Seryozha, things turned out even worse.

***

According to Dusya, her confessor Bishop Amvrosy once remarked in the course of a conversation in 1926, shortly before his next arrest, that we had all become tangled up in two neighbouring verses from St Matthew's Gospel: 'Verily I say unto you, except ye be converted, and become as little children, ye shall not enter into the Kingdom of Heaven' (18:3) and, 'But whoso shall offend one of these little ones which believe in me, it were better for him that a millstone were hanged about his neck, and that he were drowned in the depth of the sea' (18:6).

I first decided that I had to write about all this nearly thirty years ago, in Salekhard.[4] Sashenka was still alive and the world was no better or worse than it had always been, at any rate there was nobody in it whom I could never forgive under any circumstances. There was plenty of evil around, of course, but there was good as well, and with a bit of effort you could make ends meet. Besides, after five expeditions to the North I'd gained both knowledge and skills. Looking back, I can see that this was a kind of watershed in my life. The path I had taken to that point was still easily discernible, and where I was headed seemed clear enough, too. Later on, no doubt, the road would start to dip, but I wasn't too bothered.

Say what you like, but the end of June in the Arctic is really something. Blazing sunshine round the clock, night a distant memory. I'd always loved fieldwork, ever since my student days, but now it was goodbye to all that. The self-propelled barge that had left Tyumen with the stuff needed for some twenty research trips, including our own, had hit a rock and promptly sunk. The handouts we were relying on were just enough for bread and processed cheese – we could forget about booze. We weren't being thrown out of the hotel quite yet, thank God, but nobody knew how long this charity would last.

I couldn't complain about my room, though. My one neighbour, an oilman, only came back to sleep, so I was on my own, as free as a bird, with plenty of time on my hands. No

---

[4] The town of Salekhard lies on both sides of the Arctic Circle in northwest Siberia.

curtains can keep out the sun in the Arctic – five hours' sleep is the most you can hope for, then you've got the whole day to yourself. With nothing to do and no money, it took less than a week for us all to fall out with each other, and now we were doing our best to keep out of one another's way. After two days spent wondering what to do with myself, an old idea came back to me: to retell, along with circumstances that concern me personally, a cycle of modern Enets legends which I had collected not there, but in Eastern Siberia, on the Lena. And no, I don't mean their fellow Samoyeds, the Nenets: the Enets are a small northern people numbering some two hundred souls.[5] Once there were several thousand of them, but thanks to smallpox, TB, syphilis, other gifts from Europe, and above all vodka, they've been dying out one camp at a time.

What's more, just before the war, the entire North was reduced to beggary. Some bright spark in Moscow decided that the Samoyed peoples were no better than anyone else, and that it was high time to dispossess – dekulakise – the Enets. As a result, all that remains of the enormous reindeer herds that accompanied the Enets for centuries as they roamed across the tundra are eight or nine head per *chum*.[6] Most don't even have that. Some fifty or even sixty of their tribesmen have settled permanently on the outskirts of Tiksi, right behind the warehouses at the port. They huddle together in shacks knocked together from crates. Some beg, the rest find bits of work guarding this or that. They're never taken on for anything else.

Even those with regular pay can't afford to feed their

---

[5] The term Samoyed groups four indigenous peoples (Nenets, Enets, Nganasans, Selkups) whose languages are all branches of the Uralic family.
[6] A portable tent usually made of reindeer hides fastened to wooden poles.

children so their women, still barely on their feet after giving birth, go and hand them over to the state crèche. Rampant alcoholism and general filth mean that nearly one in three infants has serious health problems. In the institutions the young Enets are of course cared for, fed, treated, taught, but they leave them with no memory of their own language or customs.

The cycle I've mentioned began to take shape no earlier than the second half of the nineteenth century and never seems to have attracted anyone's attention. The older, the better, we were always taught, and that lesson has certainly stuck. The only reason I collected these legends then, was personal interest, with no particular purpose or plan. Their chief protagonist is Yevlampy Khristoforovich Peregudov, a latter-day St Paul, Apostle to the Enets. He caught my interest for the following reason. When I was ten, my father – if he happened to be at home when my sister and I were sent off to bed – read us American legends and folk tales all winter long. He read from a thick old book published, if I'm not mistaken, in the early '20s. On the one hand, these were bedtime stories like any others, so you didn't have to worry about things ending badly, only the people in them didn't get around on broomsticks or stoves but by steam train, and they didn't send carrier pigeons to each other, but telegrams. The bandits – typical baddies, only with Smith and Wessons – would rob some bank with a far from magical name, and the next moment the sheriffs would show up and after a quick shootout the good guys would triumph and the criminals would end up in the graveyard or behind bars.

For me, this coexistence of objects from one century with the worldview of a completely different era was something new and exhilarating. What was more, it said in the notes – those were read to us too – that these were stories about real people; we knew when they were born, where they lived, how they died. My father enjoyed the legends of the New World just as much as I did; it was only my sister who sometimes asked shyly for *The Hunchback of Notre-Dame* instead. Evidently, all this American folklore made a strong impression on me, because when I encountered something similar in the Russian North, I was immediately hooked.

There was one other catalyst. I recorded my first Enets legend in my fourth year at university, when I joined a group of ethnographers on a field trip to Yakutia. That experience didn't just determine my future interests – the North from the Urals to Chukotka and on to the Sea of Okhotsk, with all its 'small peoples' – it also made me more accepting of a medical problem that I'd been unable to come to terms with until then. My condition was serious and I was expecting the worst; a whole year in hospital had brought only minor improvements, if any. But now I discovered that there was no need to hurry, that perhaps my illness wasn't actually a curse, a sentence, and that everything that had come before it, and the illness itself, hadn't happened for nothing: in fact, I'd been given a master key without which you couldn't make sense of anything.

In matters like this, of course, things always move slowly. A great deal of time had to pass and a great number of things had to be worked out in my mind before I could take up this task in my hotel bed in Salekhard. Now, with the benefit of hindsight, it's perfectly clear to me that the failed expedition of '68 – that month and ten days before we were finally sent back to Moscow after endless negotiations – was far from the worst stretch of my adult life; it was then that I began to look to the future without my usual apprehension.

I'm aware that the story that follows contains too many strands. Matted and torn, they got tangled up into a ball, and it took me a long time to find the right thread to pull. From the very beginning, when I was still sketching out a plan, I knew that even the dates were a problem. So too was the jerkiness of my progress. For several years everything would go quiet, as if under wraps, then all hell would break loose; but as soon as I let off steam, the silence would return. And so, although the gist of the thing was easy enough for me to hold in my mind, work would quickly grind to a halt. Sometimes I had the impression that only a Chekist would have managed to tie this all up into a neat little story – the kind of man who prepared the Show Trials back in the '30s.[7]

Whether it was just to get myself going, or to prove to myself that nothing was off limits, I began with things that in the past I would have left well alone. But for various reasons everything I managed to write in the summer of '68 in Salekhard, and then during autumn in Moscow, had to be set aside in December. Apart from one brief interval, almost seventeen years would pass before I returned to my notes. When I did so, I was taken aback by the tone of the first twenty pages. With the passing of time, a young man's mixture of spunk and timidity loses most of its charm. But never mind: the bit that follows remains exactly as it was.

---

[7] The Cheka (acronym for The All-Russian Extraordinary Commission for Combating Counter-Revolution, Speculation, and Sabotage) existed in that form for only a few years (1917-22), but the word Chekist continued to be used throughout the Soviet era to refer to employees of the security agencies that followed it.

Be as Children

***

My own experience has taught me that being at the centre of events makes you the worst possible witness. I've seen other people have epileptic fits of course, but there would always be an aura, a warning sign, and even if it came with only a second or two to spare, the person would still manage to find somewhere to lie down, on a bed if there happened to be one, otherwise on the floor, so that, however severe the convulsion, you would still come out of it more or less in one piece. But nobody ever warns me, so I always get the full works.

My only source for what happens to me then is my family, but it's not their favourite topic and they always spare me the details. What I do know is that I begin by screeching my head off. My vocal chords have already seized up from the spasms and I barely sound human – more like a factory siren being strangled, my mother once said. During a fit I'm as strong as a madman on the rampage. So there I am, screaming away, when suddenly I stop and try, as it were, to screw myself back into whatever I'm standing on. The screw is right-threaded, because it's the left part of my brain that's damaged and it's there that everything starts. Who knows what I'm after: maybe I'm dreaming of a straitjacket, of something to squeeze me and grip me tight, with no slack at all, so that I can no longer breathe. But either the floor is made of stone, or the screwdriver itself is no good, in any case for a minute or so I jerk about like a dancer and pointlessly shuffle my feet until I finally pick up some speed and start spinning properly. Speed is an amazing thing – it sends fear packing. Just like a plane, I need it to take off and fly, even if I only travel one metre. Then it's back to the usual misery – you're hurled in the same direction that you were spinning in, and before you fall, and when you actually fall, the shaking and thrashing take over mercilessly.

My fits last for about fifteen or twenty minutes (they are categorised as *grand-mal,* or generalised, seizures), after which I'm flat on my back for another few hours, shattered, covered in blood and with a tongue like chewed paper. I wake up, fall back asleep, regain consciousness, lose it again – but there's no pain. Usually I don't come round fully till the next morning, then I start counting my losses. Patiently inspect my wounds and tell myself, in the same spirit, that I'll need another six weeks at least to sort myself out. The most painful thing, if nothing's broken, is my tongue – I can't eat properly, can't talk properly.

Even the government takes my condition seriously. Epilepsy gets you second-category disability benefits, sometimes even the top category, with a pension to boot. And it's true, you wouldn't want to trust me with anything. Certainly not a machine tool or a steering wheel. I can't even take a shower on my own – I'd be hurled from the bath and that would be that. As for life's pleasures – vodka, say – forget it: my relatives won't pour me a single shot, however much I beg them. All that remains is to live a quiet, sensible life and hope for the best. And to keep that hope alive, there's a handful of different pills, three times a day.

I should add that I didn't inherit my epilepsy, I earned it myself. When I was nineteen and as drunk as I usually was at that time, I tried to slide down the banisters at the cultural centre in the Zuyev Workers' Club. The banisters were wide enough but I slipped and took a dive, head first, from a height of six metres. The doctors at the hospital managed to return me to some semblance of my original appearance, but a month later it became apparent that something crucial had been damaged in my frontal lobe.

Convinced I was stuck with this for the rest of my life, I went downhill pretty quickly. Dropped out of university, stopped seeing friends, stayed in for weeks on end. My parents tried to help, of course, and I saw one doctor after another. But it was pointless. They all asked me identical questions as they tapped me with identical nickel-plated hammers, then took their leave without offering a word of hope. Probably only time and meekness could teach me to live with it. I had plenty of the first – no one was rushing me – and, to begin with, no shortage of the second. I lay on the couch all day long, sometimes with a book, more often just staring out of the window. I had no particular regrets, and remorse had also lost its appeal.

In short, all was calm, but then, out of nowhere, rage would come over me like a fit, any time of the day. I must have been terrifying in that state, because one day it suddenly got through to me that both my parents were far more scared of my fury than they were of my epilepsy. At that moment I was able to see myself as they saw me and I felt bad: they were suffering through no fault of their own. Which was why I asked to be put into psychiatric care. We had the famous Kashchenko hospital in our district, and that's where I was placed.[8] I spent nearly a

---

[8] Moscow Psychiatric Hospital No. 1, which between 1922-1994 was named after a previous head doctor, the psychiatrist Pyotr Kashchenko. In the 1960s and 70s, 'the Kashchenko' became notorious as the site of the forcible detention and treatment of dissidents.

year there – eleven months and six days, to be precise. That's a fair stint, and I came out a completely different man. The changes had begun back at university, but it was in the Kashchenko that the shell in which I had been growing finally shattered.

My epilepsy and raging fits earned me a bed alongside the moderately severe cases in Ward No. 2. In any mental hospital, pretty nurses are common enough. The money's always reasonable, thanks to bonus payments for this or that, it's always easy to arrange twenty-four-hour shifts if you need half a week off, and there are perks if you sign up for medical school. It was one of the nurses on the ward, Nastya, who took me under her wing after my first month of treatment. I owe her a lot. Thanks to Nastya I had a nice enough time in the hospital, better, in any case, than at home on Leontyevsky Lane. I became more stable, more cheerful, and my doses of phenobarbital and tranquillizers began to come down. Half a year later there was even talk of discharging me. But I didn't want to leave. By that time Ward No. 2 had already become my home, my burrow, and I wasn't about to go back out into the world without a very good reason. The doctors tend to be quite understanding in such cases, they don't usually just throw you out. Later, after I got tired of Nastya, I brought up the topic of my release myself, and I was moved to the convalescent ward – No. 5 – just as soon as a bed became free.

That ward, known as Kanatchikov's Dacha, is something of a halfway house between a prison and a home. It was built by the merchant of that name, or else Pyotr Kashchenko would never have agreed to treat Kanatchikov's crazy daughter. To this day the place has never been plundered: the same Empire mirrors reaching up to the ceiling in their mahogany frames, the same Louis XV-style drawing room with its authentic, superbly restored furniture. The hospital is an enormous city, and there are plenty of people around who are good with their hands. There's also a modestly sized billiard room: a German-made table with a marble base, a moderately worn cloth, and genuine ivory balls. It was all kept in order by a long-term patient, an old billiards marker who had once plied his trade in Gorky Park. He also tapered and glued excellent cues from various types of wood. Of course, in the hands of people who, legally speaking, are not responsible for their actions, cues can become weapons pretty quickly. They should have no place in a madhouse, but the head doctor in Ward No. 5, Valentin Nikolayevich Grigoryev, who was an ardent billiards player and a student of the renowned Semanov, turned a blind eye.

But there's no paradise anywhere. At Kanatchikov's Dacha it wasn't the massive, almost fifty-bed ward that bothered me, even though half the patients snored as if they were at death's door and actually passed through that same door at the rate of one a week. People give up their souls to God in every hospital and it's not so hard to get used to, especially when you have sleeping pills on tap, no questions asked. But along with all the Empire furniture, the mahogany and the billiards, the Dacha also boasts a completely insane bathroom. It, too, is quite splendid, with a stuccoed ceiling, four lancet windows – this is Moscow Art Nouveau – and lined up along the wall, fifteen standard-issue Soviet toilet bowls which, as is always the way in a madhouse, have no partitions either in front or on the sides: God forbid that anyone should hang themselves.

You can find toilets like that on any ward, of course, but here they look especially absurd. The man who sculpted them must have had excellent taste – their flowing lines are beyond reproach. But that's lost on the poor devil with chronic constipation from all the pills he's taking who clambers up on the bowl and after shifting from foot to foot, perches there like an eagle for almost an hour, vainly trying to empty his bowels. Not to mention the permanently leaking cisterns and the pure, transparent stream which flows beneath you and never runs dry, as if to mock you. Even now I remember the horror that seized me every time I entered that room: there are, after all, certain things we've been trained to do in private. In fairness though, Kanatchikov's Dacha was not the worst place to end up.

Nastya loved me. Mental hospitals are quiet places at night – apart from the patients, there's no one about. While I was in Ward No. 2, the doctors' mess, the senior consultant's office and the head nurse's room were all at our disposal. Nastya usually chose the sofa in the consultant's office, but she wasn't above using the head nurse's couch when circumstances required. She was the most generous of lovers, and if we slept together less than three times in a shift she would first blame me, then the pills, then her whole sorry life.

When she heard that a bed had become available in Kanatchikov's Dacha, she told me that she wanted a child, that she would take me out of the hospital and marry me. The little town of Naro-Fominsk wasn't Moscow of course, but she had her own room there, which if nothing else, was better than a loony bin. But I changed the topic. Nastya was caring and devoted, and I've had more than one occasion to regret turning her down. I remember her and the hospital gratefully to this day. It was the first time since I went flying off those banisters at the Zuyev Workers' Club that I'd felt protected, the first time

I knew that if things went badly for me in the world outside there was one place, one life, albeit a very different life, where I would be made welcome.

In hospital I had the strong suspicion that Nastya was messing about with my drugs – lowering the dose of some, increasing others – but I wasn't really complaining. I'd managed to go ten months in Ward No. 2 without a fit, so whatever she was doing seemed to be working. Perhaps it was Nastya herself I had to thank for my improvement rather than the drugs themselves, or maybe it was the fact that nobody has any reason to bother you in a mental hospital, but either way, once I got back home, the seizures returned within a week. I was put back on heavy medication, and the doses kept rising. I did everything the doctors told me until I realised, all over again, that ever since the Fall there has been no such thing in our world as pure good: the drugs might stave off the fits – if you're lucky, of course – but they will also turn you into something resembling a plant.

I lived like that for almost a year, struggling even to walk, until I finally decided: to hell with it all. What will be, will be. And that was when my day-to-day life became a kind of Russian roulette. When you never know when you'll be struck down or where. What you do know is that after any given fit you might wake up crippled for life with a broken spine or, having choked on your own tongue, not wake up at all. Somehow, many dozens of seizures later, my lucky streak continues – so I have good reason to thank God, after all.

I'm a gambler and an optimist by nature, but one thing my maths teacher taught me at school was that outrageous flukes can't go on for ever – probability theory has not been disproved. In other words, if fate had left me with any other option, I would never have accepted these odds. The day after a fit I understand this particularly starkly and I feel grateful, say thank you, and sometimes even cry. Once I've calmed down again, I tell myself that I'm not the only person who won't live for ever.

I used to think that if Dusya had wanted to, she could have healed me no worse than Nastya. After a seizure, when I'm pretty much out of it for hours at a time, I often dream of one and the same thing – that we're living not on Leontyevsky Lane, but in the country, at my grandma's log house, and we're fattening a pig. It's cramped in granny's *izba*, so the pig and I have been put in the sty, in two neighbouring pens. There's only a little wooden partition between us but we're still not friends. What kind of friendship can there be when I've got the black illness, when I'm possessed and flailing about, while next to me a chubby pig munches away calmly in the trough. That scumbag's sitting pretty – a whole month to go till Christmas, and it won't cross anyone's mind to slaughter her any sooner.

Then Dusya walks in. I stretch out my hands towards her, beg her, my godmother, to help me. Swear that I'll never look at another damned bottle of my beloved vodka again – it's nothing but poison. And I don't forget to cry, of course, but that's not hard: I've always been as weepy as any little girl. In fact I used to get beaten for these tears – a terrifying memory. But I'm far from confident that I'll win Dusya round. She knows better than to believe a word I say and besides, for as long as I can remember she's never been able to stand the sight of me, even if she is my godmother. But I must be putting on a good act this time, because Dusya's wavering.

Mother also starts sobbing for good measure, then father. But the pig is nice and calm, breathing evenly, chewing slowly. Empathy, you could say, is not her thing. But she's wrong, the filthy brute, if she thinks we're in different boats – we're all tied with the same thread. My tears might not be worth much, or father's, now that he's started putting it away no worse than me, but mother's a different matter – Dusya loves her to bits. Loves her, pities her and would never say no to her.

That Dusya, my godmother and a genuine seer, had no illusions about me from the very beginning, was something I discovered long ago, during a sermon given by Dusya's former confessor, Father Nikodim,[9] known in the world as Aleksei Poluektov. At the time, though, I didn't notice.

My sense of what Father Nikodim was like before his three stints in the camps comes solely from Dusya's accounts, but even in '59, when I started visiting him in Snegiri for confession and Holy Communion every Sunday, he made quite an impression on me. The house-church at which he served was located half below ground in an old brick dacha. The owners had no ties to the catacomb church and they weren't exactly concealing their activity, but nor did they want to goad the authorities, so you would rarely see more than six or seven parishioners from Moscow at any one service.[10] Though his flock was small, Nikodim took obvious joy in serving it. Twenty-five years in the camps without a church and without the proper Divine Liturgy had been hard to bear and now,

---

[9] In Russia, monks, as well as priests, are typically addressed as 'Father'.
[10] The catacomb church is the general name for the broad, disparate community of Orthodox clergy and other believers that moved 'underground' from the 1920s in resistance to Soviet rule and in many cases the official Church.

standing at the lectern, he conducted the service with deep solemnity: no abridgements or omissions at any point in the ceremony, every word sung meaningfully and without haste.

At first, I also liked the way he preached. After the service he would explain difficult passages of Holy Scripture with rare skill: you'd ask a question and he would reply there and then. Aside from the Bible, he also touched on very contemporary topics, albeit more cautiously. I'm quite certain that many of our lives would have turned out differently were it not for his teachings. When I say cautiously I don't mean that he talked in hints or allegories, just that while speaking about things that the authorities would find innocuous he would invariably integrate them into a kind of system so that something else, which had not been mentioned, would also become clear. But it's not yet time to bring in his theories. After all, Father Nikodim never spoke about faith step by step, but by fits and starts, whenever inspiration struck him, and a lot of water would have to flow under the bridge before I began to work anything out.

Now, in my dream, I see him preaching before the Holy Doors in 1960, on May 15th – my name-day, as it happens, and the day on which the Blessed Tsarevich Dmitry is remembered.[11] But my christening was meant to take place not on the 15th but on the 11th, the feast day of St Cyril and St Methodius the Enlighteners.[12] Methodius was never an option – the name

---

[11] Dmitry of Uglich, the youngest, epileptic son of Ivan the Terrible, canonised in 1606. His death at the age of eight gave rise to the long political and monarchical crisis known as the Time of Troubles.

[12] The ninth-century missionaries from Thessalonika, known as 'the Apostles to the Slavs', who invented the first Slavic script, and together with their students, translated the Bible and other ecclesiastical texts from Greek into Old Church Slavonic.

sounds far too exotic nowadays – but father was very keen on Kirill. Dusya however, insisted specifically on Dmitry. So even then, a whole nineteen years before the incident at the Zuyev Club, she already knew I would end up with the falling sickness. And even then, when I was just seven days old, she expected nothing good to come from me. Because Father Nikodim ends his sermon by saying that all the woes of the Russian lands began after the Tsarevich Dmitry was canonised, after that demon-possessed child was made a saint. The canonisation of an epileptic, it turns out, is a mortal sin. Among its evil consequences is the terrible child heresy that disturbs our peace to this day. So that was the kind of guide and intercessor my godmother had chosen for me.

But whatever her opinion of me, there's no one else I can ask for help. Especially because Dusya is in the pigsty, standing by my pen and looking at me lying there sick and miserable. Looking at me and then at the animal. The pig's snout is still over the trough, but she's stopped chewing. An open, slobbering mouth, and a look of pure stupidity in her eyes. Meanwhile godmother starts reciting a prayer. She always prays calmly and pensively, without gabbling or dropping the ends of her words. A prayer to the Lord about me and the pig, and of course I know exactly what Dusya is asking for. As I listen, I steal the odd glance at my neighbour.

The pig seems to be listening too, but I doubt she realises that the prayer's about her. Even if she does suspect something, she has no time to say anything or to object, not because animals are unable to speak but because her entire vast body is suddenly seized with convulsions. Reeling and shaking, she starts screaming the way I scream at the beginning of a fit.

Then she crashes to the ground and spasms rip through her mercilessly. All because she never showed me any pity, any sympathy, never had a kind thought for me, however much I suffered. Then, either because she's stronger than me or because father's changed her bedding – he brought in several armfuls of good straw the previous day, so you couldn't hurt yourself too badly however often you fell – she gets to her feet, trashes both our cages in an instant, and bursts out of the sty.

Father and mother run after her – otherwise we'll have no meat for six months. And that means no lavish feasts at Christmas or Shrovetide, nothing to put on the table after Lent. But they're still hopeful. It's winter, white on white, with a moon like a giant plate. A full moon, light as day, so no chance – thank God – of losing the trail left by the rampaging pig. What's more, there's been more snow than usual this winter. On low ground it must be knee-high, so you won't get far on pig legs. My parents, in other words, are in good spirits, and father's even laughing as he imagines telling guests about it. But then, before they've even walked half a kilometre, the wind picks up. The start of a proper snowstorm. Suddenly it's so dark and cold that they no longer care about the pig just so long as they find their way back. That night they return home empty-handed. The pig will only be found two days later. There's a deep ravine on the far side of our village, with a little brook winding its way along the bottom. Recently, city folk have got in the habit of dumping their rubbish there. And the dump is where she ends up, already half-eaten by dogs. They follow her tracks to the edge of the ravine: she'd run all the way and tumbled down without stopping.

I have barely a single memory of myself before the age

of seventeen that doesn't involve Dusya. At first, I loved my godmother, probably as much as I loved my mother. It didn't bother me that Dusya liked me least of all the children – I didn't like myself much either. Later I began drifting away from her, but she still remained one of the main people in my life. Then for a couple of years or more, I had other things on my mind. And after that there was what happened to Sashenka, which I don't know how to forgive even now. Most of the people around me managed to more or less accept it, at any rate nothing collapsed, no ties were broken, which I found quite astonishing, but later too, I had no wish to revisit anything linked to Dusya; in fact, given half a chance to edit my own life, I would have crossed Dusya out of it with no regrets, no traces.

Now, a good three decades on from those events, I can see that my childhood was far from ordinary. From the late '50s onwards, the authorities shut down church after church, priests were banished, and hardly any of my peers were baptised. As for me, I don't seem to have any memories of myself that don't involve Christ. I'm aware that Dusya had an entire parish revolving around her. In Moscow she had been renowned as a great seer from before the war, and in times of need her help was sought by many, many people. But there was also an inner circle – ten families or so – which included my parents. Until the '70s they all lived in close proximity in the lanes around Tverskoi Boulevard and Nikitsky Gates, in those once vast and expensive apartments on Leontyevsky and Trubnikovsky that had long since been turned into communal flats. Each one contained a large number of rooms and families, sometimes as many as fifteen, but there were always traces of the old life: a sumptuous tiled fireplace, an inlaid floor, or the most intricately stuccoed ceiling. There were also Voltaire armchairs, carved mahogany sideboards and front doors with stained glass. We didn't pay much attention to any of this but when, still a child, I ended up in a museum in some old palace, I found little there to surprise me.

My parents went to the same school that we attended later – No. 110. Until 1921 it had been the Third Girls' Gymnasium, famous across Moscow. Then, after the Bolsheviks took charge of education, it was renamed the Soviet Labour School and given a new number. But four members of staff, among them the headmaster, a literature teacher and a maths teacher known as Molekula on account of her shortness, had been there since the Third Gymnasium, whose spirit, thanks to them, had somehow survived both revolution and war.

Certainly, those of us who ended up having to move schools missed it terribly. There were many buildings in the area reserved for high-ups, and several children of Communist Party cadres in each class, but even they acknowledged the school's excellence and didn't want to change a thing. In fact, they went out of their way to protect the headmaster. I had long suspected that there must be some reason why Dusya had gathered her spiritual children from this tiny neighbourhood around the Arbat, that it was all somehow linked to our school, and not long ago I learned I was right – she completed her schooling at the Third Gymnasium in 1913.

Under Dusya's leadership, we were almost a commune. We helped each other out, got together on holy days and name-days, and having commandeered almost half a compartment of the slow train from Moscow, travelled together to Tula.

BE AS CHILDREN

Until we met Father Nikodim, we confessed and took the Eucharist in an abandoned ranger's lodge in the forest where an old catacomb priest was living – Father Iosaph. He'd been released from the camps not long before and the lodge had been bought specially for him. I can remember hearing about how all the families pitched in, giving whatever they could while godmother made up the difference. I still haven't forgotten how happy and proud everyone was to have their own shared priest. Despite Dusya's custody, many in my parents' circle felt abandoned by the Church, cut off from it, and they found this painful. But there was no solution. Everyone tried to avoid the area's one functioning church: it was known for a fact that its priest informed on his parishioners. We did attend services at Christmas and Easter, but no one ever confessed or took communion there.

This forest outpost was where Father Iosaf both served and lived. We visited him once a month, and our trips were almost always eventful. The train to Tula, then the bus, then horses if there were any to be had, otherwise a walk of some fifteen kilometres. There were three other lodges. They had also belonged to foresters, but we gradually bought them, too, after which two thirds of us children would stay on there until September with our grandmothers and nannies.

The four summers we spent there, in the woods outside Venyov, were the brightest time of my life. All the mushrooms and berries you could ever want, not to mention, just half a kilometre away, a small but pristine forest lake where we swam and fished. In short, we were almost in heaven, happy and sinless.

Every day, in his house-church in the forest, Father

Iosaf celebrated matins and the main morning service, which needless to say, was the more popular of the two. We took confession with him once a week although, unlike in Moscow, where sin seemed to stick to you however young you were, there we had nothing serious to confess. With Father Iosaf at our side, there was no filth inside us or around us – a feeling of purity I remember to this day. I remember having it in Moscow too, but never for long and only after confession, whereas there we woke up with it and fell asleep with it.

For all her holy foolishness, Dusya knew the meaning of money, and to keep our community going, she would redistribute it without asking anyone's permission. Most of the families were quite poor and even went hungry if there were many mouths to feed. The parents worked as technical specialists, junior academics, teachers, although we also had our own millionaire – a dramatist whose plays ran in dozens of theatres. Later, our quota of capitalists suddenly doubled. Our neighbour in the communal apartment was a penniless poet employed by a factory newspaper. His surname was Korostylyev. He was a kind soul, but usually dead drunk. He lived on his own – no wife or children – and I had the impression, when I was still small, that he loved godmother in a slightly different way from everyone else. Aside from his duties at the paper, he – when he wasn't drunk, that is, or perhaps even when he was – wrote strange spiritual verses to be sung, like the short hymns chanted in church during the Liturgy. He would then take the poem to the factory where he would print a copy by hand before giving it to Dusya with his personal inscription.

Three or four times a year, usually for a fortnight or

so, godmother would vanish without a word of warning to anyone. It was said she would go off to pray somewhere in the North. Well, it was during one of his muse's absences that Korostylyev committed his sin: to win a bet, he composed a couple of songs for the newspaper about the conquest of the Virgin Lands,[13] which we only found out about once the entire country was already singing them. I can see, even now, that he had a real talent for this; even his weaker poems cry out to be set to music. Unlike our playwright, though, he was plainly ashamed of his celebrity and continued to write only for Dusya, saying of those two songs that he had been led astray by the Devil. But the royalties they brought him over the next six years were a great help to him and everyone else.

Dusya arranged our financial matters so discreetly that I, for one, knew nothing about them until I was at university. She had her own key to every flat, and it was a rule among us all to leave the family purse in the most visible place, usually on a sideboard. We children, by the way, could dip into it whenever we wanted from the age of seven or so. Godmother was behind this arrangement too, and nobody I should add, ever abused this extraordinary privilege. We took only as much as we needed for a cinema ticket, an ice cream or a fizzy drink, and only if we saw that there would be enough left over.

Never ask for money and never humiliate yourself before anybody on account of money – that was another of Dusya's rules, and it was followed to the letter. She took care of everything herself. If there was a flat where the purse was still

---

[13] A campaign driven by Nikita Khrushchev after Stalin's death to boost Soviet agriculture by working previously uncultivated land in Northern Kazakhstan, Western Siberia and elsewhere.

bulging at the end of the month – in other words, just before payday, the leanest time – she would take as much from it as she thought fair, and without telling a soul, bring the money to the other homes, like a bee. Bring it to those who would otherwise have to beg a loan from their neighbours. Like some pilgrim wandering from village to village, she trod her way between the flats of Moscow, never giving less than she took.

Nobody cheated her: neither the poor, which is unsurprising, nor the rich. Both the playwright and the poet were charitable, God-fearing types, glad of the opportunity to help their neighbour – I say this without irony. There were times when there wasn't enough money to go round and then, so I'm told, my godmother resorted to the pocket of her soiled apron, which along with her rustic skirt and her woollen, equally rustic jersey, made up her daily uniform. It was there that members of her flock left money, along with requests that she pray for the success of new endeavours and for the prosperity and health of themselves and their families. But the apron wasn't needed very often: we knew that this was Dusya's personal fund and that it was earmarked for the secret monasteries of the catacomb church.

The revenue was said to be quite considerable. Many in Moscow were convinced that Dusya was a saint and that the Lord could rarely refuse her. People asked her for all sorts of things, even the most mundane, such as promotion at work, election to the Academy of Sciences or the return of their husbands. Without asking what it was that they wanted from God, what matter required her support, godmother just took the envelopes bearing the name of the petitioner as if it were a return address, and prayed to the Lord to help them.

Be as Children

We also knew how zealous Dusya was in her prayers, that it was enough to join her in asking the Lord for something and He would not refuse you. But prayers were not the only way she protected us. We went to school, joined the Young Pioneers, and when the time came, the Komsomol.[14] She was privy to everything, and everything needed her sanction. More than that, it needed her say-so: she would tell us to join, and we would join without hesitation; saving us, she took our sins upon herself. All of us, big or small, knew that she was our spiritual guide, our Elder, and that made everything easy: we were simply fulfilling our vow of obedience.[15]

She explained that she didn't want us to worry and suffer: for as long as we were children, we were pure and holy, and that was how we should remain. Like a strict governess, she made sure that our souls stayed spotless, and never tired of repeating that it is easier to keep yourself clean than to cleanse yourself once you are already stained. Godmother let us do whatever we wanted, demanding only that we never conceal anything and speak the truth without fear. Our souls had to lie open before her, only then could she be certain that she would notice our sin right away and manage to redeem it. In other words, she helped us here, there and everywhere, with the result that

---

[14] The Young Pioneers, for schoolchildren aged nine to fourteen, was founded in 1922 and borrowed heavily from the boy and girl Scout movements. It prepared children for the Komsomol (Communist League of Youth), whose membership grew to tens of millions by the 1970s.

[15] The 'Elder' (*starets*) became an influential, if institutionally controversial type following the revival of eldership in Russian monasteries in the nineteenth century. A highly charismatic figure, the Elder, to cite Ruth Coates, 'would attract spiritual children, historically neophytes, pledged in obedience, whom he or she would instruct in the mystical path' (*The Oxford Handbook of Russian Religious Thought*, OUP, 2020, p. 244).

we were all fed and clothed and knew that in times of hardship we would be supported and kept afloat. Without this, Dusya's flock would hardly have lasted a full twenty years.

Godmother called on our family three or four times a week and often stayed the night, laying down a mat by the door to sleep on. She wasn't scared of draughts. I know that my parents tried long and hard to tempt her to sleep in a more dignified spot – a bed – but eventually realised that they were getting nowhere. They told us, the children, that Dusya slept by the threshold so as to guard the home from sin. She slept deeply, though never more than three hours or so, settling down for the night only once my parents were already asleep and getting up before anyone else, even my mother. I remember her whistling through her nose as she slept – a sign that all was calm and there was nothing to fear. And in general, so long as she had no cause to be cross with us, the noises that came from her could safely be ignored, merging as they did with whatever else was happening inside the flat and outside the window – the shuffling of feet in the corridor, the sound of water, the conversations muffled by thick, pre-Revolutionary walls.

If by night she whistled, by day she muttered and jabbered at great speed – so unlike when she was praying – indiscriminately jumbling up sayings and proverbs with admonitions directed specifically at us sinners. She had no use for full stops, and no desire to separate one thing from another. It seems to me now that, for as long as you were a child, there was really no need to work out what Dusya was trying to say, all that mattered was the tone – calm if you were behaving yourself, indignant if you were up to no good. In this sense nothing much had changed from my infant years, when I didn't really understand what people were saying and thought that godmother was just twittering away like a bird. Especially because she looked just like a little bird in that grey dress she was always wearing.

But the adults distrusted her sweet murmurings and were openly scared of her. More than once she told my father, and even my mother, 'What good are the likes of you to God? You're sinful through and through, not one clean spot on you anywhere. What's there to love you for? You can only be pitied, if there's any pity left.' Sometimes she even swore at them. But we were a different matter. She would play with us for hours, especially when we were small, and treated us as equals. She would laugh, argue and get as upset as any child if a toy, which might have been given to her that very same day, was taken off her; the next moment though, she would be rejoicing, having taken away someone else's. She particularly liked playing dolls with my sister, sewing dresses for them and tacking on endless trains, ribbons and frills. A ball and a gala dinner would follow. At a table carefully laid with plates and cutlery, the dolls sat strictly according to rank, each in her own place.

My memories of Dusya stretch back to before my first memories of myself and even my mother. Mother worked as an editor at a newspaper and got home late, once the next day's issue had already gone off to the printers. As a rule, we didn't see father very often either, except on Sundays: he grabbed every opportunity he could to do experiments in the lab. By rank and qualification he was the most junior scientist at the institute, and he was always last to get the equipment he needed. So the people I remember best from my early childhood are Klasha, our nanny, and of course Dusya. With Klasha, I always knew, I think, that for all my helpless dependence on her, mother mattered more, even if she did come home late and tired. With godmother, it was more complicated. Was she more or less important than this person or that person, and who was she in our family anyway? At first, I couldn't work any of this out and often muddled things up.

Klasha was meant to be with us at all times, and if she suddenly left the room we had to yell and call her back. Dusya had no set routine. A free spirit, she could come and go whenever she wanted. If Klasha had to pop out to the shop say, or was busy in the kitchen, and Dusya happened to be with us, she would always stay with my sister and me without needing to be asked twice, in fact she seemed very glad to do so. Although none of us were well-off, many of us had nannies. The villages were completely destitute and young girls would try anything to get out of them. At first, most of them would end up working for strangers as helpers or nannies, but once they realised that they'd never find husbands in the capital, they moved out to the textile towns – Ivanovo, Kineshma, Pavlovsky Posad – where there was always demand for female workers at the factories and at least some chance of making a life for yourself.

And so, year after year, we would play with Dusya for hours on end almost every single day. It was like that before Klasha came along, and while she was with us, and after she had gone off to Ivanteyevka and been replaced by Raya. Little by little though, my sister and I grew older and from about the age of fifteen, or perhaps even earlier, we could tell from godmother's face that she was becoming disillusioned and losing interest in us. If around children she was always or almost always cheerful, gentle and caring, and if while we were still little, she loved us all as though we were her own family, she treated our parents, even those singled out as part of her inner circle, with an almost ostentatious severity, at best indifference. She could easily cut them short and would answer their questions with a curt yes or no, as if she could have nothing to say to them. She was more than capable of swearing at the adults and of doing so in our earshot, especially when she was being thanked for money or some other thing. I remember how flushed and embarrassed father became, how scared he was of saying the wrong thing to Dusya, and by contrast, how free and easy I felt around her as a child, even though I already knew that I was far from being one of her favourites.

She would give up on adults just like that, in a flash, as if each and every one of them was a lost cause and the only reason she put up with them was because she understood that we children could not yet manage without them. When my turn came to cross the boundary and I saw that I had lost my godmother, the blow hit me very hard. I suppose I must have guessed the reasons for this break even then, but in my eyes all the people I knew, big and small, were incomparably different from one another, and it was this dissimilarity that I most valued about them and that prevented me from thinking my thought through to the end.

It was only in one of his sermons several years later that Father Nikodim explained in simple, frank terms what had been happening between us and Dusya. He said that adults in our sinful world basically live according to two different creeds. For the believer, life here on Earth is a brief period of probation before eternal life. Before a life filled to the brim with grace, love and communion with the Lord. Atheists, on the other hand, are convinced that before birth and after death there is and can be nothing, there is only now, this very minute, so if you miss something, you'll never get it back and there'll be no second chance.

It's obvious to anyone that the first and second groups are so different that they will never manage to understand each other or reach agreement, yet they make friendships and families as if they were one and the same breed. The problem here is people like us, who call ourselves believers – but you can't fool God. He knows who's truly devoted to Him and who's just playing a role, as if they were on stage. What's the point of attending services, hearing the Liturgy, confessing and taking the Eucharist if the moment you step outside the church you live as if you've never heard of God at all.

I think he's right and Dusya was always waiting, always hoping that we would stop and not grow up, that we would remain children. She held us back as best she could. Coaxing and beseeching us not to go any further, she'd come with a sweet or a toy and believed to the very end that she'd manage to talk us out of it. But we kept deceiving her, again and again.

Father, mother, Klasha and godmother aside, there's no one in my life I owe more to than Seryozha. As a child, I never stopped to think where he came from or who his family was, and when I did find out I was surprised, but no more than that. There was a lot of Seryozha in my childhood, even though I didn't see him often and only ever in autumn. He spent his summers roaming Siberia on field trips, usually in the Far North, while in winter he was almost always house-sitting at someone's dacha. Maybe he actually enjoyed the nomadic life, enjoyed going wherever the wind took him, or maybe he just didn't have a place to call home and there was no other remedy.

After one of these trips Seryozha would often stay with us until he found a more permanent haven. This was usually in the first half of October, when three of us – my sister, father and mother – all had name-days in quick succession. Mother loved having guests and putting on a spread, and it so happened that Seryozha would always bring plenty of high-quality ethanol which (I already knew this then) could only be purchased in the northern regions. I remember how the ethanol, once diluted, would be infused with lemon and orange peel, walnut membrane, cranberries and horseradish, so that, on the day of the celebration, mother would lay out an entire battery of many-coloured bottles, to everyone's delight.

Seryozha was no wit, he wasn't even a particularly good storyteller, but I remember him better than any of our other guests. Thanks to Dusya, we were a tight-knit group, no outsiders, and we'd long known what to expect from each other, whereas he would be here today and gone tomorrow. Seryozha would never be the life of the party, that much I knew, but when everyone started besieging him with questions about the North he would eventually give in and I would be as enraptured as everyone else by his stories of midges you could never shake off, endless bogs covered with greyish moss, the thousand-strong herds of reindeer that grazed there, leisurely rivers that seemed not to know which direction to flow in, and the occasional dry mound of earth topped with a clump of trees.

For some obscure reason, the lands east of the Urals and the people who lived there seemed so vivid to me that a year before leaving school I already knew I would apply to the history faculty to study ethnography and that – assuming I was accepted – I would specialise in the small peoples of the North. Which, by the way, is the only plan in my life that's ever worked out to a tee. Following Seryozha's example, I spent almost thirty years shuttling back and forth along the rim of the Arctic Ocean between the River Ob and Kamchatka.

Seryozha didn't just tell us about the North, he also sent me parcels from there several times a season. Neat little cedarwood boxes would be waiting for me at the post office, and inside them, all wrapped up in cotton wool, I might find an *ongon* – a spirit-vessel – alongside other talismans and small objects carved in bone. On one occasion he gave me a pair of enormous reindeer antlers for my name-day, and the following year the tambourine of a genuine shaman. The antlers still hang over the door to my room, but the tambourine has vanished. I wasn't the only one to receive gifts like this from Seryozha. My sister, for example, once celebrated her birthday wearing full shamanic dress with countless ribbons and bells and those astonishingly intricate patterned strips in which every scrap of leather and thread is there for a reason. Seryozha started explaining it all to her, but she only listened for a couple of minutes before running off to meet her guests, and all I can remember from his commentary is that, among the Samoyeds, women are thought to make stronger shamans than men. The costume later found its way to me, and I still have it today.

BE AS CHILDREN

How this happened exactly I've never understood, but I was sixteen before I found out that Seryozha was Dusya's son. For all her energy, there was something ethereal about godmother, not to mention the fact that she seemed to belong to us all, so I could never imagine her having children of her own. I first heard about Dusya and Seryozha when I tagged along with my father to visit some distant relatives. There was the usual kind of talk around the table, but over tea, out of nowhere, the conversation turned to holy fools – who they are exactly, whether or not they still exist and so on. That was when godmother's name was suddenly mentioned. I remember my surprise at how quickly father and everyone else went along with the idea that she was a holy fool. And it was then that I heard her story, albeit only the briefest outline.

The nun Yevdokiya (Dusya, for short) was of good noble stock – the Mukhanov family – and her life got off to an entirely conventional start for people of her kind: gymnasium, marriage, two children, both boys, Seryozha being the eldest. The second son, Borya, was conceived in 1916 when godmother's husband, Prince Pyotr Igrenyev, was sent home wounded and they spent three months together for the first time in two years. Borya didn't linger long in this world, though – he caught meningitis during the Civil War. In 1918, Igrenyev died or went missing, which amounted to much the same thing. Godmother, needless to say, had no means of her own and would never have been able to raise her son without her parents and mother-in-law.

In '27, when Seryozha was thirteen, Dusya took the veil at the insistence of an Elder of the Trinity-Sergius Monastery to whom she had pledged her obedience, though she remained 'in the world'. Borya, who had died so young, was no longer mentioned at the dinner table, and as for Seryozha, Dusya was said to be quite sure he'd become a monk as soon as he reached the age of twenty. Strictly speaking, his entire education was nothing other than preparation for monastic life. But only a few monasteries survived into the mid '30s in Soviet Russia and they all supported Metropolitan Sergius, while godmother and Seryozha had long been on the side of the catacomb church.[16] What he should do was far from clear.

Seryozha wavered for a while, going from one person to another for advice, then suddenly told his mother that he wasn't yet ready to take the tonsure. Dusya, it seems, did not insist. Nobody was talking about her as a holy fool back then; it was only later, during the war, that she became the person we know. Seryozha had always been very good at drawing and his mother agreed that it would be right for him to apply to the Stroganov Institute, the only place that trained restorers (he succeeded at the second attempt). Church icons and frescoes were going to rack and ruin all over the country and it would have been hard to find a more necessary form of service.

That conversation about godmother could not fail to make an impression on me. Once I'd taken in what everyone was saying, that she was a holy fool, a saint, I realised that my entire childhood – my own relationship with Dusya, my parents' relationship with her, and everyone else's – would

---

[16] Following the death of Patriarch Tikhon in 1925, Metropolitan Sergius (born Ivan Stragorodsky) became *de facto* head of the Russian Orthodox Church, and after declaring the Church's support for the Soviet Union in 1927, remained as such until 1943. (There is no connection here with the historic Trinity-Sergius monastery, mentioned earlier in the paragraph, which is named after the fourteenth-century saint, Sergius of Radonezh.)

need to be reassessed. This proved very difficult. A year passed and I had made little progress, if any, which couldn't be said for my drinking. I'm not saying they were connected, but the setback I'd suffered with godmother coincided with me coming home drunk almost every day, to my parents' horror.

While I was small, Dusya was a kind of grandmother to me, an ordinary granny, whose oddities were neither here nor there, and now I suddenly learned that I, and everyone else, had been living all along in the presence of a holy fool, whose life could have meaning only in its relation to the Lord. By then I no longer needed to be told that a holy fool lives by God and God alone. A holy fool is even more devoted to the Lord, more dependent on Him, than a monk. But now it turned out that we too, had been playing our part in all this with our every word, our every step. Or rather, we had been made to take part.

True, the people I'd grown up with were believers and church-goers, but here a different intimacy with the Almighty was called for, and I doubt we were equal to it very often. It was a case of taking stock and re-evaluating everything, and at first I set about the task with enthusiasm. But as time passed and I was getting nowhere, I began to lose heart. So many things that I had always dismissed as petty, everyday trifles were being transformed before my eyes into serious, perhaps even mortal sins – if only because there I was playing games and enjoying myself without ever thinking of God. The world had changed its rules just like that. I'd known, for example, that Dusya loved me less than my sister, and this had never really bothered me, but now it was almost as if judgement had already been passed on me: it wasn't godmother but God

Himself who did not love me.

We – Dusya's inner circle – were her community, her flock, which she had chosen and gathered up, and was now leading to the Lord. We could try our best to back away and flee but it made no difference: part of her holiness fell on us all the same – it had to. I can't speak for others, but I was just an ordinary teenager and hardly deserving of such a gift. I spent my last eighteen months at school trying to get my head round it all, to connect the dots, however roughly. I looked at father and mother and compared them to the parents of my schoolmates, but I couldn't see anything special about them. I gradually became disillusioned with godmother too, and found myself thinking ever more often that perhaps I was just being played for a fool.

Rummaging through my childhood memories, I struggled to find more than two dozen episodes – many of which were pretty much identical – when Dusya had behaved any differently from what you would expect of an ordinary grandmother, when you could say that she really had resembled a holy fool. My recollections often began with games of hide-and-seek, which godmother loved and where she was every bit our equal. Perhaps similar things went on in other people's homes, but if so, I never saw them.

As for our home, there were plenty of places to hide. Our room was considered huge even by the standards of the time – about forty square metres, and a whole five metres high. Father, who was a decent carpenter, had built a broad mezzanine right around it, except for the wall where the windows were. It became my parents' space, while the three of us – my sister, nanny and I – stayed downstairs, which was also where we entertained guests. During our games, of course, we paid no attention to these boundaries. There was also a larder which we used as a wardrobe. As a small boy, I would go there to hide among the furs, pillows and old blankets whenever someone had upset me and I wanted to cry. Another kind of hide-and-seek, I suppose. The larder, just like the main room, was also on two levels. The winter stuff – whatever was made of fur or wool – was up at the top, with little bags of dried lavender sewn on to keep the moths away, while everything else was kept below on hangers or in boxes.

For all father's improvements, there was still something very wrong with the room. The furniture – the cupboard, cabinet, desk and mirrors – did not hug the walls as they did in other people's homes, instead they had all been pushed out into the middle, towards the dining-table, concealing the beds behind them. Thanks to this arrangement, and to the six folding screens with dragons that father had brought back from work trips to China, my sister, nanny and I each had our own nooks, real burrows, where we could be alone if we wanted and where we wouldn't be disturbed without good reason. Overall, the room was made for hide-and-seek, and Dusya, slim and lithe despite her years, always managed to find some crevice or other where no one would ever think of looking.

Godmother got as carried away as we did, which was why we loved playing with her and why we saw her, unlike other grown-ups, as one of us. We spent hours hiding and looking for each other, until eventually it was Dusya's turn to seek. Usually she'd follow the rules and we'd have no complaints, but every now and then something would go wrong. She'd begin, as she was supposed to, by going out into the corridor to give each of us time to find our hiding place. About three minutes were allowed for this. Then godmother would announce in a loud rhythmic voice, with space between the words, 'Six seven eight nine ten, now I'll catch you in your den!' repeat the counting rhyme and open the door.

Whenever hide-and-seek is being played, a home immediately becomes silent and deserted. I must have been the seeker thousands of times and I remember all too well the feeling that the room is empty and always has been and there's no point even looking. Dusya must have felt the same thing. After entering the room she'd look completely lost at first and for reasons I can't explain, call one of us by name and try to coax us out: 'Glebushka, darling, where are you, my precious, where have you got to, my little one? Out you come, don't be scared. Dusya hasn't done anything bad to you, has she? I'm never empty-handed, even now. Look – I've got a chocolate, boiled sweets and fruit bonbons. Out you come now, don't make an old woman suffer.'

She'd do the same with each of us, forgetting nobody, but we wouldn't give in, and her mood would brighten as she became ever more worked up. She walked with small pattering steps of no more than a foot, but she got around quickly and her back, supple from hundreds of prostrations, bent with almost balletic agility. Nor did she lack cunning or intuition. Two or three circuits of the room were more than enough for her to find us. The next thing we knew we'd been flushed from our lairs and were mucking around noisily by the window, trying our best to shout each other down, while she lavished sweets on us from her pocket, which really was filled to bursting. It seems to me now that in playing with us she felt the same joy that the Lord experienced, when breathing souls into His creatures, He released one living being after another into the still empty world and they, having barely touched the earth, began to bustle, chatter and chirp. But this same joy frightened her.

We run off to hide again, breathlessly giggling away, and Dusya, as usual, checks under the beds and in the cupboards, climbs up to the mezzanine, scours the larder and the cubbyholes between the windows, but then – at first we don't even understand what's happening – she loses her bearings. After calling one of us loudly, once and then twice, she suddenly becomes muddled and starts looking for either her own self or some other Dusya. She calls her with the same words she calls us – 'My darling', 'My precious' – tells her not to be afraid or to hide, that she won't do anything bad to her. Outwardly nothing has changed: godmother is scampering around the room as quickly as ever, checking all the nooks and hideouts, but now even if she finds someone she doesn't rejoice – the child is simply ignored. This was all so unfair and so hurtful that we felt like crying, but gradually we came to realise that Dusya was simply no longer playing with us, that she had her own game now and it didn't involve us.

One by one we emerged from our shelters and started some other activity. Now we were living our life, and she was living hers. It wasn't hard not to notice her – after all, many of us lived with our grandparents, some of whom were going batty with old age and could easily outdo Dusya in their eccentricities. So as children we already knew not to pay any attention to such things, whether in our own homes or other people's. The sick were just that, sick, this wasn't the theatre or the circus, and you shouldn't stand and stare.

I've long since realised, of course, that the Dusya whom godmother was calling and seeking was not the flesh-and-blood Dusya we all knew, but her own soul. She would exhort it in that tender voice she had always used with us little ones when we were ill, saying, 'Come over here, my lovely. Come, don't upset Dusya, don't make her suffer – her poor legs are all worn out as it is,' and again, 'Where on earth have you got to, my sweet, why did you go and leave me?' She asked it, 'What did I say to upset you? What have I done wrong?' Or, 'What kind of person can live without a soul? You can't even pray without a soul. And God won't listen to you if you haven't got one. He'll say, "Dusyenka, dear daughter, didn't I give every person a soul? I didn't forget anyone. Perhaps you're not a person at all, just dust, dust of the earth. Look how quick you are: everyone's light without a soul and lets the wind carry them this way and that." What will I say to Him?' And again, 'Come here, my sweet, come here, my lovely, I can't live without you.'

Seeking her soul, godmother would sob and sniff like one of our nannies, like any village woman, but she didn't really cry. At least, I don't remember any tears. For all her pleading though, nobody responded, and her searching proved unsuccessful too. Dusya of course, would never accept that her soul could no longer be found, and not only did the search continue but I even had the sense that the mechanism inside her was turning faster and faster, gathering ever more energy. Her behaviour was unpredictable: some days she would stand in the middle of the room and claim that neither she nor anyone else actually needed a soul, that it brought nothing but trouble, and it was far easier to live without one. Other days she would wander off with a bewildered air towards the window and sit down on a chair; her eyes would be blank, as if turned inwards, and her arms folded on her knees, but her fingers would fidget restlessly with her apron. She would sit like that for five minutes, then again start methodically, comprehensively scouring every area, every hideout. They had all been checked and double-checked long ago, but either she didn't remember or she didn't understand.

Sometimes she would act out entire scenes in a recitative for two or three voices: 'Dusya,' her mother would cry, 'beloved daughter, where has your soul got to, where have you left it? Go, go back and find it. I won't let you into the home without it.' 'I'll find it, mummy,' Dusya would reply, 'I'll find it right now – it can't have run away. It's found some hole or other to hide in, the little devil, and it's sitting there laughing at me.' She'd mutter something else as well, but we could only make out the odd word. At this point, two outcomes were possible. Often the soul would finally succumb to her coaxing and allow godmother to find it, and then she would calm down, contented. But when it stubbornly refused, matters could take a very different turn.

I should mention that my parents were intelligentsia types and that meant, above all, a great many unspoken taboos. One of the most important was never to swear under any circumstances. Swearing at home was simply unthinkable, as every nanny was duly warned. When they were taken on, they would all solemnly promise that nobody would ever hear any bad language from them, but back in the countryside you'd struggle to make yourself understood to your own cow without the occasional obscenity, and these would sometimes slip out in front of us children. Rarely in front of the parents, though. They were especially terrified of mother – everyone knew that she could dismiss you for it. I had it drummed into me as well. At any rate, I don't recall ever swearing at home until my stint in the madhouse. The courtyard, of course, was a different story. But I heard it at home as well, and not only from Klasha and Raya.

The soul, for whatever reason, refused to be found. It must have been far too frightened, and godmother had no more illusions. She seemed to know what was happening, understood that the soul was right: that she, Dusya, was to blame for it all. Earlier on, trying to coax the soul to return as if nothing had happened, godmother had played the fool, but all to no end. There was probably nothing for it other than to drop to her knees and meekly beg the Lord to forgive her, but Dusya it seemed, was not thinking about God at that moment. Perhaps she'd just got too carried away by the game. The flywheel inside her that let her ransack the room again and again without ever getting tired and crawl into the most improbable cracks in order to pull us skinny, slippery runts out into the light of day seemed to be saying to her: don't be scared, your soul can't run away. You'll find it soon enough, you'll coax it out with bribes if you have to. And so, caught up in the game, godmother forgot all about God, or perhaps she really was thinking that since she had no soul inside her she had nothing left to pray to the Lord with. She was further away from Him than any mute beast, she was almost a shell, a corpse.

Although Dusya's soul had abandoned her body, her body

sent outside until things settled down. But we were good kids, there was no malice in us, and no one needed to tell us how bad godmother was feeling. There was nothing we could do to help her. And there was no fun to be had either, so we were only too happy to get away. We went out to the playground in the yard and carried on with our games until nanny called us back in.

The fits would leave Dusya too weak to move, and when she did come round she would sleep through to the next morning. An evening and night must have been enough for her to recover though, because when she woke up she was her usual self, the same Dusya without whom our own lives seemed unimaginable. Without discussing or agreeing anything amongst ourselves, we all understood this to mean that Dusya's soul had returned to her, that everything was fine and that she was well again.

Seryozha began his studies at Moscow's Stroganov Institute in '34. He graduated, got a job in a museum in Yaroslavl and was sent to the front, where he was wounded three times, badly on each occasion. When he was demobilised in '45, he didn't go back to the museum but fell in with some ethnographers and spent more than twenty-five years roaming the North. He drew whatever he was asked to draw: clothes, the patterns sewn onto them to keep evil away, the faces of shamans during a ritual, the nomads' tents – the *chum* – as well as their day-to-day utensils; tambourines, *ongons*, teams of dogs and reindeer trudging through the snow. He drew wherever he found himself, from Yamal to Chukotka, first on research trips and later, when the people he used to travel with started making careers and defending dissertations, he illustrated their books for publication. I was convinced that he would roam like this to the end of his days, but in the early '70s, when he was not yet sixty, Seryozha suddenly left the Institute of Ethnography and settled permanently in Moscow. Luckily, one of his former colleagues, a member of the Academy of Sciences, had managed to secure a studio for him three years earlier in an old merchant house on Trubnaya Square.

The room was ordinary enough, except for two rows of icons on each wall. Seryozha had brought these back from the North as well. Tens of thousands of Old Believers had been sent there when collectivisation began, and by the time of Stalin's death most of them had died.[17] Seryozha had long been friendly with many of the survivors. He restored some of their icons in Moscow and did so strictly by the book, for which his work was especially prized, then he would bring them back to the sketes the following year.[18] But plenty of icons dating from even before the Schism had been given to him simply for safekeeping.

Seryozha first got to know the Old Believers in the late '40s, and the artwork that had passed through his room

---

[17] The first of many references to the consequences of the seventeenth-century Schism within the Russian Orthodox Church, when Patriarch Nikon, trying to bring the Church into line with Greek practice, introduced reforms to the sacred texts and modes of worship. Those who rejected these reforms, led by the Archpriest Avvakum, became known as the Old Believers and were frequently persecuted; those who accepted them were known as Nikonians or simply Orthodox, though the Old Believers consider themselves the bearers of 'true' Orthodoxy. (The Schism is at the heart of Sharov's novel, *The Rehearsals*.)

[18] A skete is a small, self-sufficient, usually remote community of monks living in separate cells or caves.

over a period of twenty years would have been the envy of any museum. Not long ago I was recalling the icons he was particularly fond of and our own not very frequent conversations, and I suddenly realised that Seryozha had always found it difficult to accept the adult Christ, Christ Pantocrator, Christ on Golgotha, the Christ who preached and the Christ who threatened sinners. The icons he prayed before showed only Christ the Infant, Christ the Child in the arms of Our Lady. Never, or at least never in my presence, did Seryozha express his thoughts on such topics, but for him, perhaps everything else in Christ's life was far too severe, far too strict.

There were times in those years when I also thought that, through His conception, His birth and all the miracles linked to it, the Son of God had already shown us the path to salvation. Nothing else was required: after all, Christ Himself once said, 'Be as children, for theirs is the Kingdom of Heaven'. This, I've been told, was the part of Our Saviour's life that Dusya also loved the most, when Our Lady was His entire world. When there was nobody in it apart from her.

That must have been why godmother never stopped insisting that to grow up was always to retreat from the Lord. Every day that a person spends on Earth overflows with sin and merely pushes that person further away from God. She once said that as He grew, Christ Himself began to look at the world created by the Lord in a different way. He could see that people, through their evil, had deformed it so badly that they now had no less a claim than the Almighty to be called its makers. This was the one and only reason why the Son of God, emerging from childhood, became sterner by the day and less quick to forgive, as the Gospels show us on many occasions.

That was also why He grew distant from His mother. And this continued right up until His return to Jerusalem, until the Last Supper and Golgotha.

Seryozha wasn't too willing to talk about the Old Believers. They kept to themselves, tried not to let in strangers, and he respected that. True, there were a couple of stories from before his time in the North that he did tell me. How Avvakum's followers must have felt towards the Bolsheviks who destroyed three quarters of their fellow Old Believers in prisons and camps is obvious enough, but they didn't think much of the Whites either, or the Greens, or any other colour. The prophet once said that 'A kingdom divided against itself cannot stand'; the Civil War, in which God's people slaughtered itself tirelessly, was clear evidence that the last days had come: no man without evil, no man without guilt. But then, in a skete somewhere in 1948, Seryozha heard an entirely new explanation of the Civil War. I'm not convinced that the role of the events that follow was really so great, but that's not what matters: this legend is an attempt to forgive and justify one's tribe and every person in it.

The Old Believers told Seryozha that in November 1916 – the third winter of the war, when millions of soldiers had already been killed, many million others wounded and maimed, and the lucky ones were rotting alive in the trenches – Vladimir Sabler, head of the Holy Synod,[19] informed the Tsar that His Majesty's subjects needed a sign to show that he loved them equally and held them all to be equally loyal. He was speaking

---

[19] Established in 1721 by Peter the Great, the Holy Synod replaced the Patriarchate (which was then restored after the revolutions of 1917) and increased the role of government in Church affairs.

first and foremost about the Old Believers. It was time to stop viewing them as heretics who must repent right away and must join the Synodal Church. Quite the opposite: the Old Believers should be given to understand that the Sovereign considered their faith no less pleasing to God than official Orthodoxy. And it would be best to do this without any proclamations or manifestos.

The Tsar asked what exactly Sabler had in mind. He replied that in the larger Orthodox churches one might permit the Divine Liturgy to be sung according to the pre-Schism rite every now and again. Only in one church at first, and then, if everything went smoothly, in others too, wherever there were many Old Believers nearby. After thinking this over, the Tsar agreed, and the choice for the trial run fell on the Church of the Holy Mother of God in Chukhloma.[20] The church was not chosen at random. The priest there was Father Georgy, a soft-natured man who, moreover, had a deep fondness for the Old Believers. The entire town of Chukhloma knew how close he and his family were to the Old Believer priest Father Dosifei and that their wives were sisters. Sabler had also heard all about him: the Holy Synod had received at least a dozen denunciations of Father Georgy in the last year alone. He'd been very slow to act on these, without himself knowing why, but now he saw that he had been right to hold off.

The diocesan authorities were very unhappy with Father Georgy. In particular, they blamed him for doing nothing to bring the heretics back into the bosom of the Church, and when talking to his parishioners, for not hiding his admiration of the Old Believer way of life. Especially family life. He

---

[20] Located about 500 kilometres north-east of Moscow.

liked the absence of lechery, drunkenness and foul language among both husbands and wives, liked the fact that they did not fight among themselves. That their children were well-behaved, polite and honest. This was all so much closer to what the Lord wanted from mankind. He made this last point openly, sometimes even in the middle of a sermon, and the result, according to police intelligence, was that several dozen Orthodox believers had been seduced by such speeches and drifted over to Father Dosifei.

Chukhloma's Church of the Holy Mother of God was very large. Dating from the mid-nineteenth century and paid for by the Counts Sheremetyev, it was built in the Empire style for serfs from nearby trading villages. Back then the locals were Orthodox to a man, but later on Old Believers also began to settle in the commercial suburbs of neighbouring towns. By the end of the century they numbered more than a thousand. They were all 'Priestists', who accepted, unlike their 'Priestless' brethren among the Old Believers, that salvation in our world was impossible without a clergy. As it grew, this community started submitting requests to the Holy Synod to build its own church, but twenty years later, despite generous bribes and the intercession of influential figures, matters in St Petersburg had barely moved an inch. Here was a chance to kill two birds with one stone.

This wasn't the only reason that Chukhloma had been chosen: it was no secret to the Synod that the church was half-empty even on the major feast days. Much as they respected Father Georgy, the peasants and townsfolk had taken a cordial dislike to the church itself, finding it damp and draughty. The Church of the Mother of God had one other peculiarity: from the outside it was an ordinary cross-in-square church with a dome and tall bell tower. But the architect must have made a mistake, or perhaps he just didn't know the first thing about acoustics – in any case, almost nothing could be heard in the side aisles during services. This blunder was a gift to Sabler. It meant that priests could celebrate two liturgies in the church at the same time without getting in each other's way. That decided the matter, and on 10th December 1916, during the Fast of the Nativity, Old Believer services began in the church in Chukhloma.

Still, for the first few days every measure was taken to keep the two flocks of Christ's children apart, but it soon became clear that nobody was a burden on anyone else. Seeing that the Lord was on their side, Fathers Georgy and Dosifei agreed that they would actually bring the two congregations together for the Christmas Liturgy. Even without the side aisles, the Church of the Holy Mother of God could easily fit eight hundred worshippers. There must have been at least that number at this joint service. Aside from the locals, several hundred people came from other parts of Chukhloma and the surrounding villages to hear the first Liturgy since the Schism to have been shared by both Old Believers and Orthodox. For as long as everyone was in the church, all went well. According to the accounts of the Old Believers, both priests – Father Dosifei and Father Georgy – conducted the service in a seemly, dignified fashion, the choirs sang splendidly, and the candle flames, incense and myrrh, mixing with the prayers of people whose minds were turned solely to the Lord, filled the church to its dome with godliness and transformed it into the likeness of a true paradise.

BE AS CHILDREN

By mutual agreement, the Divine Liturgy was celebrated according to the Old Believer rite and concluded when it was already past four in the afternoon, after which the priests blessed the congregation and began leading it out to the parvis for the Procession of the Cross. It was wartime, everyone had family at the front, but even so, on this salvific day of Christ's Birth, people were radiant and joyful. Old Believers, as we know, process 'sunwise' around the church, while Nikonians, just like the Greeks, walk against the direction of our heavenly body. So too on this occasion. Each procession, bearing crosses, icons and banners, followed its own priest, as sheep follow their shepherd. The parvis in front of the church was as large as a square and paved with cobblestones. Paths strewn with sand led off in both directions around the church, hugging the walls; once broad, they had become little more than a trail after the first turning. When the priests emerged, there were still plenty of people inside the church, praying or waiting their turn to kiss the icon of Our Lady of Chukhloma, which was greatly revered in these parts. Gradually, making the sign of the cross and blessing one another with the same gesture, they too came outside.

The densely packed parvis resembled a lake at high water from which two human streams were peacefully and unhurriedly flowing. Initially, both processions could comfortably absorb all the people coming out of the church, but there seemed to be no end to them. For the first few hundred metres the believers walked freely, without any crowding or jostling; not a single child was picked up and carried. But the path soon became narrow, it could no longer let everyone through at the same time, and the current of parishioners began to slow. Worse, people were being squeezed ever more tightly, as is always the case in a bottleneck. Soon, many were finding it hard even to breathe. Children were being held aloft now, to keep them from being maimed. All the same, both processions kept moving, and as yet nobody felt too frightened.

The bell tower of the Chukhloma church was famous throughout the diocese. It was renowned for two things: firstly, its three-tonne bell whose chime, against all expectation, was not a bass but a high, slightly cracked tenor – the wrong materials seem to have been used for the cast iron at the foundry. In every other way, it was a good bell, and when it was rung you could hear it many miles away. The main thing though, was the virtuoso ringer, a dumb and crippled man from somewhere in western Ukraine. As a child, the story went, he was as chatty as any woman, so one day his father, unable to make this ten-year-old kid keep his mouth shut, went berserk, and trapping his son's head between his knees, sliced through his frenulum with a utility knife. Ever since, he had lost the power of normal human speech but he had excellent hearing and quick, nimble hands. It was thanks to these that he could now communicate in chimes with the entire parish.

The narrowest section of the path curled around the base of the bell tower. Worse still, it was abutted by an old, crowded cemetery. The graves were surrounded by tall, almost chest-high railings topped by finials in the form of pointed helmets and spears. So there was no room on that side either. The Old Believers of course, could never have suspected this. Father Georgy and his parishioners were a different matter – many of them had family buried there; but the thought that there would not be enough space for the two Processions of the Cross to pass each other beneath the bell tower had never occurred to them either.

The first to realise that the Old Believers and Nikonians would soon meet head-on and that disaster would follow was the bell-ringer. Unable to scream at everyone to stop, he simply cut short the festive peals and began ringing as bell-ringers once rang in olden Rus to warn people of danger. It would have been better if he hadn't. Everyone understood that something had happened, but they didn't know what. Trapped in the crush, unable even to move their hands, they began losing their minds from helplessness.

Incidentally, some ten years later I found myself writing down Seryozha's legend almost word for word. This happened at a small Old Believer skete on the banks of the River Ob, and I was struck by the similarity between the details of the Chukhloma episode and the uprising in the town of Uglich on the day of the Blessed Tsarevich Dmitry's death. Above all, I was struck by the fact that the troubles that began on these two occasions in Russia with the ringing of church bells were almost indistinguishable.

In 1591, as is well known, Ivan the Terrible's eight-year-old son from his last wife, Maria Nagaya, died in Uglich, which had been given to him in appanage. According to the official version, the unfortunate Tsarevich Dmitry, who was prone to violent epileptic fits, accidentally stabbed himself during a game of *tychka*.[21] The townsfolk had long suspected that Boris Godunov, the country's *de facto* leader in those

---

[21] The main version of this game consisted in launching a knife (or marlinespike) so that it landed within a circle or ring on the ground, with the tip entering the earth.

years, was bent on getting rid of Ivan the Terrible's youngest son, heir to the throne. When they heard about the calamity, they rushed to the Tsarevich's residence, where they tore several of the Tsarevich's servitors to pieces, not stopping in their rage to work out who was innocent and who was guilty. There followed a lengthy criminal investigation during which one townsman after another repeated that the rioters had acted after hearing the bell, with the result that the instigator of all the trouble was deemed to have been the ringer himself. His tongue was ripped out, as with our chimer, and he was sentenced to eternal exile in Siberia. The bell itself was exiled beyond the Urals together with all the residents of Uglich, who dragged it east for several thousand versts.

In Chukhloma, meanwhile, the priests spotted each other a minute after the bell-ringer had done so. It was clear that the two processions could not pass – there wasn't enough space – so they folded their arms over their chests to tell their congregations to stop. But it was hopeless. The believers, other than those who were walking next to the priests, suspected nothing and kept on going, and the processions, like two currents, flowed ever onwards. Some shouted and begged those at the back to ease off, but their screams, along with the bell's desperate peals, all blended into a senseless cacophony. From the few isolated words that could still be made out, both flocks understood only one thing: for some unknown reason the Old Believers – or conversely, the Nikonians – were not letting them pass.

All of them, of course, were knee-deep in sin, but on this day, whether during the Liturgy, when they had listened with such faith to words of charity and love of one's neighbour, or now, as they walked and sang hymns, as best they could, to celebrate the Saviour's birth, they were as pure and innocent as infants. Righteousness is a terrible force. Forgetting all their bad deeds, they became angry and hostile. Having decided that someone was trying to prevent them from being good, they merely became more determined to stick it out to the very end, anything so as not to give way. A bloody free-for-all began. Its outcome was grim.

The first to die, like martyrs, were Father Georgy and Father Dosifei, their bodies squashed together. The police reported a further twenty-two dead, fifteen of whom were crushed underfoot, while seven were impaled on the tips of the railings, as if on spits. The Old Believers claimed that it was after this episode, in which nobody had wished anybody any ill, that the troubles began. That Rus rose against Rus.

I've related the Old Believers' tale at such length partly because I once heard Father Nikodim, the priest at Snegiri, express similar thoughts in one of his sermons. Having started to talk about the enmity of Christians towards Christians, he abruptly turned to our own Civil War and announced that nobody could be blamed for it. Those who killed in that war and those who died in it had all, in their own way, wanted the salvation of mankind. And so, filled with faith and guided by their prophets and pastors, they had walked towards their paradise – be it in Heaven or on Earth. They hadn't a single bad thought in their minds, they just walked and walked, until they suddenly saw somebody standing in their path, not letting them through. Everyone's first thought was that there was something behind this, that after so much humiliation, grief and bloodshed it wasn't humans blocking their path but evil itself. Three years of world war had been enough to convince anyone that guns were more powerful than prayers and so, not stopping to think, with sabres bared and bayonets fixed to rifles, they charged at the enemy and died, certain that they were dying for the truth. And whether they were wrong or right is not for us to judge.

There's another reason, too: the story of the Old Believers, it seems to me, makes for a good introduction to the cycle of legends about the Enets Paul the Apostle – Yevlampy Khristoforovich Peregudov – which I collected over a period of almost twenty years. The story of this man's life is remarkable in every way. What we now know about him, especially until the start of the Civil War, is entirely trustworthy. The legends contain only crumbs of myth, and I would probably have continued working on Peregudov were it not for the fact that my expeditions to the North came to an end in the second half of the 1980s and my previous interests, including the Enets, faded into the background until they were completely abandoned.

Before that, strictly once every four years, there came a series of deaths: Father Nikodim, Seryozha, Dusya. Though my relationships with them no longer bulked quite so large in my life, there was still no one in the world, aside from my mother, father and sister, whom I felt closer to. Anyway, what concerns me here is not our relationships but the things that neither Dusya nor Father Nikodim nor Seryozha, try as they might, could ever sidestep or calmly ignore. As if to illustrate the Old Believer legend, they stubbed their toes on them time and again.

BE AS CHILDREN

The first version I heard of the Life of Peregudov was very disjointed. Only this much was clear: he was a runaway soldier who in 1863 had ended up among the Enets – like all small peoples, they gladly welcomed outsiders – and promptly converted them to the Christian faith. I suspect that his own fate didn't interest him very much and he had no intention at first of telling anyone about it, but a series of circumstances forced him into greater openness. Ten years of sharing tents on the tundra changed Peregudov greatly. Within this simple soldier, who happened to become an apostle to an entire people, serious work was under way, and it didn't take long before he realised that without his past he would be unable to explain anything to his flock.

The Enets revered him as a prophet and could not imagine disobeying him, but it took the tribe some time to absorb his teachings. As compared with his earlier preaching, the Samoyeds found his sermons of the second half of the 1870s far harder to understand. The years went by, but they could hear nothing in his words except blasphemy and mockery of the same divine messenger, the same man who had brought them the true faith. The fact that he was blaspheming against himself made no difference to them. And when the Enets finally grasped what Peregudov was trying to tell them, they drew very different conclusions from the ones he'd been counting on.

Right up until his final years, the Samoyeds scrupulously preserved Peregudov's words, even when they disagreed with him. They believed that nothing he told them was, or ever could be, redundant or unimportant. Just like the colour in an icon, the arrangement of the figures, their garments, faces and hands, the way the light falls, so in his stories every detail was there for a reason and filled with meaning. If something was still unclear to them, it just meant that the time for clarity had not yet come. Sooner or later it would. Considering that not one of the Samoyedic peoples had their own written language, that at first they didn't even know Russian, and that for almost fifty years Peregudov's preaching could only be transmitted by word of mouth, its survival in the form we know is nothing short of a miracle.

Why am I convinced that nothing has been forgotten? In ethnography it's the rarest of rarities when myths can be checked against other sources. In the '20s the Society of Old Political Convicts and Exiled Settlers published several books in which one of the protagonists was none other than Peregudov. The testimonies of revolutionaries who spent twenty or thirty years with him – some even longer – are indistinguishable from the Enets legends. Sometimes you have the impression that one was just copying from the other.

Peregudov's participation in the Russian Revolution is a separate story. It began in the late 1880s under the following circumstances. A year after the Samoyeds had taken in Peregudov, a vicious plague, never before seen in these parts, swept the mouth of the Lena River. It originated somewhere along the Indigirka River, among the Tungus. The Enets, and especially their children, were hit particularly hard by the disease, which also brought many complications. In total the illness took some ninety lives, almost always of little boys. In the '70s it reared its head a second time, leaving the tribe with only half the young men it needed. There was no one to herd reindeer, to hunt, fish and above all, father children. The

Higher Power can come to people's aid whatever their woe. Newly baptised by Peregudov, the Enets prayed for husbands as the Jews in the Holy Land had prayed for winter rain, and the Lord heard their prayers.

It was at about this time that Alexander III sent hundreds of revolutionaries to Yakutia, whether to hard labour or exile. Three quarters of them were Narodniks,[22] but there were also Social Democrats and Bundists. Something for everyone, you might say. Many tried to escape, and more than once. The southern route – back west, or east to America and on to Europe – was closed off by the authorities, so the revolutionary parties all decided, one after the other, to try heading north instead. By the mid-1890s everyone had abandoned the idea but the eight years before that were sufficient for Peregudov to take in and save fifty-five people. For all the bribes, demands and threats, not one of them was handed over to the authorities. But nor did anyone manage to leave. Gradually accepting this, the Narodniks began marrying Samoyeds, starting families and having children, and it was only after the Revolution, no sooner than 1919, that some of them – half, at most – began heading back. The rest went on herding reindeer along the banks of the Lena.

In the cases where the Samoyed legends I collected in Tiksi and in nomad camps are similar to what has long been available in print, I will try to retell them as briefly as possible. I have a

---

[22] A movement that developed in the 1860s-70s, when members of the intelligentsia 'went to the people' (the *narod*), agitating among the peasantry in the hope of achieving agrarian socialism; under Alexander III, many Narodniks turned to more violent methods of resistance.

second reason for doing so: when describing his life to the Enets, all Peregudov really shared with them was the story of a run-of-the-mill murderer. Everything else became known by accident or misunderstanding. What details he gave usually served a fairly obvious purpose. Peregudov knew that without the odd vignette and splash of colour he would never be able to convince the Enets of anything, and he needed the same trust from them as when he had preached Jesus Christ the Saviour.

The sentence passed by Samokhinsky District Court on 12th January 1850 – I found it in the regional archives in Perm – states that Yevlampy Khristoforovich Peregudov was born to an impoverished priest who had lost his parish through drunkenness and negligence and had been forced once more to take up the plough. Peregudov, the third child, had been baptised in the village of Solottsy, in Samokhinsky district, eighteen years earlier, on 20th September 1832 (Old Style). The same date recurs in his certificates. Solottsy had once been a fairly large settlement: it was where peasants employed in the nearby ironworks, the third such site built by Demidov,[23] used to live.

They had been moved here from various villages in the province of Yaroslavl back during the reign of Peter the Great, but the rich ore deposits only lasted a hundred years, after which both factory and mine were closed down and half the population went away – mainly to Pervouralsk and Nizhny Tagil. Most of those who stayed lived off the forest, cutting down pine, larch and spruce, and floating the logs down the Kama. The loamy soil yielded little, it was winter half the year,

---

[23] Nikita Demidov (1656-1725), born to a peasant blacksmith, ennobled by Peter the Great, and founder of the Demidov industrial dynasty.

and there was no way of living solely off the land. You had to work hard to get by, which as Yevlampy Khristoforovich admitted, did not appeal to him one bit. When he was sixteen, a gypsy woman at a fair in the neighbouring village told him that he would kill nine people over the course of his life and that he'd do it easily, without the slightest regret, as if he were cutting heads off chickens.

Solottsy lay near an ancient highway that ran from Vyatka to Perm. There had been trouble on this road for two years. Merchants and other travellers had been robbed and even killed. According to rumours, an entire gang was operating on the highway, with a convict who'd fled the mines in the Urals as its leader. Despite strict orders from Perm, few of the brigands had been caught. Either they'd been greasing the palms of the local authorities, or the police simply weren't up to the task. All around were endless forests where any fool could hide until danger had passed.

Peregudov already had a sweetheart, a saucy soldier's widow by the name of Katya, a young peasant beauty. It was Katya who got him mixed up with these felons. By this point he'd long been thinking of the bandit life – he was fed up with slaving away for his crust from dawn till dusk. True, the thought of seeking out a bandit lair all on his own scared him a little: what if they didn't want him or just stuck a knife between his ribs? He was a strong lad and a good shot, but he was still frightened.

Six months later the brigands raided a wagon train in which two merchants were travelling from Perm, along with a lieutenant in the Guards – a courier, as it later turned out. The officer put up a manful defence and it was Peregudov who finally killed him, having joined the gang just two months before. The courier was the second of the nine victims foretold by the gypsy woman. A month earlier, to prove to the hardened convicts that he was no more scared of spilling a man's blood and committing a mortal sin than of downing a glass of vodka, he had stabbed the first stranger to cross his path – a luckless pedlar.

At first, Peregudov told the Enets, he had simply ignored the gypsy's prophesy. He'd have his fun while he was still young, then his mother would find him a good bride and everything would fall into place. He even forgave himself the pedlar and the courier, and he only realised there was no way back when he killed Katka as well.

The gang was on a bad streak, and when Peregudov got drunk he became jealous and bitter that Katka didn't want to sleep with him. Yelling that she was the source of all their troubles, that it was Katka who was grassing on them to the Chief of Police, he twisted her neck, like a little chick's, in front of the whole group. It was only when she stopped moving that he came to his senses, and appearing not to notice that she was dead and there was nothing anyone could do to help her, he kept trying to bring Katya back from the other world, to breathe life into her once more. After this, Peregudov told the Enets, he was always on the run, wherever his legs took him, anything to escape another murder. But the farther he went, the more blood he shed.

Soon after Katya's death they went into hiding. The gang had a large warm log cabin in the forest, with a proper stove and a double floor. There were plentiful supplies of the essentials – gunpowder and lead, flour, grain, salt – and everything else could be hunted, so their leader decided that they should lie low until the locals forgot about them. But he himself was the first to crack. Bored to tears, he started to pay the occasional visit, alone or with another man, to a roadside tavern five versts from their lodge. But he didn't draw any attention to himself. He'd sit down with his drink and leave soon enough. It was in this tavern that he happened to hear that a stagecoach was due to arrive in the town of Nytva in three days' time with a whole month's worth of excise tax on board. He hesitated briefly before declaring that it would be a sin to let such riches pass them by. But it was clear, Peregudov told the Enets, that the unlucky streak that had begun while Katya was still alive was not about to end. There was nothing wrong with the tip-off – the stagecoach really was carrying money, but it was also carrying three battle-hardened officers. They killed four of the gang with their first salvo, wounded two others, including Peregudov, and had the pair bandaged up in Glazov before handing them over to the Chief of Police.

Soon after, each man went his separate way. Pergudov's case dragged on for some reason, while his accomplice was sentenced within a month: he received two hundred lashes of the knout, was branded, shackled and sent off to the mines of Nerchinsk. Peregudov was also in line for hard labour, but got lucky. With the start of the Crimean War in the autumn of 1853, a new round of recruitment was announced, and among those to be called up was the son of the head of a rich trading village just outside Glazov. Desperate to keep his heir out of the army, the chief struck a deal with a justice of the peace. He bought Peregudov out of prison for a large sum and handed him over in place of his son. So instead of going down a mine,

Peregudov ended up in a dragoon regiment quartered near the Cossack village of Privolnaya and spent almost five years fighting in the Caucasus.

During his early years roaming with the Enets, Peregudov made no exception, when talking about his life, for those he killed in the war, and he never tried to absolve himself of their deaths. He said that in both cases you were taking a person's life, and the Lord had never given anyone the right to do that. As for the awards he had received for every Highlander he'd shot or hacked down and his reputation as a hero of the Caucasian War, they didn't mean much to him. He also remarked one day that when he was released from service following a serious injury to his chest and a year spent in field hospitals, he was convinced that he had long since fulfilled his quota – those nine deaths foretold by the gypsy woman – and even exceeded it.

None of this added up. After all, once he was in Siberia, the governor of Yakutia, von Stassel, also died at his hands. Then there was Ionakh the shaman, whom he killed before their eyes. But Peregudov doesn't seem to have been too worried about things fitting neatly together. As for the Enets, they didn't dare ask how it was that he'd carried on spilling human blood. Ten years passed before their teacher returned to the subject of war, and they remembered what he told them then just as clearly as they remembered everything else.

One of the things they learned from Peregudov in the 1870s was that no one could say how many Circassians he'd killed in the Caucasian War. When both sides are firing at each other nonstop, it's hard to know whose bullet – your own or someone else's – has found its target. Evidently, the Lord takes the same view: in a full-blown battle, or even a skirmish, He shares out death evenly, making no distinctions.

That the Lord might have a different reckoning, Peregudov told the Enets, was something that back then, in '55, he'd never even suspected. He killed four men in the Caucasus face to face. He spent a day and a night lying in ambush before taking out the first Highlander with a bullet, and he also used his carbine, it seems, to dispatch the second, a spy, when the poor man was trying to swim across the Sulak. Then came an episode which completely changed Peregudov's life and eventually brought him to the Enets.

In the autumn of 1854, heavy fighting erupted on the banks of the Sunzha. The Highlanders broke through their left flank and Colonel von Stassel, who was leading the Russian troops in this battle, was cut off and surrounded by a detachment of Karachays. Although Stassel put up a brave fight, everyone agreed that but for Peregudov, the colonel could not have avoided captivity. Despite losing his mount, Peregudov broke through the enemy's tightly packed ranks, wounded one Karachay in the stomach with his bayonet, killed two others with his sabre and saved his commander, injuring himself badly in the process. He received a St George's Cross for his part in the battle and was immediately promoted to the rank of non-commissioned officer.

After almost six months when no one knew whether he would live or die and when he overheard the nurses saying, more than once, that this dragoon would be crippled for life, if by God's grace he pulled through at all, Peregudov – as he told the Enets – began looking at many things in a very different way. Small wonder then, that once he completed his convalescence at the Catherine Hospital in Moscow, the first thing he did was to set out on a pilgrimage. First to Trinity-Sergius, and from there, on foot with two companions, north to the Kirillo-Belozersky monastery.

He had always loved to roam, to spend nights out in the field, and now too, as if he'd never had a single operation or a single wound, he adjusted quickly, in the space of only a couple of days, to the wandering life of the pilgrim; he walked with lightness and joy, and his prayers were also joyful. On the road and at night the same thought kept coming back to him: to walk like this to the very end of his life, simply to wend his way, without haste or plan, from one holy cloister to another.

He even considered becoming a monk himself, but this thought came and went without really taking root, and so, scared of falling into error, he decided to consult Feodor, a revered Elder at the monastery in Kirillov. He stood through matins, confessed, then went off to Feodor's cell. The Elder was very gentle and attentive towards him and asked him many questions about his life, but he sent him away with the comment that for as long as a person is still wavering, still swaying like a blade of grass in the wind, he should remain out in the world. His soul would be of no use to the Lord.

In September '57, Peregudov, now back in Moscow, took a job as a doorman in a restaurant on Neglinnaya Street. The work was easy enough and there was good money to be made from tips. Besides, Peregudov told the Enets, he had no intention of staying for ever: he'd given himself exactly a year, during which time he would calmly and carefully think over everything he'd been told by Father Feodor.

He did his job conscientiously and spent the rest of his

time reading Holy Scripture, praying and sleeping. He, like the waiters, was fed with whatever remained in the kitchen once the customers had gone, and he was also provided with a garret beneath the eaves of the same building, so he had little reason or inclination to be out and about. What was more, the drunken revelry he observed every day seemed to serve as a running commentary on Feodor's words about sin, pride and the vanity of worldly life. By spring, Peregudov had firmly made up his mind to don the monk's habit, and but for his fear that he had not yet done his time and that Father Feodor would send him straight back again, he would have left for Kirillov there and then.

According to every testimony, Peregudov spoke of his timidity with evident regret and sorrow. Realising what it would have meant for them if he'd taken his vows – they would have lived their entire lives as heathens and burned in Hell after their deaths – the Enets did not conceal how hurt they felt, that they considered his words a betrayal. Peregudov tried to make amends by adding that he would have preached Jesus Christ to them just the same, only as a monk. In fact, he would have come even sooner, by as much as a year, if not two, for the path of a man who has devoted himself to the Lord runs straight. But they were unmoved by these explanations, seeing them as no more than an excuse, and by mutual agreement they never returned to the topic of Peregudov's vows. Especially because circumstances had conspired in such a way that he left that path of his own free will.

In late May 1857, a low-ranking police officer came to see the restaurant's owner, Feofanov, a merchant of the second guild, to make inquiries about where the previous doorman had got to and who this new man was that Feofanov had taken on in the winter. Trouble with the police was the last thing Feofanov needed, and so after putting out some vodka and a bite of something, he set about explaining that the dragoon was a hero of the recent Caucasian War, had received the Cross of St George for saving the life of his commander, was wounded, spent months in a field hospital and left the service, after which he, Feofanov, had offered him work at his restaurant. He carried himself like a true soldier, was imposing, well-built and honest, so what could he say – the customers weren't complaining and Feofanov himself had never had cause to regret hiring him.

Just as soon as the policeman had jotted all this down and left, Feofanov immediately sent for his doorman. He summarised the conversation and added, with obvious sympathy, that if the soldier was hiding anything, he'd better get out of town right away, the further the better, until it all blew over. Hearing this, Peregudov decided that maybe his old exploits in Perm really had bubbled up to the surface, but he took the news calmly and decided that if they did arrest him he'd only be getting his just deserts.

But Peregudov had nothing to fear: nobody was about to poke around in his distant past in the Urals. A completely different episode suddenly re-emerged out of nowhere – the battle of the Sunzha. Five days later he received a letter by courier from Baron von Stassel. The regimental commander wrote that he too had been wounded and had retreated to his country estate to recover. He'd tried many times to track down his saviour but, whomever he asked, he always got the same reply: no idea. Now though, the baron went on, he wasn't just writing to thank the person to whom he owed his life, but because he had business to discuss.

Stassel informed him that the previous month he had been appointed governor of Yakutsk by Imperial decree, and that if there was nothing urgent detaining the soldier in Moscow, he was welcome to join him. As for what exactly Peregudov would do in Siberia, well, they'd work that out once they got there. He could stay in the town if he wanted, if not, some other job could be found for him easily enough. The region was vast and enormously rich; the gold mining industry alone was worth several million roubles and growing year on year. Embezzlement and bribery though, were out of all control, and he, Stassel, wouldn't be able to cope with it all without men he could trust. The baron finished by saying that he would be passing through the former capital in exactly two weeks' time and that if the dragoon decided to come, he would be only too glad to offer him a place in his carriage.

Yakutsk, needless to say, was about the last thing he was expecting, but it seems that Peregudov had learned to accept whatever might come his way: forced labour, the cassock, Siberia. But it wasn't easy choosing between Stassel and the monastery, and so, after obtaining leave from his employer, he went off again to Kirillov. Just like the first time, he attended a service, confessed, and went to Feodor's cell. This time round, the Elder did not keep him long and was vexed by what he heard. All the same, he let Peregudov say his piece before bringing the discussion to an abrupt end with the comment that if he, Yevlampy, was able to keep his appetites in check, then he would serve the Lord far better in Yatutsk than by taking monastic vows. And that was as much as he was prepared to say.

The Enets told me about the meeting with Feodor more than once and held rigidly to their belief that the monk had blessed the path which eventually brought Peregudov their way. But to the best of my understanding, the Apostle to the Enets could never forgive himself in his old age for leaving Moscow. And with good reason.

For all Stassel's attempts to raise the matter of a proper job, Peregudov never occupied an official position in Yakutsk. His authority though, was considerable. The baron trusted him completely and soon turned him into a kind of special assignments officer. The province occupied a vast territory – a thousand-odd versts east and west and fifteen hundred to the north and south – and Peregudov spent almost half the year on the road, assessing the situation in the Yakut encampments and around the goldmines.

Intervals between the trips were filled with a different kind of life – uneven and confused. There were entire weeks, even fortnights, when he and Stassel would drink and live it up, but then the dragoon, as if coming to his senses, would suddenly turn back into a religious zealot. Just like in Moscow, he would spend all day and night reading the Bible, the Patericon, and praying. The baron respected these eccentricities, seeing in them the stamp of true Russianness; in fact he was even a little proud of them. So it went on for two years, at which point Stassel was summoned by the Tsar to St Petersburg for almost seven months. In his absence, his duties were supposed to fall to the vice-governor, Count Stroganov, but the latter was weak-willed, and worse, staggeringly lazy, so it wasn't long before the most important decisions were being taken not by him, Actual State Counsellor Stroganov, but by an ordinary non-commissioned officer.

This development could hardly have been expected to please the local officials and the owners of the goldmines. With the state's coffers in mind, Peregudov had been squeezing them hard, even while Stassel was still around, but Stroganov didn't seem to notice anything untoward. Denunciations started arriving in the capital itself, but aware that the baron enjoyed the Tsar's favour, nobody in St Petersburg was prepared to act on them.

Stassel returned to Yakutsk from St Petersburg in the late autumn of '59. The trip had been a success in every sense. His report about the state of affairs in the province had gone down so well that he had been awarded the Order of St Anne. Even better, the baron brought back with him a charming young wife, the daughter of the merchant Batashov. A confirmed bachelor for so many years, Stassel now looked exceptionally pleased to have a ring on his wedding finger. Alas, this marriage brought no happiness to anyone. The reason was the relationship between the governor's wife and Peregudov. Back in St Petersburg, the young Batashova had heard more than enough from Stassel about his Caucasian saviour and had decided even then that her husband was giving the dragoon far too free a rein and depending on him far too much.

The Batashovs were famous for their tenacity and toughness, and it was plain to see that the young baroness was cut from the same cloth. According to the testimony of a friend, she already knew, even before the priest had crowned her at the wedding, that if she was to be dispatched to the middle of nowhere in the prime of her life, then this was Providence and she had to prove herself worthy of it. Batashova was sure that a few months would be enough for her to find out what was what and to get to the bottom of everything, and that if her husband needed a faithful helper to manage the province in the right way, he could find nobody better suited to the task than her. So it was no surprise that when Stassel introduced her to Peregudov at a party to welcome her husband back to Yakutsk, the dragoon was given a decidedly frosty reception.

Now that he was married, of course Stassel could no longer spend as much time with his trusted friend – but that's not the main thing. Batashova was working on her husband constantly, like water on stone, seizing every opportunity to turn him against Peregudov, and whenever the baron got drunk it became apparent that her efforts had not been wasted: more and more often, and for no obvious reason, Stassel would say something nasty to Peregudov, or simply mock and taunt his friend.

It became clearer by the day that the sooner Peregudov left Yakutsk, the better for all concerned, but he felt settled there, and that was something he'd learned to value; the prospect of upping sticks to go God knows where did not appeal to him. Besides, Stassel, once he was sober, would do all he could to make amends. In short, Peregudov kept putting it off until an incident occurred after which no amends were possible. Batashova wasn't directly involved, but I'm convinced things would never have reached this point without her.

In Yakutsk, the favourite haunt of both Stassel and Peregudov was a hunter's lodge built by the previous governor one verst or so beyond the city gates, on a high promontory jutting out into the river. They went there to drink and to entertain young ladies, and also in a hall hung with weapons and hunting trophies, to keep themselves fit by fencing. If they ran out of foils, they would continue their exercise routine with dancing, if they felt like it, or some playful duelling with daggers. Although the baron's years in charge of a dragoon regiment had all been spent on land, in his youth he'd trained for three years at the Naval Cadet Corps and could wield a dirk no worse than a sabre. As for Peregudov, who since childhood had carried a knife – now replaced by a dagger with a finely worked handle: a trophy from the Caucasus – he was every bit his opponent's equal.

On this particular occasion they were fencing for the first time after a long break. Stassel wasn't really in the mood, and his foil felt sluggish in his hand. Peregudov noticed this, but began cautiously enough, biding his time until the moment arrived to execute a skilful pirouette and knock Stassel's weapon to the floor. The governor was annoyed, but didn't want a revenge bout there and then, so they moved to the drawing room, where the table had already been set for them. They sat drinking there for some time, reminiscing about their days in the Caucasus, but the hall was calling them back and in the end they gave in.

The baron was no luckier this time. He failed to parry two thrusts in a row, decided that he'd have a better chance with a dirk, and cast his foil aside. Peregudov did the same and they began circling the rug with slow, smooth movements interspersed with sudden lunges. As before though, their hearts were not in it. Both it seemed, were just going through the motions before they returned to the drawing room to carry on drinking. It was then that Peregudov, after slipping on the waxed floor or catching the edge of the rug, collapsed at

Stassel's feet. As he fell he must have hit his head and lost all awareness for a few seconds of where he was and what was happening, because when he saw the baron's dirk raised above him he didn't even consider that this might be nothing more than the kind of pose that Stassel was so fond of striking.

Peregudov should probably have humoured the baron and played the victim begging for mercy, or at least lain there quietly, but instead he got such a fright that he grabbed hold of the arm hanging over him. Both men were drunk and tired, and when he felt Peregudov twisting his hand, the baron's instincts kicked in. He was on top, and no longer joking, brought all his weight to bear on the dirk. He forced the knife as far as Peregudov's neck, and even scratched the skin with the blade; only then did Peregudov manage to break his wrist.

Citing the words of their apostle, the Enets said that the governor was as strong and heavy as a boar, and although Peregudov resisted, he was convinced until the last moment that the baron would kill him – it was only a question of time. When he managed to push the dirk away he was too exhausted to move his hands or legs and just lay beneath Stassel like a mattress. It didn't even occur to him that his opponent had impaled himself on his own weapon and died. He thought he had just fallen into a drunken sleep. It was only after he wriggled out from beneath him that he realised the baron was no longer breathing.

Peregudov told the Enets that he sat next to the body for a good long time, sobbing aloud like a woman. He pitied Stassel and himself, and the senselessness of a life in which he had saved a man, lived alongside him for several years as his bosom friend, and then, after a single stupid mistake, one of them was dead and the other had to flee or go to prison. He sobbed because the war hadn't solved anything, hadn't drawn a line under the tally of those he was fated to kill, because he hadn't left for Kirillov three years earlier and hadn't taken monastic vows. He couldn't accept that there was nothing he could do to put things right and nobody to whom he could explain things. Too much in all this was awry, there was some kind of general flaw here, but Peregudov didn't dare seek it out and knew he wouldn't dare in the future either. This also made him weep.

After several hours of grieving, he thought listlessly that if he had ended up in a labour camp while still in the Urals, he would have less blood on his hands now. Then he was about to get up and leave, but he still didn't move an inch – there was no one to hide him. Only towards nightfall did Peregudov remember that he and the baron had been planning to go off at dawn to shoot geese and that right next to the house, moored to a wooden pier on the Lena, was a boat already laden with guns, powder, lead and supplies for several days under the stars. Everything, in other words, was ready for his escape; he even had a good head start.

He didn't add much to what was already in the boat: just a knapsack containing his trophies from the Caucasus – a *bekesha*,[24] a *chokha*,[25] soft mountain boots and his principal talisman: a tambourine. He also chucked in the Bible he'd bought in Kirillov, then walked down to the river, untied the rope, pushed off with an oar and began rowing out towards the current.

Of course, the dragoon told the Enets, he was aware that he

---
[24] A type of fur-lined jacket.
[25] A high-necked woollen coat typical of male dress in the Caucasus.

was unlikely to get very far before being caught, but somebody must have been watching over him even after Stassel's death. The ice often breaks twice on the big rivers of the North. That year on the Lena, just as soon as the water cleared, the river froze over once more thanks to ice from the tributaries that only thawed a week or two later. Peregudov managed to slip through just in time while his pursuers were forced to abandon their boats two days later and walk back along the shore.

The journey from Yakutsk all the way north to the trading post of Tit-Ary, just before the delta of the Lena, took Peregudov about a month. At first he rowed or at least did his best to keep in the channel, but later when his strength ran out, he barely moved for days at a time and lay half-drowsing on the bottom of the boat. Sometimes the flat-boat would be grounded by a sandbank or a spit, but the water was always high and after struggling for an hour or two he would manage to catch the current once more. He lost count of the days quite quickly, and when the food ran out he fell into a daze and remembered nothing more.

It was said among the Odans, an Enets family, that they found the newcomer lying on the sands, almost in the reeds, insensible, and for a long while, delirious. Soaked and frozen to the bone, Peregudov was in a terrible state and they didn't expect him to survive. But their future teacher recovered. By the end of May he was able to walk out of the *chum* on his own two feet, and a month later, on the day of the summer solstice, his famous duel took place with the Enets shaman Ionakh.

In contrast to what came before and what follows, the events just described are a reconstruction. My own notes played only a minor role in them. The murder of Stassel, or the accident that led to his death – take your pick – became a sensation not only in the province, but in the rest of Russia as well. The best investigators from St Petersburg were put on the case (all the files have been preserved intact) and numerous reminiscences of Yakutsk in the 1850s and 1860s were published, the baron looming large on almost every page. Peregudov and Stassel continued to be remembered for years, not least in the diaries of Batashova, published at the beginning of the twentieth century. Without all these sources, it would have been very hard for me to recreate what happened in the hunter's lodge on the night of 3rd May 1863.

Peregudov himself rarely returned to the events in Yakutsk. Worse still, in the 1970s, when I was around, the Enets suddenly began vigorously editing his stories. All allusions to their teacher's guilt were ruthlessly excised. Even so, the general picture is pretty clear. More disconcerting is the fact that the Enets imposed the same censorship on Peregudov's final murder, which they themselves actually witnessed. In the canonical version, which took shape under Brezhnev, all the blame for the death of shaman Ionakh was assumed, firmly and unconditionally by the Enets themselves.

No matter which of the Enets told me about that duel, they all said the same thing: that the newcomer set about preaching Jesus Christ pretty much from the moment he arrived in their midst. Wavering, they first leant one way, then the other, before they eventually decided to test whose faith was the stronger and whose therefore, was true, by setting Ionakh and Peregudov against each other. This redaction entirely ousted another version in which the original cause of the argument was said to have been Ionakh's wife, Belka, who had been unable to resist the tall blond dragoon. In the early legends (preserved by the Enets' neighbours, the Evens), this motif was treated in some detail, but then faded away completely.

The decision to relieve Peregudov of all responsibility for Ionakh's death was less an end in itself than the natural consequence and culmination of all their efforts to exonerate their saviour. It was the final word in an almost century-long dispute between the Enets and their teacher about good and evil, about who among us had been chosen by the Lord and for what purpose.

Some of the arguments put forward by both sides might even be found amusing now that feelings no longer run so high. Take for example, the way that the Enets kept trying to convince Peregudov that there was no need for him to castigate himself even about the people he'd killed in the Urals: the Lord had forgiven him their deaths a long time ago. It was all part of the path that God had ordained for their prophet, and he could not turn from it.

There's a superstition among Siberian convicts that if you don't slice off and keep the ear of the first person you kill, the souls of the murdered will haunt and torment you until the end of your days. Now, citing his own words, the Enets told Peregudov that all his pain and suffering stemmed from the fact that ten years earlier he had disobeyed his gang leader by not cutting off an ear of the pedlar he'd stabbed. They told their teacher again and again that it wasn't he who had spilled blood, it wasn't he who had killed, that he was wrong to think that it was evil, his own evil, that had brought the true faith to the Enets. Wrong to think in other words, that sin had seeped into the very foundations of their conversion to Christ the Saviour, and that one day it would be the Enets' ruin.

Ionakh, the former shaman, would invariably experience an overwhelming epileptic fit the day after a ritual. They knew from his own account, that with the tambourine in his hands he wielded the same absolute power over the spirits as a Tsar over his subjects, that the sounds and movements of his dance threaded space like strings and eliminated chaos, bringing order and calm to the world, good deeds and stillness. But not even Okhon, the supreme ruler of the heavens, was strong enough to keep a firm grip on the harness day in, day out, so what was to be expected of him, an ordinary shaman? When the ritual ended, he became weak and infirm, and the straps would fall from his hands. A time of troubles would begin. Inside him, as during a blizzard in winter, everything howled and raged, hurling him this way and that and knocking him over.

The world outside us, Ionakh would explain, is vast. You can walk day after day for a month and not meet a soul. Whichever way you look, there's no end, no edge. Life, like the migration of a reindeer herd, follows long-established rules: everyone depends on everyone else, and there's no particular good, no particular evil. Even the ruler of the heavens is content with this situation, and he doesn't intervene: he's probably pleased to see at least some kind of order – you can't really ask for more. A human being is a different matter. We are as densely populated with the spirits of good and evil as any Russian town, and once they've seized hold of you, the shaman would complain, they consider you their property, their appanage. This, together with the general crush, gives rise to a terrible ferocity. And so, lying in his *chum* after performing a ritual, unable to move his arms or legs, Ionakh is no longer a shaman in the eyes of the spirits, no longer a son of Okhon, but dust and dirt, the mere earth on which they are fighting. The spirits pound each other to death and whoever comes out on top makes Ionakh's body its home and does whatever it wants with its prey.

The Enets also told Peregudov that they were able to follow the course of the struggle from Ionakh's convulsions, from the straining of his facial muscles, his epileptic shrieks and wheezes, and it was clear to them which of the demons was winning; then they switched back to the topic of their teacher. There was a period of many years it seems, when the evil spirits held sway in him, and the ecstasy with which Peregudov killed, along with his weakness when he understood what he had done, were not his but theirs. Then the good spirits took hold and it was these that led him one day, as Christ once led Paul, to the Enets encampment on the banks of the Lena.

In the view of the Enets, Peregudov's duel with Ionakh was also a struggle between two dark forces. They proved almost equal, and for a long time there was no way of telling who would prevail. Only at dusk did it become obvious that their shaman was striking his tambourine ever more feebly and hopelessly, that the spirits of the underworld, whose assistance he had summoned against the enemy, were exhausted and could no longer defend him. They also said that the evil within Peregudov, in obedience to which he had slaughtered nine guiltless people, had completely expended itself in the battle, and the good, which had been hiding away in the corners in disgrace, had rallied and come out into the light. It wasn't long before it swept out whatever hatred and cruelty remained inside their teacher.

Be as Children

Stories of how the saviour of the Enets had first out-tranced and then killed Ionakh, who was famously strong, were preserved by the neighbouring peoples, especially the Evens I mentioned earlier. These stories vary, sometimes markedly, making the details on which everyone agrees all the more important. The Caucasian dress which Peregudov seems to have donned for his fight with Ionakh is one example: the soft mountain boots, polished to a shine with reindeer fat, the gold-embroidered *chokha* instead of his normal coat, and the sheepskin *bekesha* on his head. The dagger, with its blood groove and finely worked handle, was tucked under his belt. Their teacher was also carrying his little drum with jingles – another trophy from the mountains – and as he confronted Ionakh on the still solid ice of Lake Nero he seemed to be dancing the famous *lezginka* to its rhythm. Peregudov's performance of this light and graceful Caucasian dance was not just masterly: there was something bewitching about his suave movements, and when the shaman accidentally ripped his own tambourine with a fingernail, the Enets knew for certain that Ionakh's time on Earth was up.

In Yakutsk, in the '20s, one of the local ethnographers recorded several stories all of which led back, one way or another, to the slain governor. Peregudov's dancing dominates almost all of them. In particular, it was thanks to the dragoon's *lezginka* that Stassel, back when he was still a regimental commander, won a couple of victories. Two dancers – Peregudov and one of the Highlanders – would square up on the battlefield like a pair of lionhearts, and the losing side would retreat and relinquish its positions without a murmur.

All the same, the fight proved lengthy. Only towards evening did the shaman's strength run out; his legs buckled, he fell to the ground and began thrashing about. The last drops of life could be seen leaving his mouth along with the foam. The Enets understood that he was doomed, and neither then nor later did they think that Peregudov, having sliced his throat like a reindeer's, from ear to ear, had killed the shaman. Rather, they praised him for cutting short his suffering.

Some six months or so after their teacher, having killed Ionakh, took the shaman's wife Belka for himself, the Enets were visited by a plague. When people began dying one after another, Peregudov left the *chum*, went out into the tundra, stood on a mound in the middle of a swamp and began to pray. He was certain that the Enets had been punished for his sin, not theirs, and appealed to the Lord day and night to show mercy and lenience to the innocent. He addressed God aloud, and those walking past sometimes caught the words of his prayer on the wind.

He said: 'Lord, You can see that I am an outsider in this land. A wretched fugitive, hunted and persecuted, I ended up here somehow and was taken in like family. The people who live here fed and warmed me, gave me a *chum*, gave me dogs and deer, nets to catch fish and traps to catch animals – and how did I repay them? I killed Ionakh their shaman, who was so strong. Over nearly thirty years of his incantations, the evil spirits of sickness gave the Enets a wide berth – they were scared of him. Selkups and Nganasans died, Nenets died, Yukagirs and Tungus died, but as for the Enets, it was as if they were under somebody's spell. Now though calamity has reached them as well. Children are dropping like flies and there is nothing I can do to help them.

'Lord,' said Peregudov, 'You will say of course, that they were pagans, that their faith was unrighteous, that everything their shaman Ionakh did was dust and dirt, but remember: it wasn't only the rod of Moses that was turned into a serpent, so too were those of the Pharaoh's sorcerers, and even though Your serpent prevailed and swallowed them, it's clear that somebody was supporting the sorcerers as well – and that must have been enough to banish sickness.

'Lord,' said Peregudov, 'now that the Enets have turned to the true faith, now that they are walking towards Your altar, I ask and beg one thing of You: stand behind me as You once stood behind Moses, and help banish the plague. Help end this disease. Otherwise an entire people that believed in You will be no more, and a month will not pass before it dies out completely.'

So he prayed day after day, until at last the sickness abated. One in every four Enets children left this world for the next, the rest were untouched. Even while Peregudov was offering his endless prayers to the Lord, the conviction took root in him that Belka was not the only reason the plague had struck the Enets. The problem was that the path by which the Good News had reached them had been sinful through and through. And no wonder: it was brought to them by a murderer who had lined his path to their encampments not with milestones but corpses. Peregudov did not hide the way he saw himself from anyone. Day after day he told the Enets he was a murderer, and not once did he give them the chance to forget his past.

For the Enets, the preceding seventeenth and eighteenth centuries since the birth of Christ had been an era of warfare on a grand scale. They believed that in their three battles with the Russians – on each occasion the entire tribe had risen against the enemy – they had defended their lands east and west of the Lena as far as one could travel for dozens of days. Shamans had dedicated hymns and songs of thanksgiving to those wars, which had accounted for five deaths and thirteen wounded on each side, and to their heroes and lionhearts, lest anyone or anything be forgotten. They were sung by the hearth in the *chum*, and in summer at the general gathering at Ay-Tan, where the river curves round a promontory as sharp as the tip of a spear.

Half a century had not passed since that time. Less than two generations earlier they were still roaming the tundra freely and without hindrance, herding thousands of reindeer from pasture to pasture. They were masters and rulers of vast, unbounded spaces, and were treated as such by all their neighbours. They knew how this world had come into being – the sun, the moon and the Earth with its rivers and its forests, its swamps and its cold sea that was almost always covered with ice. They knew who had created them, who had filled the rivers with fish and the forests with beasts, and who had sent the reindeer – both the wild deer and those they had trained and tamed themselves – to graze in the swamps.

They were bound to Okhon their supreme god – Okhon the mighty and all-powerful, wise and indulgent, Okhon their father, who in the goodness of his heart had bestowed land on the Enets for use in perpetuity – not only by kinship and faith, but also by the most complex thoughts and feelings. There was a great deal of incomprehension and resentment, but also plenty of love, forgiveness and trust. Then suddenly they discovered that all this was no more than a pretty fairy tale. There was no Okhon and never had been. And they were not his chosen people, but pathetic, pitiful savages, weak, inept little souls, as helpless as children in the face of any evil. And like children, they could be killed with exceptional ease, just as in a spirit of mercy or playfulness, they could be left to live, at least for a while.

Peregudov understood how painful all this was for them, and trying to fill the void, to save the Enets from their loneliness, he translated for them the Book of Genesis, the Gospel of Mark and the Ten Commandments, along with a good number of psalms and prayers. If the memoirs of one of the Narodniks, Trapezundov, are to be believed, he originally intended to translate the entire Pentateuch as well as the Book of Revelation, but he stopped at Genesis, horrified by the amount of bloodshed that followed. On the whole his translation was traditional enough. True, in Peregudov's version of the Bible nobody watered sheep or rolled a stone from the mouth of a well, and lush grasslands were replaced by swamps rich in reindeer moss. People prayed to the Almighty to chase away pitiless wolves, the wind bore away clouds of mosquitoes, and happily grazing deer – not sheep – multiplied plentifully each spring.

Although Trapezundov stressed the role of Peregudov's teaching at every turn, the propagation of Christianity in the North did not of course begin with him. In the first half of the nineteenth century, several missionaries walked these lands, not to mention the fact that Cossacks and other outsiders made off with some two thousand Samoyeds. Convinced that such actions were pleasing to God, they sold them to monasteries, remained very strong. Not knowing what to do with all this strength, godmother started making fun of herself. No more recitatives, no more faint and dulcet tones, just mockery: she would bend her body this way and that, spread out her fingers, which looked just like plucked little wings, and cackling away, start making circles around the dining-table. She skirted it unhurriedly with her usual pattering gait, almost dancing, as if she wanted us all to take a good look at her – such a horrid, stupid hen, only fit for a soup – and steadily winding herself up, cackled ever more spitefully.

Sometimes it was impossible to make out a single word for two or three circuits at a time, as if the signal had been jammed, but then the crackles, noises and general gabble would suddenly die away and only obscenities, savage swearing and cursing would remain. 'Dusya, bitch, bitch, slag, street slut, slapper. You're just a whore, it's in that slutty blood of yours. No,' she'd mutter, 'you're worse than any hussy – nothing will ever stop you. There's a reason Jesus Christ accepted Mary Magdalene, comforted her – she only sold her body, but you, you've sold your soul, you shitty piece of filth.' And again, 'Weren't you the little tart who before the Lord's own altar, swore to her confessor, as if to her bridegroom, that you were giving up your soul to him for all eternity, wasn't it you who begged him on your knees to take and preserve it, or else you'd never be saved...' It wasn't all shouting, though. As her strength gradually ran out, godmother would sink into a chair and repeat in a quiet, doomed voice, 'You just kept running from one man to another, one to another...'

If one of the adults walked in while Dusya was looking for her soul, we would be taken straight out into the corridor or where they were baptised, deprived of their freedom and set to work. It was in the monasteries that the Enets were told that their rights to the lands on which they had been herding their reindeer since time immemorial, to their fisheries and hunting grounds had been bestowed on them by Catherine the Great, grandmother of the current Tsar, and that it was not their bravery but simply the kindness of Their Majesties, the grandchildren of the kind Tsaritsa, that offered the poor tribe protection. Squeezed between force and favour, they felt completely lost.

All this of course affected not only the Enets, and there were a couple of occasions, back in Yakutsk, when Peregudov heard Stassel say that the empire itself was to blame for the fate of the northern peoples and that sooner or later it would have to pay for this sin. He set his own mind at rest though, by explaining that there was no way of helping the Enets: bad as things were, they would get no better. Such were the laws of nature, and no earthly power, not even the Tsar, could do anything much about it, other than to soften the fall.

Peregudov though, wasn't particularly interested in this topic. He'd visited Yakut encampments more than once, and to his mind the people there lived no worse than the peasants of the northern Urals where he'd grown up; as for the tribes that herded reindeer further north, he couldn't be sure but he doubted there was any great difference. That may have been why he was so shocked by the wretched plight of the Enets, and equally by the speed with which what little that remained of their way of life was being destroyed.

A student from St Petersburg had ended up in an Enets encampment three years or so before Peregudov, and spent a whole summer with them. They only knew his Christian name – Gleb. Every day until the end of September, while the Enets were preparing to migrate to their winter pastures, Gleb moved like a bee, from one *chum* to another, recording Enets myths and legends, folk tales and spells, and sketching the amulets and patterns on their clothing. And now it seemed to Peregudov that the Enets were drinking themselves to death one by one, not because they found themselves in an unfamiliar, alien world to which they could not adapt, and not because in that world the story of their people no longer depended on them alone – no, the main thing was that they themselves no longer served any purpose. Everything that had to be remembered, that had to be preserved and passed on to their children come what may, had now been recorded with these incomprehensible letters and would never be lost again, even if not a single one of the Enets remained on Earth.

Some thirty years later Peregudov, now an old man, told a Narodnik from the Land and Freedom Party – his name was Sevostyanov – that the Enets he had encountered resembled a man who had made up his mind to kill himself. They lived in constant expectation of the end, they desired the end, they wanted to get right up close to that line and actually cross it. Theirs was a calm, almost tender readiness for death.

Explaining why it was that they had received Christ's faith so willingly from his hands, Peregudov twice told Sevostyanov that it was all because he, having barely arrived among the Enets, had killed a man. Killed a man in a tribe where nobody had ever killed anyone, where even the male reindeer only butted horns over a female until first blood was drawn, after which they retreated. So, from the very start, if he had preached Christ to them with words, then they had done the same to him with their life, never once resisting evil with violence. They had given his own Christianity back to him, made it into what it once had been before it veered from its path. Blood mattered so much to the Enets that when he killed their shaman Ionakh they submitted to him out of a kind of bewilderment. A man who thought he had the right to spill the blood of another became in their eyes a supernatural being, and they didn't dare raise a single objection.

Some of the other things he told Sevostyanov were more traditional. In particular, he told him that the tribe had accepted the Christian faith with such ardour because it had understood that without the Son of God it could not be saved. What was more, Peregudov had managed to tempt and entice the Enets with a path back into history. They immediately sensed, intuited that he was bringing them the beginnings of a new fate, a new life. And he added that if previously he had rejoiced at having convinced them not to die, now he feared that nothing good awaited them in their new history either.

Preaching faith in the Saviour, Peregudov had, right from the start and, above all, at one and the same time, set about explaining to the Enets that they, who had only just turned to the true faith, were God's chosen people. Persuading them that the preservation of the faith in its true fullness and integrity had been granted solely to them. Another twenty years would pass before this doctrine was definitively formulated, straight after the events of mid-June 1884. That was when four barges bearing a reinforced gendarmes unit of almost seventy men sailed up the Lena to the Enets encampments. The unit was under orders to bring the Enets to heel by whatever means necessary, and also to catch political prisoners who had fled hard labour and exile and to return them to their previous places of punishment.

While the Cossacks and gendarmes were still disembarking, Peregudov began explaining to the Enets that these were experienced, well-trained soldiers, and he urged the elders to take the tribe, along with the herds, off into the bogs and swamps, and wait there until the troops were gone. In reply the old men declared that the female reindeer had only recently calved and that by obeying Peregudov the Enets would not only disgrace themselves but lose all their baby deer. Even the resolution passed by the political exiles was roundly ignored. Most of the latter took the view that they didn't have the right to put an entire people in jeopardy and were leaning towards surrender. But the Enets told them too, that not one of those they had taken in and sheltered would be handed over to the authorities.

Reconnaissance and preparation for battle went on for two days or so, but Peregudov took no direct part in either. Just as soon as the soldiers started pitching camp he walked off to the mound from which he had begged the Lord to spare the Enets and end the plague, and asked Him to intervene once more. His hope of course, was that with the Lord's help the Enets would send the enemy back where they had come from, but far more insistent was his plea to the Almighty that less blood be spilled this time around. He said, 'I have so many souls to answer for, dead through no fault of their own. Lord, I beg one thing of You – don't let their number grow. May these children, whom I have brought to the true faith, remain unstained by murder. It's enough that I stabbed their shaman Ionakh to death for no reason. Lord, let this people never see violence again.'

Conflict between the Enets and the gendarmes began only after extensive negotiations, which of course led nowhere, and after equally lengthy reconnoitring by both sides and scouting for favourable positions. In the end battle was joined on the rocky right bank of the Kotva and dragged on for three long days before concluding on the banks of the Lena itself, where the soldiers hastily loaded the barges, cast off, and to the ecstatic whoops of the Enets and salvos fired into the air, sailed back towards Yakutsk.

Later on, in the pro-Narodnik newspapers and the leaflets distributed by Land and Freedom, this battle was described as the biggest armed uprising against autocracy for an entire decade. It was evaluated in similar terms by the leader of the gendarmes, Captain Maslov, in his report to Soimenov, Minister of Internal Affairs. Maslov, a Cossack, had seen more than his fair share of danger while fighting in Poland, Hungary and across the Caucasus, but even he noted that at times the gunfire was more like a hurricane.

The Enets were born marksmen, they could hit a squirrel in the eye at thirty metres, yet not one person died in the Battle of the Kotva and all wounds were minor. If a bullet did catch anybody, it merely grazed them. No one on either side was crippled, everyone recovered, every wound healed. It seems to me then, that Peregudov had good reason to see in all this the hand of the Lord. It was a sign, a proof that his preaching to the Enets was pleasing to the Almighty.

The cornerstone of the doctrine that the Enets were God's chosen people was laid almost by chance. Belka had two children from shaman Ionakh: Ogon and Onakh, now six and eight years old. Half a year after the shaman's death – the tribe had already been baptised – Belka complained to her husband that the boys were being bullied by their peers, who called them filthy pagans. Both then and later, Peregudov treated Ionakh's children as his own, he loved them dearly and they responded in kind. He was alarmed and decided to defend the children; by doing so moreover, he would tie his old life to his new life once and for all, leaving no gaps, no cracks.

In those years the Enets gathered almost every day in a clearing outside the *chum* of a Social Democrat called Norov. They would pray together, and Peregudov would explain Holy Scripture to them and preach. It was at one of these gatherings that the Enets learned from their teacher that shaman Ionakh, and thereby his children too, were direct descendants of one of the three Magi, who following the Star of Bethlehem, had been the first to visit Christ.

This was not just an elegant ploy – far from it. Even before the Battle of the Kotva, Peregudov had been struck by the fact that in those three wars with the Russians only five people had died, half as many as he had killed himself. Peregudov would be sure to remind the Lord of this whenever the Enets sinned and began praying for forgiveness. He also told the Enets ever more often that the Magi were the ancestors not only of Ionakh but of their entire tribe; in fact the Magi were Christ's true disciples. And the reason they had been deemed worthy of visiting Him so soon after the Virgin Mary had been delivered of her child was that they had never spilled human blood. Later, when the Magi realised that Christ would become an adult before He would have the chance to save everyone, they decided not to stay in Palestine, gathered their things and set off back to the tundra.

Peregudov kept telling the Enets not to call him their prophet: their teacher was Christ Himself, whose own people they had been ever since the days of the Star of Bethlehem. He stressed that only the Magi had managed to preserve the faith received from Christ in all its fullness; everywhere else the Saviour's teachings had led to unrest and blood, which still flowed like water. Musing for so long on the infant Christ, Peregudov must have come to see the Enets too, as immaculate children of some kind, heirs to the infants of Judea, if not part of their number, ready once more to go to their deaths for the Saviour. There in Palestine, they would have grown up and become like everyone else, but here, roaming from swamp to swamp, far away from sin, they had preserved their purity. One day he told Timofeyev, another Social Democrat, the Star of Bethlehem would rise in the sky once more, and the Enets, all dressed in white and filled with faith and exultation, would follow the Man who would save the human race.

Although Peregudov welcomed convicts and exiles without complaining or turning anyone away, he did not sympathise with revolutionary ideas. When the political exiles explained to the Enets that people in Russia were living in misery and poverty, with no reindeer to herd, fish to catch or animals to snare, and that love alone was no help to them – good deeds would have to go hand in hand with bloodshed, as is always the way, for evil is far too stubborn – Peregudov told the Enets firmly that none of this was true and they should not take the revolutionaries at their word. On the other hand, he never concealed that he had been deeply influenced by his conversations with the politicals, by the sense of guilt towards the common people that was the source of all their actions. But here too, there was a difference: the Enets knew that he was terrified of bringing disaster upon them, that the very possibility of it tormented him like the heaviest of crosses. Peregudov, needless to say, idealised the Enets: they did kill, they did wage wars. In fact their life was like everyone else's, merely softened by the distances between them, the sparseness of their population, and in his own time, by their weakness too.

Externally the Enets had little trouble separating Peregudov from the Narodniks and no hesitation in sticking with their teacher. Strictly speaking, they accepted everything he told them, even his boundless guilt. They didn't object when he explained that for all their paganism and idolatry they were better, purer, kinder than any person who had ever spilled human blood, because killing is the one thing that must never be done. Life is a gift from God, and there is no sin more terrible than to take it away. And they accepted that the only path by which any human being can atone is the path of prayer to the Lord.

But somewhere along the line Peregudov must have made a mistake. He was their teacher, they were used to obeying him, believing him, and it seems to me that the way he kept belittling himself, the way he kept trying, over some twenty years, to prove that their sins, whether taken separately or all together, bore no comparison with his own sin before the Lord – all this was just too much for the Enets to accept. No wonder that in 1885 or thereabouts, a reaction set in.

Their first retreat from their teacher was linked to those

same revolutionaries. Despite everything he had told them, the Enets were struck one day by the notion that the immense unabating guilt which the politicals had carried intact to the banks of the Lena were part of the same common wrong as Peregudov's own sins, and this sea of evil had overwhelmed them all. As a result, the Enets were in no doubt for almost a decade, that the differences between Peregudov and the Narodniks were purely tactical: on all the main points they were in agreement and singing in unison. Eventually though, during their long winter migrations, when they thought it all over and tried to piece everything together, the Enets managed to convince themselves and accept that both sides, for all their talk of guilt and repentance, were and would remain implacably opposed.

I doubt it's a mere coincidence but at the end of the 1880s (I've not been able to narrow it down any further), the Enets at Peregudov's suggestion, decided to erect a chapel to the Holy Mother of God right above the Lena, on a promontory on its high right bank. They began building at the end of November, when the lakes were already covered with a thick layer of ice. They cut out neat rectangular blocks from this layer and made walls with them. The columns that supported the roof and vault were also moulded from ice. The Enets bought some old paraffin barrels at a nearby trading post, filled them with water from the same lakes and left it to freeze.

The church was small but very festive. On sunny days it shone so bright that it hurt the eyes and you could see it ten versts away. Inside the chapel was illuminated by the same sunlight, which passed through the pure translucent ice as through good-quality glass, and on polar nights by thin sticks of dry wood. During services, hundreds of these were fixed to the walls where they burned like candles.

At the request of the Enets and with the justification in his own mind that there wasn't a priest to be found anywhere around, even if you were to travel for several days, Peregudov led the services himself, on the model of the 'Priestless' Old Believers. He was regular Orthodox himself and followed the order of service accordingly, but the very fact that he stood before the Holy Doors without asking anyone's permission, and preached at his own initiative, instructing the flock to trust only in God and in themselves, seems to have been enough to lend a kind of Protestant energy to the faith of the Enets.

Although Peregudov served with exceptional reverence, he kept repeating that his sins prevented him from being a real shepherd, and this also had a powerful effect on them, in fact it gradually convinced them, that having been converted to the true faith, it was now their turn to save *him*. More than that, it was their duty to do this, if as he said, they were truly pure and immaculate in the eyes of the Lord.

In summer when the Enets took their reindeer hundreds of versts away from the Lena, the church would be dismantled by the sun and the heat: it seemed to weep as it grieved for its flock, then it sagged like an old woman before eventually turning into a powdery greyish lump. Later, many people deemed those tears prophetic. Whether they were right or not I can't say, but I did hear that Peregudov called summer the season of sin and sorrow, and autumn, when the Enets restored their chapel, the season of repentance and forgiveness.

It must be said that Peregudov, who never forgot that one day they would be left without him, did all he could do to encourage the Enets to be self-sufficient. Perhaps that was why it took him so long to see or fully appreciate the tribe's determination to help him. To understand that he was leading the Enets into sin and that all this would soon distort his teachings about the Son of God and take its place at the very heart of their faith.

They prayed for him a great deal, when they were at leisure and when they were at work, but the years passed and their teacher's burden grew no lighter, in fact he punished himself more and more. On the eve of the Revolution, now an old, feeble man, he wept openly in front of everyone, and they despaired. It was then, seeing his unhappiness, that the Enets lost their faith that the Lord would ever hear them from the banks of the Lena, and like thousands upon thousands before them, they decided to redeem blood with blood, to give their own lives for the lives destroyed by Peregudov. To leave their reindeer and their *chums* behind, to abandon everything, to suffer and sacrifice themselves for all the wretched of the Earth, then go to Jerusalem, to the Holy Land, and appeal to the Almighty from there.

These last few years I understand Peregudov better and better. Like him I consider the crux of this story to lie in the fact that the deaths that preceded the conversion of the Enets were inseparable from the new faith. The two things became knitted together, just as in any human being the desire for salvation merges with the original sin, that since the time of Adam is always with you, whatever you do. Sadly both before the Bolsheviks and after, few of the Enets ever listened to what he was saying, few stopped and stepped aside.

The thought that prayers on their own are not enough, that

prayers without deeds are stillborn, that they would never save him just by sitting on their hands, took hold of the Enets and never left them. The very thing Peregudov feared came to pass. Ever since the Lord ordained that he join the tribe, Peregudov had been terrified by the thought that one day the Enets would replace words with actions. In his life the absence of action and the absence of guilt had always gone hand in hand, while any given deed had been mixed up with blood, no matter who or what was behind it.

Sick and infirm, he tried more than once to make them see this; it's said that he even got down on his knees before the Enets in the hope of restraining them, but to no avail. His belief in his own sinfulness was working against him and he wasn't prepared to renounce it. Peregudov's statements of those years show his growing sadness that in bringing the true faith to the Enets he had been unable at the same time to fence them off from the cruel, adult life that surrounded them, his expectation of disaster and awareness of his own decrepitude, his bitter sorrow, that however much they loved him, he would not be able to do a thing to help them.

In 1918 when he was already on his deathbed, Peregudov gathered his strength, and became for a few hours the man the Enets had known many years before. Dying, he warned them that if they involved themselves in what had just started in Russia, he wouldn't forget a single one of them, he would curse each of them by name from the next world, and before doing that he would curse the day when he had come to them and begun preaching Jesus Christ. But even then only a few of them were prepared to understand him. Most of them saw this as fear, fear for their future, but also a declaration of love, and barely had they lowered Peregudov into the grave than they agreed once more that they would save their teacher come what may.

After his death in December 1918, the Enets had a very hard time of it. When recalling it themselves, they would say that they had been unable to find the truth. As if caught in a blizzard they kept losing their way. Even though they held fast to each other, so as to save the man who had brought them the Good News, even though they were scared of splitting apart, they were unable to agree among themselves and decide once and for all where exactly it was that they wanted to go. They argued desperately about what the real Holy Land actually was: their own pastures, Russia, Palestine or the mysterious Island of Kerguelen. The captain of an American schooner had told them that nobody there had ever spilled human blood, and that as on the first day of Creation, there was no sorrow on that island, no evil, no sin.

It must be said in the interests of fairness, that the fate of both those who left and those who obeyed Peregudov and continued to roam near the mouth of the Lena proved equally hard. In '32, when collectivisation reached their lands, the Enets lost all their reindeer in the space of a few winters, and by the start of the war with the Germans there was barely a sober soul among them.

During the Civil War and NEP, nearly a third of the tribe followed the politicals – their fathers and grandfathers – to the 'mainland'. Leaving, they said that just as they, the Enets, were trying to save Peregudov, so the new rulers were dreaming of saving an entire people, of building Heaven right there on Earth, and it would be only right and honest to help them. To give up one's life for such rulers, they urged their tribesfolk would be no great loss, if afterwards at the Lord's right hand, they could roam with their reindeer across the heavenly tundra in the sky, where there would be no mosquitoes, no lack of fodder in winter, no wolves. There were several waves of migration to Russia, all probably linked, but the Enets must have perished or simply lost their way – I, at any rate, was unable to track anyone down.

I will return more than once to those who set off for the mainland and those who remained on the banks of the Lena. Here though, I'd like to retell one blatantly mythical legend that was very popular among the Enets. The idea of travelling somewhere far away, perhaps even to the French Kerguelen Island, of travelling and fleeing that which was drawing ever closer, had first been mentioned by Peregudov, or so it was said. In the last year of NEP three families came to an arrangement with the captain of an American schooner, the *Mary Holden*, the last vessel to venture so far west in search of gold and fur. He fixed his anchor to a large ice floe, and over a period of two and a half years used the wind and the currents to carry this strange ark, with the Enets and ten reindeer on board, to the island located at the other end of the Earth, near Antarctica.

The floe was melting, the crew were in almost continuous mutiny, and on two occasions, in Anchorage, Alaska, and in Manila in the Philippines, the captain put the malcontents ashore and took on new sailors. Even so, he kept his word and brought the Enets and the last pair of surviving reindeer (a bull and a cow) all the way to Kerguelen. Now they have multiplied once more and graze in the silence and plenty of the island's tundra, as though it were the Promised Land. The storyteller added – in case anyone was in any doubt – that the Enets' memories about their former homeland and their long voyage to Antarctica were written down and published in French by the famous ethnographer Léon de Blois.

As far as the American was concerned, there were many different opinions. I heard from several Enets and a Selkup called Togl that the captain proved himself a swindler and a rogue. The schooner had barely passed the Bering Strait when the floe broke into several pieces, drowning all the people and the reindeer. No one had any evidence to support either of these two versions, nor could they have done; the two outcomes as I see now, depended on one thing only: whether or not the fugitives had Peregudov's blessing. If as the storyteller believed, they did have his blessing, then they sailed safely all the way to Kerguelen; but if the Enets set out on their voyage against their teacher's orders, then their fate was already sealed, one way or another.

***

I spent June and early July of 1962 on the rehabilitation ward of the Kashchenko mental hospital. One of my neighbours there was the historian Aleksandr Vasilyevich Farabin. His was a fairly severe case. On top of depression, for which there were serious grounds, he'd also developed a persecution complex. Scared that he was about to be killed, Farabin spent the entire autumn before his admission hopping, from train to train on various branch lines, and it was only after he'd 'shaken off his pursuers' that he showed up at his aunt's place in Uglich. And that was where his parents collected him. At the age of fifty he was still living with mum and dad.

According to the doctors, Farabin was a quiet, orderly man in everyday life a proper bookworm. His true abode was not his flat but the Archives of the October Revolution, where had they only let him, he would have happily passed his nights as well as his days. For twenty years or so he calmly laboured away as a researcher at the Marx-Engels-Lenin, one of our most prestigious institutes, until something happened that left him scrambling to cover his tracks.

Farabin's department studied the last four years of Lenin's life. Aleksandr Vasilyevich was in excellent standing, had an irreproachable dossier (his father had been a candidate member of the Central Committee), was hard-working and committed, and the word from the top was that he would be invited to head the department just as soon as the State Commission for Academic Degrees approved his doctoral dissertation. But everything started going downhill even before the internal preliminary defence.

Farabin was a good, naïve man. He was over the moon about Khrushchev's Thaw and had evidently decided that now nothing was off-limits. His thesis consisted of a complete chronicle of Lenin's years at Gorki,[26] rounded off with a detailed commentary. His research was exceptionally meticulous: it's enough to say that he reconstructed Lenin's life literally minute by minute. Not that anyone doubted his professionalism. The problem was that in the wake of his study, the entire official history of the Party would have to be flushed

---

[26] An eighteenth-century manorial estate a few miles south of Moscow that became Lenin's out-of-town residence from 1918 until his death in 1924.

down the pan. No surprise then that Farabin's departmental colleagues immediately reported him to the authorities.

Luckily nobody was baying for blood, and when Farabin eventually ended up in the madhouse the decision was taken to just let him be. He was given a disability pension and forgotten about. But that came later. When the authorities got wind of the thesis, two KGB officers from the First Section searched Farabin's flat without a warrant and confiscated all his notes, drafts and other documents, chief among them typescripts of his dissertation. Whatever Farabin had circulated at the institute was already in their hands. They didn't mess around with their plunder, and following their director's orders, immediately sent it off for shredding. It was as if the young whippersnapper had never existed.

The operation was done and dusted within a single summer weekend, which like any other, the Farabin household spent at their dacha in Kratovo. On returning to Moscow on Monday, Aleksandr Vasilyevich didn't even have the chance to find out that his life's work was no more. He was met at the entrance door to his apartment block by his typist, who between tears and apologies, told him that at the request of her husband, a high-school history teacher, she had typed up an extra copy, the fourth in total. And now she wanted to hand it over to him.

Farabin spent two weeks running around Moscow with this miraculously preserved typescript. He would take it to friends and ask them to hide it somewhere, then a few hours later he'd begin having doubts about either the people or the place, and go back and retrieve the file. That of course was not very clever of him, but one way or another the manuscript survived and more copies were subsequently made. When I was discharged, I went to the ward to say goodbye to Farabin and he gave me a bag with a copy of my own. Alas, I stuffed it high up in a cupboard when I got home and forgot all about it. Although I'd never been wild about Lenin, Farabin's stories, together with the hospital setting, deserved better.

Farabin liked to share the fruits of his two decades of research during strolls with fellow patients – myself as a rule among them. A path of some fifty metres, known as Chestnut Walk, stretched from the gates to the main building. It had been laid in Kashchenko's time and was separated from the hospital entrance by a large, expertly arranged flower bed (there was no lack of green-fingered patients). Our usual route led down the path and around the bed. So Farabin would be holding forth about Lenin while in the middle of the flowers, organising the space around him, there rose a two-metre sculpture of the seated leader. Lenin moreover, was generously gilded. The statue itself, if you ignored its location and tint, was not bad at all. The massive, mighty figure was certainly expressive. The sculptor had tilted the right shoulder and pushed it forward, and you realised that Lenin was just about to ground his opponent to dust.

Farabin would wear a hat whatever the weather. Approaching the flower bed, he would always tip it and bow. There wasn't a hint of irony in this gesture, nothing except tenderness and respect. I suppose you couldn't spend your entire life studying one and the same person if you felt any other way. Lenin's skull was often graced by a pigeon. Startled by the moving hat, it would fly meekly away and you could be forgiven for thinking that Lenin was returning Farabin's bow, as if he were an old acquaintance. The hat routine didn't always come off, but when it did Farabin would be in a cheerful, jovial mood for the rest of the stroll.

The madhouse, the sight of a polite golden Ilyich[27] listening to stories about himself, along with Aleksandr Vasilyevich's narrative style, had their effect on me as well. There was no doubt, that for Farabin, Lenin was still alive, and as we walked he would sometimes swear on the leader's name or even, as if this were a perfectly normal thing to do, call on him to witness that he wasn't adding anything or leaving anything out.

Farabin it should be said, did not tell his stories about Lenin in order; he wasn't too fussed about chronology, coherence or narrative logic. One episode would replace another without any external connection, repetitions abounded, and it was only a week or two later that you began to see that there was no blunder here on the part of the storyteller. The sick Lenin kept returning – with difficulty and from different sides – to one and the same thought. There was an inevitability about it all, and it was Farabin's job to show this to us, to make us understand that fate had not left Lenin the slightest chance of deceiving himself, of somehow missing his destiny.

Slowly and without haste, he would tell us about a man who is desperately frightened of repeating a mistake, sometimes to the point of madness. Even though the Lenin he described to us has not recovered from his two strokes – he has for example, completely lost the power of speech – he still has the same faith of old and the same determination to save us. How exactly, he doesn't yet know. Or rather, he has a hunch and he has already glimpsed the path, but he can't

---

[27] Lenin, born Vladimir Ilyich Ulyanov, is often referred to in Russia with a familiar and egalitarian tone simply by his patronymic, Ilyich.

bring himself to set out on it – it's just too new, too different. During these years, Lenin thinks a great deal about God, but not because he is seriously ill and knows that death is near. This is not a one-way street. He is no prodigal son returning to his father, no sinner pleading with his last ounce of strength for salvation. Lenin's role in the Lord's mysterious ways remains as great as ever, and God does not forget this.

Trying to explain to Lenin what it is that He wants from him, God every now and again gives him some signs, He might even lead him by the hand, or just tell him straight. But when Lenin digs his heels in, the Lord sometimes loses patience and beats him cruelly, as once He punished Jonah. Every blow hurls Lenin deeper and deeper back into childhood. But more than one month will pass before Lenin begins to understand that this is not a punishment but a path, that all this is right and he shouldn't resist.

However much Lenin strives towards God, the new road does not come easily to him: it means a break with his previous life, a break with the Party and the working class. The last is especially painful for Lenin. After all, he wasn't some ordinary little man whom nobody knew about and on whom nothing depended, whose disappearance wouldn't even be noticed. He was the leader and it was for him to set the course and pave the way, while the millions who followed him trusted him more than they trusted themselves. But now here was the Lord saying that He wanted Lenin without the workers. Demanding in other words, his clear and unconditional apostasy. Telling him that this was how it had to be, that there was no other way.

Farabin managed to say a great deal more about Lenin, but alas, my memories of the hospital faded fast once I was home. The odd thing remained of course, but a year or two was enough to erase the rest. Farabin also faded into the background. I even forgot about his manuscript, until out of nowhere, a certain incident led me back to it. Now that I've read it through diligently and more than once, I'd like to give the author his due: it really is a unique piece of research.

'It's no secret,' Farabin begins when we are still in the entrance hall (this is my very first stroll), 'that when it came to politics, Lenin had exceptional intuition. But trusting it was no longer easy. The force of inertia was too great, as was the power that had come his way in 1917, and both kept Lenin in his old rut, like pincers. Both kept telling him again and again that nobody could help him reach his goal faster than they could. In the end though, they probably helped him turn off that path, maybe even forced him to do so. But as painful as all this was, Lenin behaved honourably here as well. His sister Maria testified that as he was dying, and could see that he was dying, he reproached the Lord for just one thing: that he had only been given enough time to take the first few steps, that he wouldn't even make it to the first turn before he died. The pointsman had moved him onto another track, he had understood this and accepted it, had told the few old friends he was prepared to take with him to follow him in single file, not deviating an inch, and the next thing he knew the Lord had taken Him.

'I'd go so far as to suggest,' Farabin goes on, 'that the first hint of the direction he should take, and the people he should take with him, was offered to Lenin back in the summer of 1918. The Cossack officers in the South were getting restless and had chosen General Kornilov as their ataman. Things were looking complicated, and the Party Secretariat was busy debating how to prevent the Whites from starting a civil war. The main speaker was Comrade Trotsky, who excelled in practical tasks while keeping his head permanently in the clouds.

'Trotsky believed there was still time to stave off civil war or even nip it in the bud. The main and most pressing task was to compile dossiers on all the White generals they knew about. A clear picture was needed of what each of them was capable of, and therefore, what danger they posed. Trotsky paid close attention to such things, taking the view that a commander's psychology, character and cast of mind all counted for more in military matters than guns and cannons. Lenin didn't take any of this seriously – the only question for him was whether Trotsky himself had any military talent – but it all seemed harmless enough, so he let him have his fun.

'Timing, as they say, is everything. Just the day before, Dzerzhinsky had given the People's Commissariat for Military and Naval Affairs a present fit for a king. His Chekists had raided the flat of Kornilov's niece on Mokhovaya Street three days earlier and seized the General's entire archive: hundreds of sheets on which Kornilov had sketched the disposition of troops, many of them dating back to his days in the Omsk Cadet Corps; General Staff maps with his own amendments and comments; and five bundles of letters to his wife from the front line. While Trotsky was enthusiastically explaining that without knowledge of these papers the Revolution was doomed, the bored Central Committee members were passing one another the General's letters. Alas, he was a man of few words, all of them dead. Either he didn't love his wife and only wrote to her because it was the decent thing to do, or he was just no good at it. Even the General Staff maps were more interesting, but here too, the only thing that had caught the Chekists' attention were the infant faces with which Kornilov had filled the margins. These little faces, it must be said, were very expressive, with big intelligent eyes, chubby cheeks and parted mouths that were unusually scornful. Lenin also liked them, in fact he couldn't restrain himself – which didn't happen often – from quipping, 'So now we know who's going to liberate Holy Rus!' before adding, 'Look, there's a whole army of them!' Everyone laughed, but Trotsky gave him a reproachful look and Lenin felt ashamed.

'Next came two hard years of war. Twice, when Admiral Kolchak crossed the Urals and when Denikin was about to storm Tula, it seemed to Lenin and to others, that Bolshevism in Russia was living out its final days. Preparing for it all to end, he spent several days agonising over where exactly the mistake had been made. He didn't look to God for an answer of course; he looked to Marx. But then as if by magic, the situation at the front improved, the Whites began retreating even faster than they had attacked – later they would simply flee – and Lenin's doubts subsided.

'By 1920 the Civil War was all but over; Baron Wrangel's last stand in Crimea was no more than its echo. From the Baltic to the Pacific, the time had come for this entire enormous country to pitch in and build socialism. The time had come to rout devastation, hunger and typhus even more swiftly than the Reds had routed the Whites – and it was at precisely this point that everything ground to a halt. The machine seemed to be functioning, the wheels, big and small were still turning, but they may as well have been spinning on ice.

'Lenin's brothers-in-arms thought these were just teething problems. Two or three purges would be enough to rid the Party of its bad Communists, turncoats and other selfish profiteering scum, but for now there was no point jumping the gun. For once, delay would not prove deadly. But Lenin's doubts had returned again. Revolutionary fervour lay dormant, and he understood more clearly with each passing day that they were headed in the wrong direction. He probably ought to have come out publicly and declared as much for all to hear, but he delayed. Worse still, he continued to take the Party with him as he always had.

'That was an enormous, unforgivable sin. The Party was his child through and through, he had fathered it, nurtured it. For him, it meant even more than an actual child – after all, he had never cut the cord. Over the course of two decades they had become so entwined that he was scared to even think that one day the Party would be left without him. The Party held him in place with its unconditional devotion, its absolute power over him. To break off all ties, without making a single attempt to fix anything, was inconceivable. He didn't want to be another Ivan Susanin, who led the Poles into the forest to their ruin and abandoned them there. Unsure how to get out of this mess, he just kept on going and the Party followed right behind him, never lagging.

'Just as soon as he began coming round after his first stroke, which occurred on 23rd March 1921, Lenin set about explaining in the simplest terms to Getye – his doctor and friend – that for a long time he had been unable to understand what had happened to him or where he was. All he could remember was feeling his way down dark wet passages without knowing where he was going; stumbling, falling, getting up and trudging on. His body and bones were aching, and so was his soul, it was pitch dark all around him, without even the faintest glimmer, but strangely enough he found it easier walking like that, all on his own. It was as if some heavy, heavy burden had been lifted from him. Then he suddenly asked Getye, "So maybe that was when the Lord took pity on me – and gathered the Party into His own hands?"

'From the spring of '21 onwards, Lenin really did think almost continuously about God. About the Lord Himself, but not the Church, which without the slightest regret or remorse, he either put to one side or simply ignored. He didn't even try to persuade himself that the path onto which it called did not lead to salvation – perhaps it did, perhaps it didn't. What mattered was that the road had proven far too long.

'He made only faltering progress. Both because of his illness and because the subject was new to him, it took him a while to adapt, to make himself at home in it. By nature strict and systematic, here he saw only shreds and tatters, and no way of sewing them together or making them fit. Every thought would rip down the middle, and then having lost the thread, he would spend hours scrutinising whatever was left, agonising over what it was and who it was about. And when by some miracle he remembered, he would rejoice and even start wriggling about like a child from the pleasure of it.

'He often pitied God, and he also grieved for the tribe of Adam; in fact he was ready to weep for one and all. Weeping and holding his arms out in front of himself like a blind man, he kept seeking a way out, convinced as before that a solution existed. He remarked one day – and this turned out to be a real gift for him – that if you tied a thought to one or other human being the thought became sturdier and did not tear any further, as if the person were helping him.

'Among the long-forgotten names that suddenly came back to Lenin in Gorki was that of Valya Maksakov, a high-school friend in Simbirsk. Back then everyone knew who Valya was. He'd been the first to lose his virginity and had done so without the help of a prostitute. It happened on the family estate – his parents were touring Italy at the time – when he, a thirteen-year-old adolescent was seduced by the owner of the neighbouring estate, a young widow. Later the scandal would force the poor woman out of the town. They were reunited a few years later in London, lived together for three years and only then did they part for good.

'Neither Lenin nor his friends were much interested in young ladies; society itself was of far greater concern to them – where it was headed and how it could be fundamentally, radically reformed. This, not women was what they read about, wrote about and debated at the tops of their voices, quite forgetting the need for secrecy. Still, when Lenin received a letter from Maksakov in London in 1910, he replied right away, and over a pint of beer in a pub, listened patiently and perhaps not without interest to Maksakov's doctrine of the Root of Eve.

'Valya used quite different words to those Lenin was accustomed to hearing, but he did so with great conviction. God was mentioned often, priests less so, and instead of the Church there was woman. For Valya, woman was a font, a sacred vessel in which lust and filth were miraculously transfigured and transformed into the innocence and purity of a new human soul.

'Maksakov argued that in woman, in her very innards, the justification and salvation of the human race is under way, day and night; but for her we would all have choked on our own hatred a long time ago, with no need for the flood. He did not doubt that the bliss experienced by a woman on her own with a man is a sign given to her that this salvific gift remains hers alone. And the unspeakable pain and suffering that accompany every birth also make sense: how can you not yell and howl with agony knowing that any moment now you will give up the pure and immaculate thing you have been carrying inside yourself to its ruin, that you are pitilessly forcing it out into the vale of tears and sin.

'Listening to Maksakov, Lenin thought that if only Valya's doctrine had not reeked quite so strongly of incense, it would have been a good fit for Aleksandra Kollontai and her suffragettes; as it was the only thing it went well with was beer, like rusks. Then the poor man went back to St Petersburg, where galloping consumption sent him to his grave in a matter of months, as Lenin learned a year later. By then Lenin had other things to worry about. It was only now that he suddenly remembered about him again.

'At a certain point Maksakov's doctrine led on to another theory: that after Adam and Noah the human race had made two further attempts to free itself and shake off sin, and on both occasions the Lord had hesitated for a long time, unable to decide whether man was steadfast and could be trusted. So it had been with Abraham and with Joseph, husband of Mary. After eventually convincing Himself that man was indeed steadfast, He blessed their wives, from whom more righteous men were born. From here Lenin returned to the waters of the flood and decided that those had been the same maternal waters in which, as Maksakov would have it, the transfiguration of sin into purity and innocence takes place. When the flood receded and Noah set foot on land, it was his second birth.

'Little of what Maksakov said was new of course. Not that Maksakov insisted on his originality. For example, he would speak of woman, her body, as of the Earth, which is heated less by the sun than by its own inner heat; of man, who assiduously digs up this fallow land so that one day he may sow it. The seed must come to rest on a quiet deep spot rich in warmth and moisture, so that after the mandatory nine months it can sprout vigorously, abandon the female womb and emerge into the light. He was fond of all the words that describe womanly nature and enjoyed playing with them, just like a child.

'It was then in the pub, that he explained to Lenin that the word *vlagalishche* – vagina – comes from the root '*lag-lozh*', from which are derived the verb *vlagat'* (to put in, insert) and the nouns *lozhe* (couch, bed, river-bed) and *lozhbina* (hollow, gully), before immediately contradicting himself: no, it comes from *vlaga* (moisture). The place in other words that is always moist, where the seed puts out shoots and does not wither from drought. Eventually after checking, as a courtesy, that Lenin was not against the idea, he settled on a compromise. The words *vlaga* (moisture) and *lozhbina* (gully) now shared the same root. After all, where else do you seek water, moisture – be it a spring, brook, river, lake or swamp – if not in a gully? He found this coincidence quite remarkable, perhaps even decisive: clear proof that all he had said was true. Later on Lenin would find a use for these speculations too.'

***

In the 1990s the man who'd once run the field trips I went on became a big wheel in the Council of Ministers, and at his suggestion I spent several years chairing the Education Committee of the province of Ulyanovsk. Or Simbirsk, as it was called before the Revolution.[28] In the country at large, Lenin was fast becoming a distant memory, and although his statues were still standing, many people no longer knew who they were statues of. Not so in Ulyanovsk province. Here in his homeland Lenin was still holding his ground. During my first week at work I was reminded at least twenty times that I was occupying the same position that Lenin's father had held a century earlier.

The province was desperately poor, funding for my committee was pitiful, and a good part of what we did receive was spent on residential schools, especially Special School No. 3, which was for children with physical disabilities of one kind or another. This institution was a constant headache for the town. It had once been run by a certain Lestikov, who was put away for gross embezzlement in the 1980s; now that power had changed hands, he was bombarding the Ulyanovsk administration with denunciations. He described School No. 3 as a den of iniquity, claimed that the teachers raped the children and that the children, in their turn, had sex with each

---

[28] Simbirsk, birthplace of Vladimir Ilyich Ulyanov (Lenin), was renamed Ulyanovsk following Lenin's death in January 1924.

other during lessons. As for what happened in the dormitories after lights out, the word orgy didn't begin to describe it.

This was the first case on my desk, and before visiting the school I called a Moscow acquaintance of mine, a competent child psychologist. What he told me was far from reassuring. Showing not the slightest surprise, he explained that for children in places like this sex is no different from any other natural function. There's nothing you can do about it and there's no point trying. Lestikov was telling the truth: in residential schools, especially special needs ones, pupils begin sleeping with each other just as soon as they feel the first urge. It's all perfectly straightforward – after all, they spend every day and night under the same roof. I had to realise that special needs schools are no picnic, that the children who end up there are sick, very sick, with little joy in their lives, and sex is the quickest way to find some. What I really had to worry about was making sure there were no paedophiles on the staff and that the older kids didn't abuse, not to mention rape, the younger ones. If there were no problems on that front and I still persisted in meddling and taking measures, I'd merely succeed in replacing the current teachers with others who were far worse.

Aside from general denunciations of the whole school, there were also about ten personal ones regarding a certain Ishchenko, a history teacher who'd been the first to testify against Lestikov in the '80s. Compared to the others, these looked fairly trivial. Ishchenko was charged with violating pedagogical principles by using too many words in class that even pupils at ordinary schools would struggle to understand. These principles were a light in the gloom. I remember how smug I felt when I decided to dish out an official reprimand to the unknown victim before reporting back to the authorities, with a clear conscience, that measures had been taken. I wouldn't touch anyone else, in line with my friend's advice. As it turned out though, no one suffered anyway.

I still remember my first visit to the school. The desks in the classrooms were small and uncomfortable. So as not to get in anybody's way, I chose one tucked deep in a corner and spent several minutes looking for somewhere to stick my long legs; when I eventually succeeded, I took out a notebook and pen, and as an insurance policy, switched on my tape recorder. To begin with, Lestikov's denunciations were the only thing on my mind and it wasn't until the second week that I suddenly began to understand that what I was hearing in the classroom was part and parcel of the same history that had once destroyed the lives of many people around me.

I've decided to include the stories Ishchenko told in his lessons about the last four years of Lenin's life both for that reason and because I had already heard something similar thirty years earlier in a quite different place and from a quite different man: the now deceased Farabin.

There are two other things I should mention. The class in which I was taking notes included children of different ages and very different abilities, as is usually the case in special schools of this type. But it's unlikely (Lestikov was not lying here) that Ishchenko ever stopped to think about whether they understood him. He was in no doubt, it seems to me, that his pupils needed only a hint to distinguish the true from the false. And the truth is all anyone needs. Secondly, Ishchenko's stories – I see this clearly now – contained two Lenins. One was dying a slow, agonising death and bidding farewell to his old life. But within him, within this hopelessly sick old man, another Lenin was being born before our eyes – a strong, dogged Lenin who was ready to fight.

Ishchenko had a God-given gift for teaching, no two ways about it. I can still hear him beginning every lesson with the words, 'You, the damaged, you, the famished and the frozen, the abandoned and the wretched, whom nobody loves, nobody needs, remember one thing: it was to you that Lenin came.'

LESSON ONE
A Time of Troubles

The Lenin of the early 1920s, Ishchenko said, was not his usual self, and not just on account of his illness. Lonely, abandoned by one and all, he began to understand ever more clearly that he, in his turn had to treat the proletariat in the same way. Betrayed, he had to become a traitor himself. Still unsure how to talk to God, he would get himself into a complete muddle, now begging the Lord, now demanding, now setting Him ultimata, now waving the white flag, ready to agree to anything. There were days when he spent hours torturing himself and God with one and the same question: surely a different road to Him could have been laid, one that did not lead through betrayal?

There is no path to the Lord without faith, without hope, without love, but to begin with Lenin had neither the first nor the second nor the third – only political intuition, which had never let him down. Perhaps it was because Lenin had so little faith that the Lord kept a particularly close and jealous eye on him. To say that he was herded onto the right path with a stick, though, would be unfair. He wanted to turn onto that path, desperately so, but how hard it was for him! One day he seemed to have left the old road behind him for good, the next he was turning back again. The same thing that he mocked savagely today he would try to justify tomorrow, in fact he would praise it to the skies with all the verve of a born debater. And there was no way of knowing whose side he was on or where he was headed.

It's important to understand that in the '20s, even without newspapers, books and polemics with his opponents, Lenin's political development continues. His view of the Revolution, of Communism changes. His old Marxism, with its all-saving proletariat, dies out in him. He begins to understand that it was a mistake to count on the workers. That entire class was a thing of the past and it was dragging him back like a fishing net. To build a world free of evil and sin with the workers was an exercise in futility.

Nothing it seems could be clearer, but the next day it's all change again. Arguing with God, Lenin tries, in the most touching, most determined way, to defend those he once led, to shield them from Him. Yes all right, he says, the working man is so filthy, so full of sin that no amount of baking soda will ever scrub him clean. And yes, you'll never find a down-and-out who's not a thief and a liar, a drunk and a lecher. And all the misery that's come his way has only made him worse. Avenging the world, he takes out his rage on the weak. Beats his wife and children to a pulp. But then, Lenin asks Christ, was it not He who said that '…joy shall be in Heaven over one sinner that repenteth, more than over ninety and nine just persons, which need no repentance' (Luke 15:7)? He approaches God and demands an answer, even though he has long known that a lumpenprole won't even manage to save himself, never mind others.

Trying to understand who, if not the workers, the Lord had ordained him to lead now, Lenin sifted all Russia anew at the turn of the decade. He considered the peasants, the former landowners, the bourgeoisie, the bureaucrats, the intelligentsia, paying special attention within that last category to priests and those engaged in the creative arts – but he found no one who was pure and immaculate. He had a pretty good idea of course, who the new holy people should be, but he played the fool and pretended not to understand. He submitted a sarcastic request for a clear sign from above, in case he ended up choosing the wrong lot again and led them in the wrong direction. He asked why it was that his enemies, when he had been on the side of the workers, had all called him an atheist and an antichrist, more brutal than Diocletian, yet the Lord was giving him His blessing, sending him victory after victory.

Lenin is no mystery, Ishchenko would explain to the class. He was a single-minded man, not one to spread himself thin, and until the Revolution his thoughts were entirely occupied by the Party. Opportunities to think in a measured, unhurried way about you children were few and far between. Besides, he had no cause to do so: he had no children of his own, and as for other people's kids, he knew that if Communism triumphed, they'd do just fine. Babbling babies and bubbly children were not his thing. The idea of ever having to live, let alone work near an infant horrified him. When his comrades started producing offspring and tried converting him and Nadya to their new faith, he would make light of it all, telling them that babies smelled of mice, and Krupskaya was terrified of those.[29]

But it wasn't just the mice. Runts, toerags, pipsqueaks – he gave you all sorts of names – actually seemed to scare Lenin. The little snivellers were weak and defenceless, of course, but it was your wilfulness, your innate political nous that shocked him. One would have thought that if you can't take a single step without someone helping you, then you should act accordingly, but the little squirts knew how to spin everything in such a way that it wasn't only rank-and-file workers but clandestine Party activists who began to think that nothing mattered more in the world than their runny faeces, screams and snot. Krupskaya was a good, loyal comrade, but even she told him one day that she wanted a child. Lenin's mind had long been made up on this matter and there was no point trying to argue with him; he merely observed that children did more harm to world revolution than all the Tsar's secret policemen put together. They were always getting under the feet of the progressive proletariat, hobbling it for good. Then as a softener, he added that he didn't have anything against the small fry, he just thought that a different world needed to be built for them first.

Krupskaya kept silent the first time around, then a year later she sadly observed that it was already too late for her to bear children. He started stroking her hair, but there was something fake about the whole scene and Lenin couldn't resist

---

[29] Nadezhda (Nadya) Krupskaya (1869-1939) married her fellow revolutionary Lenin in political exile in Siberia in 1898 and was closely involved with education policy after the Revolution.

saying, 'Just remember Sarah and Abraham.' Krupskaya burst into tears, but she forgave him soon enough, as she always did. That evening they went for a stroll in the park as usual.

The Revolution and the Civil War changed little. He didn't turn a blind eye to anything: he knew there were millions of children – homeless, hungry, cold, unclothed and unshod – wandering about between St Petersburg and Vladivostok. Dropping like flies from Spanish flu, typhus, cholera. But how was the Party supposed to help? Where could it find bread and medicine for them? After all, even Red Army soldiers often went without their rations. Yes of course he felt sorry for you and lamented the fact that you were born too soon, in the eye of the storm. That you turned out to be those proverbial chips of wood, which when the forest is cut down, are nobody's concern. He didn't exclude the possibility that there could have been fewer victims, but thought it unwise to waste resources on charity, on wiping away tears, and said more than once in the Central Committee that they had no right to fool around with window dressing and make-up, that the only way of dealing with the problem was to crush the White worm in double-quick time.

In the autumn of 1920, when all Wrangel had left was Crimea, Lenin told Dzerzhinsky that it was time for the Bolsheviks to turn their attention once more to the untended.[30] Here too though, progress was stop-start. Feverish activity would be followed by a month or two of treading water, then

---

[30] The *besprizorniki* ('unsupervised', 'unattended'): the millions of children orphaned or abandoned as a result of the First World War, the Revolution and the Civil War that followed. Their traumatic experience and its consequences were a major concern of pioneering educators and psychologists of the time, such as Anton Makarenko and Lev Vygotsky (see Afterword).

Dzerzhinsky would send out another volley of directives. There were plenty of clever, detailed plans, but that was as far as it went. However lucid and logical the general picture, Lenin was unable to imagine himself walking at the head of a column of children. He knew he was wrong to feel that way, but he just couldn't do it. Taken separately he could see both them and himself very clearly, but even when they were close they kept groping around like the blind, never managing to find each other. He tried more than once to make sense of this, remembered deciding that he himself was the cause of it all – he had no children of his own – and to his own surprise, felt quite upset.

Never having held a newborn infant in his arms, incapable of watching one grow and change year after year, Lenin had come to think of a child as a kind of mental blank from which a full-fledged worker could emerge only after the most thorough reshaping. There were times when he wondered whether it was even worth fussing over them; after all, the first man had had no childhood. In forming Adam, the Lord had produced a fair copy straight away.

All alone in his Kremlin office and genuinely eager to find some way to exonerate the small fry, Lenin went back over all his memories of children – but all he felt was disgust. Helpless and dependent, yet wily, timid, forever grabbing on to mummy's skirt and easily bribed: they'll yell for hours on end as if they're being tortured, but give them one cheap sweet and they'll soon shut up. Dirty, too: in '14, just a week before the war, Roza Kameneva asked him to hold her baby and it emptied its bowels all over his knees. A foul, filthy race.

Of course, they were as much victims of the old regime as

the proletariat. But what a gulf there was between them! The workers were tight-knit, well-soldered, ready to take up the struggle as one; they were, beyond doubt, born Bolsheviks, but the only people he was prepared to compare you lot with were rowdy and cowardly anarchist scum.

In '21, on his way to the Red Turbine factory, where he was due to give his first speech after Fanny Kaplan's attempt to assassinate him, his chauffeur drove him past Sukharevsky market. They'd left the Kremlin early and were in no real hurry. Lenin was idly looking out of the window, something he hadn't done for a good long time. He felt calm and cheerful. Weary of life in the office, he was desperate to be in contact with the masses again and was in an excellent mood. A horde of local roughs was facing off by the entrance to the market. He told his driver to stop the car – he wanted to see who would come out on top. They were fighting with knives and metal bars in their fists, and several young teenagers were already bleeding on the ground. Eventually he told the two Chekists escorting him to get out of the car and sort it out.

The Chekists were scared of getting mixed up with rabid street gangs and didn't want to budge, but Lenin insisted. The upshot, against all expectation, was pure vaudeville. On seeing two Chekists with leather coats and revolvers, the toerags fled in all directions. A minute later there was neither hide nor hair of them. Lenin found himself thinking once again what anarchist trash children are, how cruel and cowardly, and that evening he told Dzerzhinsky over the phone that catching the untended wasn't the problem – the main thing was to re-educate you all. To take this unpromising material and use it to forge and fashion the next shift of hardened, dedicated

Revolutionary workers.

In light of all this – Ishchenko went on – Lenin had plenty of reasons not to hear what the Lord was telling him. And this stubborn resistance continued until finally, on 25th May 1922, he had another stroke. May 25th is the turning point, when he starts to leave adult life. Doing so was not just difficult for Lenin – for a long time he found it barely comprehensible.

In July '22, via the same Doctor Getye, he complained to Trotsky in bewilderment: 'I could neither speak nor write. I had to learn it all over again, like a little boy.' Half a year later, Trotsky received another message, this time from Krupskaya: 'He hasn't been able to read for ages, but the moment he catches the scent of fresh newspaper his hands reach out for it. All the smells of the printed word – paper, ink, machine grease – seem to bring him joy and good cheer. At mealtimes, despite knowing very well how bad this is for any child, he'll wheel himself over towards the newspaper table and steal glances on the sly at the headlines in *Pravda*, like a pickpocket. Then he'll continue on his way, as if nothing has happened.'

Not being able to write was particularly painful for Lenin. He told Bukharin, 'Next thing I know I'll end up like Akselrod – what a horrible thought.'[31] On another occasion: 'You can congratulate me on my recovery. The proof's in my handwriting – look, it's almost human.'

For more than a year then, Lenin was buffeted one way then the other, not least because his family did not approve

---

[31] Nikolai Bukharin (1888 – executed 1938), a prominent Bolshevik theorist and politician who sided with Stalin against Trotsky after Lenin's death (before himself being purged a decade later). Pavel Akselrod (1850-1928), leading Menshevik and opponent of revolutionary violence and political centralisation.

BE AS CHILDREN

of him wandering off into childhood. Maria Ulyanova, his younger sister, wrote: 'I had a dream and it was as if Ilyich was his old self again. Oh, how we need him!' Krupskaya badgered him several times about why it was that now he only invited children to visit him, when an entire nation was ready to follow him. She wouldn't believe that the rest were just ballast, that their own sins would hobble them better than any straps – they'd never make it as far as the village fence.

Krupskaya kept on hoping and believing he'd get better. On 27th September 1922, she wrote in her diary: 'I spent half the night grovelling at Lenin's feet. Trying to convince him that just one week would be enough to clear out the riffraff from the Kremlin and then that would be that, I'd keep out of his way.' She kept on at him for so long that one day he almost gave in, realising only at the last moment that others would come along to take the place of the current lot and nothing would change. There was only one path to Salvation – to Jerusalem, with the children. Krupskaya was calming down in any case, learning to accept the situation, as their decades together had taught her to, and she even asked his forgiveness. But it wasn't until March 1923 that she and he were fully united once more.

Lenin was turning slowly, like a big heavy steamboat – Ishchenko continued – but there's no doubt that he was turning towards you. He saw ever more clearly that you were the only ones who had nothing to lose. Just one thing frightened him: that he might not be able to find a common language with you. You know that Lenin was no proletarian, but he never experienced any timidity before the workers; children were a different matter.

He could see that to be accepted by you he first had to

become a child himself, to bid adult life farewell for good. Otherwise he'd always be a stranger to you. Your lack of rootedness in the old life lured him like a drug. He told Krupskaya that you alone were ready, like the Lord during the flood, to raze everything to the ground, to wipe all there was from the face of the Earth. To grow up, he explained to her, is to take sin into one's soul, but there would be no sin in the world that the children would build, so there would be no growing up either.

Lenin's path to childhood also marked the beginning of his own path to the Holy Land. And that was the most important thing, even if later on, he would falter on the road to Jerusalem and sometimes wanted to leave it altogether, and when the Lord caught him he wasn't sorry but tried to justify himself, like a little boy, and asked why it was that for him, Lenin, withdrawing into childhood was the same as withdrawing into death? It wasn't fair. But the very next moment he realised that actually it was: he had spilled far too much blood in his life.

LESSON TWO
The Hand-seer

Ishchenko told the class that in early April 1920, not long before Lenin spoke to Dzerzhinsky about the untended, Getye was invited to the Kremlin for lunch and asked if he could bring a friend with him from the Military Medical Academy, a very nice man, also a doctor, who specialised in blind deaf-mutes. His surname was Demidov.

Demidov's father, an ironworks proprietor in the Urals, had

left him a considerable fortune, all of which went on building a research clinic for these unfortunate souls. It was one such patient that Demidov now wished to present. Krupskaya's first thought was that, having run out of funds, Getye and Demidov were hoping for help from Lenin, but she held her tongue. In any case, the doctors conducted themselves impeccably over lunch – not a word about food rations or clothes coupons.

It was the child, a boy of about twelve, who made the biggest impression. He ate his soup and buckwheat very nicely, without falling behind the others, and drank up his fruit juice. It was probably because they were always staring at him that the conversation failed to flow. Demidov struggled the most. Living with his wards around the clock and fussing over them as if he were their mother, he had been able to teach them to understand both himself and one another, but explaining any of this to Lenin seemed beyond him.

Lenin wanted to know how Demidov communicated with his patients and how they communicated with him, the method by which he taught them human speech. But no clear picture emerged. All he understood was that conversations would begin not with the usual phrases – 'Do tell me' or 'Ivan Petrovich!' – but with a signal, the touch of hand on hand, or finger on hand, and the same in reply. From here the child proceeds to gain its first notions of things. The teacher hands the pupil an object once, twice, a third time, then draws its outline right there, on his interlocutor's hand. Step by step, the gestures and the drawing become the image of the object. It's intricate work, and sculpting is the only activity that can bring about success. It speeds up the learning process twenty or thirty times over. In general, blind deaf-mutes use their hands to speak, see, hear. Their hands, Demidov repeated, replace everything else.

After dessert, Krupskaya gave everyone a red apple and sat down at the piano. To everyone's surprise, the boy got up from the table, and without a moment's hesitation, followed her over. Krupskaya was in an excellent mood and played piece after piece while he stood beside her, placed his hand on the smooth cold lid of the grand piano and listened in rapture to the vibrations of the wood.

After she had finished her little recital, the conversation around the table returned to the subject of hands. Lenin asked the boy, through Demidov, what else he could do with them. He replied that feeling the tension in a person's muscles, or just feeling their pulse, was enough to tell him what mood they were in: nervous, agitated, hiding something, telling the truth, or on the point of telling a lie. He explained that if someone is feeling bad, if a person is suffering, this instantly communicates itself to the person holding their hand. From then on the conversation flowed smoothly. The boy spoke particularly well about the movement of air and about smells, which also rarely deceived him.

Lenin and Krupskaya noticed, as early as the soup course, that whenever the domestic staff entered the dining-room, the boy gave a barely perceptible shudder, and now Nadezhda asked, through Demidov, whether the boy was bothered by something. He gave a broad smile and said that Lenin knew as well as he did that no one could survive for long without reliable informants. The boy had air waves to tell him that a person had walked into a room. The wave having reached him, would press against his cheek, then drift down together with the smell. He added that he would know when a political demonstration was happening from the powerful movement of smells. But there was no chaos here: the currents of workers' columns would advance in taut, powerful streams, and it was only during a rally that they became entwined in plaits. He said he liked it when the strong and harsh smells of men – tobacco, freshly chopped wood, metal, grease – marched side by side with the mild smells of the labour and flesh of female workers, the smells of fresh laundry, milk, sweat, soap.

But it wasn't this that Krupskaya remembered for the rest of her life. When they were saying goodbye and were already halfway out the door, the boy suddenly grabbed Demidov's hand and began feverishly tapping something on it with his long strong fingers. Krupskaya was sure that it was about Lenin, who had stayed behind in the room, that he had something terribly important to tell her husband. But Demidov surprisingly enough, didn't say a word; instead he began to fuss and hurry. He was clearly pleased with how the visit had gone and he didn't want to risk spoiling the good impression they'd made. The boy though, proved himself quite sly. Ingeniously, stubbornly, he started dropping one thing after another – hat, gloves, scarf – and putting his feet into someone else's shoes, and Demidov just wasn't able to usher him out.

After observing all this for a few minutes, Krupskaya lost patience and asked Demidov to translate for her what exactly the boy was after. Unfortunately Demidov had been right and the boy's request was not a very pleasant one. He was begging that Lenin let him touch his face, otherwise he was worried that, when the time came, he wouldn't recognise him. Krupskaya, needless to say, was never likely to pass on a request like that, but Lenin had heard Demidov's words, and to her surprise, agreed.

In the evening Krupskaya wrote in her diary that after Demidov and his ward left, Lenin took her hand, held and stroked it for a few minutes, then suddenly said, out of the blue, 'Don't be sad: to each their own fate. We are the makers of transient forms on the path to the Communist order – but we were essential: without us the others would not have come along, the ones who are already Communism itself.'

LESSON THREE
The Treachery of Words

After the first stroke, Ishchenko said, thinking no longer came easily to Lenin, and he lacked confidence in doing so. His thoughts would wander away and break off and there was no point trying to bring them back by force. At best, he would be sent back to square one, as in a children's game, and begin all over again, only with less hope. Anything could bother him: a creaking floorboard, a snatch of conversation, a stray fly. Every sound enraged him; spluttering with hatred, he would shout, bang his walking stick, and when he could manage it, stamp his feet. But it got him nowhere. All that yelling did not make Lenin any less feeble, he just became weaker and weaker until he suddenly drooped like an old man. A minute later he would be fast asleep, slumped to one side in his wheelchair. His constant terror of never managing to finish anything, of having to abandon it halfway stemmed from these sudden ruptures. True, every now and again something would come back to him and restore itself just like that, as if someone had taken pity on him and thrown him a few coins. But such gifts brought him little joy.

Lenin, Ishchenko said, was in the most obvious, most categorical way, a man of words. Without words, without mentally articulating what he was feeling, he could neither tell the taste of his food nor even know whether he felt hot or cold. The same went for music, which he had adored since childhood. Before letting it enter him, he would first picture it in edifices of letters, from which the sounds would release themselves only gradually.

He was aware of his dependence on language, but he never regretted it, in fact he was proud of it. It was as if he had signed an eternal pact with words, and together they had no trouble dispatching any opponent. For all that he burred and lisped, he was a born orator who knew how to make his listeners pin back their ears, how to make them afraid of missing a single word, above all – how to make them trust him. Reading and writing mattered even more to Lenin. But after the stroke, everything changed. He was suddenly transformed from a human being into a mute beast. One by one, the words deserted him. They went away without turning back or showing any pity, and Lenin was stunned.

Six months later, as he gradually got used to his new situation, Lenin suddenly realised that the reason the world was so foul, so vile, was that we had no qualms about constructing it with words, words that were always ready to betray us. He himself had been no mean builder. Lenin remembered the first words of St John's Gospel: 'In the beginning was the Word, and the Word was with God, and the Word was God.' But one fine day man had decided that the word was greater and stronger than God, that for as long as you had it by your side, for as long as you and it were one, you had nobody and nothing to fear. But that's wrong. It's enough for God to take one step away from the word for it to turn into a pretender, a thief.

When Lenin understood that words had betrayed him for good and would never return, he wept inconsolably for three days, literally choking on his tears. Even Krupskaya could not calm him down. In fact, right up to the last days of his life he could not forgive them their treachery. For all his vows to the contrary, he came back to this subject again and again. Still crying, he would either curse words or tell himself that he would be better off without them. Like Job, he needed to lose everything, deprive himself of all he'd ever had, before the true path would be revealed to him. Whether or not he really believed this is not for me to say.

During the second half of 1922 and throughout 1923, Lenin didn't just vilify words, he also thought about them long and hard. In the past, too, he had tended to the view that all the senses that the Lord had given man before the Fall – everything he saw, smelled, touched, heard – were perfect and had no need of being translated into words. But once Adam was banished from Paradise it was a different story. It was then that we switched to the deceitful language of mere convention and frittered away God's gift with talk. We probably took fright at the brilliance of creation, the brilliance of the world, and concealed it by concealing ourselves beneath a blanket of verbal husks. Tried to hide our sin, just as Cain had sought to hide the slain body of Abel. Telling himself he was glad that words had run away from him as if from a leper, that he himself should have fled from them even faster a long time ago, Lenin no longer doubted that the sole purpose of words was to think about God and talk with God, that all else was the work of the Devil. True, for a whole year he believed that under Communism people would manage to wash words clean, but later he realised sadly that there was no remedy – the human tongue only had to touch a word in vain even once for it to be ruined evermore.

He told Krupskaya that the Lord is good, but that from the very start the world had been made in such a way that it was enough for Him to find Himself near a sin for the latter to turn to ashes. Along with the sins, He would incinerate us as well, even if we were as righteous as Moses. The Lord knew human nature, He had few illusions, yet he still had faith in our repentance. He was waiting for us no less than a father waits for his prodigal son, and before creating the universe, before dividing light from darkness, He created words to help us. We were filthy and bloody from head to toe, we didn't even dare approach Him, but we could still turn to Him. But then we closed off this path to salvation as well.

Now it was the sheer clumsiness of words that astounded him. There were millions of them, yet you could never use them to convey a taste or a smell. Obviously winemakers and perfumers manage to understand one another somehow, but isn't it better just to pour the person you're talking to a glass from the same bottle you're drinking yourself? Words, he told Krupskaya, are and always will be a surrogate and a lie, and the only way of returning to the world the Lord has given us is to renounce them.

There are five primary senses, each with their own

language: touch, smell, sight, hearing, taste. We must learn to live only with them. Track down our prey with them, identify diseases with them, use them to understand the person standing next to us – does he believe in us, is he honest, or is he an enemy?

He reminisced about the hunting he had loved so much. There you are, waiting in ambush with your gun, and all of a sudden your partner points with his eyes to where some bushes are being parted by an animal – and no words are needed. What he sees, you see, and when you go, all this will end, and that's no disaster. There'll be some other animal and some other bird, some other tree and some other grass.

The word, Lenin thought, is born from the desire to convey to others what they have not seen with their own eyes, not touched with their hands, not smelled with their nostrils. As under socialism, to make the world equal for each and every person. But is this really necessary? It's the same with thoughts. But when has one person ever understood another? Of course, Lenin thought, words have many virtues, and these have always seemed to outweigh their faults. With words we could just about preserve what we were so scared of forgetting. These were not empty fears. The problem was that words proved to be poor tools. Crude and unwieldy. And so one day, despairing of ever adapting words to the world, we energetically, even ecstatically began simplifying the world, adapting it to words.

Lenin was at the forefront of these adjustments, but he knew that his sickness was not a punishment; on the contrary, it was the token of fast-approaching freedom. A year or two would pass and the world would rid itself of words and become as it had been at the time of its creation. He often saw it now, vast and bright, like a water-meadow at noon. And upon it joyful, innocent people, babbling away as if they had just been born.

LESSON FOUR
Lenin and the Doctors

During his first lesson devoted to Lenin's physicians, Ishchenko said the following. Lenin died on 21st January 1924, after almost two years of illness (the worst strokes occurred on 25-27th May 1922 and 10th March 1923) but throughout this time he was no living corpse, no vegetable: he was fighting for all he was worth. And it's incumbent on us to know who and what he was fighting for. His medical record and the recollections of the professors who treated him and of Krupskaya herself can clear up a great deal here.

Lenin made his last public appearance in November 1922, when he gave his Report to the Fourth Congress of the Comintern in the House of the Unions. He spoke in German. Whenever he forgot a word, he would snap his fingers to jog his memory. A large group of the Party elite was standing by the tribune, headed by Kolya (Nikolai) Bukharin – his paramedics, as it were. It was Bukharin who recalled that when Lenin had finished his speech and they led him backstage, supporting him all the way, the shirt under his fur coat was drenched from the exertion. Despite the cold, the sweat was dripping off his forehead too, and his eyes had sunk so deep you could barely see them.

Lenin's first stroke and sudden dumbness sent his

comrades into blind panic. Most of them were convinced that they couldn't stay in power without him. Desperate to get him back in action, his Central Committee colleagues dispatched doctors to Gorki in droves – forty-three in two years.

How he hated them! In April 1923 he wrote to Trotsky, through Krupskaya, that they were true demons and that he knew that earlier, at the beginning of time, they had been the guardian angels of sinners. The Lord had inflicted a flood on humankind and punished them by casting them down into Hell. Now they were doing all they could to exonerate themselves, to prove to the Lord that the descendants of the survivor Noah, were no better. He complained that there were so many of these medics that they had literally buried him beneath themselves.

Lenin's condition was unpredictable: he would lose one faculty but might recover another. What's more, in many cases it was unclear whether the losses were genuine or simply part of a conspiracy to deceive the Central Committee. For example, his unusually methodical sessions with his speech therapists, especially Professor Dobrogayev, raise all sorts of questions.

I want you all to write down, Ishchenko told the class, that after his first stroke, which hurled him back into childhood, Lenin became just like you, just like any of the children sitting before me now. Teachers, pupils, anyone in our school would recognise him as one of their own. Just like you, Peristy, he suffered from complete auditory agnosia at the beginning. But just like you, Kamkin, he gradually started understanding more and more of what people were saying to him. On the other hand, for a long time, just like Ustavin, he retained the ability to read to himself, and it was only after the second stroke that for him, as for Volodya Polsky, the image of letters – the syllabic and syntactic patterns of the written word – disintegrated. This is known as agraphia. But although he never regained the skill of lexicographic scanning, his visual-analytic scanning function remained strangely intact – one glance at a headline, at the space occupied by an article on the page was more than enough to tell Lenin what was in it.

During the second attack in March '23 he experienced total aphasia, shouting one and the same sentence for several hours: 'Help me, ah, dammit, the iodine's helped, if it's iodine'. But a month later the aphasia became milder. It returned to how it was before, except that is, for Lenin's body language. His eyes – and this is mentioned by everyone who was around him at the time – became particularly expressive.

On the whole, though he kept looking backwards, Lenin was wandering further and further away, and between glances, tossing everything he had gained year by year over his shoulder, with no regrets. In the space of two short years he forgot how to read, write, count, speak, and at least partially, to understand words. Sometimes the speed with which he was re-entering childhood actually frightened him. From January '23 he was no longer able to dress himself or use a toothbrush.

Still, there would have been fewer agonising lurches one way then the other, were it not for the doctors. Even after Krupskaya herself had retreated, they continued to urge him onto the path which Lenin had already walked once before and which – he knew full well – led nowhere except ruin. Still tempting him with power, they didn't merely repeat that it would fall into his lap instantly, just as soon as he agreed to become an adult once more; the main thing was that the Party and the entire country were begging him to do this. And they dangled before him a picture of total apocalypse if, God forbid, he refused.

While looking after Lenin, the doctors imitated his mother with fiendish skill. They'd heard somewhere that during lessons she used to encourage her son by saying, 'Valik, my dear, beloved Valyusinka, what a clever boy you are', and they copied this so precisely that Solomon himself would have been deceived. Even their smiles were hers, and he was taken in by them, he couldn't fail to have been. After the stroke he was far too weak not to yield to them, thinking that the sooner he did what the doctors wanted of him, the quicker they would leave, but when one left another arrived and it never seemed to end. They merely attacked with greater conviction, explained to him in louder, more resonant, more vigorous tones that soon, very soon he'd be back in action – one more push was all it needed. When they saw that Lenin was digging his heels in, or simply struggling with a particular exercise, they began to torture him. Humiliated him with false hopes, with their loathsome, trite jokes and their concerned, patronising tone, their chuckles and fake smiles.

No wonder that Krupskaya wrote in her diary more than once that her husband's reaction to the doctors on this or that date was overheated and unhealthy. His hatred for this infernal band was truly savage – he may never have hated anyone quite so much – but there was no way of getting rid of them even for a day. Not everyone who treated him of course, was a scoundrel and a scumbag. I've already spoken about Professor Getye – his friend, confidant, liaison man – and there were also some run-of-the-mill fools who wanted what was best for him and were convinced they were helping. Lenin could barely stand them either. True, the last six months of Lenin's life did bring him some relief. By that point the Central Committee (CC) members felt confident that even without him their hold on power was secure, after which, as if by command, every second doctor became an ordinary stool pigeon. We'll return to that later – Ishchenko continued – but for now it would be beneficial I think, to compare the success rate of the professors who taught Lenin with my own achievements here at school and those of my colleagues.

So what did they try to teach him and to what extent did they succeed? What did he master and for how long? Following a set system, the doctors began by modelling voiced sounds and sibilants as if they were teaching a one-year-old. Lenin, as we know, had spoken with a strong burr ever since childhood. When talking to workers, he had always been very embarrassed by this failing, but now he pronounced his 'r's better than any other sound. There were other achievements too, and gradually the professors advanced to the next stage, where they began arranging the letters alphabetically. Next they moved on to syllables, just as we do here, then a little later to entire words. Sometimes getting carried away and forgetting that he was being led into temptation, he made astonishing leaps, but luckily he soon came to his senses and remembered none of it the next morning.

Truth be told, the doctors who did the most harm were the honest ones, the ones who rejoiced over the slightest progress on Lenin's part. The wounds they inflicted went deeper than any others. When Professor Kulakov demonstrated that there was a mismatch in Lenin's mind between the graphic image and the acoustic image, Lenin literally wept, but later, after working with the same Kulakov, he wrote proudly to Mikhail Tomsky, in a very respectable hand: 'I've been given permission to read the papers: old ones today, new ones from Monday.'

Only a month later though, Kulakov's adversary Professor Ferster reaffirmed, just before heading back to Germany, the complete ban on newspapers, meetings and all political news. This verdict was issued during lunch, in front of everyone. As Lenin listened, his lips quivered with resentment. But Ferster had helped him: thanks to this snub, Lenin managed to pull himself together. By 10th March 1923, he had taken the painful step of renouncing meaningful writing for good. Any concessions that Lenin subsequently allowed himself were trivial in nature. He might for example, spend the afternoon copying out letters and sometimes entire phrases, his tongue hanging loose from the effort. Under dictation (from Professor Feinberg) he would write out the entire alphabet, not without pleasure. The only thing he could replicate with any success though, was his signature, and each time he would laugh with joy.

If the main danger came from the honest doctors, then those who fawned on him, such as the famous CC spy, Professor Gunther – according to the domestic staff, he would spend hours on his knees by the keyhole when everyone else was having lunch, fearful that his appearance would bring on a fit – and those who mocked him, such as Dobrogayev, actually brought him to his senses, made him finally remember which way he was going and to whom.

By and large, Ishchenko continued, the doctors' exercises

were based on rote learning, on endless repetition. It wasn't just sounds, syllables, words (in particular, the Spanish-Russian dictionary) that Lenin learned by heart, but also poems and even, later on, some very short stories. This was meant to give him confidence and allow him to move on to reading aloud and writing from dictation. But none of the doctors could claim any great success. Vast quantities of time and energy were expended, with almost no results. True, he did try more than once to retell a two- or three-page story from memory, but he kept forgetting the words and losing his way. The gist was also beyond his reach, leading to verbal paraphasia: instead of 'cockerel' he'd suddenly say 'pear', instead of 'spoon', 'house'. Within a day or two the entire text had been forgotten.

After a year of studying, only seven phrases had stuck. Here's the complete list: *off you go, drive on, ooh-la-la, guten Morgen, Lloyd George, conference, impossibility* – but even these popped out without rhyme or reason, like devils from a snuff-box. There were only two real achievements: Professor Strakhov taught him to add and subtract quite tolerably with numbers up to ten, and at the dinner table at Gorki, where at least thirty people might gather and where, on Krupskaya's orders, only small talk was permitted, Lenin was capable of very deliberately chipping in 'that's just', subsequently adding the word 'it'.

For various reasons, some of Lenin's plans concerning children came out in the last months of his life. The CC members got wind of them and began considering retaliatory measures. Fortunately Lenin wasn't caught off guard – all thanks to Trotsky. It was Trotsky who communicated, via Professor Getye, that there was a plan to poison Lenin and that the venom would probably be added to his quinine. Which is why we read in Krupskaya's diary that from the summer of '23 onwards Lenin refused all medication except laxatives and iodine. In another entry, Professor Kadastrov brings quinine and Lenin shakes his fist at him in rage. 'If you don't want to take it, then don't, no one's forcing you,' Kadastrov jabbers as he backs out of the room, accompanied by a burst of laughter and an expression of complete satisfaction on Lenin's face.

The CC members, needless to say, made sure that Lenin's doctors were proper all-rounders. They treated him and snooped on him, taught him and poisoned him. The hardest job though, fell to just one of them, Professor Osipov. In the autumn of '23, Osipov, a specialist in paedology, experimental pedagogy and neuropsychiatry, published his first article (of dozens) in the *Bulletin of Psychiatry* under the title, 'On the Counter-Revolutionary Complex of the Insane'. Patently alluding to his patient, he wrote that, 'A case history of this sort is primarily typical of those in the advanced stages of syphilis', and then, 'Such patients show great commitment to overthrowing the Soviet order. There's barely a single expansive paralytic who doesn't try. As a result, counter-revolutionary ideas and the entire counter-revolutionary complex have spread with almost pandemic speed in our country.'

LESSON FIVE
A Clean Break

1923 proved a very painful year for Lenin – Martov's death, Vorovsky's death, Gorky's illness. Becoming ever more sad and pensive, he watched on hopelessly as the last threads tying him to his former life broke one by one. 'There are times,' Krupskaya wrote in her diary, 'when he sits for hours without moving, without noticing or hearing a thing. He just stares at a fixed point and his eyes fill with tears.' It was with despair too, that Lenin received news of the debate later that year which culminated in the decisive defeat of Trotsky. It was precisely then, Krupskaya wrote, that his illness took a fateful turn. Lenin stopped laughing and joking, and sank into his own thoughts.

Until then he had followed every stage of the struggle for power, and whenever he saw a newspaper – it didn't matter where – he would always try to scan at least the headlines. When it became clear that the Party had chosen Stalin, he saw at once that everyone he knew would soon become members of anti-Party factions, counter-revolutionaries, sectarians, saboteurs and murderers, become creators of a cult of personality, and if they got lucky, become little cults of their own for a short while – and he no longer wished to see them.

That same May of 1923, Ishchenko recounted, was marked by another important event, which outwardly has much in common with Lev Tolstoy's flight from his family estate at Yasnaya Polyana. On the fifteenth, a Monday, Lenin moved out of the manor house in Gorki to one of the wings, without even telling Krupskaya. Despite his paralysis, he climbed the steep staircase on his own, locked the door behind him and spent three days there entirely alone. That wing is the point of no return. It was then that the definitive break took place with the old world, the old comrades and ideas.

Unsurprisingly, we know very little of what Lenin spent

those three days thinking about. We probably wouldn't know anything at all were it not for some new topics that begin to appear in Krupskaya's diary in the summer of '23. To judge by these entries, he must have said one day that the Gospel account of the temptation of Christ on the high mountain in the wilderness was incomplete: the most important thing had been left out. The Devil tempted Christ not with the power to rule the world – it would have been difficult to entice the Son of God with that – but with the boundless power to work miracles, save people and do good. Christ had stood firm, but he, Lenin, had been wavering for so many years, tempted by a far smaller prize.

In another entry (June 1st) Krupskaya recorded the following conversation. After lunch, when they were sitting together on the terrace, she said to him, 'Remember, it's been exactly a year now since you declared – when you had barely recovered from your stroke – that you no longer counted yourself among Russia's active politicians, that you were senile, that you'd entered your second childhood. But just this morning some extremely interesting papers arrived from Moscow. A general survey was carried out across Russia last month on the orders of the Orgbureau of the CC. All sorts of questions were asked, including some about you – what you'd been up to and what you were doing now. It turns out that more than 90 percent of the population are convinced that not only are you still leading the country, but that everything good that happens in it is your doing and anything bad a result of your occasional poor health. When they were asked what would happen to Russia without you, the response was sheer panic. Look what they recorded in Belarus: "Them Bolsheviks always wanted to bring in vouchers for every meal – and if you've not got one, tough: you can starve. Lenin found out and put a stop to it. Now while Lenin's still breathing, they carry out his will, but not all of it, 'cos Lenin never wrote down his last testament – he just whispered it in Trotsky's ear. When Trotsky kicks the bucket too, he'll tell it to everyone else. And then the Bolsheviks will conquer the whole world." So you're not just an active politician – you're loved and respected more than ever.'

For a few moments Lenin stared into the garden without saying anything, before he finally replied, 'What I told you back then was true: it's the old Lenin they're talking about, not me as I am now.'

LESSON SIX
The New Revolution (*Problems of Organisation*)

Krupskaya's diary, in which she recorded everything that Lenin wanted to communicate to Trotsky and Dzerzhinsky via Getye between '22 and '24, contains dozens of entries about the new revolution to come.

1st May 1922, to Trotsky: 'The millions left orphaned and homeless by world war and civil war, by hunger and typhus, by Spanish flu and cholera are the true proletariat. The last and most proletarian of all proletariats, the most abused and the most defenceless, yet the salvation of humanity lies precisely in them. In the past, generations of parents tried to justify themselves by forcing their children to take the path of sin – as if there were no alternative – but these ones are free and will choose good. Your world revolution is a revolution of children.'

15th May 1922, to Trotsky: 'Hungry, cold, without a shirt to their backs, they are revolutionaries to the core, whatever their family history. We could not hope for more trustworthy successors. Not one will betray us, not one will leap into the arms of the enemy. And if in the past, Lev Davydovich, you and I always stood up for the working class, now it's time to admit that both we and the Party made a strategic error. But the children will forgive us – no one in the world is more merciful, more noble than they.'

18th May 1922, to Trotsky: 'The workers in the West have sold out and become completely bourgeois – no use expecting anything from them. Homeless children are a different matter. They alone cherish nothing about the old life, they alone are ready to start from scratch. It's the children we should be counting on. But there's one danger: just like the bourgeoisie with the proletariat, so the parents – if they turn up again – will almost certainly start trying to lure away their offspring, to butter them up with warmth, full stomachs and home comforts. The children need to understand that this is a trick and a lie. The only person waiting for these pure and innocent souls is Christ – a child Himself.'

And immediately to Dzerzhinsky: 'The juveniles from the children's homes have even less to lose than the proletariat. Setting little store by life, they alone are ready to burn to ashes the sin from which all of it is made. And they will show the enemies of the Revolution no pity – of this I am certain. A further advantage, from our point of view, is that they can be herded together so easily.'

Thinking of children as the new chosen people, Lenin recalled Demidov and his ward ever more often. The research that Getye's friend was carrying out could prove extremely important for him – almost the key to everything. The main thing Lenin felt, was to see the boy again, and as quickly as possible, before the first directives were issued. But he had to proceed cautiously.

On Monday morning (29th May 1922), an hour before breakfast, Getye came as usual to check Lenin's blood pressure and heart and to tap him with his little hammer. Lenin loathed these daily examinations, but on this occasion he bore them meekly. When the doctor was about to leave, Lenin held him back. To emphasise the strictly confidential nature of the conversation ahead of them, he put a finger to his lips several times and then, to remove any lingering doubt, pinched them tightly together. Only once he saw that Getye had understood did he begin. Explaining what he wanted though, proved far harder than warning Getye to keep his mouth shut. He had to sweat blood before he got there, but his efforts were rewarded. The boy was brought to Gorki the very next day.

The entire meeting took less than five minutes. Lenin asked the child just one single question: 'What must communards do, whatever the circumstances, to be strong enough to walk all the way to the Holy Land?'[32] The boy gave his answer without a moment's hesitation – by tapping it out on Demidov's hand: 'Before every major stage of the journey, they should hold hands and sing.' Then he added: 'The warmth and vibration that passes from hand to hand when they sing is nothing other

---

[32] The short-lived rule of the revolutionary-socialist Paris Commune in 1871 was a vital precedent for the early Bolsheviks, who often adopted the term 'communards' to describe those fighting for their cause (one Civil War ballad is entitled 'The Shooting of the Communards').

than the Holy Spirit. It will help them overcome any obstacle.'

This meeting was the last time Lenin and the boy saw each other, but Demidov's visits to Gorki became almost regular: fifteen in one year, some lasting more than three hours.

Of course, Ishchenko said, very little of the last two years of Lenin's life has come down to us, and even then only by chance. Far too many people would prefer to bury that time together with him. All the same, bits and pieces have survived, and the first conclusion – it's enough to glance at a couple of the notebooks in which Krupskaya kept her diary – is that it was precisely after the conversation with Demidov's ward that the real work began.

30th June 1922. Lenin, discussing the march on Jerusalem, writes to Dzerzhinsky: 'I positively insist that every brigade walking to the Holy Land should have its own Cheka:[33] it's the only way of avoiding betrayal and treason.' He explains: 'You are right to reproach children for being too kind, too soft, too quick to forgive. And besides, you find all sorts in children's homes: at least half are not orphans at all. Some were left there by parents who couldn't feed them, some got lost in the chaos of the Civil War, others ended up on the streets when their parents were taken off to prison or the typhus barracks. As far as I understand it, Felix Edmundovich, you also consider them unreliable. However clearly they see the overwhelming sinfulness of mankind, children are all too quick to make an exception for their parents. Squeeze them a little and

---

[33] The Cheka, the first iteration of the Soviet security agencies/secret police, was headed by Felix Dzerzhinsky. Its immediate successors, mentioned later, are the GPU (1922-23) and OGPU (1923-34), both also run by Dzerzhinsky (until his death in 1926).

BE AS CHILDREN

they'll start howling and blabbing, "My mummy's good, my mummy's good", like a broken record. Mothers in general are exceptionally dangerous: children are ready to forgive them at the first opportunity and go back home.'

Dzerzhinsky hesitates briefly before agreeing, and goes on to ask who will organise each Cheka, how they will go about it and who will be in them. Lenin, as if he hasn't even heard the question, begins by recommending a new adviser – Demidov – and only then tells him a few crucial things. Their purpose is to dispel Dzerzhinsky's doubts.

First, who will be in them. For Lenin, the reply is obvious: blind deaf-mutes. And only they. He writes to Dzerzhinsky: what we have here is a special path of development and a special type of human being. It is of course a terrible thing, a tragedy, when a child cannot see or hear, but every ordeal that hasn't killed you, that you've endured, pushes you onwards. And he cites the words of William Stern, 'What doesn't destroy a person makes him stronger.'[34] It's wrong to think, Lenin continues, that for a child born deaf and blind none of what we see and hear exists at all. The belief that to be blind is to abide in eternal darkness is no more than a misguided, pointless attempt on the part of the sighted to penetrate an alien world.

Were it not for the circumstances of the revolutionary times, Lenin maintains, we would have no right to intrude upon their lives. He explains that, in exchange for all that's been taken away from them, such children have been given a sense of warmth and cold, a sense of vibration, far sharper

---

[34] Stern (1871-1938), a German psychologist, did influential work in the field of child development. The original source of the quotation is Nietzsche.

senses of smell, taste, touch. So their knowledge of the world is no lesser and no coarser than ours. If the children in question were to mix only with one another, a nation would appear on Earth free of any of the sins of ears and eyes. Above all, Lenin stresses, propaganda is wasted on them and they can't be recruited by the other side. The next day though, he adds a note of caution: 'Regrettably, there are reasons to believe that blind deaf-mutes are excessively sensitive.'

On July 5th he returns to the same idea. Letter to Trotsky: 'Those who have parents are weak, thanks to their constant readiness to forgive. In the brigades that will march to Jerusalem, they can be among the led, but not among the leaders. Only those with no parents at all can be trusted.' A brigade, Lenin concludes, will be solid only if at least a third of it is composed of orphans. Still, the matter of how the Cheka of blind deaf-mutes will actually operate remains unresolved in the minds of his correspondents. Lenin carries on trying to talk Dzerzhinsky round, explaining that even among proletarians and regular Chekists, blind deaf-mutes can easily identify one another by their smell. Referring once again to Demidov's ward, he writes that thanks to their astonishing sense of vibration, they can hear sound with their fingers. A song is an unusually pure and genuine thing, and it's enough for a deaf Chekist to grab a singing communard by the throat to know there and then whether that person is faking, whether he is friend or foe.

Krupskaya notes in her diary that Lenin, though well-disposed to Trotsky until the very end of his life, thought him doctrinaire and dogmatic. In particular he couldn't forgive him the moment when, during their first discussion of the child

BE AS CHILDREN

Cheka, Trotsky sent him, by way of a reply, a typewritten copy of Christ's parable of the blind leading the blind. After receiving this from Getye, Lenin told Krupskaya that for all his enormous military and organisational talent, Trotsky would almost certainly be of little use. He insisted that the children's march to the Holy Land must not, under any circumstances, become a purely military venture and that it would be better to take his own return to childhood as a model. When the three of them discussed the question of who the overall leader of the campaign would be, who would lead the brigades, and how all this would be done, Lenin demanded categorically that there should be no adults in charge of the communards. Teachers, educators, commissars, however good and however devoted to the cause they might be, had to remain in the past: sin could not lead righteousness. The columns of communards were to be headed by those among them who had been chosen by the untended themselves, or even better, why not delegate the whole matter to God.

Trotsky asked him to clarify how this would be done in practice. Lenin replied that nothing could be simpler: the commander could be chosen by casting lots or by using children's counting rhymes. Lenin made a very similar comment about the General Staff of the campaign. Krupskaya passed on his message: 'Children will be children. Nobody can know when they will be ready, which road they will take and at what pace. Consistency is not their forte, and they are as superstitious as they are fearless. They could easily panic for no reason and flee in all directions.'

'Let me assure you,' he told Dzerzhinsky, 'that there will be squabbles in every brigade. About nothing. There will be fights, knives. In the end the brigade will break up, and each part of it will find its own way to the Holy Land. Former brothers-in-arms will be completely forgotten.'

To Trotsky once more: 'During adult campaigns of course, organisation – good organisation – has a decisive role to play, as you, Lev Davydovich, showed so brilliantly in the Civil War. But here – and I am quite certain of this – the brigades must march independently, without conferring with one another and without knowing anything about anyone else. Otherwise the Centre will destroy them and that will be that, whereas a movement like this one is impossible to control. Overall,' he concluded, 'in this instance I am on the side of anarchy.'

Nevertheless, Ishchenko said at the next lesson, some kind of auxiliary General Staff was created in mid '23 at Trotsky's urging. Lenin was also involved in its work. The role of the Centre is far from clear, but I will tell you about it all the same, though not now, but at the end of the second term of teaching. Then Ishchenko continued: you mustn't think, as Ivanov did yesterday – he pointed at the pupil sitting at the first desk by the window – that Lenin, Trotsky and Dzerzhinsky, in ruling themselves out as leaders of the expedition to the Holy Land, also ruled themselves out of the necessary preparations. On the contrary, this is the time of unprecedented activity on their part. Keeping a close eye on progress, Lenin demanded almost daily reports from Dzerzhinsky personally and from his agency, the Cheka. In the space of two short years, an enormous amount was achieved.

To ensure that the blind would safely and successfully lead the sighted to Jerusalem, verst-by-verst maps were drawn up of the smells on each of the thirty roads stretching from Central Russia to Palestine (this was the responsibility of the Transcaucasian and Central Asian sections of the Commissariat for Internal Affairs, with Comrade Vinnitsky in charge) as well as equally detailed maps of their gradients and surfaces – stone, clay, gravel, earth – so that the guides would know with their feet whether the column was on the right path (European section, Comrade Zagnitsyn). The blind were also supplied with a map of every turning, so that they could work out their location from the warmth of the sun on their face (Far Eastern section, Comrade Myasoyedov). Myasoyedov was also ordered to share out the Hermitage's collection of Swiss chiming watches among the children's homes. The blind would be able to tell the time even at night, from the vibration of the cases.

If Dzerzhinsky was in charge of practical matters related to the preparations for the expedition, Lenin delegated ideological questions to Trotsky. But here too he retained general oversight. From Krupskaya's diary: Lenin to Trotsky (15th September 1922): 'We must give the communards a firm, clear and categorical promise that no sooner will the first of them set foot on the Holy Land than the lame shall walk, the blind shall see and the deaf shall hear. And the dead, they too shall rise.' 'You can even tell them,' he continued in a letter dated the following day, 'that in Jerusalem they will see their mummies and daddies.'

To Trotsky again, two weeks later: 'The columns of communards will set forth for the Holy Land at different times and by different roads. Some roaming this way and that on mountain paths, others making a beeline for it, as if their path had been drawn with a ruler, but that doesn't matter. In fact, none of it matters: neither hunger, nor cold, nor even wild beasts. So what if tens of thousands are killed, so what if thousands of others are captured and sold into bondage? If even one person makes it and turns to the Lord, he will beg the forgiveness of all and save all.' And he concluded with the words that would soon become the oath of the Young Pioneers: 'One for all and all for one!!'

The bulk of the preparations took a year, ending with a general inspection. It was then, from 30th April to 6th May 1923, that the entire country – every city and settlement from Petrograd to Vladivostok – celebrated the Week of the Untended and Sick Child, with Lenin's blessing and in the face of desperate resistance from the Party's Orgbureau. Lenin said nothing when he was informed that more than three million children had taken part in it, but that evening when he was already drifting off to sleep, he told Krupskaya: 'You know, today I understood what it was that we, and not only we, were working for. In order that their nation should multiply before the Exodus from Egypt to the Holy Land, the wives of Israel gave birth tirelessly – up to six infants at a time. We, it turns out have laboured just as hard.' And added: 'Perhaps somebody really will make it.'

LESSON SEVEN
The Glukhov Brigade (*Problems of Linguistics*)

Lenin continued to make preparations for the joint expedition of the communards with every ounce of his strength, but there was only so much he could do. Half-paralysed and frequently bedridden for months at a time, he could make the odd proposal or demand but he was rarely in a fit state to carry out everyday tasks. On the other hand, he knew better than anyone that good organisation and the recruitment of the right people for each Cheka were not enough on their own: it was imperative that the untended should have a secret language known only to them. Then the enemy would be kept out of your plans and would not get in your way. He explained to Dzerzhinsky that if each communard brigade had a lingo all its own, one that was easy to use and felt familiar to them, this would be the best possible solution. He instructed the Cheka to gather argots from all over the country, and they did so. To judge from Krupskaya's diary, Lenin received a whole stack of notes from Dzerzhinsky a month before his death. But Lenin was convinced that, aside from criminal slang, a shared communard language was also needed. By this point he had already gained some basic experience in such matters.

In March '23 Lenin suffered a further stroke. His recovery was slow and difficult. He lay in bed for days on end in a state of total apathy. He didn't want to see anyone, didn't want to know about anyone or anything. Krupskaya was told by all and sundry that this was the end – he was fading away. A bevy of doctors swirled around him to no purpose. In the past he had always got rid of them at the first opportunity, and now Krupskaya had the impression that the professors were exulting. They found one excuse after another to stop her seeing her husband, turned him this way and that like a rag doll, administered endless injections and lavages, then gathered in groups of three or five for their conferences at which, fully aware that he could hear everything, they argued until they were blue in the face about whether he was already a corpse – or not quite yet.

Even on this occasion he found the strength of will to pick himself up. And not just to get back on his feet but to organise a brigade of his own, his first. In April he had barely come to his senses when he recalled that one verst away, in neighbouring Glukhov – another former country estate – there was now a children's home, and as he himself returned ever more definitively and irrevocably to childhood, he couldn't stop thinking about its residents. At first he couldn't find even the smallest toehold, but he didn't give up. It wasn't long before his plan was ready.

Lenin of course was a great plotter. Take, for example, the way he discovered the size of the future brigade in one fell swoop, without arousing anyone's suspicion. At lunch on July 17th he summoned the commandant of Gorki, who knew everyone in the vicinity, and through Krupskaya asked him, among other things, how much milk was allocated to the Glukhov children's home. The reply came instantly – twenty litres. Next Lenin asked how much milk each child received. After the commandant told him, Lenin sketched TOO LITTLE in the air in large letters and quickly changed the topic. When everyone was busy eating dessert, he calmly did the sums and found that there were roughly one hundred communards. That suited him perfectly.

Now he had to find a way of making contact with them, and this is where the story of his first, still syllabic language begins. It was clear to Lenin that language had to be his main priority now, otherwise both he and those who agreed to follow him would always be at loggerheads. The new language, from its very first day, had to be no poorer than any venerable, long-lived tongue; most importantly now that they had all become as one and were determined to stick together to the end, it had to be easily understood by everybody without exception. It was precisely language, he told Krupskaya, that would bind them together, push them towards each other day and night. Without it they would fall out and wander off in different directions before they were even halfway to their destination. Never mind, thought Lenin, that he himself still found it hard to get along without words, that he bowed to them at every turn – what mattered was to ensure that the communards marching to the Holy Land no longer depended on them.

In '21, when the CC members were convinced that without Lenin their number was up, that they would never hold on to the country on their own, the Sovnarkom (Council of People's Commissars) tried to ingratiate itself with its chairman by sending for an excellent chef from Paris (he also happened to be a member of the French Communist Party) to run the Gorki kitchen. Ilyich greeted his appearance with indifference. He was no snob when it came to food, and if you ask me – Ishchenko said – Lenin probably never noticed who was cooking his meals or what was in them. Small wonder that in '23 he showed little doubt or hesitation in changing things around for the good of the cause, and if that meant sacrificing his cook, so be it.

Seeking a channel of communication with the Glukhov children, Lenin now started shouting and spitting during every meal, however tasty the food, and throwing dishes to the floor. A month later he was already celebrating his first success: the poor chef announced that he was returning to his homeland.

And so it went on, with Ilyich repeating exactly the same stunt with all the Frenchman's replacements, and if he did deign to eat anything, by way of an exception, then only simple soups, kasha or kissel.[35] Eventually, Krupskaya realised that his tastes had changed and so, once it became clear that good chefs would never agree to devote their life to kasha, she had a word with Lebedyev, the deputy commandant at Gorki, and decided to recruit the woman who cooked for the nearby children's home in Glukhov.

The first line of defence had been breached, but everything still hung on a thread. Fortunately, the cook was no fool and returned Lenin's lead almost immediately. Realising that Ilyich wouldn't last long and that she'd be thrown out of Gorki the day after the Sovnarkom chairman's funeral, she demanded that her position at the children's home be kept for her. This was just what Lenin needed.

Now things started moving of their own accord. From endless soups, whether hot soups: borsch, meat, fish, cabbage (fresh or sour), mushroom, sorrel, pickled cucumber, potato, pea, bean, noodle; or cold soups: kvass and meat, kvass and salmon (with ice cubes), lenten, meat, fish, beetroot, cold borsch; or sour milk soup with herbs, cherry soup with dumplings, cranberry and apple soup, purée of fresh berries, fruit and rice soup, redcurrant soup with semolina dumplings; from kashas: oat, semolina, pearl barley, crushed-grain, buckwheat, corn, sago, rice, fine-ground barley, millet, wheat; and from the kissels he was so fond of: cranberry, milk, oat, bilberry, cherry, strawberry, raspberry, apple, rhubarb (which

---

[35] Usually made with fruit, sugar and starch, kissel can be eaten as a kind of jelly (or made thinner for drinking).

helped with his stomach), hips (drunk at night, to help him fall asleep faster) – from the first syllables of this entire children's-home recipe book he constructed a language no poorer than Esperanto, and then, to attract the cook's attention, he started either frowning with displeasure or seasoning each dish with immoderate amounts of salt, sugar, vegetable oil, vinegar, pepper, mustard and horseradish. He would demand seconds or the chunkier part of one soup (act now, no time to waste), then push away a different one or ask for it to be made thinner next time (ease off, lie low and wait), and he knew that Krupskaya, a good, trusty helpmate, would make a note of everything without perceiving what lay behind it and would pass it all on, down to the smallest detail, when discussing tomorrow's menu with the cook in the evening. She might even scold her. In reply the cook would burst into tears and start saying, 'I didn't ask for this job. I'm a simple woman and I know my place.' Krupskaya would feel ashamed and rush to console her, assuring the cook that in fact Vladimir Ilyich couldn't be more pleased with her. To make it up to her once and for all, she would even give her one of her woollen shawls.

The cook kept it all to herself for a month or so, marvelling in silence at her master's whims, but then her fear wore off, and as if guessing what was wanted of her, began spreading the story far and wide. By May, Lenin's eating habits – what he ate and how he ate – were known not only to the staff of the children's home, but to every boy and girl there. This channel proved entirely reliable. Undiscovered, it continued to function without a hitch until the last day of his life.

At that lesson Ishchenko also described how Trotsky, like some doubting Thomas, continued to lurch this way and that, never fully persuaded by Lenin's ideas. On July 11th he gave Krupskaya a letter for her husband, in which among other things, he wrote to Ilyich: 'What if the communards, having already set out, become scared and give up in the face of difficulty? Children's moods change quickly: one moment they can be ecstatic and jubilant, unable to contain their joy and tearing around like crazy, but a minute later they'll be sobbing away in the bushes somewhere. You know as well as I do that the proletarian movement has always stood on the rock of *Das Kapital*. This foundation was firmer than the arms of Atlas or the three turtles and two whales on which the Earth rested in ancient times, but as for us, what will we tell the kids from the children's home if one day they suddenly begin to doubt and lose faith that they and only they are fated to save the human race? How will we convince them not to stop, to keep going?'

According to Krupskaya, Trotsky's letter made a very powerful impression on Vladimir Ilyich. He had only just started coming round from the March stroke and any excitement was categorically forbidden, but there was a great deal of truth in Trotsky's words and he couldn't just brush them aside. Even worse was that for the first time Lenin didn't know what to reply. Not only did the terrible strain make his temperature shoot up and his pulse go berserk, but that evening he began vomiting almost nonstop.

The one memory that Krupskaya retained from that night was of Professor Kunts, the most alarmist of the Gorki doctors, putting his arm around her shoulders, taking her aside and telling her that Lenin's death throes had started. Fortunately, Krupskaya paid no attention to Kunts or any of the others;

ignoring all attempts to get rid of her, she sat down next to her husband, took his hand in hers, and as if refusing to release him from this life, held it till morning. And when at dawn she understood that the crisis had passed and he was sleeping peacefully, she burst into tears. She cried and cried and couldn't stop. He carried on sleeping while she, still gripping his hand, cried her eyes out like a little girl.

Lenin came round only towards evening. He was wide awake, but just as weak as before. He lay motionless, unable to twitch so much as a hand or a foot, but his eyes were open and there was nothing in them except sorrow and hopelessness. She had never seen him like that, had never realised he could even be like that, and unable to bear it, blurted out in her distress, 'Volodenka, perhaps I can write to Lev Davydovich myself?' Twenty years later she was still astonished by that act of boldness, and above all, that Lenin hadn't become angry, hadn't frowned, and had even managed the faintest of smiles.

Krupskaya was under no illusions: she realised that he had simply been touched by her concern, and she herself doubted that there would be any real substance to her reply. Nevertheless, three days later her letter to Trotsky was ready. In it, Kruspkaya was among other things the first to formulate the founding principles of the new Communist faith. When she read the letter out to Lenin before sending it, his response was ecstatic and he immediately insisted that she share its theses with the pupils of the children's home the very next week.

Krupskaya's speech, Ishchenko continued, went down tremendously well, as all the witnesses agreed. Unfortunately, it went no further, since nobody took it upon themselves to spread or promote her ideas. Nevertheless, the essence of her proposals has been preserved. Four of the Glukhov communards describe Nadezhda Konstantinovna's speech in their memoirs, three of them in some detail, but there are serious discrepancies between their versions, and so – Ishchenko explained to the class – I decided after some hesitation that it would be best to confine myself to the draft of the letter to Trotsky. It can still be found now among Krupskaya's diary entries for July 1923.

The letter contains four points concerning the children's march to the Holy Land. One: the communards are those same children of Bethlehem who went to the slaughter in place of Christ. Who gave up their lives with joy, concealing Christ from Herod, the criminal who had sent for the newborn King of the Jews to be killed. In saving the Son of God, they will also save the entire human race. Two: free of sin and slain through no fault of their own, they are those young bullocks without blemish or defect that are meant to be offered up in sacrifice to the Almighty. Three: the sufferings which they, pure and unstained, have undergone in their lives will give them the strength to reach Jerusalem. Four (and this is very close to what Peregudov told the Enets; there is a plump question mark before it in the draft): Christ, perhaps, should not have grown up at all. The disputes with the Pharisees, the miracles, the healings, even death on the cross and resurrection – none of this was strictly necessary: had the Son of God remained an infant, His sacrifice, like theirs, would have been more complete, and the race of Adam would already have been saved.

BE AS CHILDREN

LESSON EIGHT
Language Work

As regards the second Gorki brigade, Ishchenko continued a week later, we are better informed. But before turning to that, I want to speak about the languages Lenin worked on throughout the final year of his life. The first, syllabic language – sometimes known as Glukhovian – was, when you got down to it, also made of words, so it could hardly have satisfied him. Different approaches were called for, and Lenin sought them ceaselessly. More than once, for example, his thoughts turned to the language of gestures, of bodily movements. This in turn, made him cast his mind back to 1901 and the Ball of the Victims of the Jacobin Terror. Only the descendants of families whose members had been put to death by Robespierre were welcome at this occasion, but Lenin, an ardent admirer of the French Revolution, was brought there by a new friend of his. Also a socialist, he came from a celebrated aristocratic family, and as they were making their way to the ball, told Lenin that a whole swathe of his ancestors, ranging from old men to a seven-year-old girl, had gone to the guillotine.

The event itself was held in Saint-Denis, just outside Paris, in an ancient cemetery in the middle of the night. The flame of one hundred and fifty candles fixed to the cornice of the Montmorency family tomb bowed to all sides with the movement of the people, and the air, illuminating now the dancers, now the musicians, now a few spectators. The music was very sad, and Lenin was especially struck by the violins, which sounded like Scottish bagpipes.

The couples were dressed in the usual fashion: gentlemen

in tails and cambric shirts, ladies in long silk dresses with plunging necklines and exposed backs. They danced all over the gravestones, though really it was only the women doing the dancing. The gentlemen merely kept them from falling, and their partners, having executed a step, hung limply on their arms as if dead. The ladies' movements bore no resemblance to any dance Lenin had ever known. In the lurching light, the female figures replicated all too realistically the spasms of a human body whose head has just been chopped off by a guillotine. Vivid though these memories were, Lenin thought it all through and regretfully abandoned the idea. None of the blind would ever have understood the language of dance.

Conscious of the shortcomings of Glukhovian, he spent most of 1922 mulling a language built entirely on touch. He even experimented a little. When for example, he wanted to show Frosya his cat, that she was being good, he would stroke her along the lie of her fur and she would snuggle up to him, as if drunk, but when he was cross with her, he would stroke firmly against the fur and Frosya, acknowledging her error, would jump off his knees and make herself scarce.

Later he tried out these techniques on Krupskaya too. He would slowly pass his hand down his wife's arm, as if along the fur, and Nadya would smile, understanding as well as any animal, that he was pleased with her. Matters took a different turn, when as if reining her in, he drew his fingers sharply upwards. There were different points on the arm, from the completely soft spots inside, where it flexed, to the hard, almost stony knuckles, and one touch on your part was enough to tell your interlocutor what it was that you wanted: concessions, compromise, or on the contrary, obduracy, revolutionary severity. Soft and hard alternated on the face as well, so one could make use of the communards' unseeing eyes, deaf ears and wordless mouths. It was then, stroking Krupskaya's arm, that he realised that by drawing a line on the skin with his nail he could separate one thought from another no worse than with a pause or a paragraph break.

One night Lenin dreamed of Valya Maksakov and woke up imagining his wife – woman – as a land across which the children would walk without fear to Jerusalem, as a vast, boundless plain with hills and hollows, a land heated by inner warmth, soft and moist. For himself, he knew that he had to walk all over it, go everywhere, survey the fields and pastures, the meadows and vegetable rows. See what was what, decide what was ready to be cultivated and what should be left fallow, so that the earth could rest, replenish its moisture and bring a good harvest for years to come.

He was a prudent, shrewd peasant, not one for cutting corners. Everything had to be properly evaluated, totted and weighed up, so that there would be enough for both himself and his descendants. But he understood that he was in very poor health, that he was old and feeble, and feared that he would no longer manage to till the land himself. His time had run out.

From her hair and the lock that fell over her forehead, he was slowly making his way down. Trying not to wake her, he stepped cautiously, barely touching her skin, and he was glad that Krupskaya was breathing quietly and evenly, as she always did when asleep. But even so he soon tired, and after cupping his hand like a ladle and filling it to the brim with her cheek – from eyelids to chin – he lay down to rest and gather strength once more. Doing so, he, as once in his youth, accustomed himself to Nadya with his hand, and with the same hand he explained that now she was a wife, she was his, and Krupskaya herself realised and memorised through her sleep that she was no longer a stray picked up God knows where, but belonged somewhere, to someone, and her master could and would treat her as he saw fit. Her job was to give herself to him entirely, and believe, and pray for him, and love him. She was ready to do all of this, she had said yes to it all some thirty years earlier, and now, making herself cosy in his ladle, she repeated her yes, confirmed that nothing had changed, that they were one, and where he went she would go too.

Lying with his hand on her cheek, Lenin thought that under Communism people would live without remembering anything or anyone; instead they would see, hear, touch and sniff the world as if after a long winter. Like newborns, they would feel the world with all they had. The unimaginable happiness and exultation would never end. Refusing to grow up, they would deliver themselves from evil, and from end to end the Earth would become one big paradise teeming with little children.

Having gathered his strength, he stood up on his index and middle fingers, and slowly, totteringly walked on. This was hard both because his illness had left him so weak and because the soil swayed beneath him with each step, as if it were swamp. Soft and yielding, it sagged and sank, as if it were trying to absorb and submerge him wherever he went. Only when he walked along the collarbone or one of the ribs, as if along a ridge, did he find the going any easier. But soon the bone would vanish into the depths and once again he would have to climb his way out of this living flesh, which was literally begging him to stay and stay put. His palm, along with the other three fingers he had to carry, also felt too heavy to lift. His former self, youthful and strong, would have coped even with a load like that, but the best he could do now was drag them along until eventually, too weak to take another step, he sank onto the knuckles of his middle and ring fingers, as if to his knees. He didn't pray and didn't ask the Lord for anything, he just waited for his strength to return. A breather was certainly needed, but he noted that he'd done a better job of maintaining his dignity in the past, hadn't surrendered just because he was tired like now, hadn't prostrated himself in front of anyone – on the contrary, he would have straightened out the fingers he walked on as if they were crutches, brought in the thumb for support, and stood in place like a tripod, rocking slightly from side to side as he waited for his heart to become calmer and his breathing more even.

Krupskaya it seems, woke up when he reached her nipple. But the road to get there had taken so much out of him that he himself didn't notice. Wheezing and whistling, he still made an effort to straighten up by resting on his thumb, but he lost his balance, and toppling over, covered her breast with the same hand with which he had cupped her cheek before. It was warm and snug there; worn out by the journey, he settled down and it seems, dozed off.

Sleep refreshed him, and from the nipple he began descending towards the stomach. The slope made the going easier, and albeit slowly and with frequent pauses, Lenin kept walking. He even seems to have cheered up a little. By this point he already realised that Krupskaya could feel his fingers, that she knew where he was going. And no wonder:

she was shaking, as if with fever. Sensing that soon, very soon, she would become an instrument for the transformation of the world and feeling aroused by the very possibility, she was trembling almost continuously and couldn't hold a single thought in her mind. It occurred to her that if that was where he was going then he was probably getting better; but why 'probably', she wondered with a burst of sardonic laughter – of course he was getting better! Then her mind leapt to Armand.[36] She blamed neither Inessa nor him for anything, but she rejoiced and thanked the Lord that her husband had remembered her, his wife. And not merely remembered her – she suddenly believed that the time had come, that today the promise made to her so long ago would finally be fulfilled: that like Sarah, she would conceive.

Alas, Ishchenko concluded sadly at the end of the lesson, Krupskaya was wrong. On that occasion Lenin only got as far as her navel. The soft flesh of the stomach, her fidgetiness and restlessness, had completely exhausted him. He had no strength left and could no longer climb out of the pit into which he had fallen.

LESSON NINE
The Second Gorki Brigade

The morning before Christmas Day 1924, Lenin ordered his guards to find a nice, bushy fir tree in the forest and chop it

---

[36] French-born Bolshevik Inessa Armand, whose activity in Tsarist Russia led to her internal exile near the White Sea in 1907; she escaped and moved to Paris, where she became very close to the exiled Lenin both as revolutionary ally, and it is widely assumed, mistress.

BE AS CHILDREN

down. Both he and Krupskaya had been trying all week to get the Gorki commandant or steward to do it, but either they pretended not to understand or they feigned forgetfulness. The previous day, he had received a visit from Krestinsky and his young daughter.[37] He ordered Krestinsky to be told that he was sick and in no condition to discuss serious matters, but played with the child for a long time and with great enjoyment. As a goodbye present he gave the girl a doll he was especially fond of, together with three dresses for it, toy boots and a little hat decorated with phlox. All Christmas Eve, Ishchenko recounted, was spent arranging and decking the tree and by ten o'clock, when the children were due to arrive, almost everything was ready.

In the end, it looked like an ordinary Christmas tree with presents, the kind that in years gone by were put up in manor houses every December for the children of relatives living close by and of the servants. At eleven o'clock sharp, when the kids were dancing in the round, and for the purposes of camouflage, singing 'The Varshavianka'[38] rather than 'Glory Be to Our Saviour', while Lenin sat in his wheelchair and smiled at them, his sister Maria got up on a chair and pinned the Star of Bethlehem to the top of the tree: it would show them the path to the Holy Land. The next instant, as if on cue, everyone started clapping, kissing and wishing each other Happy Christmas. At that moment it became clear, and not

---

[37] Nikolai Krestinsky (1883-1938), a CC member who had served as People's Commissar for Finance, 1918-22.
[38] The Russian version of this Polish socialist song enjoyed mass popularity from the 1905 Revolution onwards, the word 'Warsaw' having been replaced with 'working people'.

only to Krupskaya, that Lenin was burning all his bridges, that he had made up his mind and was solemnly declaring that this was his communard brigade right here and he was ready to lead the children personally to the Holy Land.

In essence, that Christmas Eve was Lenin's true testament, and the CC members were quick to grasp its meaning. In their efforts to conceal Ilyich's final wish and muddy the waters, they would in years to come keep changing the date and claim that the tree was put up for New Year, or Old New Year, or for no obvious reason, on the eve of January 3rd, but certainly not for Christmas. And the star that would be drawn on Soviet pictures would not be the Star of Bethlehem but just the ordinary Soviet one, red and five-pointed.

But the main thing, Ishchenko said, is that the memory of the testament drawn up that Christmas Eve was nevertheless preserved, albeit with a generous sprinkling of lies, and that is why, in every kindergarten, in every school and in our own classroom, you always find the same picture hanging on the wall: a seated Lenin, surrounded by cheerful playing children, with a lush green fir tree in the background. And it doesn't matter what kind of star is on the tree, or that in Gorki Lenin sat not on an ordinary chair but a special therapeutic one, or that the hand with which he was stroking one of the young guests was not, as we see here, his right one – which he could no longer use – but his left. Such a foolish error: the artist must have been an icon-painter once and had decided that stroking with the left hand would be a sacrilege.

The Gorki fir tree, Ishchenko continued after breaktime, was at once a farewell and a blessing and an inspection of the troops before the start of the expedition. That's why all the children we see next to Lenin in the picture must be named. Those called to the tree are his apostles.

Why, by the way, have the photos from that time not survived? After all we know that Lenin, with his fear of fakery and trickery, had specifically asked Krupskaya to invite a *Pravda* photographer to Gorki, and that she had carried out his request. But according to her account, the children were so overjoyed to have Lenin with them at long last – and this time for good – that they kept tearing around the room like crazy and there was no way of getting them to sit down. But I doubt he minded too much: Krupskaya recalled in her memoirs that when the doctors decided that Lenin was too tired and were about to send the children home, he demanded brusquely that they be left to enjoy themselves.

Here then are the people around Lenin in the picture (from left to right): 1. V.D. Ulyanov (nephew); 2. O.D. Ulyanova (niece); 3. G.Y. Lozgachev-Yelizarov (adopted son of A.I. Ulyanova-Yelizarova); 4. A.V. Yustus (son of a Hungarian revolutionary, taken in by the Ulyanov family after his father's death); 5. N.A. Preobrazhenskaya (daughter of A.A. Preobrazhensky, manager of the state farm in Gorky); 6. Vera (identity unknown); 7. N.I. Khabarov (son of I.N. Khabarov, head of maintenance at Gorki); 8. G.A. Leitman-Volostnova (daughter of A.M. Leitman, an employee at the sanatorium, and E.B. Attal, a laundress at Gorki); 9. S.V. Letalin (son of the stoker at Gorki); 10-12. A.S. Gorsky, N.N. Skokin, A.F. Kalganov – children of inhabitants of Gorki village.

There's something else that must be mentioned. That night Lenin made each child a personal gift of a picture book – a keepsake for their travels.

Lenin had barely woken up the next morning when he received more glad tidings from Dzerzhinsky. It turned out that their fir tree had not been the first. Three years earlier just such a tree – with a Christmas star pointing the way to Jerusalem – had been put up in an assembly hall by the children of the Shatsky commune near Nizhny Novgorod.[39] Forsaking the flesh for the spirit, and not breathing a word to anyone, they went a whole day without bread in the midst of the terrible famine of '21, then bought the star at the market with the two rolls they had saved.

After Christmas and until the very day of his death, Lenin (according to the testimony of his sister Maria) was in an almost permanent state of unusual excitement. Especially in the mornings, when he tended to feel stronger. Sitting himself up in bed, he would start gesticulating and fidgeting. I think, Ishchenko said, that he was under the impression that their brigade would set forth any moment, and he wanted to hurry somebody up, or else they were already on the move and he wanted to fix something. But by evening Lenin's strength would desert him, and as Krupskaya writes in her memoirs, often it would all end in an epileptic fit. She adds that his excitement would not pass even if he had a raging headache.

He was unable to spend even a minute lying peacefully in his bed, however much they tried to talk him out of it; he would always be shouting something or waving his hands. He would only calm down if Krupskaya dragged him over to his

---

[39] The ambitious educational initiatives of Stanislav Shatsky (1878-1934), which drew on the ideas of Tolstoy and had much in common with the progressivism of John Dewey, included a large network of schools and reading rooms known as The First Experimental Station (1919-32).

wheelchair with the help of an attendant and started pushing him as quickly as she could around the room. He probably thought that the march had begun and that he was at least one step, one turn of the wheel, closer to Jerusalem. But just before his death, Krupskaya noted his facial expression changed: he looked at people without recognising them, as if he were blind. He seemed to foresee a different, better world, and the world Lenin was preparing to leave no longer interested him.

At his funeral, added Ishchenko, drawing the lesson to a close, a great deal was said by a great many people. But I would single out the words of L.B. Kamenev, whom Ilyich had lost touch with long ago, just as he had with the other CC members. 'Lenin,' said Kamenev, standing over the coffin, 'never spared himself, scattering his brain and his blood with unheard-of generosity, giving even the poorest of the poor their fair share. We can be sure that soon these drops will sprout like seeds in the souls of the proletariat, and numberless regiments will grow from them all over the world.'

LESSON TEN
The March of the Enets

During his lesson on November 9th, Ishchenko began speaking, to my complete surprise, about Peregudov and the Enets, the same people I had been researching for almost thirty years. He gave a coherent account of whatever in their history was remotely related to Lenin and Trotsky, but seemed to know little about the rest of it. In class at any rate, he merely said that in the 1860s the Enets, roaming with their reindeer around the mouth of the Lena, were baptised into the Orthodox faith by a certain Yevlampy Peregudov, whom they had since revered virtually on a par with Christ. And that later this same Peregudov took in almost forty revolutionaries fleeing Siberian prisons and hard labour.

The Lena delta though, is a kind of trap: it's not so hard to end up there, but few, even now, manage to get out. Those whom Peregudov had made welcome and looked after understood this quite quickly and within three or four months they were only too happy to take Enets women from him as their wives. These brides by the way, were in most cases shapely, good-looking women. In fact, the Enets were famous for their women among the neighbouring tribes. By 1917 the number of descendants from mixed marriages – the children and grandchildren of Narodniks (Land and Freedom, Black Partition, Socialist Revolutionary), socialists (Menshevik, Bolshevik, Social-Democrat) and assorted anarchists – exceeded three hundred souls.

Under Peregudov's leadership the tribe lived and multiplied in peace, tranquillity and plenty for more than half a century, but by 1917 as in the rest of Russia, their bliss came to an end. It was destroyed by the Enets prophet himself who, as if weary of calm, suddenly announced to the tribe that he was a great sinner, almost the Devil incarnate. From this point on the history of the Enets was no longer that of a united people. In 1920, despite their late teacher's categorical prohibition, some hundred Enets set out across Russia for the Holy Land, where their new faith was born, to pray to the Almighty and win forgiveness for their teacher.

Not long before the March stroke, Lenin's personal

security staff was doubled. The Cheka had learned through its informers that the Whites – no one could say how, who, where or when – were preparing an attempt on Ilyich's life. Lenin was guarded almost entirely by Latvians and he was perfectly satisfied with them, but Dzerzhinsky had learned that they were talking more and more often among themselves about taking some leave. About how nice it would be to spend a week or two back home in Latgale. There was nothing bad about these conversations but Dzerzhinsky decided, simply as a precaution, to water the Latvians down a bit – especially because he now knew whom he could use. And that's where Peregudov comes into the picture.

It so happened that five months earlier a dozen children and grandchildren of political prisoners (mainly from the earliest populist group, Land and Freedom) had reached Moscow from the mouth of the Lena. The Enets received a warm welcome: they were provided with clothes, food and medical treatment, and thought was given about what to do with them. The last remnants of the old revolutionary brotherhood were long gone, yet people were queuing up to take care of them. Even the fact that the parents of three of the Enets were still alive and on the other side of the barricades didn't bother anyone.

At first, Dzerzhinsky was planning to bring the Enets into his own organisation, the Cheka, but he soon realised there was no point – it would take too long for them to find their bearings in Russian life. For now, if they saw an automobile in the street they would just stop and stare. The car would be long gone, but they'd still be standing there gaping. Then it was suggested to him that the Enets would make a splendid folk ensemble, after all they had already put their throat-singing and shamanic dances to excellent use in the Kremlin, with three performances over the past month, all met with rapturous applause. So why not let them sing and dance until autumn, after which they could be assigned to the Communist University of the Peoples of the North? The decision to open this university had been taken after Lenin's announcement at a CC session that the world revolution was not just about Europe and Asia and that commissars would also be sorely needed in, for example, the Arctic. But where were people who really knew the North inside out to be found, who were at home in its mire and murk?

While Dzerzhinsky pondered what to do with the Enets, they began to work a few things out for themselves and decided that if they succeeded in returning Russia, this country that had strayed from the true faith, to the Lord, Peregudov would be well pleased with them. Above all, when the hour came to decide his fate, Christ would remember their service and lighten their teacher's lot. This time too they split up into groups of five, and wherever they found themselves – in the Kremlin, in factory clubs, in cinemas – they set about fearlessly bearing witness to the Saviour.

Denunciations came pouring in. Though the Chekists were inclined to view the whole thing as a mere curiosity, they still took the Enets down to the Lubyanka[40] and set about explaining to them, as if they were little children, that their missionary work was nonsense from start to finish and they couldn't have chosen a worse time or cause for their propaganda. But when the Narodniks' offspring refused to give in, Dzerzhinsky tried

---

[40] A building in central Moscow, headquarters of the Soviet secret police in its various incarnations.

to knock some sense into these idiotic Samoyeds by locking them up for a couple of days. But the slammer didn't help either; on the contrary the Enets decided that this was the beginning of their path to martyrdom and that by suffering for Christ they could be even surer of winning forgiveness for their teacher.

Fresh martyrs though, were not in demand. Dzerzhinsky briefed Lenin, and the latter agreed that these five strange preachers would be of little use to the Communist University. A week later the Enets were put on a steamer bound for Perm, whence they were to be transported across Siberia back to the Lena. The group of five left, but the other seven liked what was happening in Russia and stayed, and Dzerzhinsky liked them just as much as before: no ties to the counter-revolution and to foreign spies, not a single relative who might set them on the path of betrayal – such advantages were not to be sneezed at. No wonder that when the Cheka decided to reinforce Lenin's security detail, they settled on the Enets.

Lenin was a keen hunter, and the Samoyeds were initially employed as his huntsmen. The Enets were superb shots: when hunting squirrel, they hit the animals flush in the eye to save the pelts. Lenin became fond of them for their excellent knowledge of the forest and their reticence. They didn't fuss and they gave him space to think. Later the Enets started performing other duties too: like all his guards they stood sentry and kept him safe during his strolls.

When Lenin wasn't feeling well enough to work, he would enter into long conversations with them. Asked them all sorts of questions: what their life had been like, who Peregudov was, how he'd ended up in their neck of the woods, how a *chum* was arranged, how many reindeer a family needed to get by. In turn they told him how many animals they would kill and what kind, how much fish they would bring in during a single season. Told him about their old faith and how they managed to get on with their wives when the parents were always around, there were children everywhere and they had no space of their own. He found this topic neither awkward nor taboo, and the Enets didn't see anything wrong with it either – they replied willingly and in detail.

Lenin took a serious and sympathetic interest in relations between Samoyeds and Russians. Was it worth trading with the Russians, were there squabbles, and how did they usually end? Knowing that the Enets generally bartered furs for vodka, he asked whether they drank too much and whether anything could be done to help them. He understood even better than the Enets themselves, that alcohol was their curse and explained to them in the simplest possible language that it was because of all their drinking that two thirds of the children born in the encampments died as children.

In the autumn of '21 they spent an entire week telling him their myths and legends and singing songs about the great shamans. Sadly though, that was the most he could get out of them. Lenin was very disappointed and kept asking whether the oldies at least, remembered bygone days. But the Enets didn't come up short very often. He was thrilled for example, to learn that they could all count back a dozen generations. The names and family legends instantly stuck in his memory, and whenever a Russian revolutionary appeared in the family tree he was so happy he couldn't help roaring with laughter. After all, he'd known many of them back in the St Petersburg underground.

BE AS CHILDREN

Lenin kept returning to the five Enets Dzerzhinsky had recently sent back to the Lena. He was clearly baffled by their preaching of Jesus Christ and to get to the bottom of it all he asked one question after another: who was whose son or grandson, was the family well-off, and so on. The Enets had known each other since the day they were born, and weren't given to secrecy, so once again Lenin was pleased with them. Some of the stories he heard from them he would later repeat in cigarette breaks between Politbureau sessions and each time he would marvel at the fact that entire peoples existed to whom there was no need to say, 'Be as children'.

Six months were enough for Lenin to become so friendly with the Enets that his old Latvian guards became jealous. Gossip began to spread quickly and Dzerzhinsky was even forced to admonish him. After all it's unseemly to offend people who are ready to give up their life for you at the drop of a hat. Lenin admitted he'd been foolish and promised to make amends. And in fact the grumbling soon petered out.

Lenin's offer to share the leadership of the All-Russian Children's March to the Holy Land was accepted by Trotsky without a second thought. A week later Trotsky suggested adding a few dozen child-nations, and specifically the Enets whom Lenin now knew so well. He particularly stressed their skill at shooting and tracking down animals. Initially Lenin was sceptical. He asked whether they really were entirely without sin: after all that would be far more crucial to the success of the Jerusalem expedition than any hunting prowess. He was very worried that they would stick out from the rest. But Trotsky, through Getye, insisted with his customary enthusiasm that their participation was both right and necessary. He explained to Ilyich that the Samoyeds were without a doubt, children, the most genuine children imaginable.

To resolve the issue once and for all, Trotsky, in the space of a mere six months, compiled and published an entire *History of the Enets*, which made it clear that for centuries they, like other nomadic tribes, had lived a normal adult existence, only for fate to make an abrupt about-turn and push them back into childhood. The book told of the battles and heroic deeds of the Samoyeds and of the gradual realisation that all their brilliant victories were no more than fun and games. Yes, they too spilled a little blood, real blood, but you can gash your finger just by messing about with a penknife.

There was a bit about how and when the Enets began to understand that they could have been ground to dust a long time ago, but had been allowed to survive as a natural cabinet of curiosities. Ever since then they had been treated like children, both in the way they were punished and in the way they were protected and pitied. Nor did Trotsky forget about the ethnographers who had fallen in love with the small peoples of the North and whom the latter had helped to record their own legends until one day it suddenly became clear that even this task of preservation no longer required the Samoyeds themselves.

Lenin however pressed on with his interrogation: how could Trotsky be so sure that the Enets would not change once they left the tundra behind them? Rather than answer this question directly, Trotsky merely arranged for Lenin to be informed that according to top-secret intelligence, the Enets were even prepared to march on Jerusalem on their own and that their aim was to exonerate their teacher, a certain

BE AS CHILDREN

Peregudov, before God. The Revolutionary War Council, he told Lenin, had decided to help them, and in return the tribe would help the Bolsheviks rout the chief enemies of Soviet power – the Polacks. The Samoyeds were headed that way anyway, and the Poles wouldn't detain them for long. Overall he concluded the participation of the Enets in the march on Jerusalem would be beneficial in every conceivable way.

Still there are different accounts as to when and why Trotsky took an interest in the Samoyeds. According to one version he was unable to forget that Lenin had once called children 'anarchist scum' and wanted to begin with the more organised northern 'child-nations'; according to another he simply wanted to take advantage of Lenin's expedition to the Holy Land – he'd decided what to do with the Enets himself a long time before. Back in 1919 he'd been very impressed by the success of Makhno's horse-drawn machine guns, the *tachankas*, and when Soviet Russia was routed by Piłsudski, he immediately remembered Makhno's lightning-quick attacks and equally rapid retreats.[41]

While wondering where to strike against the Polacks, Trotsky realised that there could be no better place than the Pripet Marshes in Polesia and decided there and then that the tiny peoples of the North, with their deer and sledges, would be a hundred times more useful in the impassable mire along the banks of the Pripet than any cavalry. It was a small step from there to the Enets. The plan that Trotsky had prepared

---

[41] Nestor Makhno (1889-1935), an anarchist leader whose guerrilla army had wide support among peasants in south-eastern Ukraine during the Civil War. Marshal Piłsudski (1867-1935) was Polish Chief of State, 1918-22, and commander of the Polish forces during the Polish-Soviet War of 1919-20.

by the start of 1921 and which he brought before the Revolutionary War Council on January 17th was notable for its rare simplicity. But Trotsky was in no doubt that it was this same quality that would lure the Poles.

Essentially, the plan was as follows: on the Don, in the Kuban and in Stavropol, the Cossacks become extremely restless. Comrade Budyonny is in charge. The main military force is his First Cavalry Army. Two demands: 'Freedom for the Cossack Republic!' and 'Away With The Communists!' Under pressure from the rebels, the regular units of the Red Army abandon their positions and the fortified areas in the North Caucasus and fall back to the Voronezh-Simbirsk line. The Cossacks lack the resources to advance any further, but the Red Army is not yet ready to launch a counterattack.

A truce is agreed. At a general meeting of the Cossack Circle, Budyonny is announced Hetman of all the troops. His popularity knows no bounds. Every second Cossack wears a Budyonny moustache. For the first time since 1917, the Cossack lands are united, independent from Moscow and free of Communists.

Budyonny proclaims the Cossack Republic and earns international recognition almost instantly. But the situation is unstable: the Red Army has an overwhelming superiority in artillery. Realising this, Buydonny dispatches couriers to Marshal Piłsudski to propose a two-pronged attack on the Reds – the Cossacks along the line Voronezh-Tula, the Poles along the line Kharkov-Kursk-Oryol-Tula – before advancing on Moscow together, to destroy the Bolshevik vermin once and for all. In the event of success (a foregone conclusion) peace eternal will ensue between Moscow and Warsaw, along with equality of the two Slavic peoples, while Poland, by way of a bonus, will receive all the lands on the right bank of the Dnieper including Kiev.

The Poles trust neither Budyonny nor the Cossacks, but the temptation is too great. They hesitate, but by spring, Trotsky explains, as if peeking into the Book of Fate, they make up their minds. Preparations for a joint expedition begin, and thanks to the general chaos, drag on for almost eighteen months. While this is happening the Polish General Staff discusses the routes by which to move its army to Ukraine and sketches detailed maps of the campaign.

Opinions will differ, Trotsky told the Revolutionary War Council, but the Pripet Marshes option will win out due to one clear advantage – it's the safest. Of course it's not easy to move a 300,000 strong army along two roads, but at least no one will be able to attack you. Being more scared of your ally than your enemy is already something. Besides, the Poles see no reason to hurry: the Red Army is stuck near Voronezh with no back-up.

In January '23 the Polish Army finally sets out. It traverses Polesia in two months, and after crossing the Desna, takes Chernigov without a fight. Soviet Russia protests, but the memoranda sent by its diplomats are roundly ignored. It's obvious to all that for as long as the Cossacks are camped outside Voronezh there's nothing much it can do. Meanwhile the Poles begin their advance on Kharkov in the most relaxed of moods. The generals exchange Muscovite and provincial newspapers carrying reports of savage Cossack attacks at Borisoglebsk and Stary Oskol.

The papers will continue to cover the battles on the

Middle Don for another month, but the masquerade is well and truly over. By this point the turncoat Semyon Budyonny is no longer walking the Earth, nor are his Cossacks, those traitors to the ideals of the Revolution, and the Free Cossack Republic has also vanished like a mirage. In their place – Trotsky continues in triumph – are the legendary commander and Civil War hero Semyon Budyonny and his invincible First Cavalry Army, which our railway forces are covertly transferring to the city of Priluki at full speed. From there, without even entering the city, they attack the rear of the Polack forces. On its own, needless to say, the First Cavalry Army lacks the resources to rout 300,000 Poles. But that's not the aim. All that's needed is for the Poles to lose the maximum amount of men and equipment, panic, fall into disarray and begin their retreat.

Meanwhile, spring will have arrived, the snow will be melting, the Pripet will have burst its banks, and unless you count those same two roads, you won't get through Polesia either on foot or by horse. Nobody will get through, Trotsky repeats emphatically, aside from the Enets many of us remember so well. For the Enets and their reindeer, the Belarusian marshes are like the cobblestones of Red Square for a Red Army soldier.

But for now the Cossacks, having completed their task, stop at the edge of the bogs. Emerging from battle, the surviving Poles also become a little calmer, which of course plays right into our hands. The soldiers lick their wounds as they march, all is quiet, and soon they are already halfway to Lublin. It's at this point that the Samoyeds burst onto the scene. Now it's their turn to crush Piłsudski as Makhno once crushed Denikin. So, Trotsky summed up, if the plan is properly executed, only shreds will remain of the 300,000 strong Polack army. For Soviet Russia, the threat from the West will have been removed for a long time to come.

After a break the details of Trotsky's speech were discussed and Frunze asked him:[42] 'Lev Davydovich, how many Enets will there be and why are you certain that they will agree to go? It's obvious why the Poles will swallow the bait but what do the poor Samoyeds have to gain from the swamps of Polesia?' 'As to the size of the Enets expeditionary force, I anticipate approximately three or four hundred fighters,' Trotsky replied, 'and in view of the circumstances I consider that ample. As to the question of what they will be fighting for, Comrade Dzerzhinsky is best placed to answer. He brought seven northerners into Lenin's security staff two years ago and knows all the ins and outs.'

'Perhaps you didn't hear the kind of things the Enets were preaching in the winter of 1920, when they had only just arrived in Moscow,' said Dzerzhinsky turning to Frunze. 'Well, they have two aims in mind. The more distant one is to convert the entire world to the true faith – but we won't concern ourselves here with that; the other most pressing aim is to save their teacher, a certain Peregudov, who died in sin. To make their way to the Holy Land, and there in the place of Christ's birth, win his forgiveness through prayer. Polesia, as it happens, is on the way to Palestine, and the Sovnarkom has already reached an agreement with the Samoyeds: they'll help us with the Polacks, and we'll return the favour by helping

---

[42] Mikhail Frunze (1885-1925), a leading Bolshevik and Central Committee member who, during the Civil War, distinguished himself as commander of the eastern and then southern fronts.

them with Jerusalem,' Dzerzhinsky concluded.

On Monday, January 24th, just a week after the meeting of the Revolutionary War Council, Dzerzhinsky sent three of the Enets on Lenin's personal security staff back to the Lena with the task of agitating among their fellow tribesmen and persuading them to help Russia stand firm against the global counter-revolution. Aside from Trotsky's written promise that they would receive a free corridor directly to the Holy Land and Jerusalem just as soon as they defeated the Poles, they were also told that in the upper reaches of the River Jordan, on the boundless swamps overgrown with reindeer moss around Lake Hula, Abraham's direct descendants – the Jewish settlers – had long been waiting to welcome them as brothers. There are no mosquitoes in Palestine, no midges, no cold, snow or wolves; like the flocks once tended by the Jews in the land of Goshen in Egypt, the reindeer would be left in peace to graze on those swamps all year round, to love their female mates and bring up their calves. And in the Holy Land, when the time came, they would see, on the right hand of God the Father, from the direction of Jerusalem, their teacher Peregudov, forgiven and exonerated through their prayers.

Dzerzhinsky's envoys did not reach the Lena until the end of May, and by their own admission achieved little over the three summer months. But by September their propaganda was already bearing fruit, and despite the late Peregudov's categorical prohibition, almost a third of the tribe had volunteered to march on Jerusalem and to help the Bolsheviks settle their scores with the Poles along the way. From the very beginning, it seems neither Trotsky nor Frunze had any doubts that the recruitment campaign would succeed; by September at any rate, preparations for the operation were already in full swing.

Things started moving even faster in February, when the Enets and their reindeer were transferred closer to the centre of the country, to the lichen pastures in the mouth of the Pechora. They were to advance to their starting position in the swamps of Polesia only in February or March of the following year. There, on the left and right banks of the Pripet, to ensure that the reindeer would maintain their usual diet and manage to withstand six to eight weeks of intense conflict without their spirits flagging, the Institute of Experimental Plant Breeding (IEPB) in Petrograd had been planting reindeer moss at record speed since the previous summer. To everybody's delight, the lichen took very well to its new surroundings.

March was the most favourable month, whichever way you looked at it. The Poles and their horses would be good for nothing, while the male reindeer – the bulls – would be lean and strong. True, the duels of the mating season would be over, but they would still be in fighting form. Jumping ahead though, Ishchenko continued, I'll add that in the year leading up to the Polish campaign the decision was taken to graze the reindeer separately: the bulls were to be kept apart from the females to preserve their strength. And the bulls, to give them their due, accepted and understood this. I expect they even guessed that they were probably going to die, but they still agreed unhesitatingly to lay down their lives for Peregudov. And so as in the days of Adam, man and beast spoke the same language once more, served the Lord and understood each other without words.

Over the course of the winter of 1921-22 however, military

exercises revealed serious flaws in planning. The consequence, to Trotsky's annoyance, was that the entire Budyonny-Piłsudski operation – in the files it goes under the label 'Slav Brothers' – had to be postponed for another year, to the spring of '23. The General Staff had failed to take into account that although reindeer antlers remain strong until mid-April, their velvet becomes thin and delicate, and the machine guns that were fastened to them tore it in a matter of hours. Unable to bear the pain the reindeer tried to free themselves from the weapons. Ignoring the herders' yells, they tossed their heads like madmen and rubbed their antlers against roots and trees, and that was that as far as accuracy of fire was concerned. Moreover, Frunze reported back to Moscow, if the cartridges in the belts had not been empty during the exercises, the teams of reindeer would have annihilated one another instead of the enemy. It was another year before these failings were eliminated. Engineers at the Votkinsk Machine-Building Plant began producing machine guns that were only half as heavy as ordinary ones; in addition, the Enets themselves made strong sheaths for the antlers out of birch bark – they looked a bit like corsets – and soft fasteners specially made of leather. All this taken together helped solve the problem.

Aside from the blunder with the machine guns, the operation was going to plan. A year before the start of the campaign, the Enets migrated east from the Pechora to the swamps of the Valdai Hills, from where they began trickling into Polesia, having arranged themselves into small groups so as not to alarm anyone. There, keeping well away from the main thoroughfares, they quietly tended their reindeer and waited to be called.

Be as Children

Everything we know about the battles themselves comes from the reports of the Polish generals. Their army was destroyed, in their own words, by terrifying horned monsters with furry snouts. These fire-spewing beasts – there were rarely more than seven or eight of them at a time – would emerge completely unexpectedly from the predawn mist hovering over the road, then a few minutes later, leaving a mountain of corpses behind them, disappear back into the mist and the impassable mire.

The Enets did indeed fight in small, well-trained units, usually of no more than five sledges. They would intercept the enemy from both sides of the road and right down the middle, and unleashing round after round of machine-gun fire on the exhausted, barely advancing Poles, mow down entire squadrons without even stopping, then retreat to the swamps. Each unit carried out up to a dozen such raids a day. The losses suffered by the Enets themselves were few, and as a rule, random. All the same, by the end of the campaign barely a third of the expeditionary force remained; the rest had met their deaths in the swamps together with the Poles.

The surviving Enets waited another fortnight for the reindeer to shed their horns along with the machine guns, so that they could walk to the Holy Land in peace, and then, still unsure whether there were any swamps on the way to Palestine – some locals said there were, others claimed there weren't – they finally started out. Beyond Chernigov however, they didn't find a single swamp, nothing but arable land and dry feather-grass steppe. The reindeer died within three days, near Vinnitsa, which was also where the Enets ended up in a typhus barrack. No one knows whether any of them got out alive. True, I have had occasion to read that two Samoyeds were brought back to Moscow in Trotsky's personal armoured train. They returned to Gorki and resumed their service on Lenin's personal security staff. Later they both walked off to Latgale with the Latvians. This last claim however, strikes me as highly dubious.

LESSON ELEVEN
Testament, Death and Funeral in Moscow

A separate topic, Ishchenko continued in the next lesson, is Ilyich's testament and death. This is where we should seek Lenin's farewell to his entire life as it drew to its close, and his turn towards new life. The debate about the testament continues to this day, and let's not pretend it will be cleared up any time soon. The most likely candidate in my view, is the short letter which Krupskaya gave to Trotsky for safekeeping in '24. The letter is unaddressed, but there's a date – 1st December 1922 – so it must have been written a few days after the speech I mentioned earlier, which Lenin gave at the Congress of the Comintern. The letter was intended for all and sundry, but there are hints in Krupskaya's diary that its formal recipient was meant to have been Trotsky himself.

In that letter, after cursory analysis of the state of affairs in Russia, Lenin wrote the following: '1917, however painful this is to admit, was not a revolution: it merely marked a turning point. The proletariat and the Party proved capable of taking only the first step, although that was already a lot. Revolution,' he went on, 'occurs when society can no longer bear the complexity of its own life, whose senselessness and uselessness it suddenly grasps. After years of fumbling their way down paths and passages leading nowhere, of ending up time and again in traps and dead ends, people become utterly exhausted and no longer believe that they will find the road to Salvation on their own. They fall to their knees in despair and turn to God. They beg God to enlighten them, and the Lord, seeing their suffering, their sincerity and remorse, grants them their wish. He says that the world they have built, a world where, as the philosophers acknowledge, good must give birth sooner or later to evil, and evil to good, is merely a refuge for sin and must be razed to the ground. Committed to the flames like Sodom and abandoned without a backward glance.

'Revolution,' Lenin continued, 'is a decisive renunciation of the entire path that man has walked, the path from birth to unavoidable old age and death. We must freely and sincerely reject the temptation of independent adult existence and repent; we must admit that we are prodigal sons. Each of us is a small child who has lost its way, and the Lord, the true Father and Saviour, is waiting to press us to His chest. However far we may have strayed, we are obliged to return to childhood, because the life of an infant is simple and straight, and there is nowhere for sin to hide. Only like so, by becoming children once more – this time for good – may we be saved.'

Lenin was just as clear-sighted about what was waiting for him after his death. He told Krupskaya more than once for example, that a Judas kiss was inevitable, if not during his life, then straight after his death. He also said that though the Lord had once told man, 'For dust thou art, and unto dust shalt thou return,' this same 'Judas' would prevent him, Lenin, from doing precisely that. Krupskaya, who disliked such conversations, always tried to cut them short and it was only at her husband's funeral that she understood what he had been trying to tell her.

Lenin, Ishchenko went on after the break, lay in state in the Column Hall of the House of the Unions. The members of the Central Committee formed a closely packed ring around him, even several rings, lightly bumping hips to get that little bit closer. It was then that Stalin appeared, as if from nowhere. Short, quick, nimble, he broke through the living cordon without even stopping and threw himself at the head of the coffin. 'Goodbye! Goodbye, Vladimir Ilyich! Goodbye!' Pale-faced, he seized Lenin's head in his hands with an impulsive, passionate movement, raised it and pressed it to his chest, to his very heart, then let it fall back a little and kissed Lenin very hard on both cheeks and on his forehead. He ran his eyes over everyone in the room, and just as abruptly, as if chopping off the past from the present, walked away.

When Krupskaya informed the Orgbureau the next morning that Lenin had asked for his body to be cremated, this same Stalin replied firmly that cremation was not in keeping with the Russian understanding of love and reverence for the deceased. It would be an insult to his memory. The Russian mind had always viewed burning and the scattering of ashes as a kind of final, supreme judgment over those who had been subject to execution.

But never mind Stalin, continued Ishchenko, and let's get back to Lenin. Krupskaya wrote in her diary that throughout his last year, whenever she took him out in his wheelchair beyond the confines of the garden, Ilyich would go out of his way to bow to every peasant and worker they met, and even to some painters up on the roof of the Gorki manor house. The moment he caught sight of someone walking towards them, he would hurriedly remove his cap with his good arm and bare his head. In her diary Krupskaya reported somebody's opinion that these ruses of his – the constant baring and bowing of his head before representatives of the most impoverished peasantry and proletariat – were a form of unconscious repentance, but she was right I think, not to agree with this interpretation.

LESSON TWELVE
The Latgalian Brigade (*Lenin's Funeral in Latvia*)

Reliable information about the third brigade organised personally by Lenin himself – it's usually called the Latgalian Brigade – is scant. Hence, Ishchenko said, all the rumours and speculations. In the parts of this lesson in which we are trying to stick to the facts, in so far as we can, I will permit myself a series of conjectures only when those facts dry up completely. The date of the foundation of the Gorki commune – the direct precursor of the Latgalian Brigade – is generally held to be 3rd February 1923, and the first thing that must be said about it is that nobody would ever have allowed it to be organised and to come into existence, were it not for Lenin's conspiratorial talents. Everything was arranged in such a way that, formally speaking, he had no connection at all to its creation. His cover in this instance was Krupskaya, who excelled in her role as naïve, idealistic enthusiast utterly drained by her husband's illness. A person, in other words, from whom little was to be expected. What was more, to keep suspicions at bay, Lenin himself would continue to spread rumours about the commune, each more absurd than the last.

Over lunch one day towards the end of January '23, Krupskaya suggested that they see for themselves what living in a commune was actually like. The doctors had already been informed that she was simply trying to distract her husband and that she was counting on their support. Lenin was in a bad way. His last stroke had taken a particularly heavy toll on him and even eating, never mind speaking, had become difficult. Appearing not to notice his exhaustion, Krupskaya pestered him for a whole hour to tell her what he thought of the suggestion, until Lenin waved her away like a fly. Around the table though, there was unanimity: Lenin had clearly intimated that he was not against the idea.

That was a Saturday, and the next Friday, also at lunchtime, Krupskaya triumphantly announced the names of those who had firmly agreed to join the commune. I will list them wholesale, as it were, rather than one by one. So: the Gorki communards included, on the one hand, peasants from the nearest village, also called Gorki (forty souls altogether), and on the other, all the residents of Reinbot's[43] estate (the Ulyanovs, including Lenin and his young nephew Yelizarov – nine in all), the domestic staff from commandant to cleaners (twenty-three people), and the guards, who as I've said, were mainly Latvians (in total, thirty soldiers from a special secret-police unit, under the command of Pakalne). Incidentally, a

---

[43] Before being nationalised by the Bolshevik government, Gorki was owned by the wealthy aristocrat Zinaida Morozova. Her third marriage was to General Reinbot, whose corrupt practices saw him deprived him of his post as Moscow governor in 1907.

third of the villagers were also refugees from Latvia, and these Livonian communards often acted in unison.

The next day saw the first meeting of the communards, at which Krupskaya, after congratulating everyone on the start of their new life, proposed that the commune adopt the scientific organisation of labour, which would include, among other things, a mandatory day of rest. She subsequently complained to Lenin that she had never expected this harmless suggestion to lead to such heated arguments, nor, more importantly, that after all the cursing and making up, the participants would settle on such a peculiar compromise. The peasants had started it all by debating at such length whether or not the livestock should also get a day off. They eventually decreed that they shouldn't since they were not members of the commune and could not yet be admitted on account of their insufficient political awareness.

They had only just dealt with the livestock when a young peasant stood up and declared that they, the village folk, were annoyed that their church in Gorki had been destroyed two years earlier. There was nowhere for them to pray and as a result the rain never fell at the right time. The crops would be either too wet or too dry, and even after mowing there was no way of drying out the hay. But Krupskaya refused outright to pay for the church from communal funds and the peasant dropped his suggestion, though in exchange he demanded that one additional member be elected to the commune, namely God the Father. He began explaining that the Lord was a working element if ever there was: He made the sun, the Earth, Man himself – you couldn't just ignore Him. Krupskaya was about to object, but the peasant cut her short by adding tartly,

'You know, it weren't you Bolsheviks what started it all. He was the first to work for six days, before resting from His labours, scientifically-like, on the seventh.'

When the matter was put to the vote, the guards sided almost unanimously with the villagers, and the Lord got in easily. As Krupskaya later told Lenin, the reason for this alliance soon became clear. At the same session, Palkane's men tried to build on the villagers' success by demanding almost categorically, that in addition to the Lord, the Mother of God should also be included among the communards. On what grounds, asked Krupskaya with a sinking heart. They dithered a little before explaining that the Virgin Mary was terribly merciful; in fact, in Latvia and Russia many people believed that between Easter and Pentecost she relieved all sinners in Hell of their torments. Having a person like that in the commune would be very useful. The guards' proposal also sailed through.

Communal life continued as unpromisingly as it had begun. On February 11th, for example, Krupskaya wrote in her diary that earlier that night, when it was time to go to sleep, it became clear that there was no bedding in the house. She was about to blame the laundrywomen, only to be told that at the meeting the previous day the sheets, pillowcases and duvet covers had been divided equally among all the communards. Then a week later the lounge and some other rooms suddenly became larger and brighter overnight, which Lenin, by the way, was very pleased about. On this occasion the Gorki authorities, led by the commandant, had decided to do up their homes and had confiscated half of Reinbot's furniture. What shocked Krupskaya most was that even though she was still deputy chair of the commune, nobody had even thought of keeping her informed.

The most unpleasant episode however, occurred in March, in the fifth week of Lent. Having just got out of bed, Krupskaya discovered that the house had been emptied of all its crockery, nickel silver, ordinary silver and rugs. She summoned the commandant right away and was told that it had all been carried off at dawn by ten riflemen from the guards. They had piled the stuff onto five sledges, said it was an order and left. The commandant hadn't dared wake her – he'd assumed this was supposed to be happening.

Krupskaya immediately telephoned Dzerzhinsky, who rushed over to Gorki in a car. He arrived three hours later, spitting with rage. The loss of property bothered him much less than the ten deserters who had abandoned their posts without permission. In Krupskaya's presence he told Palkane, who was standing at attention, that the ten Latvian Riflemen under his command would be shot in accordance with the laws of the revolutionary period.[44] Having given instructions by telephone to intercept the string of sledges outside New Jerusalem,[45] return the goods to Gorki that afternoon and arrest the runaways along with the peasants who'd gone with them, he was just about to head back to Moscow when Lenin, who had been woken up by all the shouting, conducted himself in an unexpectedly gentle way. He wanted to know all the details,

---

[44] Regiments of highly skilled Latvian riflemen played an important part in containing German advances on the Northern Front in the First World War; after the war many were incorporated into the Red Army and fought in the Civil War.

[45] Site of an important seventeenth-century monastery outside Moscow (and one of the settings in Sharov's *The Rehearsals*).

chuckled, then said that none of them should be touched. 'If they want to leave, let them.' As for the silver: 'If they've taken it, they must need it more than we do. Let's call it their share.'

Such odd behaviour on the part of the leader gave rise to a wave of gossip in Moscow. Arguments raged between those who thought that the children's march had nothing to do with it – were it not for their resentment of the Enets, the Latvians would never have quit such lucrative jobs – and those who claimed that Lenin had simply taken advantage of the conflict to brilliant effect. It was he who had insulted the Latvians, having foreseen and calculated everything in advance. Some thought that the base in Latgalia had been a decoy from the very start, with the sole purpose of distracting the enemy. Others countered that the Latvians, on leaving the commune, had taken their share – the Gorki gold and silver – with Lenin's tacit consent, so as to organise an expedition of their own to the Holy Land.

The majority though, was convinced that there had never been any talk of creating a headquarters and leadership for the expedition. They frequently cited Trotsky, who in his speech in the Polytechnical Museum, had apparently said that yes of course it would be no bad thing if there was a centre coordinating the campaign. People feel calmer and more confident when they know there's someone in charge – that's how it has always been and that's what we're used to, but this is a different matter. The communard brigades will be led to Jerusalem by the Lord Himself, and any attempt to interfere with His deeds is the work of the Devil. The chattels meanwhile are relics: the plates Lenin ate from, the clothes he wore. For those who end up going, Ilyich's personal items are the best proof that the expedition has been blessed.

The Latvians' departure, Ishchenko continued, is the last mention of the Gorki commune I have come across. It appears to have fulfilled its task and was disbanded. Its heir – the Latgalian centre – made one more splash, and a loud one at that, but still, it's not for me to say whether it lived up to expectations or what those expectations were. The story begins on 26th January 1924, when the former Latvian Riflemen and some Komsomol lads from the village of Dautsen, fifteen kilometres outside the city of Rēzekne, learned that their beloved Lenin had passed away in Moscow, after a long and difficult illness.

Having lived for many years in Russia, the Latvian Riflemen understood that Lenin's death needed to be properly lamented – not to bewail the deceased would have been shameful. Had they decided simply to bury him, people would have said that they were glad that Lenin was gone, that they couldn't wait for his grave to be dug. But the guards themselves didn't know how to compose a death wail on their own, so they decided to walk to the neighbouring Russian village of Pochinki and ask the old women who lived there and who were famous throughout the region for their especially mournful wailing.

The Riflemen visited the women en masse. They went four times in total, doing all they could to talk them round, but it got them nowhere. None of their lavish promises, arguments or even threats seemed to help: the old women categorically refused to wail for Lenin. Night was falling and they were still at square one. Suddenly one of the Latvians remembered that just outside Pochinki, in a farm beyond the common pastureland, there was a nice working girl called Katya Maslennikova, who despite her youth, was also known to be an excellent wailer. Many still remembered how, on November 17th, when her grandfather died, she fell on his coffin and sobbed, 'Oh how can I speak, I'll weep, I'll weep, this dear old grandpa of mine…' They went to see her. Fortunately, Katya was home, and after asking the Riflemen all sorts of questions about the man that needed bewailing, she smiled, and without playing hard to get, agreed. She even promised that if one of the Komsomol lads rocked her baby sister's cradle for her and the little one went through the night without screaming, the wail would be ready by morning prayers.

The leader of their cell was one Karl Langen. He was happy with this schedule and immediately assigned Komsomol member Stasiulis Ritmanen to babysit Maslennikova's sister. The others in the cell were also given tasks. In particular, Komsomol member Artūrs Skaltsnis was charged with knocking together a reliquary along the lines of the symbolic coffin of Christ that is carried in the procession for the Bringing out of the Shroud on Good Friday. It needed to be quite small: about five or six inches long, as if it were made not for an adult but a child born the day before. Langen asked for the wood to be trimmed with black crape on all sides, while the inside was to be adorned with red fabric, ideally silk or velvet, if Artūrs could find it. He also told the Riflemen that the coffin they would be carrying would bear an unclothed doll; we are, after all, born naked. One of the Komsomolers had a recently printed postcard with Lenin's photograph, and after a brief discussion, they decided to stick it directly on the lid of the coffin. Lastly, Langen announced that everyone should attend the funeral in black.

With everything settled, Karl Langen and the others were already on their way out and saying their goodbyes when Katya suddenly said with some embarrassment that it's hard to have a good weep on your own. This was serious and the Komsomol members, after weighing up Maslennikova's words, agreed with her. At Langen's suggestion, the group left Ritmanen with the baby girl and brought Katya back with them to Pochinki. All the village girls were sitting outside an *izba* and were delighted to see the visitors, especially because many had known each other for a good long time. The Komsomolers said hello and ordered them to 'jump down from that bench before your bottoms freeze.' The girls tittered and got up. The lads went on, 'And now let's pretend this isn't a bench but a table, and it's not out here, leaning against a fence, but inside the hut. And on the table there's a coffin with Lenin inside, and you're walking around it wailing for him. Not any old how mind, but really pitifully.'

As soon as the girls heard this, they all began saying: Lenin, Lenin… yes, all right, let's do a death wail for him. Katya stood at the head and the others lined up behind her and started singing. Circling the coffin, they walked behind Katya in single file, stepping carefully in her tracks, just as you are supposed to. As they walked, they composed the wail for the deceased line by line, as if laying new logs for a hut. It was well past midnight when they finished.

The next day, when the good people of Dautsen started coming out of church after morning prayers, they all saw before them a funeral procession making its slow and solemn way around the church railings. There was a long string of carts, on the first of which stood a superbly crafted black coffin. The Komsomolers, rifles slung across their chests, pranced around them on horseback.

The parishioners asked each other who was being buried with such ceremony, such gravity and majesty, and heard in reply: Lenin, Lenin himself. And for a long time afterwards, almost until the early hours – despite the bitter frost – the girls, under the trusty protection of the Riflemen, travelled from village to village all over Rēzekne district with their dirges and endless keening, their eulogies and their death wail composed by Katya Maslennikova. Who knows what the Komsomol lads were counting on. Perhaps they weren't just saying goodbye to Lenin but believed that they would also manage, finally, to awaken and rouse the people and lead them to the Holy Land. Their hopes however came to naught. Although a fair few locals joined the funeral procession in every village, they would generally accompany the coffin only as far as the village fence, after which they turned back, frozen to the bone.

Still, it was probably only the old Lenin and his life's work that the Komsomol lads were burying. The former adult Lenin had to die and be buried in the earth for him to rise again, for a new Lenin to be born: the child-Lenin who would lead them to the Holy Land. All in all, there's plenty of scope for conjecture, but the truth as usual has remained in the shadows. The one thing that's definitely come down to us from that January is the death wail composed by Katya Maslennikova. Somebody wrote it out, thanks to which it survived. It goes like this:

Poor ol Vladeemir, poor ol Illitch!
O whood you get angry wiv now

BE AS CHILDREN

O whood you get cross wiv, o who.
O whool be ruling over us now,
O whool be taking care of us now,
O whool take care of ar problums.
O thares only Leff Daveedavitch
Taking care of evrifing now.
O is poor liddle eadll be spinning
O is poor liddle artll be sadning,
O sadning and worying it will.
O ee wont no witch way to turn
O eel turn this way then eel turn that.
O warel ee turn is ead, is ead,
O its is soldjers wot made it spin,
O its is soldjers, is soviet soldjers.
O is soldjers wont listen no mor.
O wotl we do wiv you now, o wot,
O howl we get you back on yor feet,
O howl we wake you up, o how.
O youv orfund us all, you ave,
O ar deer ol masters no mor.
O iff only ee woz still alive,
Alive an kikking, alive an well,
O eed diffend us all ee wood,
O eed put evrifing in ordur.
O whys your deff come for you now,
O whys it made us suffer so bad,
O whys it made us suffer for you.
O weev even bigun to fink,
O weev even bigun to wonder,
Ware to turn ar eads wivout you,

Wivout ar master, ar master.
O wen you get back up, clever ead,
O wen you take yor place again,
O pity yor soljers, yor army.
O ware can we go now, o ware…
O weel turn ar eads yonder, we will,
Yonder wiv Leff Daveedavitch,
An weel listen only to im, to im.
O weel remembur you olways
O weel nevur furget you, Illitch,
O weel nevur furget yor deff
An weel remembur you til we dy.

***

My three years in charge of education in Ulyanovsk were more than enough to rid me of any illusions. There was clearly no hope for me: however long I sat in my office, the demands of my post would continue to defeat me. Worst of all, the regional governor eventually cottoned on to the fact that even though I'd been sent from Moscow he had nothing to fear from me, after which the funds dried up completely. All those at my beck and call – from the university to the local schools – howled in protest.

Once I'd realised that things were only going to get worse, I had no other option than to write my letter of resignation. It was accepted instantaneously. I arrived back home in Moscow at the end of October and spent all winter resting up and licking my wounds. I did a bit of this and a bit of that: tidied up some things I'd been working on ages ago, sorted through my letters, read some periodicals, even began thinking about summer at the dacha. But I was getting ahead of myself: in March I suddenly felt bored, and after considering two or three options, settled on Ishchenko. I'd go and visit some provincial archives and dig around about all the things I'd heard from him. I wanted to find out what had come of Lenin's plans. Especially how far he, Trotsky and Dzerzhinsky had got in organising the crusade of the children's-home kids. It was this that fascinated me most.

Between April and November I visited fifteen towns in Ukraine, Central Russia and the Volga region, but left them all empty-handed. It was as if nothing of the kind had ever happened. By autumn I was feeling totally discouraged and returned to Moscow, where I lamented my failures to a friend over a vodka. It was a good thing I did. He told me there and then to forget all about the archives and not waste a moment more on them: the local authorities had feared stories like this since time immemorial, which was why they went out of their way to erase every last trace of them. Newspapers were a different matter. If he'd understood me correctly, the children's-home movement peaked in the first half of the '20s, the years of NEP, when the press had not yet been squeezed to death.

The Russian pilgrims would surely have faced the same problems as their brethren in the West. Seeking a direct route to the Holy Land, they must have gathered in their thousands in the South, by the sea. In Europe, the children had walked to Venice, to Genoa, while our lot – this much we can be sure of – would have headed for the Black Sea ports. Your children, my friend told me, must have moved across the country like wildfire – one day you saw them, the next they were gone – but down there weeks could pass before you found a ship and struck a deal with the captain: a gift for any local hack. Besides, unlike archives, the press is easy work. All the interesting stuff is always on the front page under a banner headline. It was good advice, and what I learned more than made up for my previous disappointments.

Between 1996 and '98, usually in winter, I travelled from one Black Sea town to another: Odessa, Nikolayev, on to Yalta, Feodosia, Kerch, then leaving Crimea behind me, Berdyansk, Taganrog, Novorossiisk, Tuapse. Lastly, the South Caucasus: Sochi, Sukhumi, Poti, Batumi. Every visit turned up something or other. I usually managed to get to four or five towns a year and brought a sheaf of notes back from each of them. There were plenty of good stories but I'll tell just one of them now, and even then only because one of the people caught up in it was Father Nikodim. The events took place in Taganrog, between the 19th and 23rd May 1923. But the *Azov Herald* wouldn't let go of the story even when it was all over. Its punishment was to be shut down for a whole month. The issue of July 1st celebrates the resumption of publication.

If we try to reconstruct the events in Taganrog day by day, we end up with something like this. The town has a large children's home for the untended – almost three hundred of them. Its official name is Commune No. 1. The home is right in the centre, not far from the seafront, in a house that had previously been used for the district's Assembly of the Nobility. This sizeable building occupies an entire block, if you include its various extensions. Locals recognise it by its columns and marble lions by the main entrance.

Be as Children

The teachers and pupils are as ever a motley bunch. Approximately half the staff once worked in ordinary schools. As for the management and those in charge of military classes and physical education, they're all career Chekists. Some have been maimed or shell-shocked during the recent Civil War and have now been moved into the reserves. Among the teachers who collaborate with the security services, the children are especially fond of Father Nikodim, who goes under the name of Aleksei Nikolayevich Poluektov in the school records. Nikodim teaches maths and geography at the commune. Various rumours circulate in the town about this man – Dusya's confessor – but little is known for certain. Still, the *Herald* asserts that he spent several years as a novice in one of our northern monasteries, but that after the Revolution he broke all ties with the Church. Poluektov's role in the events I am about to describe is undeniably large, but if the newspaper is to be believed, somewhat ambiguous.

Two thirds of the pupils really are orphans or have been abandoned by their parents, and for them the commune is their only home. The rest are children of the local Chekists and military men. By '23 things have settled down along the coast of the Sea of Azov and the local Chekists begin to be sent off in large numbers on distant missions, usually to Turkestan to fight the Basmachis. Some of the Taganrogians have previously served in cavalry brigades alongside North Caucasians, so they know a thing or two about Islam, and this is highly prized. They are posted to the Far East as well. As a rule, they're considered experienced and dependable: the Caucasus is close by, with its two languages for every dozen people, then they've got the port with its smugglers on their doorstep, to keep boredom away.

The missions last a good two or three years. Taking wives along is permitted and even welcomed, but the couples are encouraged to leave their offspring at home, in Taganrog. In the new place there's often no permanent lodging, never mind schooling, and any child would be a major burden. Besides, the Party as we all know still views the family as a relic of the bourgeois past; those untouched by its influence are raised within the collective from the cradle onwards, after which the future lies open before them. Overall then the commune offers a privileged education, no worse than the Page Corps of old, and there's no shortage of higher-ups wanting to send their children there.

So on May 19th, with no hint of a warning, strange disturbances begin in our forge of Soviet cadres. An hour or two before dawn, a group of older pupils eliminates the guard on duty, breaks into the munitions room and arms itself. The commune has plenty of weapons and supplies. Almost one hundred rifles with bayonets (mainly Mosin-Nagants), five German machine guns (the latest models) and even a light field-cannon. As yet it's far from obvious what the communards are after, nor is it clear whether all the pupils are in revolt or only the orphans.

The townsfolk subsequently learn that the journalists were not mistaken: the untended started it all, but by morning the Chekists' children had also decided to join them. They'd even vowed to stand shoulder to shoulder with them. Apparently the untended had tried to talk them out of it ahead of time. Explained to them that they understood how proud they were of their fathers and how scared they were of getting them in trouble. If they had fathers like that, they would be sure to keep out of it – and that would be the right thing to do. But the Chekists' children answered that it was precisely because of their fathers that they were joining. Every one of those men was up to his elbows in blood, and this was the only way of begging forgiveness for them, otherwise they would burn in Hell until the end of time.

These events were of course a complete scandal, and that very same morning, May 19th, the Taganrog Party committee demanded that the head and teachers of the commune restore order in the school within two hours, return the weapons to the munitions room and throw the ringleaders into the detention cell. It's not known whether the head made any attempt to carry out the order – I expect he did – but he wasn't even allowed into the commune building. There were guards at the door, a canon and two machine guns on the stairs, and pupils standing at the windows with rifles.

The Party committee was informed, via the head, that if any attempt was made to storm the school, the communards would meet fire with fire, with all the ensuing consequences. The building was sturdy enough and the chief of the Taganrog OGPU office knew exactly how well stocked the commune was with weaponry and munitions. But if nobody touched them, the communards would leave the city in no time, without any noise or trouble. The head was also told that from now on the communards would only agree to talk to the committee through their geography teacher Aleksei Nikolayevich Poluektov, whom they asked to be recognised as their official peace envoy.

At first however, nobody was prepared to listen to

Poluektov or any other peacemaker. The Party committee secretary ordered a battalion of special operations units to be transferred to the town to blockade the building. This was done by the following morning, whereupon the pupils were presented with a further ultimatum to lay down their arms immediately and unconditionally. But this too had no effect. When it became clear where things were headed, the Taganrog OGPU chief, who had been keeping a low profile, tried to talk the Party secretary out of storming the school. He began explaining to him, as if to a young boy, that a peaceful solution was essential, that a shoot-out in the middle of a large town would only play into enemy hands, and that the pupils, despite their youth had been superbly trained: 'Try to get this into your thick skull: we trained them up for our own use. They can hit a bottle top from ten metres, never mind a special ops officer. Then there's the school itself, sturdy as hell, built the old way – even direct cannon fire won't bring the walls down. Just think how many men we'll lose to corner these shits.'

But the secretary wouldn't budge. He declared that a full-blown counter-revolution was brewing in the town and needed to be nipped in the bud, after which he told the commanding officers to ready their troops. The Chekists carried out this instruction, but that was as far as they would go. However much the secretary threatened them with a military tribunal and execution, they categorically refused to order their men to attack. It's not hard to see why: shooting your own children is no fun. At midday, having achieved precisely nothing, the belligerent secretary left the scene. He gave the OGPU chief a further twenty-four hours to sort things out.

Poluektov's moment had arrived. He spent the first half

of the night shuttling between his pupils and the Chekists, trying to find some semblance of common ground. At first the negotiations were hard-going and on the verge of collapsing more than once, but then things started moving. Shortly before dawn the Chekists, who had already made several concessions, accepted the communards' final demand – to sign a written agreement. The rest was easy.

The document that came out of all this was published by the *Azov Herald* in its entirety. It's certainly an odd-looking text. The meaning of several articles in the treaty seems deliberately obscure, but one thing is beyond doubt: not only did Poluektov play the main role in the drafting of the agreement, he is also the central figure in the text itself. The treaty stipulated the following obligations on the part of the children: to surrender by the following evening all heavy weaponry (the cannon and five machine guns) along with half the rifles, and to leave the building. The communards were allowed to take fifty rifles with them, plus a dozen cartridges per gun, and go wherever they wanted. A footnote specified that this article would come into force only if the evening was clear and calm. The second article directly concerned Poluektov: the latter undertook, without any explanation whatsoever, to pray for the communards for as long as proved necessary. According to the third, no less baffling article, the OGPU chief agreed within the next hour to supply the commune with a roll of thick brown paper, one hundred metres of tape and a further five rolls of white satin chiffon fabric, all of which the newspaper notes, he provided right on time.

It was a near twenty-four-hour wait until the next stage, and the Chekists and special ops forces had nothing to fill the time with, which made them extremely jumpy. What bothered them most was the fact that following a special edition of the *Herald*, a large crowd of townsfolk had massed on the seafront, the beach and all around the building. A cordon was set up and threats were issued, but the bystanders were pushed back fifty metres at most. One single cavalry squadron would probably have scattered them without the slightest difficulty, but no order was given and the crowd grew by the hour.

On May 23rd, the sun sets at 21:52 according to the calendar. There wasn't a breath of wind but the sun was red when it set and the moon in the sky was just as red and just as round – a sure sign that the wind would pick up by the morning. Nevertheless, the condition stipulated by the children had not been violated and the Chekists were told to prepare themselves: the communards might start emerging from the building at any moment. And indeed, they appeared in the doorway soon enough, but when the soldiers, all simple village lads, caught sight of them, their eyes leapt from their sockets.

The standard uniform at the children's home was military: tarpaulin boots and greatcoat, only without piping, bars or stripes. But the figures bearing down the main staircase towards the special ops forces, with rifles slung over their chests, were skinny and half-naked. They were wearing masks over their faces – that was what the brown packing paper was for – and to complete the disguise, white chiffon tunics and nothing on their feet. The aim of this carnival, the *Azov Herald* speculated in its next edition, was purely pragmatic: to prevent the Chekists from identifying and reclaiming their children. But I doubt that this was the only reason.

Be as Children

Split up into seven brigades, the communards marched in this strange attire as if on parade, with a confident, even sprightly step, despite their bare feet, and the crowd was so impressed by their proficiency that many clapped. Then, keeping their formation, the brigades calmly crossed the seafront one after another, marched down the granite steps to the beach and made for the sea. The sand was white and fine here, and in summer the beach was always crammed with bathers. In May 1914, out of concern for their safety, the Assembly of the Nobility had drawn on its own funds to erect a seven-metre lifeguard tower on the shore. One hundred townsfolk, at the very least, had this tower to thank for their lives. Ever since those same war years though, the beach had been considered closed in the evenings, even in high season, and the tower was unmanned.

But when the first of the communards reached the water, the crowd realised that there was somebody up there. The silhouette of a human figure facing the sea stood out clearly against the bright round moon, and the sharpest-eyed onlookers claimed that the person at the top of the tower was without doubt the much-loved children's-home teacher Poluektov. It didn't bother them that Poluektov was famous in the town for being almost two metres tall, while this man was only half that height. The reason, they explained, was that Poluektov was kneeling. Which was probably true: the man praying at the top, like Simeon Stylites, was indeed Father Nikodim. The *Azov Herald* was in no doubt about this, and its correspondent was even able to reconstruct one of the prayers from the scraps of words that occasionally reached the crowd. It was very similar to those that Father Nikodim would offer up to the Lord in our presence.

He said, 'Oh Lord, my dearest Lord, remember how You once walked upon the waters and they did not part, they held You no worse than the Earth. Without sin or the burden of evil You were light, almost weightless, and it was a joy for them to cradle You. Look, Lord – are not these children as righteous and as pure as You Yourself? Even if one or other of them has broken the commandments in the past, they have suffered so much that they have long since atoned for their sin. Lord, my God, my one and only God,' he beseeched Christ, 'work a miracle: let not the deep open up beneath their feet, for their intentions are also pure. It is not vanity that has made them take to the road, they are walking to You, to Your Holy Land, they believe in You, and like You, they are ready to lay down their lives to save all sinners, even the worst.'

When the first of the communards stepped onto the path of moonlight that led due south to Jerusalem and had been laid down for them by the Lord, it strained, sagged and quivered like some flimsy piece of matting; the crowd froze. But Poluektov began praying ever more fervently, ever more loudly and vehemently, and the path, as if taking fright, became as even and as smooth as before – not that there was ever any danger for the communards by the shore, in the shallows. So then the children's-home brigades walked along the path almost to the horizon with strong, confident strides, as if marching along the coast, and only at the line that divided sea and sky did the path begin to play up again, whether because of a sudden squall or simply because it was tired of supporting them. But this danger also passed. On the one hand, some people in the crowd managed, at the very limits of their vision, to see the children cast off their rifles into the water with a precise balletic movement, as if in a silent film; on the other, Poluektov's prayers, which he was now reciting with almost feverish speed, seem to have been heard again. One way or another, the path smoothed itself out once more.

The communards had long disappeared over the horizon, but the crowd was still standing on the shore and watching; only at dawn did it begin to disperse. Though there seemed no cause, the general mood was one of sadness. The bystanders did not even say goodbye to one another, they just quietly wandered off home. It was as if the Taganrogians no longer cared what happened next, they were weary of this story and wished to forget it, the sooner the better. The reporters were convinced that people would gradually accept it all and digest it all, and that the communard crusade to the Holy Land would be the main topic of conversation in the town for many a year. But later they had to admit they were wrong – the kids from the children's home were barely ever mentioned.

As to whether any of the communards made it to Asia Minor – personally, I have my doubts. I wasn't the only one interested in this question, but we don't know the answer to this day. Although the *Azov Herald*, following its closure was reluctant to return to that night at any length, it did report in the issue of July 5th, that some fishermen from Feodosia had caught seven drowned bodies in their nets – children's bodies by the look of them, but they had been in the water for more than a month and could no longer be identified. The newspaper did add however, that this happened almost two hundred kilometres west of the road the children were walking along. That the corpses might have been borne to Crimea on the current was never mentioned.

A month after the article about the drowned bodies (though there's probably no connection here) a committee from the Office of the Procurator General arrived from Moscow. It subjected both the city authorities – from the secretary of the Taganrog Party Committee, to rank-and-file special ops forces – and the staff of the children's home, to a whole new round of interrogations. Poluektov was of particular interest to the investigators. They didn't learn anything much about him from the Chekists, but the former schoolteachers – Father Nikodim's colleagues – were a different matter. When questioned they proved surprisingly forthcoming. Their testimony made it very clear that it was precisely Poluektov who had first led the children to the idea of crossing the Black Sea on foot. In fact he'd done such a skilful job of it that the communards began to think that they had taken the decision all on their own and that Nikodim had sought to restrain them.

They said that Poluektov had spent several months convincing his pupils in the commune, that they, and only they, could save our unhappy world, and most importantly, that the only way to do this was to liberate the Holy Land. Being a geography teacher, he was able to show them the shortest routes from Taganrog across the Caucasus, Anatolia and Syria to Palestine. He even got them to learn these routes, tested them and recorded the marks in his journal. When the communards began to believe that the salvation of the world depended solely on them, Poluektov suddenly changed his tune and began telling them that crossing the Caucasus on foot was a recipe for disaster: there were no proper roads, only caravan paths, which few people knew well, even among the locals. Not to mention the fact that it was a huge detour. Better to walk straight over the sea.

Some of the children weren't convinced by this and asked: how can ordinary people, not Christ, walk on water? Won't they drown? In response he called them doubting Thomases and patiently explained that belief is the cornerstone of the universe, that it fortifies not only Man but also the elements around him, while unbelief destroys everything. If they are righteous before God, if they are truly pure and without blemish, then they have nothing to fear: water or flagstones will be all the same to them. The deep will swallow up only the sinners, those unable to save themselves, as well as those in whom there is too little faith. Then, in the same breath, he began to taunt the pupils, asking them whether all this was simply their boundless pride. What had made them think that they could save the race of Adam? And he added mockingly, 'I've never hidden this from anyone and won't do so now: pride is a sin, a great sin.'

In the townsfolk's view, all this was enough for serious charges to be brought, but the Moscow commission didn't seem to notice the statements made by Father Nikodim's colleagues. What it was after, both from the teachers and later from Poluektov himself, was the answer to a question, that in the context of Soviet justice, sounded very odd indeed: why had he stopped praying and climbed down from the tower a full three hours before dawn? By doing so, had he not doomed the communards to certain death? All the children's-home teachers were flummoxed by this suggestion, and the commission was unable to get anything useful out of them.

As for Poluektov, who had remained perfectly calm

throughout the investigation, he asserted that, firstly, the procuracy would find it difficult to prove such charges: after all, who said that the children had died and weren't still marching across Asia Minor somewhere? Secondly, the statement that he had stopped praying for them was also unproven – if you sincerely believe in the Lord, then He is always close at hand, whether you're on the top of a tower or in your own room. Thirdly, it was absurd to think his prayers could mean more to the Lord than the prayers of the communards themselves. These arguments must have sounded quite convincing – at any rate, no arrest or trial followed. All the same, Poluektov didn't want to remain in Taganrog and left the moment the case was closed.

The Azov episode reverberated as far as Tuapse, where the local *Observer* wrote that after an unexpected and very powerful storm broke over Taganrog in the middle of August, all the untended left with the rainbow, to the jubilation of the townsfolk. There are a few other reports I want to add here too. The *Nikolayev Telegraph* explained to its readers, in a very heartfelt piece, that the untended were trying to escape the clutches of blood-soaked Russia, and on reaching the Holy Land, to beg forgiveness for her in Jerusalem. But only a few would manage to reach Palestine. The rest would continue to wander like the blind from place to place, until they perished in exhaustion.

The *Telegraph* was echoed by the *Novorossiisk Courier*, which informed its subscribers that at the sight of any town the untended would say to one another, 'There it is, Jerusalem! That's it!!!' hoping and believing that they had finally arrived. The *Kerch News* noted the communards' conviction that the shells and bullets which they had cast from melted-down bells preserved their holiness. There was no need even to take aim – the bullets would find sinners by themselves. The untended from another brigade explained to the correspondent that words of all-forgiving love should be scratched into the bullets, and not because forgiveness is good. It's simply that a sinner, having absorbed a piece of hallowed metal, will at the very moment it enters his body, believe and repent. By beholding death with an infant's purity, he will be saved.

As to the question of how many communards would manage to touch the Holy Land, the newspaper's predictions made for grim reading. Those vessels that did agree to take the children on board (for what reasons I cannot say, but I suspect the deliberate dereliction of duty in all cases) were dilapidated and barely able to keep afloat. Worse, they were shamelessly overloaded, so sometimes they would already be sinking when they had barely left the port. It's not impossible though, that one or two of them still made it to Constantinople.

The overland route – the Caucasus, then the Anatolian peaks – also proved difficult: the untended perished from hunger and cold, or fell to their deaths. Some were taken captive by the locals, often ending up in servitude or harems. Almost ten thousand of the strongest and most healthy were seized by Atatürk and sent off to his military colleges. Even the communards seem to have understood that only a few of their number would ever reach the Holy Land. Among themselves they would say that it would be nice of course, if everyone could endure the hardships of the journey – you can't have too much of a good thing – but what mattered most was that at least one innocent person should force their way through evil and turn to the Lord.

One last thing. When the communard brigades arrived in the coastal towns, the local papers wrote about them willingly, but they knew nothing as a rule about the children's past. Everything I managed to find by skimming through the folders of ten publications over a period of five years (1922-26) was cursory and bitty. The one exception was an article in the *Russian Trader*. The issue of 15th February 1924 gives a very full description of a communard's funeral that had taken place a fortnight earlier, on the very same day that the children walking from Yekaterinburg to the Black Sea had learned of Lenin's death. Such reports are few and far between. Even so, I wouldn't have chosen to summarise it here were it not for its obvious connection to the Kremlin visit of Demidov and his ward.

This funeral happened near Feodosia, on 1st February 1924. That morning the Mikhail Frunze Children's-Home Brigade had learned of Lenin's passing in Moscow, just an hour after the death at dawn of the communard Ivan Kostandinov. The decision was taken to bury them together, high up on a hillside, where there was a view of the port and the boundless sea. A cross was planted at the head of Ivan's grave with the modest inscription, 'Here rests communard Ivan Kostandinov, who was walking to Jerusalem and could walk no further', while a small distance away on a ledge in the rock they placed a bust of Lenin – the work it seems of our acquaintance. The newspaper gives an expert account of how it was sculpted. A small, graceful head of Apollo was used as a template in the drawing class at the high school in Feodosia. A quarter of a pound of nails was knocked into it to support a thick layer of terracotta. And that was what the boy worked with. He sculpted all night long and by sunrise he had finished, just as he had promised.

The sighted children had seen plenty of photographs of Lenin of course, and said that the likeness was quite astonishing. And that the reason Lenin wore such a kind, sad smile was that he already knew, that just like Vanya Kostandinov, he wouldn't make it to Jerusalem himself. Then it was the turn of the blind children. Demidov's ward had once used his fingers to commit the face of the living Lenin to memory, preserving it just as it was; they too now ran their fingers slowly and carefully all over the head he had sculpted, so that nothing would be forgotten.

***

In her second to last year at the gymnasium, Dusya Mukhanova became close friends with Masha Apostolova, the daughter of Father Vasily, senior priest at the Church of St Peter and St Paul, on the Yauza. Dusya was growing up quickly at the time, and unable to cope with what was happening inside her, badly needed someone to confide in. Masha, a taciturn, sympathetic girl who was in love, just as Dusya was, with their literature teacher Nikolai Porfiryevich Pokladov, proved a real find. They were almost always together: they sat at the same desk in class, and after school, since they lived in the same neighbourhood – Masha in the clergy house by the church, Dusya two blocks away in a big new apartment building on Solyanka Street – they would do their homework and make music together. Sometimes, when their parents agreed to it, they would even stay over at each other's place for the night. In her quiet way, Masha was a very ardent, devoted girl, and Dusya guessed that it wasn't so much their literature teacher that she loved as Dusya herself.

Their friendship continued like this throughout the seventh year of gymnasium, but in August, on returning from her holidays at her uncle's estate on the Don and calling Masha, Dusya learned that Father Vasily had passed away unexpectedly in June, and that just a month later, Masha had been hurriedly married off to none other than their literature teacher, who by way of a dowry, had inherited the position of senior priest at St Peter and St Paul's. This double betrayal broke Dusya. She shut herself off from the world and stopped attending school. It was only towards spring that she slowly began to recover.

She had spent her summer at the estate with a cousin five years older than her. Bored of country life, the cousin would plague Dusya from noon until night with stories of her marriage and her new lover, a friend of her husband's from their time together in the Horse Guards. Now, as she began to feel stronger, Dusya made it a rule to attend Divine Liturgy at St Peter and St Paul's every week, and to stay on to receive confession from her former teacher. Mixing up her own fantasies with the stories she had heard from her cousin, she would repent thoroughly and unhurriedly before God. She did not leave out a single trifle, a single salacious detail, in fact she savoured them to the full. Father Nikolai must have had feelings for her once, because now, forgetting that he was a priest and she a penitent sinner, he would shut his ears, literally beg her to stop, just stop, saying that's enough, I absolve you of everything anyway.

Even before all this, Father Nikolai, from the very first days of his priesthood, had been overwhelmed by the weight of evil and sin that had fallen upon him. There was so much grief in the church, so much suffering and hopelessness, that in the evening he would lament to his wife over dinner that the gymnasium now seemed a heavenly oasis. It was as if his colleagues and pupils, every single one of them, had been specially chosen for their kindness, intelligence, decency, and above all, their high ideals. Of course, Father Nikolai was still very inexperienced, with a poor sense of how a priest should conduct himself during confession, what he was supposed to say and how. Besides, he was a gentle, sensitive man who took things too much to heart, and who most importantly, did not yet know how to mediate between God and Man; when people came to him to confess they were, albeit before God, repenting and baring their souls to another human being, and it was from him that they expected mercy and forgiveness. Small wonder, that for Father Nikolai, Dusya's every appearance was sheer torture.

Of Dusya it would be fair to say that even as a young girl she was already a whore. Her fantasies, together with everything that happened between her and the priest during confession, brought her genuine pleasure. She wanted him to see everything just as vividly as she did, and she seems to have succeeded; she wanted him too, to sin with her, not just listen to her calmly and disinterestedly. Just as a man adjusting to a new partner gradually begins to understand what she responds to and how, so Dusya adapted herself to Pokladov. She was helped in this by her eye for small details and her quick reactions.

At times though, the encounters in the church began to pall and were no longer enough for Dusya, and then after a quick telephone call, she would walk the familiar path to Masha's home. Her friend was almost due, yet despite her size and sluggishness she offered Dusya the same joyful welcome as ever. For Father Nikolai these visits were even more excruciating than the confessions. Fond of play from a young age and with a keen understanding of its laws, Dusya would get carried away and become completely pitiless.

Once, during his time as a teacher, Pokladov had been very keen on wordplay, which he considered an excellent pedagogical tool. While telling a story in class he would change one particle, prefix or preposition and everything would instantly be turned on its head. He was even fonder of reading out soliloquies from famous plays, having warned the girls in advance that the hero already knew how it was all going to end and was just playing the fool. After this, every line, however innocent, became bitterly sarcastic or taunting. Now, as they drank tea in the sitting room, Dusya showed him that she had forgotten nothing.

In his desperation, Father Nikolai even resolved to talk about Dusya Mukhanova with his wife, but fearing for Masha's health, he put it off once, twice and then, a year later, learned to his relief that his tormentress was engaged to be married and would soon be leaving. For all this, the priest couldn't fail to notice that Dusya's visits were not just revenge – she was clearly in love with him.

Marriage put an abrupt stop to it all. Dusya it seems had said all she had to say; building her own nest and raising her first child made a model wife of her for a good long time. She barely ever cast her mind back to her schoolgirl exploits. If she did stumble upon them, she would be surprised at her own actions, but in the end dismiss them all as childish pranks of no importance. It was only after she discovered that her husband was already on his third affair with nurses on the front line, and after she also took a lover herself, that distant memories of her relationship with Father Nikolai began to disturb her once more.

She spoke about those confessions to all her current confessors, including both Pimen, her Elder, and Bishop Amvrosy. She begged them to show her how she could obtain forgiveness for them, but the penances they imposed brought no relief. The only person who truly managed to help her was Nikodim. When he started demanding that she tell him her entire life to the last drop and confess her every sin, no matter whether in thought or deed, from more or less the cradle onwards, his words in essence, were the forgiveness she sought. And it turned out that during those confessions with Father Nikolai she had been right not to hide anything, not to keep anything back.

Dusya had been prone to exalted, even mystical moods ever since childhood. Her father had been a member of the Synod, and at home over dinner and at other times, there was always plenty of talk about the Church; but what she heard there could hardly have enthused her. The clergy was managed by an ordinary ministry – without spirit, without faith, and naturally, without God. Dusya's father took a sympathetic view of Christ but considered His flock very hard to control, which in itself was good reason to see Jesus as something of an anarchist.

The Church of course had had its own system of seniority for almost two thousand years and even now conversations were taking place about making it whole once more by restoring the Patriarchate. But the people on whom the decision depended were worldly men by nature who had no desire to rock the boat. They were being sincere when they said that the Church was as anti-state as it had ever been. To God what is God's, to Caesar what is Caesar's, Christ had once said – consenting in other words to put up with the state but certainly not to like it. Not for nothing were so many of yesterday's seminarians now throwing bombs for the Revolution.

Such topics were discussed in an entirely matter-of-fact way, and at times with more than a hint of cynicism. The conversations to which Dusya had been privy almost since her swaddling days had contained not a drop of respect for parish priests, monks or bishops, only endless stories about intrigues, bribes and power struggles behind the scenes. This was how she saw the Church too, and when she began to pine for the Lord it was not the Church she remembered but the Elders. They were almost never mentioned in her father's conversations with his guests, and yet to all appearances, they were the last living shard of the faith that had come down from Jesus Christ.

From the age of about fifteen she had become ever more fascinated by hermits and anchorites who had gone off to live in sketes, and one day she even told her mother of her wish to be guided by an Elder. She was helped in this by a journey she made with her godmother to Optina Pustyn once her marriage to Pyotr Igrenyev had already been decided.[46] She spent six weeks at the monastery, confessing every other day to Pimen, an Elder and highly respected monk.

She remembered all the things he told her to the end of her days, and shared them with us. On confession: never be ashamed to reveal your sins; the more mercilessly you repent and condemn yourself, the lighter you will feel afterwards. The same went for life itself, which he saw as the continuous circulation of souls: some descend to those born anew, while others – those who have just died – rise to the Lord's throne. And if the sins are not too heavy, the soul, radiant and renewed, will find itself one day in Heaven, all sufferings forgotten. On another occasion Pimen said that to live is always to leave the Lord in a state of purity and to return to him in a state of filth, black with hatred and evil, so as to be cleansed in Him once more. This is the Greater salvation; the Lesser is confession with its repentance and mercy.

It was from him that Dusya learned that without a shepherd repentance might fail. Without a guide you can never know whether you have taken the true path or if you are straying towards danger, to places that oppress the spirit. He returned to this topic at their every meeting. Told her that a spiritual father has many spiritual daughters, but an Elder can have only one or two. There's a mystery here, he said, which you can spend years trying to penetrate, but whether you will succeed, only God can tell. Once she pressed him to tell her how she could know – were there any signs, at least? – and he smiled and told

---

[46] A celebrated Orthodox monastery in Kaluga region, known in particular for its Elders, who were visited for their guidance by, among many others, Gogol, Dostoevsky and Tolstoy.

her that if God deemed her worthy of receiving an Elder, she would feel him beside her wherever she was and whatever she was doing.

It was from Pimen that she first learned that if you obey and follow your confessor there can be no sin in anything, but if you stray and act as you please, there can be nothing but sin, and that an Elder's Liturgy is an ocean of mercy. But however much Dusya begged him to take her under his wing, Pimen refused, and rightly so. She couldn't get to Optina often, a couple of times a year at best. But she did write to him every week without fail.

The link was broken only at the end of 1917. Her letters rarely made it to Optina; the post was in a terrible state but the main reason was that Pimen had fallen seriously ill that autumn, and according to his cell attendant, was finding it hard to reply. All the same, when she found herself at a fork in the road – this was seven years later – she travelled to see him once more, and the Elder helped her.

Dusya's family was very fond of her, but thought her frivolous. They took the same view both of her trips to Optina and of her sudden craze for the theatre, which it so happened, started at the same time, in '17. In 1913, after the wedding, she had moved to Pskov, where her husband was named Official for Special Assignments under the local governor. Not far from the town, on the right bank of the Velikaya, the Igrenyevs had a large estate, and every summer the famous theatre director Slipavsky would rent a dacha close by. After they met and became friends, Dusya managed to persuade Slipavsky to help the Igrenyevs with a production of *King Lear*. She would play Cordelia.

Be as Children

There was nothing particularly special about Dusya – she was pretty, quite graceful – but after several rehearsals the director suddenly told her mother-in-law, also a passionate theatre-lover, that the bride could go a long way as a professional actress. She had a rare ability to surrender herself to another person, the gift of trust and non-resistance: you could work her like wax, then sculpt whatever you wanted. This lack of fear in the hands of others, perhaps even sympathy towards them, is an extremely unusual thing; a person like that can walk along a ledge like a lunatic and not be scared.

It was her mother-in-law, old Princess Igrenyeva, who first predicted to Dusya that one day she would take the veil. That was in the winter of 1918. At the time they were living in the village of Gustinino, on the border of Pskov province and Estonia, seventy versts from their former estate. They had quite a large place – two log-houses joined together. Thanks to its size and especially, of course, to the lady of the house, it soon became a shelter for wayfarers, both those fleeing Moscow or Petrograd for Estonia and Latvia, and those on a pilgrimage to the Pskov-Pechory Monastery. Later, as emigrés, many would remember it fondly.

Following a bout of typhus in the autumn, Igrenyeva had almost completely lost the use of her legs and could barely stand. Dusya would be busy nearby with the children, washing clothes, tidying up, while the princess, lying in the corner by the stove, would train a pair of theatre binoculars at a pot of porridge that was taking forever to cook. The stove was useless, burning through stacks of wood to little effect. The millet could take two hours to soften. Igrenyeva was still very young when she ended up in these backwoods and she missed St Petersburg, its theatres and balls, and above all her friends, to the point of tears. Luckily God had blessed her with an active, lively temperament and she soon found a way of keeping herself occupied: she started putting on amateur plays, usually based on German and Scandinavian history, something her father, who counted a Teutonic knight among his forbears, had been very interested in. On stage, to the music of Wagner, funerary boats would burn on bonfires, the wind would scatter the ash, and all things disappeared and drowned in the mists drifting in from the north, so that in the end, nobody knew which way to sail, which way was the shore, which way the open sea.

The porridge lived its own life, like any human being: one moment it would give a deep sigh, the next – a loud splutter from deep within, while the steam, which rose ever more densely as the porridge cooked and was illuminated by the soft velvet glow of the coal beneath it, seemed no less magical and mysterious than the vapours that Ivanov, the local pharmacist and amateur chemist, had once created in Pskov. When the pharmacist worked himself up into one of his frenzies, there was no point arguing with him: Ivanov was ready to release his freon onto the stage, along with some other harmless gas, every single minute, not least because the audience loved it, and she was wasting her breath when she tried to convince him that such effects served a purpose only at the very end, otherwise they just got in the way. The actors were especially put out by Ivanov's behaviour: after all, who would want to see at the moment of greatest tension, when you're wringing your hands in torment, or worse, preparing to take your own life as a result of those same inescapable torments, illuminated wreaths of steam suddenly emerging from a booth, so that the stage, the set and you yourself, with all your pain and suffering, are swallowed up by a white shroud, as if there had never been anything there in the first place.

The porridge snorted and grumbled in muffled satisfaction, as though it had been eating itself and had eaten its fill. Dusya knew how much the princess enjoyed making fun of the fact that she had once had her own theatre, audience, ovations, and now look – just a stove and a pot; and yet while the porridge was cooking, she couldn't take her eyes off it, no doubt because she like everyone else had been so hopelessly, permanently hungry for such a long time.

Sometimes there would be a knock on the door from one of the travellers heading west. This scene – a princess watching porridge through theatre binoculars – was witnessed by many, and Igrenyeva, in the hope of appearing not entirely mad, would explain to everyone that it was her nanny, born to a gypsy mother, who had taught her to read fortunes in burning lumps of coal and in the vapours rising from a pot.

It was a time when nobody could make sense of anything or decide on anything. People didn't even dare ask themselves if they and their loved ones would survive or if tomorrow they would be lying in some ditch with a bullet in the back of their heads or in another ditch used to dump corpses from the typhus barrack. They weren't sure whether to leave this blood-maddened country, to flee headlong without a backward glance, or to stay, because if not today then tomorrow everything would settle down, sort itself out, and people would come to their senses and begin living again as they had lived ten or twenty years before.

As soon as they heard the word gypsy, visitors immediately wanted to know their fate, and Igrenyeva, not in the least surprised, would agree to tell their fortune. The princess had a way with words, as well as a good understanding of human nature, and much of what she said struck home. Within a few months her fame had spread throughout the district. Igrenyeva only ever used porridge for telling fortunes, and only while it was still cooking: remembering what her guests had been through over the past year, she never let it burn. Aside from that she openly warned everyone that she could only foretell their fate for a few months into the future – half a year, at most. But at that time, even a day was plenty, and nobody minded.

In the summer of 1919 her nephew, a former colonel of the General Staff who was making his way from Moscow to Riga, stayed with them for three days. By that time General Mamontov's offensive had already petered out and the Whites, who had controlled more than half of Russia only a few weeks before, began falling back to the South. The colonel knew all this but he still couldn't accept that the Reds would win and spoke about the regrouping of forces, reserves, and help from Allied powers.

Igrenyeva though, could see that the game was up. The Reds, who until recently had been no more than an ordinary rabble – aside from the Latvians and the Chinese, they didn't know the first thing about warfare – and who at the sight of officers and Cossacks, would desert the front, one brigade at a time, scattering every which way, had finally learnt the basics. The tide had turned: from now until the very end, the Reds would fight better and better and the Whites worse and worse. She wanted to explain all this to him, but the only thing the nephew wanted to ask her about was his sweetheart Marusya Ardashnikova. Igrenyeva knew very little about her. She said that she was alive, but as for where she was and what she was up to, there was no one to ask – the porridge was already cooked and it would be a sin, a great sin, for her to spoil it. Nephew: 'Come on, Auntie – what does it matter!' Igrenyeva: 'It does matter, my dear. No truth will come of sin – you can't read fortunes in burnt porridge. You can ask it till you're blue in the face but you won't see a thing.'

Fortune-telling did not just brighten Igrenyeva's days; it also allowed her, Dusya and the children to survive the two hardest winters of '18 and '19. Not that the princess ever asked to be paid – that would have embarrassed her – but people still brought something, usually grain for the porridge. They all knew that unless you 'gilded the hand' no good prophecy would ever come true.

In 1918 Dusya vowed obedience to a former hegumen of the Pskov-Pechory Monastery, and then from '21 on to Father Amvrosy, Bishop of Pskov. Even before Estonia had definitively gained its independence, several monks, Amvrosy among them, had moved from the monastery in Pechora to some caves three versts outside Gustinino and founded a skete there.

Dusya told us about the first time she went to Amvrosy for confession and how long she kept everyone else in the queue waiting. She had suddenly decided the day before that she was greatly at fault before her husband: she had short-changed him badly and she was ready for the harshest penance. She repented almost as hysterically as she had to her parish priest during the war, three years earlier, for fornicating during Lent. It was a confession she would never forget: even while she was still on her knees pleading for pardon, she had known full well that she would carry on fornicating, that there was too much desire in her womb to resist and refuse her lover. The priest had imposed a penance of one hundred prostrations a day for two weeks and she could still remember swaying this way and that like a pendulum, as the blood ebbed and flowed in her head. After the first four or five prostrations she was already unable to take anything in; even her own voice reciting *Our Father* over and over again seemed to come from somewhere outside her.

From December 1919, whether they happened to be living in Moscow or in Gustinino, Dusya no longer saw Amvrosy three or four times a week, as she was used to doing, but rarely and irregularly. Sometimes half a year could go by between meetings. Neither of them was to blame. In the two years that followed, Bishop Amvrosy was transferred three times to a new diocese, and arrested three times. After the first investigation, which lasted about a month, he was unexpectedly released, but later, after twice retrieving the old interrogation reports from the archives, the authorities exiled him to the North – first for six months, then nine.

These were relatively brief terms and Dusya went off to see him on both occasions, but her mother-in-law could tell that the absence of constant care was a torment to her. Dusya complained about this herself to Amvrosy during her visits and when she wrote to him. Deep down Amvrosy understood that he should find Dusya somebody else to take his place, not least because his terms of exile could turn into prison sentences at a moment's notice, but he had become very attached to her over the previous two years, and calling to mind all the spiritual guides he knew one by one, he was unable to decide on any to whom he could entrust her.

In 1920 Amvrosy was arrested again. For a while Dusya tried going to the village priest, Father Vladimir, for confession, but he had a large flock as it was – the local Church of the Most Holy Trinity, in which he served, was the only one in the district to have survived, and he couldn't devote time to her at the expense of others. Even the confessions in his church were generally communal, and Dusya, with no guidance at all for the first time in several years, felt totally at sea. Even then of course, she continued talking to Father Amvrosy in her own mind, making mental confessions to him, but she sorely needed real dialogue too.

By that time the stream of refugees had given way to pilgrims hailing from Moscow and Petrograd. When she wasn't at church, she would spend all day cooking, washing clothes, cleaning the house and taking care of the children, but it wasn't the chores that brought her down – it was the bitter, nasty row that was raging almost continuously in Gustinino. What approach should the episcopate take to Soviet power, and how should it treat the Renovationists?[47] Was Patriarch Tikhon running the Russian Orthodox Church in the right way? Was it enough simply to protest the plundering and closing of churches, the arrests of priests, or was it time for a clean break with the Bolsheviks?

The ill-feeling and hatred among those they were taking

---

[47] A modernising movement within the Russian Orthodox Church found congenial by the state authorities in the 1920s (see Afterword).

in kept growing, and as she listened to one group, then another, Dusya despaired. Unsure where the truth lay and feeling utterly confused, she stopped attending church and didn't let the children go either. The loss of the Holy Liturgy was especially hard for them. Brought up to attend mass every day and to confess no less often than once a week, they asked and begged her to take them to church and were incapable of understanding their punishment.

She did yield on one occasion to her mother-in-law's entreaties to let the children receive confession, and that same night Father Amvrosy appeared to her in her dreams. He spoke very tenderly to Dusya and did all he could to comfort her; above all he told her that soon she would be given the guide she needed and was asking for. He would be with her for four years, and when he too went away and Dusya found herself alone again, she should not be afraid: before leaving he would set her on the true, straight path where you can no longer err – you just walk and walk, never needing to turn. She would go along it calmly year after year, and when that road also went bad, when it too began to twist and turn, to go round and round, the time would come for Dusya herself to decide whom to obey.

Dreams are all very well, but the questions to which Dusya urgently needed answers, about the Renovationists in particular, seemed to her impossibly complicated. Terrified of making a mistake, never knowing who was right or whom to believe, she spent every minute in the despairing awareness that without a shepherd she could not be saved. So much fear had accumulated inside her that no sooner did Father Nikodim, who was well-known in Pskov, agree to take her confession there one day than Dusya, choking on her words and tears, poured everything out to him, mixing up the agonies of the Church with her own personal torments. It wasn't simply that one seemed to explain the other: they were she felt, one whole, for in both cases the suffering was born of faith in the Lord and was directed towards Him, and above all, in both cases nobody knew whom to follow or which way to go.

When recalling Nikodim in our presence, Dusya would say different things about the monk at different times. She didn't contradict herself exactly, she just changed the emphasis. We and our parents were not the only ones to see her shuffle her stories about in this way – evidently Father Amvrosy and her other shepherds saw it too.

At the end of the Civil War, not long before the death of her youngest son, three admirers came to Gustinino to seek Dusya's hand. Two of them moreover, had been in love with her ever since the gymnasium. This series of marriage proposals left her filled with doubt and hesitation until eventually, still undecided, she went off to Nikodim to confess. And to hear above all, that there was nothing wrong with any of this: she would never manage to raise two children on her own, especially boys.

Later she would say that Nikodim seemed to have known in advance what she was bringing him. He had dug a pit, set some snares and was patiently lying in ambush, waiting for her. The question of why she wanted to remarry didn't seem to interest him all that much, instead he would always begin by asking whether she had already lusted for her new admirer, already fornicated with him in her thoughts. Having ascertained that something of the kind had happened, he would fly into a rage. Then during confession, she would tell him everything, keep nothing back, no matter how paltry. Often she would even throw in some extra sins, otherwise it might turn out that, albeit fleetingly, albeit glancingly, she really had imagined this or that and not told him, and then the sin would never be forgiven, however much she prayed.

Nikodim it seems, loathed fornication in thought even more than in deed, because he would execrate her and literally drag her through the dirt, releasing her with the words 'Go in peace' only when she had no hope left, when she wanted nothing more than for the ground to swallow up all her suitors one by one for ever bringing such torments upon her. And this wasn't so much fear of Nikodim as the fact that during confession, with every minute that passed, the sin that she had committed grew larger and larger in her own eyes, and compared to that sin any act of obedience and penance began to resemble unattainable mercy.

And this perhaps was Nikodim's gift: in his presence any transgression, however petty, was transformed into some kind of diabolic temple, enormous and utterly black, without windows, doors, candles or icon-lamps, into which you stepped like Jonah into the belly of the whale, and from which – this much was certain – nobody could emerge without his help. It wasn't even worth trying. And so, whenever she realised that it was all over for her, that she had perished, and not here and now on Earth, but for all eternity, there right on cue, was Nikodim, her last hope. No matter that he was stern with her and that his words were also stern and hard: he had come to help her, to stretch out a hand and save her, to drag her straight from the abyss.

BE AS CHILDREN

Meanwhile Nikodim would continue to explain – not that it entered her mind to contradict him – that for the Lord imagined sins were not a whit less loathsome than ordinary ones, and it was no use her thinking that some lascivious thought had gone away as fast as it had come; this was all sin, real, great sin, and unless it was redeemed through prayer, Dusya would burn in Hell. But how small her fear of God must have been at that time, for there were occasions when not even a week would pass before she was running to Nikodim once more, hoping yet again that today he would finally tell her: yes, you can remarry – I can't see anything wrong here, you weren't the worst wife, but your husband has been killed and no longer has any need of your marital fidelity. He is in Heaven now, next to the throne of the Lord, because he died for a just cause. You have in other words, fulfilled your duty towards him and you are free to do with yourself as you please.

Father Nikodim did not just punish, he also promised Dusya that by pledging her obedience, by renouncing her will without regret and submitting to her shepherd, she would see before her in broad daylight, the path to her salvation. Moreover, she would instantly feel an unheard-of, almost angelic lightness. About that, alas, he was mistaken: the path to the prize proved long and agonising for Dusya. As to why she experienced so much difficulty and distress on her way to God, Dusya would come to blame both herself and her teachers, each of whom had called and pulled her soul in his own direction. For almost five years, she had kept Amvrosy and Nikodim hidden from one another, kept them secret, an indubitable sin which she blamed on both men, who had undertaken to guide her without ever managing to reach an agreement among themselves, to decide once and for all whose she was.

Dusya was always desperately scared of the slightest disharmony, she knew that she must not under any circumstances become an apple of discord, like some Helen of Troy, but after spending almost two years in daily dialogue with Father Amvrosy, she came to realise, three months after his arrest, that she wouldn't manage to get by on her own. Father Amvrosy had done so much to raise and nurture her soul, brought it so much closer to God, that it seemed to Dusya now that without her teacher's help she would be sure to destroy it. To do something that could no longer be undone or redone, for which she would never be able to forgive herself. It wasn't that she could no longer catch up with her own soul, but it had of course gone much further along the path that led to the Lord and was directed much more intensely towards Him.

When he received his sentence, Amvrosy, thinking he would soon be back, did not let her go. During their brief meeting a day before his exile, he said that the chance to test herself would actually do her good, a chance to see whether she could walk at least part of the way to the Lord without a guide.

But either she was not yet strong enough or she was just constitutionally incapable of coping with this life on her own – the first seems to me more likely – but Dusya, with no one to watch over her, with no person to whom her every corner lay open, completely lost her way. She told us some time in the '60s, that when the news reached Gustinino that Father Amvrosy had been given a new term and would not be returning any time soon, she, all worn out with waiting, began to drift. Like a madwoman, she was hurled one way then the other, and she couldn't stop thinking of the Church, torn like her between different paths to salvation, unsure whom to obey, which way to go, whom to believe.

Many people told me that when Dusya talked about anything to do with faith, she struggled to separate herself from the world outside her. As if she was always no smaller than the biggest, no bigger than the smallest. I no longer remember who told me that this muddling of dimensions, this almost steppe-like absence of borders and barriers first appeared in her around 1919 and became ever more marked thereafter.

All this time Dusya floundered between Father Amvrosy and Nikodim, thrashed about as if in a cage, lied to them even during confession, before God. She had already promised herself and told each man that she was surrendering her soul precisely to him, that it was for him that she was renouncing a terrible burden – her own will. She could see no great sin here, after all, both the first and the second man had been given to her by the Lord to help her, it was to Him that they wished to lead her. But they were too different from one another, and the roads they were choosing for her differed just as starkly.

One of them spoke to her tenderly, sometimes even meekly. Told her that until her soul had been strengthened and hardened in the Lord's service, he was scared of frightening it or wounding it. The other considered her a great sinner in need of an iron fist, and repeated over and over that harsh penances and the kind of severity that chills the bones would only do her good: the more the better, or else she would perish.

Dusya understood how much it meant to each of them to have somebody whom, God willing, they could save. Whom they could take in a state of sin, wash clean and return to the

Lord as free of taint or blemish as any sacrificial animal. She was devastated by the thought that either of them could so much as think that she had betrayed him and left him. Much later, in our time, she recalled with deep horror what she went through when the Cheka arrested Amvrosy once more. She would say things – and not only when she got carried away – that were completely blasphemous, she would say, again and again, that she was a whore, a proper whore, a slut, even worse than a whore, because a whore traded her body – a piece of flesh – while she had passed her soul around left and right. Told us that she had begged the Virgin Mary day after day to help her, to show her the way.

My view now is that Dusya had good grounds to heap such abuse on herself. The Lord said more than once that He is a jealous God, and the Elders, as if following His example, were also exceptionally touchy. If they agreed out of necessity to entrust Dusya's soul to someone else, then only for a time and only after making it look as if they had been forced into it. Dusya sometimes had the impression that for them her soul was, as it were, not actually hers, that it was in their custody, that it had been pawned with them, that perhaps it was even a part of their own soul, and now they were having to tear out this living lump, put it in the rough hands of others, hands you wouldn't want to trust with a plate, never mind a soul. There was far more jealousy and suspicion here than in an ordinary human relationship, their ways were sterner, and like some partisan fighter she, frightened, hounded, loving each of them and desperately fearing for each of them, began hiding and keeping them secret from one another even during confession, before the Lord.

Be as Children

Everything had got mixed up in her: both the terror that they would reject her, that she would not be saved, and the fear of offending them, and she could not separate one from the other, even if she had wanted to. Not knowing what to do, Dusya started keeping quiet about whom she saw and when, whom she talked to and what they discussed. But the Elders had keen eyes and piercing minds, and when they caught her lying, they raged. She understood though, that Amvrosy and Nikodim were right – having assumed responsibility for her salvation, they could not watch on calmly as their spiritual daughter destroyed herself. And so however harsh the penances they imposed on her, she accepted them meekly.

When Dusya first asked Father Nikodim to be her constant helper, he demanded from her a full and written confession, from the age of six onwards. She found it unpleasant and shameful to take up this task, she'd already forgotten a great deal and had no wish to recall it. But Nikodim said such repentance was essential, he had to know everything about Dusya or else there was no point. She hesitated for a few days, then agreed – she couldn't see any other way out.

After that diary he never refused to see her and confess her whenever she was in need, usually not in church though, but simply during a walk. He was especially fond of the high bank of the Velikaya and the path that led through the woods from Gustinino to the neighbouring village of Strunniki.

Mortally afraid of leaving something out and thus depriving herself of true absolution, Dusya spent these confessions in a state of desperate anxiety and confusion, which resulted, however absurd this might seem, in anger. Still it wasn't long before she could rely not just on her crib notes but on a whole set of techniques by which to structure her confessions: first her big sins, then the small ones, subject by subject, in alphabetical order. But it wasn't the most reliable of systems and in all her years under Nikodim, not one confession came easily to her. Incidentally, it was then, according to Dusya, that she got into the habit not only of seeking permission for every thought, but of carefully choosing her every step in life, her every word, of only doing things that she would not be ashamed to tell Father Nikodim about later. But even then, until she had told the monk every last thing down to the smallest detail, until she had seen, heard and felt whatever had happened to her with his eyes, ears, touch, and above all, until she had found out whether it was a sin or it wasn't, and if it was, whether it was pardonable, a sin that could be remitted and atoned through penance, or whether it was mortal – until then she was completely helpless.

Without her almost daily confessions, without her fear, that monstrous fear – would she be absolved or wouldn't she? – without God, who was always right there but, so to speak, in the shadows, behind the monk, everything became tasteless to her, incomplete, unfinished. Life itself began to seem unmoulded, mere possibility, and it was only now that it gained flavour and colour, became faceted and shaped. However blasphemous the comparison, the difference between one and the other was no less than between her girlhood daydreams about men, which were almost continuous – she was nothing if not passionate – and those same dreams once she had become a woman. Hence her dependence on Nikodim, which over those three years that Amvrosy spent behind bars and in exile, turned into a complete inability to get by without him.

Be as Children

She was, by the way, fully aware of how wrong so much of this was, she had had her share of holy men in her life intelligent enough to warn her and even attempt to stop her. And it wasn't just that Dusya now thought that real life began only with confession, when she revealed herself and all that was inside her to the Lord, that it was precisely the smallest sin that could prove the most terrible, the one that would bring eternal torments, but if you could only dig it out of yourself and repent, forgiveness and grace would follow. Rather it seems that for as long as she was still experiencing something she wasn't able to make the slightest sense of it. Events flowed far too quickly, and like a negligent schoolgirl, she needed to repeat and carefully pick apart everything she had already been through.

She discovered quite quickly that she could tell Nikodim things that she would never have dared tell her closest friend. And he didn't just listen and nod: nowhere could she have found a more interested audience, more attentive and devoted. Nikodim really was the confidant, the person closer to her than any child, husband or mother, for whom she had begged the Lord for as long as she could remember and for whom she had long given up hope. And now he had been given to her, just like that.

Her spiritual father filled her life with meaning, according it a significance she had never even dreamed about. The fact that she was his only novice, and above all, the candour with which she was supposed to speak about herself gave a peculiar character to their relationship. He knew so much about her, surely even more than she knew herself, that there were times when Dusya was unable to grasp where she ended and Nikodim began. Her confessions had erased the border between them, as if it had extended and expanded towards him, which was why she felt calm and assured. Over three years such relations began to feel natural to her, almost habitual. And when she defended Nikodim to Father Amvrosy, she said exactly that.

But she told us other things too. Remembering how she would confess to Nikodim, she might say that she often had the impression that Nikodim was simply interrogating her. That the questions were chosen not to absolve her sins, nor to make her repent, but to better understand sin as such – what was its nature, its appeal, and why did people turn away from God for its sake? And when at the end of the confession Nikodim kissed her with cold monastic exultation, she understood that he was grateful to her for the experience and her candour. She said some other, even scarier things. Such as that for Nikodim, who had never been with a woman, her confessions were a chance to be alone with one. For this Dusya hated both him and herself; she would never forgive the fact that she had led him into sin and temptation. Further, that they would maul each other for hours on end and it needed the Lord to take pity on them in their complete exhaustion and separate them. Nikodim would absolve her of her sins, and she would leave.

***

In '24, when Amvrosy returned from his third term of exile (he served it in Kem, on the White Sea), he had a long talk with Dusya about Nikodim. Amvrosy was haggard, frail, and worn out from the journey, and as a result there was something hazy and blurred about their conversation – such at least, was the impression it left on Dusya. She'd already written to him in Kem about Nikodim, about her intention to pledge her obedience to him, but Amvrosy had let her know through a mutual acquaintance, that without first seeing her, without talking it over with her face to face, he couldn't give her his verdict. While he was still away from Moscow, she could leave things as they were; she would receive his definitive answer whenever God saw fit to let him return to the old capital.

The lack of certainty was excruciating. Try as she might to drive away such thoughts, Dusya knew, even while praying alone in her room, that where Nikodim would impose a new penance, Amvrosy would comfort her and gladly show leniency. She never forgot this for a moment, which was why, not knowing whom she should obey or whose she was, she suffered so intensely. When the message reached her from Amvrosy, a month before the end of his sentence, that he would be unlikely to be freed – either his exile would be extended or he would be sent to prison – she got herself ready to travel to Kem to talk it through with him and even bought herself a ticket as far as Arkhangelsk. But she was stopped in her tracks by a telegram from Amvrosy himself: he wrote that the camp boss had just spoken to him and confirmed that he would be released at the end of his term and not a day later. There would be no restrictions either – he could go straight to Moscow if he wanted to.

After meeting Amvrosy at Yaroslavsky station, Dusya brought him to an old friend of hers, a reliable and devoted woman who happened to have a free room. It wasn't a fasting day and her friend had spared no effort for the occasion – there was a carafe of vodka on the table, various hors d'oeuvres, and pies she had baked herself. But Amvrosy, citing tiredness, didn't touch a thing; he just had a few cups of tea and said he was turning in. Dusya came back the next morning. He was pleased to see her and generally looked much brighter, but he didn't want to talk things over in the flat so they walked to Petrovsky Boulevard, found an empty bench opposite the Vysoko-Petrovsky Monastery and sat down.

Nikodim had recently been transferred to the monastery, and it was there that Dusya came to confess to him. She had written to Amvrosy about this, and as they turned into the boulevard, she was scared that he might be taking her to see him. But now, on the bench, she calmed down and started telling him about the most recent developments in the Church. He knew much of it already, but he listened attentively, even stopping her occasionally to check something.

It was only mid-May but it was already hot, and though they were sitting in the shade of a big, ancient lime tree, the sun was beating down on them through the scanty leaves. But Amvrosy, who had been starved of sun and warmth for so long, had no wish to leave this spot. He liked everything about it: the throng of people, the frequent screech and scrape of trams coming down the hill, the clatter of cartwheels on the cobbles, the sharp klaxon of the occasional automobile. The bustle and muddle of the street was a joy and comfort to him after the camp. He was gentle with her too: he didn't blame or reproach her for anything, said that he understood very well that prison and exile hadn't given him the chance to tend properly to her soul, then immediately added that he would need some time: handing her over to the care of Father Nikodim, a man Amvrosy had only ever spoken to once and whom he knew nothing or almost nothing about, was something he wasn't yet ready to do.

Dusya had heard about that one meeting. They had been introduced to each other six years earlier at the Trinity-Sergius Monastery at the funeral of Father Simeon, Metropolitan of St Petersburg and Ladoga. Amvrosy had taken a dislike to Nikodim, finding him hard-edged and haughty. 'Of course,' Amvrosy continued, 'your confessor came up often in the letters you wrote to me when I was in the camp, but the written word is one thing, the spoken another. In short, it would be a great help to me if you could give me a full, detailed account of all you think about Father Nikodim. I'm particularly interested in how he confesses you and the kind of person he is in general. And please, don't be surprised by my request – this is extremely important both for me and for you.'

The conversation up to this point had been an uncomfortable one; they were no longer used to each other and it was an effort to recover the habit now, to reattune themselves. But during the two minutes or so that Dusya spent choosing the words to speak about Nikodim, going over what she would say and what she would try to leave out, Amvrosy wilted. Perhaps he had already resigned himself to the fact that Dusya would leave him one day and this whole conversation, which he himself had initiated, was a mere formality, or perhaps he was just tired. He sat with his eyes closed for a quarter of an hour or so – Dusya even thought he'd fallen asleep – but then with eyelids still lowered, he began saying all over again, just as listlessly, that he needed to understand whether it really was the case that she wanted to stay with Nikodim – wasn't he too strict? – and as if forgetting his own question, began explaining that to be an Elder you have to know life as it really is. Otherwise you yourself, being as weak and fragile as any child, will make strictness your crutch.

Before withdrawing to a monastery, he said, almost all Elders had lived a full, long life in the world. They had been soldiers, which meant they had killed, fallen in love, got married, had children, and only then had they shut themselves away in their cells. That was why they could understand people and help them. But what could Father Nikodim know, a man who had taken his vows when he was all of eighteen years old?

Evidently these arguments had little effect on Dusya, and Amvrosy went back to the topic of confession and asked what kind of questions Father Nikodim would put to her. Dusya: 'A lot about lust, but actually he asks about everything. Insists I leave nothing out, because Your Grace, sin is everywhere: in deed and thought.' Amvrosy: 'And you don't hide anything from him?' She: 'No, Your Grace, I tell Father Nikodim about all my sins during confession, down to the smallest detail, especially anything to do with lust. Otherwise, he says, I can't be saved. Because until you have put what you've done into words before the Lord, until you feel horrified by your own self, you will keep on sinning. And it's true Your Grace' – Dusya was doing her best to rouse Amvrosy – 'that there are times when I drop my guard, when desire stirs in me again, as if my husband were right beside me. It comes then it goes, but the minute I start talking about it during confession with Father Nikodim my sin becomes bigger and bigger and then it's as if it's not me standing there in the church but the Devil incarnate. Anyone would start shaking.' Amvrosy: 'And you've never wondered why he, a monk, is so interested in such things?'

Be as Children

She: 'Of course I have. At first I even feared – just like you Your Grace – that the questions he was asking did not come from God to seek out my sins, but because he took his vows when he was little more than a boy and now he himself was being lured and tempted by lust. I was terrified that I might lead him into sin.' Amvrosy: 'But you still answered.' She: 'I did, although it was hard at first, unpleasant, like getting undressed before a stranger. But now I probably wouldn't be able to confess any other way. Life – what I've done, what I've thought – just slips away as if it had never been, like water into sand. Don't you think Your Grace, that this shows immense disrespect to the Lord, to all Creation? And now, when I know that Father Nikodim will ask me for every last item, that he won't forget a thing, I, like some Plyushkin,[48] make sure that nothing goes to waste. I keep the most detailed diary, write crib notes as if I'm back in the gymnasium, and at the end of it all I see that I'm more than some tiny insect to be crushed and ignored: in my life everything is from God, or if I've sinned, against God. And in order that I be free of sin and be saved, Father Nikodim will stop at nothing.'

There was of course a great deal that Dusya kept silent about back then on the boulevard, but still, as she finished speaking, she was clearly expecting Amvrosy to approve of the way she had conducted herself. Hard as it had been for her, she had stuck at it, obeyed all the Elder's instructions, responsibility for which was borne by he who had given them. Even better if Amvrosy were to add, that having been Dusya's spiritual father since she was twenty-two, he was now handing

---

[48] The miserly landowner to whom Nikolai Gogol devotes a central chapter of *Dead Souls* (1842).

her over to Father Nikodim. But Amvrosy merely repeated that in the current circumstances, while he was still unable to tend to her properly, Dusya was not forbidden from availing herself of Father Nikodim's guidance. But he wasn't prepared to give her up completely, nor did he think it correct to do so.

'In the first place,' Amvrosy went on, 'because I can't understand why he is so severe. Father Nikodim doesn't sense that people have different natures, different characters – he treats everyone alike. Doesn't see that his pressure might end up breaking you.' Still, Amvrosy finished on an unexpectedly conciliatory note, saying, 'Well, all right, if you want to go to Father Nikodim, go, it's not the end of the world. But if it gets too much, know that I am releasing you from the vow you gave him. The same goes for his rules: if they are too much for you, you don't have to follow them.' Amvrosy didn't ask her about anything else. They sat for a little while longer on the bench before slowly making their way home.

That time round, Amvrosy spent a little under nine months at liberty. Then he was rearrested and died in prison in Vladimir in the winter of '27. But while he was still in Moscow, right up until the following spring, Dusya alternated between him and Nikodim. Cutting ties was something she had always found hard, ever since childhood, and now too she just couldn't make up her mind one way or the other. In November she wrote a letter to Optina Pustyn, to her first Elder, Father Pimen, whom she hadn't seen for almost five years, and begged him to help her, but she received no reply. A month later she sent a second, even more desperate letter. No sooner had she done so than she set off for Optina herself, right before Christmas.

Be as Children

Little was left of the former hermitage. A year had already passed since the monastery was plundered and closed, and the brethren had scattered far and wide, but the most elderly and infirm of the monks, including, she was told, Pimen, were still living in the surrounding villages, renting little bathhouses or rooms, or just a bed in a corner. At the Optina market, she quickly found out that she should look for Pimen in Onufriyevka, a large village seven versts away, on the road to Tula. He was living there with his old cell attendant, Anfinogen, also an Elder. But there was little chance he could help her: he was too sick and Anfinogen wasn't letting anyone visit him. But Dusya paid no attention. Walking round the market she found a peasant from Onufriyevka in the meat row, and he agreed to take her there for a rouble. The peasant, it must be said, also tried to talk Dusya out of it, saying that much as he respected the old man, Pimen was now little more than a child and couldn't even pray properly.

The journey through deep snow to Onufriyevka took a very long time and they arrived in the village when it was already dark. The peasant drove her right up to the homestead of the landlord who was renting out a bathhouse to Pimen and Anfinogen. She asked him if he could put her up and he took her in for nothing, out of Christian charity. But here too the news was all bad: the landlord told her that it had already been two years since the Elder had fallen back into infancy and confirmed that his cell attendant wasn't allowing any visits. If it was a simple question, Anfinogen would answer it himself, but if anyone started begging to see Pimen, he would curse them and kick them out. Dusya understood that the landlord was telling the truth, but for some reason she didn't lose heart.

The next morning she walked down the path that cut across the snow-covered kitchen garden and began knocking on the door of the bathhouse, first just with her hand, then harder, with a stick she'd picked up from the ground. But nobody opened, so she sat down on a step and decided not to go anywhere until they did. There were signs of life – someone was walking around inside and groaning, and you could even hear a tinkling from the washstand. At times Dusya had the impression that somebody was spying on her through the sooty window.

Eventually though, she managed to wear Anfinogen down, the bolt slid away and she was let into a small, square inner porch. The attendant wasn't cross with her for pestering them, in fact he went out of his way to say that he remembered Dusya very well and understood that this was about something important, but here was the problem: Pimen was very frail and didn't wish to see anybody. He, Anfinogen, couldn't think of any way of helping her. A gold coin though, was enough to change all that. He said that the next day was Christmas Eve and Pimen usually felt better on feast days, not that there was really much difference. So she could come tomorrow if she was so keen, but nice and early at first light, and if it didn't go well she shouldn't take it amiss or ask for her money back. Firewood, bread and potatoes were expensive, and it wasn't easy for the two of them. There were days when they had nothing to light the stove with.

What Dusya saw the following day differed little from what she had heard from the sledge-driver and the landlord. Pimen was sitting at the table in a faded, patched-up cassock. Old, decrepit and with a long matted beard, he was picking over little woodchips, sticks and scraps of fabric, in fact there was a whole mound of this stuff in front of him. Dusya thought he was using the rubbish and rags in place of a rosary, until she worked out that Pimen was trying to construct a kind of toy manger for the Saviour. But his fingers were stiff, his hands trembled, and he was getting nowhere. He'd place one chip of wood on top of another, reach for the next and then ruin it all with a swipe of his arm. She was sitting opposite him, waiting to see if he would raise his head and recognise her, and then she would tell him why she had come.

Pimen worked away in silence, and she didn't say anything either, she just prayed and asked the Lord to help him. Told Him that Pimen, after all, was not building a shelter for himself, but for the Virgin Mary and her Son. Maybe the Lord really did hear her, or maybe the Elder's luck had turned at long last, but Pimen suddenly managed to put the last two bits of wood in place and cover them with a piece of fabric, like a tent.

Dusya knew that Pimen had been a famous Moscow architect before his tonsure, and now as he completed his structure, he gave the same gentle smile she remembered from their meetings – first to his cell attendant, then to her. Realising that the moment had come to earn his gold coin, Anfinogen started telling him that you see, Father, your spiritual daughter Dusya has come to visit, she is begging you to intercede for her, to help her, I mean. She's having a hard time of it, she can't take any more. Like a matchmaker, he egged Dusya on too: go on, tell him, tell him why you're here, he might be able to do something, might even ask the Lord, and the Lord won't say no. Think how much money it's cost you. You'll be telling people that you were keeping it for a rainy day, then I turned up and licked it off like a cow with its long tongue. But Dusya wasn't sorry about the gold coin, she was gazing at the smiling Pimen and felt happy and calm.

In the end though, Anfinogen won out, and Dusya started talking about Nikodim. She began by saying that when after her first confession, he had recited the prayer of absolution, the relief she had felt with him was greater than with her other confessors. Then, following no particular order, she described Nikodim's view of how necessary the persecutions were for the Church, otherwise the Augean Stables would never be cleaned. Of how the Revolution had raised the bar as it were, by making the past with all its quarrels, resentments and betrayals, seem petty and trivial. She'd become so confused, she said, that she had even stopped going to church or letting her children go, but he brought her back into the fold, explaining that the trials and tribulations that the Church undergoes are of two kinds: *akribeia* – the rejection of all compromise, and therefore the voluntary acceptance of the martyr's cross, and *oikonomia* – adaptation to circumstance, another form of martyrdom but with a different cross: abuse, incomprehension, mockery, humiliation. Both sets of fetters serve one and the same aim: the salvation of the flock which has been left without its shepherd, Jesus Christ.

She said that throughout this time there had only ever been one sin which Nikodim, stern as he always was with her, had refused to absolve. Once, getting very angry with her eldest son, she had snapped, 'The Devil take you, for all I care – I've had it up to here with you today!' When he learned about this, Nikodim said that no penance could atone for this sin; if there was any salvation for her, it was only through the prayers of the child she had cursed. She also spoke about Amvrosy. Explained that it was only when he came back from the camp that she had realised how hard it was to cope with Nikodim's severity and how badly she had missed Amvrosy's gentleness and tenderness, before adding that Amvrosy could be arrested any day and she wouldn't survive without someone to guide her. So now she didn't know whom to stay with. Then she repeated yet again that she no longer had the strength to keep running from one to the other.

She spoke and spoke, and the Elder kept smiling and looking at her, smiling and looking. Every now and again he would even start babbling away to himself like an infant. She carried on confessing to Pimen until late in the evening, then she went back to the *izba* and straight to bed. She had made arrangements the previous day for the same peasant to take her back to Optina the following morning. It was easier to reach Kaluga from there, then on to Moscow by train. When the sledge was already at the gates and she was on the porch saying goodbye to the landlord, Anfinogen came up and pressed into her hand a little icon wrapped in paper, adding that it came from Pimen. Anfinogen had written some words on both sides of the paper, but it wasn't until she was on the train that she managed to decipher them.

On one side it said that the previous day Pimen had spent a long time praying. He had entrusted her to Our Lady in Heaven, so she need not fear. He had also prayed to Our Lord Jesus Christ with the request, 'Send my child Yevdokiya an Elder after her heart', and was sure that Christ would not abandon her. As for Amvrosy and Nikodim, he had instructed

Anfinogen to tell her: to each his own. He himself, Pimen, had once stood for strictness, though only moderate strictness, but the main thing now was the fact that without a guide she would not be saved. And again, coming back to Nikodim: this monk just didn't know whether she was his or someone else's spiritual daughter, hence his insecurity, his excessive harshness. But Nikodim's severity was merely external – beneath it lay an immense desire to save her. On the other side, Anfinogen had added a note of his own to say that he had been living under one roof with Pimen for thirty years now and knew what the Elder was talking about. She should have no doubts: this was precisely what Pimen had been trying to say as he babbled away during her visit. These were in any case good words to take away with her, and Dusya drew comfort from them as she arrived back in Moscow.

In December 1920 – by then they were living partly in Gustinino, partly in Moscow – Dusya's beloved brother Pasha, an exceptionally pure and ardent man, decided he should go to Siberia to begin the task of assembling a militia of Christian crusaders. It was the only way he believed, of saving both Russia and Orthodoxy. The fate of the Church worried him terribly. It was enough for someone to mention it and he would begin quickly pacing the room; the nervous twitch in his shoulder which had first appeared in childhood, would get worse, his face would turn pale, and by the time he spoke he would be virtually in tears. But the fit of anguish and anxiety would soon pass and he would fall back into that light, exuberant mood of which his family was so fond.

Their mother was desperately scared of Pasha leaving,

she was convinced she would never see him alive again, and in her attempts to stop him, managed to talk him into going to see Father Amvrosy with Dusya. Amvrosy, predictably enough, was none too pleased by the idea. After coolly hearing Pasha out, he said that the demon he wished to fight could be banished only through prayer and fasting, never brute force, and considered the matter closed.

A month after this conversation with the Elder, Pasha did nevertheless leave, and shortly afterwards Amvrosy was arrested once more. Then six months later, Dusya lost yet another of the people closest to her. A young novice from the Vysoko-Petrovsky Monastery came to their house to tell them that due to a combination of circumstances, Nikodim had had to leave Moscow in a hurry the day before. It seems unlikely though, that these three events were in any way linked.

Short letters from Pasha, usually brought back by acquaintances, occasionally by post, continued to arrive from various Siberian towns for about half a year, then he went quiet. Their mother kept waiting for these letters, pretending that nothing terrible was going on, that everything was fine, but one day something inside her seemed to snap and she began visibly losing her mind. Not knowing how to support her, Dusya decided to go to Siberia herself, to try to find her brother.

As for Nikodim, in February '22 he bumped into her on a street in Khabarovsk,[49] and that chance encounter undoubtedly

---

[49] A large industrial city and port in the Russian Far East, founded on the Amur River in the eighth century but coming under Russian rule in the mid-nineteenth century, when it was fortified to defend the Russian-Chinese border.

saved Dusya's life.

Bringing her into his room, Nikodim embraced her joyfully, almost jubilantly, kissed her on her forehead and immediately began retrieving heaps of cut-up paper from the pockets of his coat. Scrunching them up so as to grab more each time, he pulled them out by the handful and stuffed them into a soldier's knapsack lying right there on the table. Eventually the supplies must have run out as his pockets emptied, but the knapsack, which had become a kind of way station, was bulging. Nikodim now started fishing out the paper from there but without the same haste. He carefully uncreased the scraps one by one then laid them out in rows on the dining-table, as if serving them to guests. Calmly, pensively, he picked a place for each of them, constantly straightening and adjusting the rows as he did so.

It was warm here, Dusya felt cosy, and leaning back against the headboard of the bed, dozed off. She didn't sleep long, probably no more than an hour, and when she woke, Nikodim was still performing his sacred ritual. She repeated this ironic phrase to herself a few times and was about to close her eyes once more when he suddenly exclaimed, as if from the pulpit, 'Read, Yevdokiya!' In her surprise she couldn't think what to say and asked, 'Aloud, Father Nikodim?' 'Aloud,' he confirmed.

Each bit of paper contained a children's counting rhyme. Dusya knew Father Nikodim's handwriting, she could even understand his shorthand, but she felt unsure of herself now as she began to read. This particular instruction seemed far too strange. She diligently read out each word in turn, but she was thinking about the starving cold town which the Whites had left three days before, about the brother she hadn't found, about not having had a crumb of bread in her mouth for twenty-four hours. She remembered walking down a snowbound street, her legs frozen so stiff that she couldn't even feel them, she could only move them around like crutches. That morning she had wept till dawn in the flower shop, sat on a box filled with earth and howled, because even in the shop there was nobody left to help her. The owner, a friend from the gymnasium, had fled during the night with the last White troops.

Dusya could also remember what happened next, but less clearly. She seemed to be making her way out through the back door, trudging along a path trampled down between snowdrifts. The road leads downhill and there are moments when Dusya's legs seem to be carrying her by themselves, but whenever the snow has been trodden to ice, she falls, and even if she makes a soft landing in the snow, it's a long time before she gets back up. She just lies there, and as in the shop, weeps with pity for herself.

The path brings her out to a dark broad river which even though it's February, has not yet frozen over and steams in the frost, like a bathhouse. The trembling woolly mist makes her think it must be warmer there and she slides down on her bottom to the sandy shore. But it's very windy by the water and even colder. Dusya raises her arms to shield her face, but she can't keep them hanging there for long and lowers them submissively. It's already getting dark when she leaves the river and starts wandering aimlessly down narrow little streets. Not many houses, just lumber yards on both sides, one after the other, their gates lying open or knocked off their hinges. She has never set foot in this part of town before, but it makes no difference – she's got nowhere to go.

It's quiet here among the warehouses and that must be why she hears familiar voices, Moscow voices. Looking for them, she turns right at the corner, right again, left, but finds nobody. Many voices, different voices, but one is more frequent than the rest. Sometimes it's ahead of her, behind her and off to the side all at once. The voice is hurrying her, calling her, crying out to her, it's all around her, but Dusya doesn't even try to make out what it is that it wants from her. Eventually she tires of this hide-and-seek, leans against a fence and slides down into the snow.

The flower shop, the river, the moment she had found herself outside the *izba* where Father Nikodim had been renting a room for a year already and where he bumped into Dusya by the gate when returning home – Dusya went back over all this in her mind, just to be sure, then she added the counting rhymes which she was reading aloud right now, one after the other. It was all sheer madness of course, but it was only there in madness, that there was life: everywhere else there was only cold.

She has no fight left in her, she has suddenly understood that she is accepting this, acknowledging it, that she will go on accepting it, on and on until the very end, until the instant when somebody closes her eyes. And now she feels within herself, for the first time, the humility that Father Nikodim has demanded of her ever since she pledged her obedience to him. It's warm all around and she knows that with Nikodim she has no need to fear anything, to go anywhere, to search for anybody without his help. She feels calm but she is counting ever more loudly, with ever more zeal, even chanting some of the lines. In fact it feels fun, like in childhood. She tells herself happily that soon they'll start playing, otherwise what's the point of counting.

'You see, Yevdokiya,' Father Nikodim says when she reaches the final row, 'I've worked out that almost one in five counting rhymes must come from Aramaic and Hebrew prayers. Do you have any idea what that means?' Dusya shakes her head. 'It means,' Nikodim solemnly repeats, 'that from the time of Sinai to our own day the rhymes before you have retained without a single interruption their devotional character. In other words, you are not reading but praying. Take for example, one of the most ordinary of them – you must have also counted with it once:

Ene bene res,
Kventer menter zhes,
Ene bene rabo
Kventer menter zhaba.

Ene (from the Aramaic – *ano, Ani*) – I; *ben* – a son; *res* (*airaiso*) – the Five Books of Moses, the Torah; *kventer* (*k ven toir*) – a son of his times; *menter* (*mentar*) – have mercy; *zhes* (*es*) – me; *rabo* – God; *zhaba* (*abo*) – father. In a free translation: "I am the son of the Law and the son of my times. Have mercy on me, oh Lord my Father".

Or:

Ene bene
Torba sorba
Entse zvaka
Teus eus
Kosmateus.

I've already explained *ene* and *bene*; *torba* (*toir bo*) – the present time; *sorba* – I resist, struggle, try not to give in; *entse zvaka* (*noits z oko*) – vulgarity; *teus* (*tous*) – mistake; *kosmateus* (*kesem*) – mirage, fancy, mist. In translation: "I, a son of my times, try not to surrender to the vulgarity and lies that surround me, not to be distracted by flights of fancy and illusions". We adults, like Noah's descendants, have retreated from God, become pagans and idolaters once more, but the children, saving the world, prayed for both themselves and us. The Lord grew to love them so dearly precisely because, in their fear of sin, they cleansed themselves through prayer of every kind of filth, day in, day out.

'There's one other thing,' Nikodim continued. 'Remember how vehemently the Renovationists curse us for using Old Church Slavonic, saying the parishioners don't understand the Divine Liturgy. I, too, wavered for a year, thinking that perhaps they were right. But the counting rhymes took away all my doubts. The point is that the Lord cannot be reached by reason and all our intellectualising is hollow and superfluous – it can't satisfy or save a single person. In their counting rhymes children treat rationalism in just the same way.

'Seen through somebody else's eyes, from the outside, the words of the ditties have not the slightest meaning, only the tension and the music of the sounds themselves, but it's what stands behind this tension that matters – the Lord, to whom you are speaking. And also: by simultaneously counting and praying, the children whom we are so used to criticising for their wilfulness and disobedience are actually saying one and the same thing with their every syllable: "All is in God's hands – the seeker will be the person on whom the lot falls". There are no calculations here, no tricks, no lies – nothing except trust in Divine Providence.

'I know what you're going to say,' Nikodim went on. 'Are children really praying and speaking to God when they're playing games? But that's the whole point: by joyfully and merrily repeating the words of the counting rhyme line by line, in chorus, they are praying with all the simplicity of their hearts. Everything they do, they do simply – whether sinning or following God. Children are the true poor in spirit. And that's why the Lord says they are blessed. Says to each of us: unless you accept the Saviour as a child, unless you humble yourself and become as they are, you shall not enter the Kingdom of Heaven.'

Nikodim went on about children and counting rhymes for a long time, but when he saw that Dusya was no longer following, he took out some bread and lard, heated up some tea on the paraffin stove, and began feeding her. As she ate, he told her that the room was at her disposal for both that night and the entire month ahead. No need for her to worry about him – there was another home where he would be made very welcome.

Towards evening the following day, he appeared again with a large, round white loaf and a bag of potatoes, and after dinner, once she had made an entire cauldron of tea and poured some out, he started telling Dusya about a very important task he wanted to set her – to start collecting counting rhymes in Khabarovsk.

He was speaking with her as he used to in Moscow, when she would come to see him almost every day, when she was his true spiritual daughter, because whatever she might be doing, he was always in her mind. But then he had left: he had snapped the bond between them just like that, without a word of warning, and a whole year had passed without so much as a line from him. She understood, given the general circumstances, that there must have been serious reasons for him to take such a step, she was in no doubt about that, but it still seemed wrong for him to have abandoned her as he did.

She wasn't about to say any of this to Nikodim of course, but nor was she prepared to go back all at once to the way things had been between them. She hazily recalled that the previous day she had even taken him for her guardian angel, and she had not forgotten the delight she had experienced on catching sight of his figure through the dusk and the cold, his face bent over her. Dusya felt an immense gratitude for the warmth, the food, the room, which was why, as she prepared to refuse Nikodim's request, she spoke confusedly and guiltily, finding one excuse after another for almost half an hour, explaining that if she could be of any use to him, she would gladly do whatever he wanted, but she had come all the way to Khabarovsk from Moscow for one reason only: to find some trace, however faint, of her brother. And if she couldn't find anything here, she'd go on to Kharbin, Vladivostok, after all it was simply impossible that no one had seen him or heard anything about him.

The moment Nikodim realised that today he wouldn't get what he wanted from her, he abruptly changed the subject and began recalling how in 1915 he had intended to serve as a military priest at the front and still regretted not going. At war people quickly grow wild, especially without God, without words of loving kindness and support, and all the things they go on to do later, when the war is over, are its continuation, its trace. A bit like phantom pains: the wound on the body has healed, but the soul remains crippled.

Then out of nowhere, he began praising contemporary literature. By his account there were plenty of new names, and people were writing more simply now, without the preciousness of the recent past. He had two books with him, including a certain Shklovsky's reminiscences of the Caucasian Front,[50] and said he was leaving her both of them. Dusya hadn't read anything secular for a long time, but this was special – the Caucasian Front was where her husband Pyotr Igrenyev had died, but despite repeated efforts it had proved impossible to find out where or when. Not that she was expecting to read about him here – her husband had been just an ordinary, entirely unexceptional artillery captain, one of the 300,000 strong army that was trying to reach Baghdad from the east, without entering Turkey. Seemed unlikely that anyone would have remembered him. Even so, any eye-witness accounts of the people he fought alongside, of the land in which in all probability he now lay, were also important to her.

It was already evening by the time Nikodim went. Left alone, her first thought was that she wouldn't read Shklovsky that night – she would say her prayers and go to bed. But she couldn't fall asleep. She tossed and turned for an hour, then lit her lamp once more. Sticking out of the Shklovsky book, some forty pages before the end, was a beautiful embossed leather bookmark – she'd been given a dozen such bookmarks by Masha a couple of years before the war. The summer of 1912 had been a good, kind time for the pair of them, and now

---

[50] Contained in Victor Shklovsky's *A Sentimental Journey* (1923).

she couldn't resist and opened the book a few pages before the mark. She wanted to do what she'd always done as a child: flick through and see what it was all about before reading properly.

Opening the book at random, she immediately found a fairy tale she enjoyed about a devil who rejuvenates a woman by first burning her and then restoring her from her ashes, with a comment about the Bolsheviks, who had burned everything down in just the same way and now had no choice but to continue putting their faith in a miracle. Next came the last months of the war. Strictly speaking, the war was in fact already over. The soviets that had been formed in St Petersburg and Moscow almost six months before had announced the end of the Great War, peace without annexations or indemnities, but as ever this news took a long time to reach Northern Mesopotamia from the capital. When it eventually did, the army left its positions like a hen from its perch, abandoned its trenches, and started moving back along the same route by which it had come.

Though the route was familiar and the soldiers were ready to walk twenty-four hours a day if it meant reaching Russia any sooner, the divisions moved slowly, in endless crush and confusion. Shedding men and equipment as they went, and having first eaten the horses, abandoning their artillery – sometimes whole batteries at a time, along with ammunition and carts – they were leaving this alien, monstrously hot country in the belief that the war really was over. They walked along tangled paths that clung to rocks above a precipice and were for some reason called roads, crossed one mountain range after another, and were already forgetting, and could no longer begin to understand, why they had been sent and what it was all for.

Sometimes they would come out and say this, and Shklovsky quotes them time and again, but the soldiers' comments seemed unimportant to Dusya, because the army's current movements did after all have an obvious purpose. And since all was now going as it should – the soldiers were heading home – she read an entire chapter without fear and even with relish. She only became frightened, for no obvious reason, when the soldiers – tattered, drunk and in complete disarray – emerged onto the banks of a border river, the Araks, and began crossing the bridge.

It was a clear, mild spring day. The river was very full from the snow melting on the mountains, and the famished infantrymen were stunning fish with dynamite. Many of them were already on our side of the Araks. The road along the river terrace was so much broader there, not to mention the single-track railway line running along the rock face right beside it and overflowing with locomotives and wagons. Essentially, this was the first page without any fighting that she had read in the entire book so far, and for precisely this reason, because this page was so unlike the others, she immediately sensed danger.

Still not knowing what to fear or where, Dusya suddenly began to guess that Shklovsky, or Father Nikodim, or the two of them together had set a trap for her, cast a hook with some bait on it, luring her to turn the page. Dusya would remember to the end of her days how much she had wanted to close the book at that point and never read another page of it again. She usually trusted herself in such cases, but this time she couldn't resist. What followed, just a paragraph later, was addressed directly to her.

Two soldiers knee-deep in water, wearing burnouses stuffed with sticks of dynamite, are stunning fish. Looking for the most promising holes, they climb higher and higher upstream. There's plenty of beautiful trout glittering in the sunlight, and their comrades are laughing gaily as they gather their catch. They make their way unhurriedly over the pebbles close to the shoreline, but on the other side of a tall promontory the valley claps shut all at once and the river, turning sharply, now hugs the road. The railway embankment, which has been skirting the far edge of the fields and villages, is now squeezed by the mountains and almost suspended over the river. The Araks has become deeper, the water still foaming only over the shallows.

After lighting the fuse, the soldiers throw another bundle of dynamite into the river. They're using a long cord as a precaution and wait almost a minute until they hear a brief explosion, muffled by water, after which silence sets in once more. No different it seems from the previous time, except that now instead of silence the explosion is followed – not just where they're standing, but all around them – by a kind of frenzied cannonade. Those who've managed to drop to the ground in time press themselves by force of habit into the earth, into the shallow water between the rocks, while artillery shells keep bursting one after the other, as they would during a general offensive. When the firing eventually subsides, they wait a long time just to be sure; only then do the survivors of this inferno begin to get to their feet. Stunned, concussed, still incapable of understanding what's happened, they look at the mangled rails, at the wreckage of the wagons carrying the shells detonated by the dynamite sticks, and at what remains of the large composite battalion, which during the blast fishing, had been marching alongside the railway tracks and had now fallen, almost to a man.

In essence, Shklovsky was describing an ordinary scene of war, with a lull between battles, a pause granted in order that people can collect and bury the dead. Without exchanging a word, the unmaimed drag the wounded to the roadside, in the shade of the rock face, and then working industriously and diligently, as if they were picking cucumbers on a vegetable patch, they set about gathering the ripped-off arms, legs and heads scattered all around in a half-kilometre radius. They find them in the ditches by the road and among the shrubs, pull them out of the water together with fish floating belly-up and carry them unhurriedly to the road, where their comrades, working as tidily as the battalion had been marching, are laying out crippled bodies.

In order to bury so much human flesh, they now have to dig a common grave, and three of the soldiers seek a spot for it by testing the ground with their shovels. It's not all stone, thank God – there's bits of earth here and there, and sand and loam carried over by the river. The most convenient plot is right under the rock face, just a short distance from the wounded, and there, after sketching out the pit they start digging. A soldier's entrenching tool is quite small – you can't grab much earth at a time and the work goes slowly. Especially because the others have no intention of joining them. They've got their own job to do, one that from a distance looks very much like a children's game. Something along the lines of the popular German Shuco construction kits that appeared not long before the war. Having decided perhaps, that a soldier can only be buried in one piece – in other words, as your mother first saw you, as you lived and went off to war – they walk around as if lost, carrying a head, an arm or a leg fished out from God knows where and trying it out now on one torso, now on another. Sometimes, unable to agree, they argue wearily and exchange a few insults.

Everyone's hands and feet look alike: palms rough and cracked from dirt, work, sun; soles calloused and crushed by boots. The uniform is also of little help, although the cloth of the greatcoats and the imitation leather on the boots have proven far sturdier than human beings. But somehow or other they manage to tell them apart, and after several failed attempts to reunite them with the correct torso; then they go off to fetch the next human stub. Strange as it sounds the work is moving quite quickly. Either they've just got the hang of it or three years of war really have been enough to train them to tell which bit is whose, so that everybody gets what's owed to them. Mistakes happen though, and for the strapping artillery captain who is closing the ranks of the recumbent – the little stars still intact on his epaulets – only two small, very elegant hands remain: left hands both, neither of them his.

No sooner had she read about the captain's epaulets than Dusya realised that the armless artilleryman was her husband, Prince Pyotr Igrenyev, but to her own astonishment she felt nothing at first. Although she now knew how he had died and where he was buried, nothing inside her had changed. The prince was from a good family, but a carouser and a drunk: he loved women and cards, taverns and drinking-bouts, and from the very first day of their life together she had the impression that this great clod of a man had nothing even remotely aristocratic about him. She was the mother of his two children, but the marriage had not been a happy one. Dusya had suffered greatly with him and told her friend more than once that she had never been fond of her husband simply as a human being. For her he was in every sense, too large, loud, forceful.

It didn't even shock her that, as things turned out, it was she who was to blame for his death. Once, confessing to Father Nikodim, she described how in 1916 after learning that Pyotr was having an affair with yet another nurse from the Martha and Mary field hospital, she had also found herself a lover: she began seeing an old admirer, the brother of a friend from the gymnasium. It wasn't long before his uncle, the war minister Sukhomlinov, decided to prevent Dusya's husband from getting in anyone's way by transferring Pyotr from the Western to the Caucasian Front.

In truth, the Turkish theatre was considered less dangerous than the German one, and Pyotr, who had been fascinated by the East since childhood, had himself submitted three requests to His Majesty to be transferred to the Caucasus. But without Sukhomlinov's involvement nothing would have moved, and as she knew very well, would never have done so but for her ill-fated love affair. In other words, it turned out that although Dusya bore him no malice, her husband had died because of her and her lechery. But Nikodim had said, when he started watching over Dusya, that infidelity was a lesser sin than the cursing of a son, and for her too that sin had shrivelled up and faded.

Now, as she read about the exploding wagons and shells, about those insane burials, all she could think of was the sheer absurdity of Pyotr's death – to fight for four years on the front to give her – only a sack of potatoes and an agreement with the landlord to let her stay on for one more week. After that she'd have to manage on her own. In any case, Nikodim said, whether Dusya carried on looking for her brother or tried to return to Moscow, he understood that she was in for a tough time, which was why he wanted to suggest an idea that might prove helpful. It would guarantee her a roof over her head, rations, and perhaps if she got lucky, the chance to learn something about Pasha without even having to leave Khabarovsk.

A week earlier, Nikodim explained, the former branch of the Siberian Bank of Trade and Industry, on Bolshaya Pochtovaya Street, had been requisitioned as a commune for the untended. The Bolsheviks were currently attaching enormous importance to children's homes of that kind. Although they called the proletariat the new chosen people and said that the Revolution had brought it out of capitalist slavery and liberated it, the stamp of bondage, all its taints and birthmarks still remained, and there was no point hoping they would ever be washed clean. In short, for the proletariat, Communism was already out of reach. Like the sons of Israel, the working class would roam the desert at the very rim of the Promised Land of Communism, but would never set foot inside it. The ones, who according to the Word of the Lord, would reconquer the Holy Land, regain it as their eternal possession, were precisely the untended. Hence all the attention.

'I realise Dusya, that the Bolsheviks use different words when writing about this, but I've given you the exact gist. The commune,' Nikodim went on, 'already has a name, chosen in honour of the famous bomb-thrower Yekaterina Konstantinovna Breshko-Breshkovskaya, also known as the *babushka* of the Russian Revolution. The head of the children's home has been appointed too, and he's no slouch either – he's the deputy chief of the Cheka here in Khabarovsk. And the commune can count on the patronage of the secret police in the future, too.'

The Chekists were planning to turn the untended into the new nomads, the cadres of the world revolution that was about to happen. Clearly the teaching of foreign languages would need to meet the highest standards, so they were in dire need of good language instructors, especially in German which as he knew well, was Dusya's second language, and of French too. The terms were generous but there were few volunteers: the old teachers were frightened and lying low. In short, she should go there the very next day at the latest and mention a certain Gury Pavlovich Shamayev – who he was and what he did was irrelevant – and she would almost certainly be taken on.

Dusya was short, but quick, spry and quite strong. She was initially asked to teach German but recalling the instruction that Nikodim had given her, she soon began collecting and writing down what the pupils said and how they said it, the customs and rules they followed both inside and outside the commune, their slang and bawdy songs, spells, ditties and games. The result was a fascinating ethnographic study; following Nikodim, she also viewed the untended as a special people.

Living in a room at the children's home, and barely ever apart from the communards, Dusya soon saw that Nikodim had been right about something else as well – many of the ditties and counting rhymes really did derive from Aramaic prayers. She found herself thinking ever more often that this

BE AS CHILDREN

was because when the untended had lost their parents and family, and were left without hearth or home, without a soul in the entire world, they had called the Lord and He had come to their help. The Almighty would save them, take them under His personal care, and now, convinced of the communards' devotion, He had decided to make them His new chosen people. Having inherited His blessing since time immemorial, they had also preserved and kept alive the language in which the Levites had once spoken to the Lord. That this should be so would not have surprised Christ, who told his disciples on more than one occasion, 'Be as children, for theirs is the Kingdom of Heaven'.

The head – the Chekist – had studied at a seminary before the Revolution and had a decent knowledge of ancient languages. When Dusya showed him her notes, he wasn't surprised, saying that he also thought that if there was anybody who had never ceased to serve God through prayer, then it could only be the untended. The most indigent, the most hungry, orphans and paupers, they and no one else were the true proletariat. And it didn't matter whether the communards realised that they were praying and appealing to the Lord many times a day: responsibility for keeping the thread intact had been assumed by the Almighty Himself.

She established a close relationship with the head from the very beginning. Among other things he promised Dusya to help find her brother, assuming of course, that he was still alive. What was more, he raised the topic of Pasha himself – she didn't even need to ask. Over cups of tea in his office every evening, they would discuss the day gone by and the things that would need to be done tomorrow, talking not just about lessons, food, bathing, clothing, but also about communard self-governance. The Chekist asked Dusya in depth about every pupil and every communard brigade: who were the leaders, who were – and would remain – the led, who were the people with a collective spirit and who were the loners who went their own way; then he would look over the notes she'd taken that day. They would also chat about life in general.

Eight months went by in this way, and then on one of the last days of November, the head called her into his office straight from a lesson, without even bothering to find someone to take over her class. As soon as she walked in, he apologised for interrupting her lesson, but said he had no right to delay. An urgent and exceptionally serious assignment had just arrived from Moscow. A month ago he had sent part of the material she had collected directly to Dzerzhinsky, who had just confirmed, by secret telegram from Moscow, the significance of the work that Dusya had begun. What was more, the head continued, Dzerzhinsky was asking him whether he could spare several colleagues to carry on with this work and whether one of the children's-home teachers – ideally, one who had already dealt with such matters before – could be dispatched, strictly on a voluntary basis, to gather new materials 'out in the field', right among the town's hoodlums.

After mentioning fieldwork, the head looked expectantly at Dusya, but she said nothing, so then just as Nikodim had predicted, he added that if she agreed to do this, the Cheka, with Dzerzhinsky's permission, would search all Siberia and the Far Eastern Republic for her brother. And if they didn't find him there, they had permission to use resident spies in Kharbin, Shanghai, and if necessary, even Europe.

Dusya nodded her agreement. Deep down, she had long known that the consequences of her conversation with Nikodim and the night spent reading about her husband's death would be little short of cosmic, and she wasn't frightened now by the prospect of becoming a hoodlum or by the fact that the search for Pasha would involve almost a dozen countries. It even began to seem to Dusya that her teacher had planned this all along.

At the children's home the next day, in order that the new chosen people would not immediately reject her and would even take her for one of their own, she was given a 'number one' haircut (her first tonsure, as Dusya would become fond of saying). After this sudden loss of her long and very beautiful ashen hair, she discovered on glancing in a mirror that she looked decidedly younger, that she had become a gaunt but very fetching teenager. One of the thousands, who against all odds, had survived the typhus barracks. In short, she could take heart from this first stage, in fact she even began to think that the role might suit her. Next, Dusya was passed to the school housekeeper, whose storeroom turned out to contain a heap of tattered rags. She got changed, foolishly worrying more about cleanliness than warmth, was fed to bursting and at dawn – when the pupils were still sleeping – she was let out through the commune gate.

Finding herself alone on the snowy street, Dusya took a while to get used to her new circumstances, to the cold, and shifted hesitantly from foot to foot, then out of the blue, she felt a sudden conviction that God's blessing was upon her, that she would cope with whatever trials were sent her way. Armed with the knowledge that she would be accepted and would not be mistreated, she set off with light, even cheerful steps in the direction of the town market. She was followed all the way to the market square, just in case, but on reaching the first row of stalls, she, in the words of the shadow, 'put on a spurt', and like a seasoned thief, melted into the crowd.

She had agreed with the head to call in at the commune every few days, in order to leave the materials she'd gathered and have a wash and a meal while she was at it. For the two months that she spent on the streets, she kept strictly to this routine. She returned to the commune for good only towards the end of December, right before Christmas, when there was already snow on the ground again. As far as I know, the head was pleased with the results of her mission and she even received a letter of commendation from the Khabarovsk Cheka. In total, Dusya recorded some dozen languages and fifty-odd prayers (ditties and counting rhymes) during her time among the hoodlums. I'm in no doubt that the collection of languages Lenin received from Dzerzhinsky in an envelope shortly before his death would never have existed were it not for her.

In January 1923, after spending almost a year in Khabarovsk, during which, whether on her own or with the help of the Cheka, she had found no trace of her brother, Dusya returned to Moscow. She thought that, as after the death of her son, shared sorrow would bring her and her mother even closer together, but the opposite happened. Somehow her mother had understood from her letters from Khabarovsk that Dusya knew where Pasha was and would bring him back with her, so now, stripped of her last hope, she could not forgive the deception. Dusya could see that whatever she did provoked a kind of dull irritation, even loathing, in her mother. As if she really was to blame. Even more hurtful was the fact that Seryozha had become distant towards her. He welcomed her back with open arms, but there was no longer the same trust between them.

In Moscow she attended the Church of the Holy Trinity in Kitay-Gorod, and confessed there too, but it proved impossible to find a priest to whom she could open up as she once had to Father Pimen, His Grace Amvrosy or Father Nikodim, and Dusya was in no fit state to go looking for one, at least not then. Her spirits were low, even if from the outside things were going well for her. The recently established Young Guard publishing house had commissioned her to translate some fairy tales from German, as well as from Scandinavian languages. There was plenty of work and they lived comfortably enough, sometimes even sending money to her mother-in-law and her mother-in-law's niece, who were still stuck in Gustinino. Dusya enjoyed translating, not to mention the fact that it allowed her to spend all day at home, near Seryozha, and their relationship began to recover.

Even though Pimen was no longer alive, she would travel once a month or so to Onufriyevka to see his cell attendant Anfinogen. She would bring supplies and bits of clothing for him and for several nuns from the former convent near Optina who had bought themselves two *izbas* in the neighbouring village and were still living in strict accordance with the charter of Mount Athos. Anfinogen and the nuns helped take her mind off things, but still, life without a confessor was so wretched that at times she gave way to complete despair.

Several years passed in this way until two events, one after the other, abruptly altered the course of her fate. First,

Father Nikodim returned from Siberia. Dusya went to see him and Nikodim, on learning that she had not remarried, that she was still bringing up her child on her own, said that the dead – he obviously meant her husband – see everything, that they feel sad when we do something bad and joy when we do good. Then, in Onufriyevka a week later, Father Anfinogen let slip that every morning for the past three months Klasha – a holy fool known to them both – had been performing a full burial service for the repose of her, the living Dusya's soul. She was very frightened by this and on the train home, repeating what she'd just heard over and over again in her mind, worked herself up into near hysteria. On reaching Moscow she didn't even leave the station to walk home, she just waited for the first morning train and travelled back to Optina, to the nuns, hoping for some advice.

The nuns, sure enough, welcomed Dusya back as a sister and did all they could to calm and comfort her, explaining that it was only her secular life that the holy fool was burying, and that she should see it as an honour. 'Klasha probably had a vision about you,' they told her, 'where it was said that soon you would also become a bride of Christ, just like us.' They were joyful and gay, kissed her and said that the Lord had finally heeded Dusya's tears and prayers, had decided to lighten the burden that He had heaped upon her. But she was no longer listening – she was trying to imagine herself in a nun's habit.

From that day on Dusya began thinking more and more fixedly about taking the veil. Only one thing held her back – fear for her son. But when six months later she spoke about Seryozha to Anfinogen, he replied that though he understood her misgivings, the monastic life could be lived in different ways; she could become a nun yet remain in the world while she was bringing up her child. This form of service had met with the Church's approval in the past, not to mention now, when monasteries and convents were being shut down all over the country.

Anfinogen's words removed the main impediment, and on 22nd January 1927 she took the veil. She was tonsured by Father Nikodim under her own name, Yevdokiya. Her veil was held by Father Anfinogen and she was given her new clothes for the ceremony by Klasha, who blessed her on her path to God.

Later we learned from Dusya herself (this seemed important to her) that her life as a nun was tainted and there was no way of putting things right. The reason for this was not some violation of her vows – she knew she was innocent of that – but the weakness and untruth that had preceded her retreat from the world. She was a fugitive bride of Christ, who had fled to the convent to save herself from the lies that had filled her confessions to the brim for so many years and from the equally false promises she had made to each of her Elders. Even here it turned out evil had paved the way for good, but Dusya was certain that neither time nor anything else had ever managed to cleanse this good of its sin; the sin was still there.

When Seryozha, against her wishes and all her prayers, refused to take monastic vows after the war, it convinced her for good that the reason was always the same – her own birth in the spirit had been tainted. If she would manage to save anyone, then only herself. In fact after her son returned from the front, Dusya came to understand and accept a great deal. Previously she had not believed Father Nikodim when he told her that the most terrible of all her sins were the words she had said, in the middle of a sleepless night to little Seryozha: 'The Devil take you, you vile little boy!' This curse, which had slipped out in the heat of the moment, hadn't seemed worth a second thought – what won't you say to a child who's driving you mad? But now she agreed that she really had handed over some of the rights to his soul to the forces of Hell, and that however much she repented, those forces would not release her son to God.

But if Seryozha, despite his vow, failed to continue their family's service to the Lord, Dusya – and I have little doubt about this – did her level best to adopt the relationship with Christ maintained by the holy fool Klasha, who in 1926, had prayed for Dusya's soul while she was still alive, had made her understand that it was time for her to leave this world, that if Dusya dithered and delayed, the chance to save her soul would be gone.

***

I visited Father Nikodim in Snegiri over a period of almost thirty years, albeit with interruptions. I liked the way he celebrated the services and took confession, even if it surprised me that during his sermons he would avoid any mention of his own fate – prison, the camps – and would speak as if the Revolution had never happened. The Church of course had been attacked many times before then – there had been entire epochs of persecution and punishment – but the Bolsheviks had played their full part in this mournful history, and he seemed to have forgotten all about them. But the reason I kept distancing myself from Nikodim, then coming back to him, was not his preaching.

I usually travelled to Snegiri for Sunday mass and when after the service, Father Nikodim invited me for tea in his living room upstairs, it would be late evening before I returned to Moscow. Nikodim was very different after mass, even to look at. In church he wore a monk's black habit, but for tea he changed into the clothes he always wore when walking around the village. Old linen trousers and a marginally less faded jacket – pretty much the uniform, to judge by paintings and photographs, of Soviet agronomists of the '30s. Over tea Nikodim no longer avoided talking about the camps and I remember feeling troubled by this sudden change, although I don't think the reason was a fear of informants in church and a fresh sentence. It was probably all a question of time. Life in the camps had broken off so abruptly – Nikodim wasn't even halfway through his third term – that he still didn't know what to make of many of the things that had happened to him as a *zek*.

It was at the dacha in Snegiri that I heard what follows below, heard it from his own lips, and I'm no more ready than I was before to separate it from him. He linked some of the ideas he spoke about to his cellmates, that is he gave the thoughts both a name and a biography, sometimes a rather extravagant one, but never with a happy ending; he took issue with others and tried to refute them in our presence, often with our help, but all the same I didn't much like hearing a priest, straight after a service tell us things that lay outside Orthodox teachings, and that more often than not, were outright heresies. Nikodim, whether or not he meant to, was seeding doubts in our faith, as if putting it to the test, and our doubts were made all the bigger when we saw that for him too these questions had not gone away, that they were troubling him as much as ever.

Nikodim told us about a cellmate who had been with him in pre-trial detention in Barnaul, an Amur Cossack by the name of Nikolai Yevstratov. They'd tried to execute Yevstratov on three occasions – once they had even fired a bullet into the back of his head to finish him off – but he had got out alive and explained to Nikodim that every ordeal had been granted to Rus for one purpose only: so that the Lord could show her His miracles. That every person who had not died in the First World War, or the Civil War, or the Great Patriotic War, who had been through trial, prison and the camps, was alive by divine miracle. And there was no other nation in the world that could say, in such numbers, that it lived beneath the protecting veil of God's Grace. The sufferings were great, but the redemption no less so.

On another occasion Nikodim started talking about an Old Believer he'd met in a camp near Abakan, where there were almost a dozen such men in one barracks, all from the 'Priestless' strain of the Old Belief. This man taught that the freedom to choose good and evil is pretty much the most important gift granted to man. We are made as the Lord's interlocutors, as those who when the time comes and by inner necessity – not like soldiers by external command – will choose good and reject evil. Miracles though are fatal, said the Old Believer, and if the Lord stoops to them every now and again, then only out of pity and compassion for human beings. It's not just that miracles violate the laws of the world created by God, but – and this is even more terrifying – that people give up and resign themselves to evil, purely in the hope of further handouts.

One name that came up often in Snegiri was Paisy Velichkovsky.[51] Much of what he wrote it seems to me, was close to Father Nikodim's heart. Especially Father Paisy's view that all the world's evil is in our souls, that's where the struggle unfolds. When in the darkness of his cell a monk goes to battle against temptation with only the name of the Lord upon his lips, these are not just his temptations, his seductions, but those of the entire world. Wars, the struggle against God – these too are in our souls, while the world's uprisings, hatred and murders are secondary and derivative. Merely reverberations, echoes. One day, he took our recent past as his example: 'The Revolution is a series of convulsions, an epileptic fit. The struggle with evil in the soul and body of man has reached its limit, its utmost degree of tension, and nobody knows who will win.'

Nikodim was fond of saying that prayer is the umbilical cord which joins us to the Lord. For as long as we pray, it lives; through it the Lord nourishes us with his mercy and grace. That when we confess, we are giving back to the Lord not just evil and sin, but everything we have lived through, returning it in the hope that He will forgive us, wash away our stains, and in order that nothing be lost. He would say that we are not created in God's image, that the external likeness between Him and us which is taken for granted by the icon-painters does not in fact exist. But we are similar to the Almighty. Similar in the ability to create, to distinguish good and evil, to

---

[51] A Ukrainian monk (1722-1794) who played a vital role in reviving monasticism in Eastern Europe and Russia in the eighteenth century, especially the traditions of hesychasm and Eldership.

understand how good one thing is and how foul another. And also: it is given only to us to see the full complexity, the full inconceivable beauty and perfection of Creation.

I can recall three occasions when from a different angle each time, Father Nikodim came back to the idea that the Lord speaks to Man in such a way that the Son of Adam may understand Him to the best of his ability. And so that the sinfulness revealed during the sacrament of confession does not annihilate the repenter. After all, what is Holy Scripture if not the cloud through which the Lord addresses His people? Had the Lord appeared outside the cloud on Mount Sinai, Man would have instantly perished.

Aside from this, we must not forget as we read the Bible, that people reconcile themselves to evil more easily when it comes from outside them. When we are not doing it ourselves, but being punished by it. 'My comments,' Nikodim continued, 'are especially important for those chapters in which evil is attributed to God Himself. The Lord is infinitely good, and the evil that exists in the world is done only by Man. The most the Lord can do is to allow it to happen. The flood is the evil wrought by Man, and it is Man who chokes on it. The ark is the good deeds of a righteous man, deeds that do not drown in sin, and Noah and his family wait patiently for the Lord to show His mercy and send evil back to the netherworld from whence it came. As with the flood, so with the infants in Egypt. The Almighty did not kill them. Protecting His people, He placed a looking glass, and the Pharaoh's evil, reflected in the bronze, fell back on Egypt. The hardening of the Pharaoh's heart, his refusal to let the seed of Jacob go out into the wilderness are all part of the same bondage, filled with torment and persecution, in which he kept the sons of Israel.'

Once, as if echoing Lenin, Nikodim said that revolution, its aim and meaning, is a return to childhood. People become infinitely weary of life's complexity, of the thousands upon thousands of gaps, nooks and dead ends in which sin conceals itself and from which it can never be scraped out. Eventually they reach the conclusion that the sole purpose of complexity is precisely that – to hide evil, to give it refuge – and until you destroy it, you can forget about salvation.

Revolution is the attempt to separate good and evil all over again, to make the world as simple and clear as before the Fall. Hence the certainty that you are right, the joy, ecstasy, jubilation, that for all its calamities, revolution engenders. I'd already heard similar things in those years; what surprised me was the sadness and remorse in the voice of our priest.

I knew that Father Nikodim had never supported the Revolution, but his words could be understood to mean that the enemies of the Revolution also came from the same childish camp. In 1917 the old world collapsed and faded away overnight. It had not the faintest chance of standing its ground, because the Revolution offered each and everyone the real thing – God's own paradise. You were being promised a life free of taint or blemish, a life without temptation, torment, doubt. A happy, joyful time; after all, if you had faith, if you were committed and conscientious, you knew that whatever you did would be completely blameless. This really was a good, sincere world, filled with youth and enthusiasm. Your faith had stored up incalculable reserves of strength, you were literally bursting with it, and as a result everything inside you was singing, and living felt easy and light.

There was another idea that also absorbed Nikodim. At a transit prison, once he had heard a military engineer – a captain during the First World War, who had laid pontoon bridges in Galicia – explain to his cellmates that each of us is a prodigal son, that faith is a path to the Lord, a journey marked by every conceivable retreat and change of tack. We are granted revelation in proportion to our progress; only to and by the extent that we walk that path can we understand the words of the Lord. Otherwise all we have is a collection of everyday precepts and lessons. Otherwise nothing touches us deeply, nothing hurts us, torments us. No doubts, no betrayals, no running away: you are just a star pupil who learns everything by heart and rattles it off in class.

In the Bible, the captain said, faith pushes its way up through human weakness. It is proportionate to our conceptions of the world, of the world's justice, of the power of sin: only in this way can it help us, point us in a better direction. The way the people chosen by the Lord withdrew from Him – not only in Sinai, but earlier in Egypt, and later in their own state – the way they complained and groaned are the surest evidence that this was the most of which Man was capable. The cowardice and taintedness of the sons of Adam established limits, and those limits were narrow.

Faith, in other words, is not something ready-made, it's more like the moulding of Man from clay, the gradual creation of a sculpture step by step. Both Testaments show a path that is uneven and faltering, a difficult journey in which everything is necessary and everything inevitable. Only by walking it from beginning to end may we hope to be saved. He himself, a commissioned officer, maintained that Russia's military campaigns were the mediastinum of her history. The advance towards Jerusalem was, as her people could see very clearly, a reflection of her slow, inner reform. Before Christ can make His second appearance, we must repeat the path by which faith came to us and ourselves walk back to the Holy Land.

There were many on the General Staff who wanted to take the most direct route, to march to the true faith and the land of the One God with barely a single deviation, not even on the map: Moscow – Kiev – Constantinople – Jerusalem; and with the destination almost in sight, to transfer some forces to a second front in Mesopotamia, and following Abraham's footsteps, march to the Holy Land from there as well. But the court and the Guards took a different view. Their strategic plan was based on the following principle: since holiness now resides in Moscow, an advance on Jerusalem would mean little in itself. We are already marching to Jerusalem in every direction you can think of: the expansion of the empire is the only certain and reliable path to the Lord. Say what you will, but until the entire globe – Palestine included – finds itself beneath the sceptre of the Russian Tsar, the Kingdom of God will not take root.

From about 1970, Nikodim's health took a clear turn for the worse. His cell attendant at the time was a tough and deeply devoted old woman called Raya. But she couldn't look after him, day in, day out, she had a daughter living in Moscow with two small children, not far from Preobrazhenskaya Square, and old Raya was constantly shuttling from Nikodim to her daughter and back to Snegiri. Nikodim had returned from the camps with high blood pressure, in fact he was at risk of a stroke at any moment, which was why whenever Raya went away, somebody would always fill in for her. From late autumn to mid-spring – between my annual field trips, in other words – I was more than happy to assume these duties myself. And it wasn't a question of gratitude – I just found him interesting.

Nikodim's decline was uneven. As soon as the doctors managed to get his blood pressure down, the lethargy and confusion in his speech would disappear, and even if he was no longer the vivid, forceful preacher we knew from church, he still excelled in conversation. And we had found a topic of common interest – the North.

Nikodim would ask me for hours about the Enets and other northern peoples. How they had lived both before Peregudov and after they had taken him in and been baptised. How they saw their own history, their own fate. Nikodim added one or two stories himself. It turned out for example, that he had spent several months in Tomsk living under one roof with an Enets by the name of Noan. He didn't give any other details, but this was already something.

By this point I knew the names of almost the entire tribe going back about forty or fifty years from the census of 1924. I had a thick notebook bound in good calico and filled with a veritable forest of Enets genealogical trees as well as various jottings on matrimonial topics. It was all based on the memories of the elderly and on documents from the archives: from the reign of Alexander III onwards – so from 1881 – record-keeping had been standard practice in the Lena delta. The rest of the nineteenth century was of course much trickier. You could count the available documents on the fingers of one hand, and there wasn't a single old man who had lived back then and had survived to tell you anything about it. And yet, thanks to this man's name – Noan – and a few dozen other bits and pieces, I soon began thinking that Nikodim's acquaintance must have been the great-grandson of the elder of the two sons Belka had had before even meeting Peregudov. A direct descendant in other words, of Ionakh the shaman, whom Peregudov had killed. Incidentally, despite the circumstances of Ionakh's death, this Enets, according to Nikodim, had spoken about Peregudov with love and profound respect, describing him as a new apostle to the pagans, a second Paul.

I should mention, that whenever the topic of the North came up, I would plunge into it with my usual enthusiasm, while Nikodim would struggle to hide his irritation towards the Samoyeds and the Ostyaks, as he still called the Khanty people.[52] But he wouldn't cut the conversation short, in fact he clearly wanted, at least at the beginning, to win me over to his side, to persuade me that their faith was sheer ignorance and atavism, and always had been.

Arguing the same points month after month would soon have palled were it not for the colourfulness of the topic, and we were both moths to its flame. The protagonist of our debates was of course Peregudov, and we would work back from him to the local tribes – how they had lived before the Great Russians started settling in Siberia – then turn to other preachers of the North. I can remember our second and perhaps prickliest conversation. Nikodim started railing against Peregudov almost immediately, calling him a heretic

---

[52] The Khanty (their own self-appellation) live in north-west Siberia around the River Ob, or *As* in the Khanty language, from which was derived the term Ostyak, long used by Russians and now often seen as derogatory.

and a killer. Unable to restrain myself, I shot back that maybe he was a murderer but at least he brought the Enets to the true faith by peaceful means, without the use of force, while the missionary path of Filofei Leshchinsky,[53] whom Nikodim dubbed the Apostle to the Pagans, had resembled nothing so much as the Crusades. No wonder the Ostyaks still hated him. Back then they had shot one of his travelling companions through the head and another through the chest, and they had wanted to kill Leshchinsky as well.

In fairness Nikodim might not have known that this same Father Filofei, together with Luka Vologodsky, had ransomed dozens of non-Russians from the Siberian Cossacks who were holding them captive, and then having converted them to Christianity and ensured their complete dependence, had forcibly settled them on monastic lands. Or that many missionaries, in their efforts to prevent the Samoyeds from falling back into paganism, had taken away their children, usually boys, and sent them to a special orphanage in Tobolsk. Apparently they weren't treated too badly there – they were kept warm and clean, taught to read and write – but even so, just as soon as the children were let out again, they immediately realised that they were suspended between one world and another, that they would never belong to either. Virtually all of them drank themselves to an early grave.

Besides, where Peregudov had translated Genesis, Mark's Gospel and many psalms and prayers into the language of the Enets, the missionary Luka Vologodsky – namesake of Luke the

---

[53] Born in Ukraine in 1650, Leshchinsky became Metropolitan of Siberia and Tobolsk, and despite illness, continued his evangelising activity across Siberia deep into old age (d. 1727).

BE AS CHILDREN

Evangelist – had only tackled the Creed, the Commandments and the Gospel of Matthew. Listening to my passionate speech, Nikodim grew darker and darker; fortunately I realised I was going too far just in time. Determined to lighten the mood, I resorted to the usual Russian topic – vodka. I mentioned that people in the North still believed that this accursed substance granted the most blissful death and that the person who managed to drink himself to the grave was the envy of all. That they often strengthened their vodka with tobacco and that alcohol had even altered the Samoyeds' notion of the afterlife: if previously they had believed, in accordance with their faith, that the dead went off to a realm of misfortune and hardship, now, following the example of the Yukaghirs, they held that the afterworld, though similar to this one, was kinder and gentler. The deceased go to their supreme god, Num, once almost inaccessible to mortals, and drink each day to their heart's content.

Then we talked until evening about amok and *miryachit*, entire epidemics of which were described in the '20s in Kolyma region, and about so-called *uch-gurbul* – the mental state of a shaman. About the fact that, as a rule, these people are from birth unusually highly strung and excitable, and that almost three quarters of them suffer from epilepsy, often in a very serious form. Hallucinations, somnambulistic states, blackouts followed by random groans and wails – all this is frequently observed, and their natural constitution has nothing to do with it: before entering a trance, many shamans chew dried fly agarics – potent hallucinogens. Sometimes the mushrooms are chased with more vodka.

Most of the people I spoke to considered shamans to be

gloomy, solitary, secretive types, though they also told me about some who were more like our own holy fools. But it wasn't the shamans' character that mattered most here: the Ostyaks, just like the ancient Greeks, Romans and other pagans, were impressed above all by the prophetic and poetic gifts of the shamans, their facility – comparable to the oracles of antiquity – for improvised verse. Here too though, I quickly backtracked and said that this was probably just my sympathetic view of the Samoyeds and their faith; from the outside, you could easily think that the tribes were bowing down to patients on a psychiatric ward. During the rituals, even I had sometimes felt as if I were surrounded by the more violent inmates of a madhouse. Especially because the shamans used fly agarics and vodka quite deliberately to provoke genuine fits. That second conversation was the crisis we needed: having overcome it, we chatted quite freely from then on, rarely getting stuck on anything for too long.

Our talks became unusually amicable. There was the odd argument of course, and there were some issues we couldn't agree on, but we readily – even gladly – made concessions. During the eighteen months of the priest's illness we discussed dozens of topics. Nikodim for example, was convinced that shamanism is not a faith, not even a pagan faith, and that it is better understood in medical terms as a kind of hypnosis, a form of psychotherapy. We both knew that the Samoyeds attribute illness to the abduction of one of the sick person's souls by wicked demons; another pack of demons takes up residence in its place, like a foetus in a woman, and begins gnawing the body from the inside and drinking the patient's blood. So then they call the shaman. Yes: shamans in Siberia are what doctors are for us, and they don't invoke good spirits all that often – they use up almost all their powers fighting demons – but I was still convinced that if we ignored the Upper World, the world of light, we had no chance of understanding the religious beliefs of the Siberian peoples.

I explained to him, that as the Enets see it, evil spirits hunt human souls by a variety of methods, all very similar to the way that humans themselves hunt animals or trap fish. They catch them with nets and rods, they harpoon and lasso them, then bag their prey, take it home and give it to their women, who dress the human souls, cut them into pieces, fry them and feed them to their husband and children. The Enets, I told him, think that if a shaman fails to help someone, then the sickness, like an evil spell, will leave that person only when they die. Like a genuine shapeshifter, it can turn into a worm or a cockroach, become a cat, crow, mouse, or even another human being – a small hunchback dwarf.

We picked apart the entire ritual by which the abducted human soul is exchanged for the soul of a sacrificial animal, and I even remember saying that so too did Abraham, following the Lord's command, offer up a young ram caught in the thickets in place of Isaac, but Nikodim didn't like this parallel. We spoke about how in the past the shamans had stopped at nothing in their struggle with evil spirits, how the two sides had been evenly matched, with victories on both sides. But the shamans, like everyone else had become weaker and pettier, and now their main weapon was a combination of bribery, unctuousness and abasement. The cleverer, less cowardly ones just set the spirits against each other, and when the fight was over, took great pleasure in dealing the final blow to the defeated party. Embarrassed on behalf of the shamans, I added apologetically, that however noble their aim, their behaviour was of course beneath contempt.

Once I happened to mention that in the past, before a legal system was established, the representative of law on Earth, in the eyes of the Samoyeds, was the bear, and Nikodim, as if taking up this thought and linking the two subjects, began describing how in 1930, in the Far East, a Nivkh woman picked up two baby bears – their mother must have abandoned them, or perhaps she had been killed by hunters – and after bringing them into her *izba*, began to suckle them herself. Later they ate the same things as everyone else – fish, meat, berries. The bears were between eighteen months and two years old when they broke down the door and wanted to go off into the taiga, but the Nivkh woman begged them to stay, saying, 'I love you so much. I'll be sad without you. I'll cry.' Unfortunately they did as she asked. That autumn, the woman's father, husband and three eldest sons were arrested, on the grounds that if they had voluntarily taken in two bears, they must be rich, they must be kulaks. At first they were going to be tried in Blagoveshchensk, but heavy rains set in and the roads became impassable, so they were just led out of the village and shot in a meadow. The bears, having been classed as kulak beasts, were executed with them.

Sometimes I had the impression that Nikodim knew as much as I did about the North – at best, I was stronger on detail – yet even so, he chose to play second fiddle in our conversations, right from the beginning. For example, he could interrogate me for hours about how shamans earned their status among the tribe. He was especially interested in their life stories. Having recorded several dozen such stories myself, I had much to tell him.

I remember that once we spent an entire day discussing the life and death of a shaman: how they could die only at the hands of an equal, and how as the Ostyaks testified, they were actually immortal. Ordinary people are like dogs – they die as they live, and where they die they will lie, but shamans are born many times over and in different places. They can spend their first life shamanising for the Tungus, the second for the Yakuts, the third for the Nenets; their powers just become a little weaker with each birth.

The notes I took in the North contained both real stories and legends – and no wonder: the people we were interviewing drew little distinction between them. Take for example the story of the celebrated shaman Ga Paan. At first he was just an ordinary child. When he was about ten, he went off to cut grass, fainted and spent seven days unconscious. By the time he came round he was a shaman blessed with rare powers. He just had to look at someone – whether man or beast – for them to drop dead. Ga Paan did not perform any rituals himself, and to avoid killing anyone he shielded his eyes with an iron visor at the request of his tribesfolk. He lived a long time, almost to the age of ninety, in a village on the left bank of the Ob, downstream from the confluence with the Sosva.

According to popular belief, every shaman has a mother: a bird-beast with a beak resembling a small iron ice-breaker, with hooked claws and a tail six metres long. But the mother's not enough on her own – you can't become a shaman without an initiation, and those are not easy to pass. First, demons take the soul of the future shaman and imprison it in the underworld for three years; the actual person does not die, but without his soul he loses his mind. When the first trial is almost at an end, the evil spirits kill the man back here on Earth, and cut him up into pieces. Three days will pass before he comes back to life. All that time the demons will tear at his flesh with iron hooks, setting aside the joints and bones, scraping out the meat and letting the juices flow out and soak into the earth. They remove the shaman's eyes from their sockets in advance and place them nearby, so that he can see and remember everything that happens to him. Only towards nightfall on the third day do they gather up the remains of the unfortunate, and having sewn them together with iron threads, return the shaman to life.

There's no doubt that after such violence, such vicious desecration of your own body before your very own eyes, you will never be free of fear, of the sense of your own weakness, fragility. You may not seem to look any different from before, but that changes little.

We had several quite detailed conversations about the supreme deities of the Samoyeds: about the Num of the Nenets, and the Torum of the Ostyaks, who can't be bribed with any sacrifice and for whom only one thing matters – the good deeds of a human being. About the Tengri of the Turki people, a wise and just master of the heavens, and about his assistants, the bright spirits whom he sends to help those praying for children and the survival of their herds. Once, in a remote Tungus reindeer camp, I wrote down a pregnant woman's very beautiful prayer to Tengri and now I began reciting it from memory to Nikodim, in a faintly sing-song voice: 'You, gazing down from above at every step of the reindeer tribe – you see woe and fear. If you are merciful, then take pity on the little one, still unborn, that inspires pity in beasts and people. Allow it to be nourished with the milk of my breasts. Lead away the spirits of sickness and death and make the lying sit, the sitting walk, the walking run, make it the swift-footed guardian of the herds.'

We also spoke about the enemies of the good spirits – the evil *chitkury*, the spitting image of our own devils. About *ongons* – the souls of the dead, which rove between the world beyond and the world of the living, and which unless you indulge them and butter them up, kill children and adults without distinction, inflict illnesses and lean harvests. I managed to exchange goods for a figurine of one such *ongon* in an Enets reindeer camp in 1960. A small god of carved bone, whose garments miraculously accommodated depictions of twenty-seven shamans – nine of them blind, nine lame and nine without arms.

Passing from one topic to another, I might start talking about the circle as the symbol of the sun and the shaman's soul, while Nikodim – again, almost as an aside – might recall the June sun in Yakutia, which sets over the nearby mountains like an enormous ruby-red ball before rising entirely white in the East just two hours later, as if it were a human soul that the Lord had finally cleansed of blood. Then on to the '30s, when collectivisation began in Siberia, and the shamans, who were declared accomplices of the kulaks, were shot or imprisoned by the hundreds; the few who survived made statements at special meetings or on the pages of a national newspaper, *The Atheist*, to renounce their faith.

On that day, as I recall, we moved on from Yakutsk, where Nikodim had served his sentence, to the way that the nomads measured the passing of time: he told me for example that they would describe a filly as being not two years old, but two grasses old, so then I started telling him that the very same cry of *Khoru-u!* with which the Yakuts gather a herd of fillies had in days gone by been used by shamans on the eve of a military campaign to distant lands from which few would return. Its purpose was to announce the beginning of an orgiastic ritual. To return victorious to their native *chums* and pastures, the men had to remember the love of their wives, while the women had to wait out the long months of war by carrying their husbands' seed beneath their hearts.

And so, spinning around in a dance and beating out a rhythm on a tambourine, the shaman would remove one garment after another, until fully naked and still moving to his beat, he would fall to the earth and begin imitating sexual intercourse on the grass. At the beginning, the women who had gathered round – the men were excluded from this ritual – looked at his shuddering body with an almost detached air, but then they too began shaking ever more violently. Their faces turned red and a thick sweat covered their bodies. A minute later, roaring and neighing like horses, they too set about ripping off their clothes, until stark naked and mad with desire, they started rolling in the grass with the shaman.

Needless to say, I never attended any such rituals myself, but in the course of my first expedition to Siberia I did record an account of them by two old Yakut women, who had taken part in many mystery rites in their youth. I remember Nikodim agreeing that it was no coincidence that the shaman summoned women and fillies with one and the same cry, nor that the women, driven to frenzy, should neigh like horses, and we began talking about the cult of animals, which remained strong wherever shamanism had not yet been obliterated root and branch – from the Far North to the Altai Mountains.

He explained that to begin a ritual for the prosperity of the herds, a shaman in Yakutia would usually open his mouth wide, so that the spirits of the animals for whom he would be praying could enter, and then, as if turning into one of the animals himself, he would start making its movements and sounds. On the Lena, the shamans imitate horses by putting on a harness and using a broad leather strap that goes across their foreheads before being looped under their arms, but this is only the start; like a stallion that has not yet been broken in, the shaman rears up, neighs, snorts, tosses his head, and then, to tame his fury, sticks a piece of iron in his mouth, like a bridle.

The horse is becalmed, and now dancing to the rattle of the tambourine, the shaman recreates the patter of hooves and a leisurely, gentle trot. Then with his legs slightly wider apart, his buttocks and hips working faster, and the tassels of his coat – a horse's tail – switching this way and that, the shaman's gait becomes more expansive. A minute later, he's still trotting, but as a bull. The legs are close together and the clatter of hooves and the taps of the tambourine become frequent and shallow. The shaman is wearing a different cape now, a wavy woollen fabric dyed in shades of greyish blue, its surface all speckled. The bull breathes heavily as it runs, puffing out its flanks, slows down, and filling the air far and wide with its bellow, begins a slow, tottering saunter around the pasture.

We found it curious that during both the orgies and the other rituals the male shamans quite often behave like women, even though female shamans are something of a rarity. Much of a shaman's activity is far from manly. The need for shamans to fawn and cringe before evil spirits as they beg them to leave the sick, the lengthy negotiations, the bargaining and bartering – none of this had much in common with the nomads' notion of a man: herder, hunter, warrior.

The shaman's hysterics and fickleness, feminine by their nature, his ability to adjust and accommodate himself to others, to feel just as confident among evil spirits as among good ones: there was in the rituals I happened to see a great deal of theatre and roleplay, an almost actorly plasticity. Quickness of adaptation was a given, permitting the shaman with the tambourine's help, to move between worlds in the blink of an eye. It was no wonder then, that shamans, especially in Chukotka, considered the degree of their femininity to be equivalent to their strength. To reinforce it, they did women's jobs and wore women's clothes, kept their hair in plaits and even had official male 'husbands'. For their rituals they sewed metal cones onto their clothes and even adopted women's voices.

We spoke a lot about shamanic dress, which from the colour of the threads used for the tassels to the smallest detail in the patterns, is filled with meaning and represents an exact model of the universe. There is the Upper World, inhabited by the ruler of the heavens and the good spirits petitioned by those wishing for more children and cattle, the spirits who reject blood sacrifice and are just and merciful; the Lower World, inhabited by evil spirits and the spirits of the dead, who aside from everything else, are touchy and capricious, who might even take exception to a shaman's posture during a ritual, who don't like loud speech or sudden movements – with them you're best off keeping a low profile; and finally, the Middle World, the place where human beings reside from birth to death, the place of their labours, joy and grief. It is from here, when the hardest days arrive, when sickness, hunger and other woes assail them, that they call for help.

But clothes are not just a map of Creation, they are also hearth and home for the spirits who have agreed to assist our shaman. The same goes for the tambourine – this is no mere likeness of a drum but a perfect device permitting journeys to the remotest corners of the cosmos; and simultaneously, a weapon in the struggle with evil spirits. I heard from the Enets that only shamans of the highest orders can use a tambourine for their rituals; the rest are only permitted sticks (*orbu*) and brooms to scare off unclean forces.

For eighteen months, with one interruption for my annual field trip, we explored topic after topic, never hurrying and never letting our emotions get the better of us. I got used to this tempo, it became part of my life, and I didn't seem to notice that Nikodim was fading. He really was dying, leaving us bit by bit, and there was no longer anything we could do to help him. Five days before his death Nikodim asked me to bring Dusya to see him in Snegiri. She could not confess him, of course, or absolve him, nor was he expecting her to. If he wanted anything, it was the chance to repent before the end, to place Dusya and himself on an equal footing, to open up to her as she had once opened herself to him. The conversation proved long – it lasted almost five hours – disjointed and hard for them both.

Nikodim was exhausted and emaciated by illness; to find

the strength to go on, he needed rest, or at least a short break. Besides, he was clearly nervous and even, it seemed to me, frightened of Dusya. But there was nothing to fear: too much time had passed, a whole lifetime more or less, and it was too late to put things right: the people he was speaking about had been in the ground for a long time now and their fate lay in the hands of God alone.

He told Dusya about the people closest to her, the people she loved, told her important, often crucial things, but I could see what she was thinking: why tell me all this now? She was trying in her anguish to work out how much of what she considered good and right, of what she liked to repeat and recall in her mind, had been destroyed in the bud and would never recover. Still, she understood Nikodim too – to take to his grave, to leave without repenting before God and humankind was something he could not do.

After bringing Dusya to Nikodim, I didn't bother taking my coat off – I was planning to take a stroll around the village so as to keep out of their way, but Nikodim stopped me and in the end he made his confession to us both. What he told us was that some time around the winter of 1920 he had begun to think that neither the Church, nor the Whites, nor the Reds, but children, only children could save a world so sunk in sin and hatred. Nothing else had any answer to evil, and there was nobody else to count on. For weeks on end he had spent entire days, sometimes even nights, at Moscow's Khitrovka market,[54] and had made great strides with his collection of children's counting-rhyme prayers. Soon he believed he would have

---

[54] A district famous for its rampant criminal activity, and the dosshouses and slums that surrounded it.

enough of them for an entire liturgy, and it was with this liturgy that salvation would begin. But he was forced to break off his work for Easter. Straight after the Feast of the Annunciation, when the Whites were already in retreat on every front, he and eleven other monks from the Vysoko-Petrovsky Monastery were arrested. There was no real investigation and three of them were shot, but he, Nikodim, chickened out, signing up as a collaborator in exchange for his freedom. Still, they left their new agent in peace until Pentecost and nobody seemed to want anything from him. He was as they say a 'sleeper'.

The Chekists appear to have been very confident that Nikodim – a monk from his youth, born moreover to a long line of priests – would rise quickly through the ranks, and they would soon have another bishop to call their own. Back then this was certainly possible. But on this point, Nikodim explained, he managed to hold firm. Terrified of sin, he could see what they were after and however much they nudged him, managed with God's help to resist temptation. He would die, it seemed, as he'd lived – a simple monk. 'Overall,' he summed up, 'I wasn't as weak as all that.'

Eventually the Chekists realised that they could forget about Nikodim ever becoming a bishop and were very annoyed. They started calling him into the Lubyanka almost every other day. Nikodim's personal handler, Groshev, who was one of the top men in the section that dealt with the Church, was beside himself with rage: he yelled, swore uncontrollably, and threatened him with another arrest. Ducking and diving, Nikodim ended up mentioning the untended – so it wasn't just his brethren he pawned, but the children too.

To his surprise the untended worked like a charm. Perhaps

the Chekists had also been thinking along similar lines, or maybe they just liked the idea. In any case the tone of the interrogation changed and they were perfectly polite as they said goodbye and let him go. Then, at a safe house a month later, they told him they held nothing against him, and to prove that they trusted him as much as before, suggested that he travel urgently to Khabarovsk and see what he could learn there about certain people in Kolchak's entourage.

As far as the Whites were concerned, Nikodim went on, his journey all the way out to the Chinese Eastern Railway was pretty much a waste of time, but he did learn a great deal about one of Dusya's relatives. Which was why he had called her out to Snegiri now. Timewise, Nikodim continued, the assignment in Khabarovsk was easy enough: shadowing the Kolchakists took about an hour a day, two at the outside, so he was able to get ahead with the children too. There was a whole horde of hoodlums roving around Siberia and the Far East at this period, so there was no lack of material.

At first, the tasks set by Moscow were all one-offs, and Nikodim, aware that he was being closely watched, tried to carry them out conscientiously. 'In general,' he emphasised, addressing Dusya, 'you should know that I worked for the Cheka in good faith, without cutting corners.' His honesty was clearly appreciated, because a month later it was suggested that he focus on the search for a man, who, they stressed, was a serious target. The only information the 'Services' had on him was his underground alias – Ilya – and his purpose: to assemble, from all the officer and Cossack units that had split off from Kolchak's army, a militia of Orthodox crusaders, and to march on Moscow once more.

Be as Children

As soon as this militia was mentioned, Dusya realised that she was about to hear about her brother, Pasha. Four years younger than his sister, Pasha had been idolised by his family. He was clever, poetic, refined, an excellent musician, not to mention the rare gentleness that had been evident since the first year of his life. Dusya, who had found her mother's pregnancy hard to deal with – she was sure she would be forgotten – fell passionately in love with him just as soon as it became clear what kind of brother she had. She played with Pasha for hours and insisted that she be allowed to give him his bath and read him his bedtime story. Then all of a sudden, before he had even completed his second year at university, this charming boy, who had been turning women's heads since the age of fifteen (she'd often noticed how they looked at him), began talking about becoming a monk.

In those years, for all her family's close links with the Church, the thought of such a future, whether for herself or any of her loved ones, had never entered her mind. That her brother might retreat to a monastery seemed completely impossible to her. He was sensitive and thin-skinned, without a hint of rigidity or fanaticism, yet hardness of character was precisely what monastic life, as Dusya understood it, demanded. She made this point to him more than once, to which he would explain, with his usual guilty smile, that he understood perfectly well that it would be tough at first, but he couldn't see any other path for himself.

She – and her mother too for that matter – literally threw herself at his feet trying to talk him out of it, or at least make him wait, thinking he would fall in love and forget the whole idea, but none of it made the slightest difference until one day

Dusya remembered the words that Amvrosy had said about Nikodim. Now she repeated them to Pasha: he was too young to flee the world. The Elders, whom they both revered, had seen a great deal of life, thanks to which they understood people and were able to help them. But what would he be able to say to those who came to him, if he knew nothing about human beings or anything else? Amvrosy's words seemed to have done the trick. Pasha went to see the holy man, then told his mother that he had decided to put off taking his tonsure for another five years.

The Civil War had been going on for a long time. At first Pasha wanted to travel south and join up with the Volunteer Army, but there was no way of reaching Crimea; for some reason though, the trains were still running to Siberia, where Kolchak was still fighting.

Up until the summer of 1921, Pasha sent occasional letters to them from Irkutsk, Chita, Khabarovsk, usually through acquaintances, but then the link snapped. Until October, she and her mother carried on hoping he was still alive and about to walk in at any moment. Especially because there were rumours in Moscow that he'd been seen in Kharbin on the China Eastern Railway, or in Burma running a tea plantation for the British. Eventually Dusya, who had talked Pasha out of becoming a monk in the first place and blamed herself for his fate, could take no more. In November '21, she left her son and sobbing mother, and following in her brother's footsteps, set out for the Far East.

In Khabarovsk, Nikodim continued, he thought he'd located Ilya's hideout on two occasions, only to draw a blank both times. Then a whisper of a rumour reached the Services that apparently Ilya had taken off for somewhere in the West. Seeking a needle in a haystack, Nikodim traipsed around the Far East and Siberia for six months, trying to piece things together, but without any leads he made no progress. Then, just as he was losing hope, Moscow ordered him back to Khabarovsk without delay: according to the latest intelligence, this Ilya's go-between, a woman, was expected in the city at any moment. There'd be no better chance of running him to ground.

So actually, he explained to Dusya, there was no miracle here – neither big nor small. How could he have failed to bump into her, frozen in the street, when he had just spent the previous five hours tailing her like a well-trained police spy. By this point it was clear to Nikodim that 'Ilya' was Dusya's brother, Pasha, but she, like Nikodim himself, was also searching for him in the dark. So although he knew he was breaking the rules by bringing her to a safe house, he felt no guilt. 'Or maybe there was a miracle,' he said suddenly, 'otherwise it all seems far too convoluted: as if the Lord and the Cheka were working in unison to entrust one and the same soul to my care.'

When he had gone to the town's railway station two weeks earlier – Nikodim continued – and scanned the crowd for a lady who might fit the description, he was of course stunned to discover that she was his own spiritual daughter, but he felt no particular anguish, convinced as he was that it made no difference anyway – the children would save everyone and wipe the slate clean. He wasn't ashamed of the Shklovsky either. When, back in Moscow, he read Shklovsky's memoirs of the Caucasian Front – a remarkable piece of writing – he understood that one of the events described there was the death of Dusya's husband. But in the end he'd decided to keep it to himself for a while, just in case. Then in Khabarovsk, when he would have given his right arm to have a helper for his 'children's liturgy' and all he could see on her face was indifference, there was nothing for it: it was time, like it or not, to put Shklovsky to use.

Nikodim left Khabarovsk on 7th March '22. Regarding Dusya, he already had an agreement with his handler – who was also head of the town's recently formed Breshko-Breshkovskaya commune – so he had nothing to worry about there. According to the latest reports, Ilya had been sighted in Tomsk several times, and Moscow, unsure of how far everything had gone, was getting decidedly jumpy and demanding further information from the local Cheka as a matter of urgency. Which was why Tomsk needed Nikodim so badly.

The Church channels used by Nikodim worked very well in Siberia too. Thanks to them Nikodim, without raising suspicion, could enter houses that would have been out of bounds to anyone else. These connections gave him a significant advantage: they allowed him in the space of less than a week, to search some half-dozen hideouts in the industrial districts on the edge of town. It was in one such district, in a ramshackle, draughty little hovel, that he found Ilya. He'd got lucky. The fact was that Ilya, a born conspirator, never stayed longer than forty-eight hours anywhere and would have been miles away from Tomsk by now, were it not for a bout of typhus. Nikodim found Ilya on the floor in a completely helpless condition – he must have fallen while trying to get out of bed – and running a temperature of over forty. Found him, and as he explained to Dusya almost apologetically, ended up nursing him. The illness had taken a bad turn and Ilya didn't recover his senses for a full five days; he just raved and offered up garbled prayers, asking the Lord to give him the strength to recover and finish what he had begun.

Then Ilya seemed to be on the mend; he was still bedbound – he couldn't even make it to the sink – but at least he was eating a little. But either this was just a lull, or else his typhus was of the recurrent kind – in any case a week later his temperature began creeping up again, and this relapse was more than Ilya could cope with. Still, during the ten days in which he was conscious, they managed to talk about a great deal. 'In the end,' Nikodim went on, 'we wanted the same thing: to help people, to save them, even if we'd chosen different paths.'

As she listened to all this, Dusya remained calm. Perhaps Nikodim had been expecting a different reaction or he was just tired, but from this point onwards he spoke less fluently. Ilya had no reason to distrust Nikodim, even if at one point he did marvel at fate, which had brought his sister's beloved confessor to him as he lay dying in Tomsk. Well, the Civil War, which had mixed everyone and everything up together, loved pulling stunts like this, and they never returned to the topic again. Nor did Ilya name his contacts – just as Nikodim never asked for any.

Overall, Ilya was quite candid, and Nikodim quickly realised that no new Holy Crusade against the Bolsheviks – the Chekists' great worry – had been or would be organised by him. Some mistake or misprint must have found its way into the intelligence received by the Cheka – the whole story wasn't worth the paper it had been written on. Ilya's aim from the very beginning, had been not a Holy Crusade but a Holy Cross procession of officers and Cossacks, of people, in other words, who had committed a mortal sin: the spilling of their Christian brothers' blood. Bearing icons, candles, and above all, prayers of remorse on their lips, they would walk from Siberia to Moscow. He envisaged many such processions, which would be formed of those who had killed in the recent Civil War, whomever they had fought for – Reds, Whites, Greens – and would advance from all corners of Russia on Moscow, where beneath the Kremlin walls, the believers would beg forgiveness from their former enemies and make peace with them. Alas, he had no success with this plan either; he was dying in Siberia in the same way that he had arrived there – all alone.

As though to justify himself, Ilya said that he realised there was no longer any chance of rousing people to his cause. He kept repeating that everyone he met was tired to death, wanted to leave, flee or just find somewhere to hide and lie low. That they were scared it would all end in more shooting. But they didn't want to shoot anyone ever again. He also mentioned that His Grace Amvrosy, with whom thanks to Dusya they were both acquainted, had long known this. When Ilya had asked him for his blessing before leaving Moscow, Amvrosy had flatly refused. As for the Bolsheviks, he'd said that this was a demon that could not be banished by force or by collective action, but only by the fasts and prayers of each individual soul.

That conversation with Amvrosy depressed him deeply; he couldn't stop coming back to it. He even seemed to have decided that the human exhaustion he had mentioned was irrelevant, just a pretext; the real reason was that people felt they had been denied God's blessing.

Ilya wasn't much interested in what Nikodim had to tell him about the untended. However much Nikodim tried to prove to him that it was those same unfortunates, those same long-suffering children who had taken the world's evil upon themselves, that only they had preserved a connection with the Lord and could become the supplicants of the human race, Ilya just shrugged. 'But on one occasion,' Nikodim continued, 'I must have really got on his nerves – this was three days before his relapse – and he said a few things which however heretical, I remember to this day. Ilya claimed that Man – here on Earth – lives not as if he were created in God's image and likeness, but as though he himself had sculpted the Lord in conformity with his own sin-fouled nature. As if echoing the Old Believer whose bunk was right next to mine in the camp near Abakan, Ilya took the view that all the evil, all the deaths and punishments that can be found in Scripture, are our own human evil and bear no relation to God. Specifically, he said the same about Egypt too, and when I reminded him of what the Lord had said about Himself – "And I will harden Pharaoh's heart, and multiply My signs and My wonders in the land of Egypt" (Exodus 7:3) – he replied that this "hardening of the heart" is the same slavery, the same bondage that the Pharaoh had imposed on God's chosen people, and that like a faithful dog had returned to its master.

'He didn't believe in the waters that had swallowed up the human race on the Day of Judgement and that had held the ark afloat; before the flood, in Ilya's telling, people themselves line and perish so stupidly. And also: that it was no accident that Nikodim had placed the bookmark right there, on the page about the River Araks. He probably no longer found her sense of guilt to be strong enough. She turned these two thoughts over in her mind for a while, then fell asleep.

That night she had a dream. She's playing with the children after supper in Moscow, in the living room, when there's an unexpected ring. She walks down the corridor and opens the door. On the threshold stands an unshaven, uncombed Pyotr in a tattered filthy greatcoat. In her dream she's happy that he's alive, that he's come back, her legs buckle from joy and tenderness towards him, he rushes towards her, wants to embrace her, sweep her up, and suddenly she realises that there's something wrong with him. The only thing she liked about him from their very first day of intimacy were his hands: they were large, as soft as a doctor's, and she liked it when he grabbed her with them, held her close, but the hands that extend towards her now are someone else's, fine-boned and puny, and they look like tentacles.

Feeling wronged, disgusted, deceived without obvious cause, Dusya starts crying, tries to wriggle out and slip away. At first Pyotr thinks that she is just toying and flirting with him, but then after one look at Dusya's face, he understands everything. He turns away and draws several loud breaths through his nose, but she has nothing to say to him and so without hearing a single word from his wife, Igrenyev leaves.

Just as he had promised, Nikodim let Dusya live in his room for a whole month, even a little bit more, then told her that unfortunately he had to leave Khabarovsk. He had no money had been filling the Earth with their sins day and night, until the Lord despaired, gave up on the tribe of Adam and left it to choke on its own evil. But now, when He has sworn that there will never be another flood over the Earth, we have completely let ourselves go. Murders, hatred, greed without limit or end, while He, like some patient nanny, keeps indulging Man's entreaties. Believes our false repentance, forgives us, wipes away our tears. And this makes us no better.

'As regards children,' Ilya continued, 'we needn't take our orders from them. Too worn out to endure evil any longer, the Lord works a miracle, and from us, covered as we are in mortal sin from head to toe, are born pure, unblemished souls. Sadly, as they mature, these souls also succumb to evil, so great is its charm. Worse still, after gawping for so long at children and seeing how much the Lord loves them, we too have no wish to grow up.

'We are tormented, century after century, by the demons of pride and chosenness; thanks to them we shed our own and other people's blood as if it were water, yet we refuse to answer for anything. Try nudging us and we'll shriek that we're only little, only foolish, and you really shouldn't expect too much from us. Whatever we may have done, we're as innocent as we always were. As a last resort we'll shift all the blame onto others, onto those who, like the Devil, tempted us and lured us into evil. None of us know what real repentance is, but you can't atone for your sins without it.

'In Tomsk,' Nikodim went on, 'the GPU knew almost nothing about me for almost a month. Right until the end I believed I could get Ilya – that is Pasha – back on his feet, and I didn't want to hand him in. I understood of course, that the only thing I was nursing him for was a Chekist's bullet, but when you're caring for a dying man, you don't stop to think about what comes next. But I didn't manage to save him. I remember to this day how he kept begging the Lord to let him live, to let him join the procession with the Holy Cross, but then, once he understood he was dying, he became sluggish and indifferent, merely repeating that Amvrosy seemed to have been right all along: his path had not been blessed.

'On the eve of his death, after I changed Pasha's sheets – they were dripping with sweat – he thanked me for such a long time I felt ashamed, and then, just like that, without the slightest warning, he asked me to confess him. I offered to go and find another priest the following morning – I had nothing with me either for the Eucharist or the Holy Unction – but he cut me short with a shake of his head. Pasha's confession was quite brief and after I absolved him – this must have been some time between two and three in the morning – he lost consciousness.

'I sat beside him and watched the flame flickering in the potbelly stove, until the wood burned out and the *izba* began to cool. I had to go out to the shed – we'd been using its floorboards to heat the stove for the past two days. I must have hacked away for an hour, breaking off and chopping up boards, and when I came back and began stacking them by the stove I suddenly realised that the *izba* was strangely quiet. All those days Ilya had been wheezing and groaning in his sleep, but now, not a sound. At first I thought Pasha's fever had come down and he was sleeping peacefully, and it was only when I went over to the bed that I realised his ordeal was over. The following morning I read prayers for Pasha's soul and slipped up on two occasions, when I commended to God's care His recently departed servant "Ilya".

'A peasant lived with his wife in the next hovel along; they had once been workers at the long-closed hardware factory just across the road. I already knew them and had given them some money a few times. When I couldn't leave Pasha's side, they would buy supplies for us at the market. Good, God-fearing people. Now, for a gold coin, they agreed to knock together a coffin from pine boards, dig a grave at the local cemetery near the Church of St Nicholas, which had been plundered the previous summer and was now closed, and help lay the deceased to rest.

'Making the grave was hard work, the cemetery soil was all clay and stone and had frozen through during the winter. The pit couldn't be dug, it had to be gouged out with a crowbar. They laboured away almost until dusk, but it still came out shallow, with barely enough space for the coffin. There, at the cemetery, I recited a last prayer for the repose of the deceased and we lowered Pasha into the ground. Then we put out some vodka on a nearby bench and hastily drank to his memory.

'The day after the burial I ordered a memorial service for Pasha in the city's cathedral, after which I went to the local GPU office to give myself up. I didn't think anything too terrible lay in store for me, after all I was the bearer of good tidings: I'd come to say that Ilya was dead and no longer a danger to anyone. But they listened to my report stone-faced. Just as soon as I'd finished, the most senior person there, a commissar of some kind, pressed a button to summon an escort and I was taken off to a cell. They were in no mood to mess about.

Be as Children

'That time I was only given three lengthy interrogations, but the first was more than enough for me to see that in their eyes I was a traitor and Ilya's accomplice, and that the Holy Cross procession seemed just as dangerous to the Soviet authorities as any crusade.

'Nor did Ilya's death mitigate my guilt in any way. The investigator in charge of the case actually made fun of me at one point, saying that even if Ilya's torments were over, mine were not.

'Man's a funny creature: for as long as the investigation was still under way, I was scared of only one thing – that they would want to check what I'd said and go and dig up the grave. But clearly they already knew about the Procession of the Holy Cross, just as they knew that nothing had come of this whole idea – so there was no point in putting themselves to unnecessary trouble. However shameless a double-dealer I'd shown myself to be in Tomsk, I'd still been sent by Moscow, and they dared not shoot me without its sanction. So they asked the Lubyanka, where it was decided after some hesitation that, badly as I had behaved in Siberia, they could still find a use for me.

'As soon as I was released from the house of detention, I left town as fast as I could. Never staying in one place for long, I spent two years roaming between St Petersburg and Central Asia. I lived in Vologda, Tashkent, Yerevan, but mostly I wandered around Russia's South. Much of my time was still spent on the untended, but without my frenzy of old. I'd lost any sense of urgency – in fact, I found myself thinking more and more often that there was a good deal of truth in what Ilya had told me.

'Before I settled down,' Nikodim went on with his story, 'they kept half an eye on me at most, and never bothered me. I can see now that I should never have put down roots, I should have carried on with my vagrant life. But I was tired, and in '24, as Dusya knows, I returned to Moscow again. Got a job at a school in Miusy,[55] teaching biology, geography and even, if I was asked, physics. I got on fine with my colleagues, no dramas, and I also found a nice enough room to rent – warm and close to the school. I wore ordinary clothes of course, so the thought that I might be a monk never crossed anyone's mind.

'I worked at the school for more than five years, but in 1930, when I was coming home from mass on Christmas Eve, they grabbed me in the middle of the street. Came up to me, introduced themselves, showed the warrant for my arrest and took me off to Lefortovo Prison. And from there, a month later I was transported to Tomsk, where the local Chekists still remembered me.'

Father Nikodim said nothing about what was happening in Siberia at this time, during collectivisation, but I didn't need him to tell me that beyond the Urals churchmen were being shot in droves. There were two other men in his cell, which was a small pre-Revolutionary solitary, and the first he mentioned was the priest Father Nikolai. The same priest, I quickly realised, whom Dusya had fallen in love with at the gymnasium. In Nikodim's account he was a sorry fellow aged forty-five or so, maybe fifty, but much older to look at, a wreck of a man. He reminded him of Job, not the Job who rebels

---

[55] A small area in central Moscow north-east of Mayakovskaya metro station.

though, but the Job who has been crushed and has long since resigned himself to his lot.

Before becoming a priest, Father Nikolai had been a competent schoolteacher, Nikodim explained for my benefit. He would probably have stuck at it, had his father not gone bankrupt. In 1912, under pressure from his family (he had five sisters, for a start), Father Nikolai held out for a month before agreeing to take holy orders and to replace the recently deceased senior priest at the large church in Moscow that his betrothed had, so to speak, inherited. Father Nikolai had graduated with distinction from a seminary before entering university, so no objections were expected on the part of the diocesan authorities. Only one thing was still needed before he could join the clergy – a wedding.

Despite the period of mourning, everything was arranged by mutual agreement within a matter of days. But it's not easy to be the wife of a priest, and Masha, still just a young girl who loved concerts, theatres and balls, proved unprepared for it. Like Dusya, she had dreamed of a prince, but the man she got as her husband was already going grey and bald. She remembered that she had once liked him, that she had found him exalted and poetic, but now she thought that she had simply been tricked and taken for a ride.

Both before and after the Revolution she conceived easily, a child every year, but with each new baby she saw more and more clearly that her life was ruined. When in 1920 the church was shut down and the family started going hungry, she came to loathe him. He knew this, and according to Nikodim, could not forgive himself for ignoring a friend's advice never to marry a young girl. He used to say that he was irredeemably guilty before her.

From then on they moved from one village parish to another. Twice he escaped only by a miracle. Every Chekist, every special ops cadre had a mother, aunt or granny among his parishioners, and they were the ones who warned him, who let him know that he had to leave that same night or else he'd be seized at dawn. The warrant had already been signed. While Father Nikolai would wander off in search of a new parish, his tender-hearted flock helped feed his family as best it could. Eventually he would find a church that was not yet destroyed and begin ministering there, but just as soon as Masha arrived with the children, the same thing would happen all over again.

Nikodim described how Father Nikolai would pray aloud in the cell and ask the Lord over and over what he had done to deserve such a punishment: a wife who does not love her husband. He would cry and keep asking whether his sins were truly so great. He would tell Nikodim that he had often thought that maybe they really should seize him, arrest him, shoot him, anything so as not to see that hatred – and then he would curse himself without mercy. The children needed bringing up after all. In prison he began to recover his spirits a little and described how one night, during a savage frost, he had walked almost thirty versts across the taiga to shake off his pursuers. Wolves howled around him and he, for all his unceasing prayers, had been sure that right now, straight after that fir tree, they would jump on him and tear him to pieces. But that surge soon petered out and he began talking once more only of Masha, the children and how they were coping without him. He'd been taken a hundred versts from town, deep in the countryside, and hadn't had the faintest chance of finding out what had happened to them. Overall he was a very dignified, very sad man, and Nikodim said that he counted him among those who had been given a rough ride in life, perhaps even unfairly so.

Earlier on, Nikodim had been confessing to Dusya; now it seemed that part was over, and he, completely drained, slumped back against the wall and closed his eyes. He hadn't asked, but I brought some hot tea from the kitchen just in case, and next to it, on a saucer, I laid out the pills he usually took during the day. Nikodim ignored the pills but drank a little tea, clearly glad that it was sweet and strong. The tea revived him, and leaning on some cushions, he sat back up again. As if by inertia he was still looking at Dusya, but it was clear to us both that now it was my turn to receive Nikodim's confession.

His starting point was the same topic I'd been going on at him about for two years from different angles. He said that Noan Yefimov, whom he'd mentioned when talking about the North, had been in the next bunk along in Tomsk City Prison. Throughout the four months of the investigation, during the winter and early spring of '31, the three of them – Father Nikolai, Noan and Nikodim – had shared the same cell. What I'd heard so far from Nikodim was Noan's stories about his tribesfolk; now it was time to hear about Noan himself.

'There was a long period,' Nikodim said, 'when the three of us were in different cells, on different charges: I as Ilya's accomplice – they hadn't forgotten; Father Nikolai, God rest his soul, for trouble-making – he stood accused of opposing the local authorities and attempting to foment an uprising in the village of Stolbovoye: for two hours some thirty peasant women, most of them elderly, had prevented the police from closing and sealing the church where he was ministering; while the Enets, Noan Yefimov, hadn't actually been charged with anything at all.

'He'd been arrested at a remote reindeer camp at the head of the River Sym, a thousand versts from where we were now, and getting him to Tomsk by one means or another took almost half a year. His documents, if there ever were any, got lost on the way, and the Procurator's Office wasn't at all inclined to start working on his case. It was only much later, when we had already spent at least six months in the town's remand prison, that some brainbox came up with the idea of connecting us and lumping us together for a big trial. We were labelled the Counter-Revolutionary Organisation of Clerics, CROC for short.

'Any other prisoner would have said that Noan Yefimov had been dealt the worst possible hand, but with him joy seemed to spring eternal – he had enough of it to last him till his dying day, whatever fate placed in his path. Having said that, things didn't look too bad for Noan at the beginning, in fact he even seemed to have struck lucky. There was no way of establishing why he'd been locked up – Yefimov himself had no idea – and as for fabricating something serious out of nothing, well, the Chekists were already drowning in work without him. Noan had the most trusting, sincere eyes imaginable; no wonder that the first idea that occurred to Volkov, the prison agent in charge of Yefimov, was to recruit him as a stool pigeon.

'He was moved to a nice warm room – it had been a solitary confinement cell until the Revolution, but now the bunks stood three high – and other detainees were put in with him, first one, then two. Volkov's calculation proved accurate: people couldn't resist confessing and baring their souls to Noan. But if the agent had made no mistake there, what followed proved far trickier: Yefimov did not wish to give away anything of what had been confided in him. Volkov tried all the baits he could think of – a double ration, other perks, and later on, a nice cushy position. When carrots failed, he tried the stick, first taking away Noan's shamanic amulets, then putting him in solitary. Gave him a three-day break to weigh everything up, then sent him back to the punishment cell for two weeks. But nothing helped, and the decision was taken to make an example of him.

'There was one cell in the prison, entirely made up of non-politicals, where a sadist and murderer ruled the roost, one Sergei Paranyanov, nicknamed Pike. He certainly stood out from the common run of criminals. In Irkutsk, in the '20s, he had killed at least a dozen people – even more, Dima,' said Nikodim, looking at me, 'than that Peregudov of yours. The criminal investigation department in Irkutsk had it in for him, and when they managed to catch him in '24 his arrest was held up to the city as a great triumph for the GPU. Pike's trial was covered in the local press and no one expected any other verdict than the death sentence. Which is exactly what he got.

'He was meant to be shot that same day but the presiding judge decided to put on a show of legality, and in accordance with regulations, gave Pike a month during which he could appeal to Moscow for pardon. Paranyanov made the most of it. He sent a letter in verse to the head of the All-Russian Executive Committee, Mikhail Kalinin, which began as follows: "I've thought it all through with a cool head, and swear on the grave of Lenin the dead, that I'm only an accidental offender, and

I'll reform like any honourable pauper." Inspiration ran dry at this point so Paranyanov carried on in prose, vowing that if he was forgiven he would make amends and become a shock worker to recompense his countrymen for every kopeck he'd ever stolen from them. This gibberish was sent off to Moscow, and strange as it may seem, did the trick: Paranyanov's death sentence was commuted to ten years in prison.

'In comparison with what would happen five or six years later,' Nikodim continued, 'ours was still a vegetarian time: you got beaten, of course, beaten black and blue, but the "conveyor belt" and other such delights were still a rarity, and the Chekists liked to complain that their hands were tied. In Tomsk they were helped out by Paranyanov and his desire to atone.

'His cell became an out-and-out torture chamber, a kind of private hell for prisoners who didn't want to sign the statements that the investigators needed. The agony and humiliation meted out in that room were such that of those who passed through Pike's hands over many years only a few managed not to crack. As for Noan, though,' Nikodim said, 'it seemed at first as if he might survive even Pike unscathed. There were rumours that in his previous cell he had complained to his bunkmates that he was being forced to endure evil. That without a man to call his own, he was unable to call on his true shamanic power and reward everybody according to their deserts.

'In general the precept "Ask and it shall be given you" is not made for prison, but in this case, somebody, I don't know who, heeded Noan Yefimov's request. In ordinary life,' said Nikodim, turning to me once more, 'a shaman, having chosen a husband, might pretend to be living with him just by chance, but prison mores are simpler, and Pike, who for the first time in five years had seen something resembling a woman, could not resist. It was love at first sight. Wearing multicoloured ribbons in his hair and with clothes copiously adorned from top to toe with ruffles, flounces and fanciful tassels, Noan moved around with grace, gently swaying his hips and wiggling his bum. On the threshold of the cell he really did look like a girl waiting to be given in marriage.

'Pike made a wife of him on the very first night. From then on, for all that he was now a "bitch" and so an untouchable in the prison hierarchy, Yefimov had no one to fear, not with a gangster like that to defend him. Pike lived with his Fimochka – that was his pet name for him – as if they had been together for years. Noan also felt sincere affection for Pike and catered to his every need; luckily their bunks in the corner of the overcrowded cell were screened off with a length of cotton fabric.

'Whenever Yefimov saw that Pike had no need of him for the time being, he would make himself comfortable on their bunks and craft some new amulets for himself. He was good with his hands and did everything himself from start to finish. Pike had a lot of influence in the prison: thanks to him Noan enjoyed a regular supply of beef femur bones, shins and knuckles, on which he carved entire scenes of Samoyed life. He was just as skilled at wood carving, but he preferred bone. His favourite subjects were reindeer drivers and teams of dogs pulling sledges, shamans mid-trance, various spirits good and bad, and herds of reindeer slowly making their way along riverbanks. Once he'd finished carving, he would take a good knife and scrape either an aluminium spoon or a piece of tin from a can, producing a silverish powder which he would then heat up with a blowtorch and rub into the bone like amalgam.

The effect was very beautiful. These were not mere trinkets, but genuine amulets, and nobody in the cell dared touch them, not even Pike.

'One strange story linked to Yefimov's amulets caused a stir throughout the prison. After moving him to his new cell, Volkov carried on calling Yefimov into his office every now and again, to see whether this "stool pigeon" had changed his mind. After one such visit Noan suddenly found himself in possession of two collections of amulets: in addition to a new set, he had also recovered the old, confiscated one, down to the smallest little bell. Apparently they'd been returned to him by spirits.

'Well, it certainly wasn't the agent. The day before, Volkov had spent a long session yelling obscenities at Yefimov and threatening him with every kind of unpleasantness, the like of which would make even Pike seem a soft touch. An investigation into how exactly Noan got hold of the amulets was never held. No one wanted that less than Volkov, who had clearly messed up in a big way. Perhaps that was why this episode continued to accrue completely fantastical details, until eventually it led to the ruin of our shaman himself.

'Among the competing versions, two proved most popular. The first was mundane and perfectly harmless: the shaman "shafted" the agent when the latter went out of the room for a couple of minutes to talk to a friend. Seeing that he was alone in the office, Yefimov grabbed the opportunity to open the cupboard and take back his amulets. Volkov's account was pretty similar, but with one amendment. He hadn't gone out to the corridor, and as per regulations, had not left a prisoner alone in his office – instead he had spoken to the chief security officer, Senior Lieutenant Gudin, from the doorway. Besides, the cupboard in which he had placed Yefimov's amulets was locked and the key remained where it had always been – in the safe. The agent was also the source of the other version, which at first he told only to his wife, but then after one too many at work, he ended up sharing with his colleagues as well. It certainly put a different spin on what happened.

'According to this second version, Yefimov responded calmly to Volkov's filthy language by saying that in the past, before Pike became his husband, he had been an ordinary shaman and a far less potent one than his forebears. One of those, who had roamed not far from Lake Uvs Nuur,[56] had his beloved white stallion stolen by a cruel rich landowner, a *bai*, who lived in the vicinity. The shaman was upset but waited patiently for two months, hoping the *bai* would think better of it. But when it became clear that no one was planning to give the horse back to him, he took his revenge, destroying the *bai*'s entire clan with the help of the spirits. Did he, Volkov, want to bring about his own ruin too? After all he had a wife and children. But these were just words and the agent burst out laughing. So then, as if he had every right to do so, Yefimov got up, went to the door, opened it, and in a loud voice summoned the guard currently on duty on that floor, Senior Sergeant Tuchka. He appeared. Yefimov told him to lie down. The sergeant lay down. Yefimov told him to turn onto his back. Once again the guard obeyed him, as if hypnotised. Then Yefimov bent over and with a single sweep of his hand

---

[56] The largest lake in Mongolia, the Uvs reaches up into Tuva, a contested territory in the inter-war period before being integrated into the Soviet Union in 1944.

ripped out both of Tuchka's eyes, then placed them on the table next to the inkpot, right under Volkov's nose. Though there was no blood, the blinded Tuchka wailed like a woman and only calmed down when Yefimov took pity on him and put the eyes back in. The agent was offered the same treatment, but didn't want anything to do with it.'

'Volkov paid a heavy price for that booze-up. Three days later, with the words *For Bringing into Disrepute* added to his military record book, he was dismissed from the Services; then after another seven days, as if someone was out to remove unwanted witnesses, Pike was stabbed with a shiv during daily exercise.

'Yefimov's fame as a crafty thief,' Nikodim continued, 'did not last long however. Just as soon as Pike was wheeled into the morgue, dark days set in for the shaman. A power struggle began in the cell, and the *zeks* literally ran amok. Without his protector Noan became just another bitch. A couple of times he was "passed down the tram" and raped by the whole cell, and even the ritual "registration" of Yefimov on the floor next to the piss bucket, after they'd shoved him off his bunk, was not enough to calm them down.

'They seemed to be making up for all the vicious humiliations they'd been unable to inflict on him while Pike was still alive. Meanwhile the powers with which he had frightened the agent,' Nikodim noted, perhaps to me, perhaps to Dusya, 'were in no hurry to come to his aid. He was shy and meek, as submissive and slavish as bitches are meant to be, but still the cell did not tire of bullying and torturing him. Endless kicks to the groin, knuckle sandwiches, jeers. And the thing that enraged his cellmates the most was the idiotic way

Noan had of finding excuses for the men who were making him suffer. Every time he was hit or spat at, Yefimov would tell his offender that he didn't blame him for anything. That he forgave him all the bad things he had done and was doing to him, knew that he was cold, sick, hungry – collectivisation was already into its second year and just recently the rations, miserly enough already, had been cut by a third, so every other *zek* had scurvy or diarrhoea. In short, such cruelty was understandable.

'These words of mercy and forgiveness were loathed with a passion by the entire cell. The minute Yefimov started off on his preaching, the *zeks* would turn into clowns and fools, mimicking and interrupting him. Playing his words back to him almost to the letter, they cackled away and congratulated themselves on their new understanding of why it was that they had stolen and killed, why they had caused so much pain and grief without showing an ounce of mercy. Poor souls, they had never had money, shoes or clothes, they had been no better off outside prison than they were now on the inside, and this injustice, which had touched each and every one of them, had been too much for them to bear. Others had accepted it, managed to convince themselves that there was nothing to be done about it, such was life, but they could not, and having lost their way, had turned to crime.

'Evidently there was something about their mockery that Yefimov's brain could not cope with, and the cell having found his weak spot, learnt the quickest way of making Noan lose his self-control and of bringing on an epileptic fit. Trying desperately to forgive them and save them while he still could, he would shout, sputter, start choking and emit some terrible lifeless cry, whereupon, after spinning like a top he would be thrown to the floor.

'The fit usually lasted about a quarter of an hour. He would shake violently throughout and groan, though you could barely hear him – the spasm kept the sound in, like a noose around his throat. Then the convulsions became less frequent and strong, but for another two or three hours he would lie half-dead on the floor, unable to get up. Consciousness returned unevenly – it came and went. As he recovered, Noan would sleep for almost twenty-four hours if the guards let him, then he would need another two, long, agonising weeks before he was himself again.

'Usually his tongue would be badly bitten – as if the Lord were warning him of something. He couldn't chew, gave his rations to his cellmates, ate only thin gruel. He remembered nothing, was feeble and quiet, but his willpower was something else: whenever anyone went past him to the piss bucket, he, as if apologising for himself, would always croak that he didn't blame anyone for anything and as for the fits, they were essential, otherwise the spirits that were making the *zeks* sick would get the better of him. These fits were becoming ever more frequent and it was obvious, even then, that Yefimov already had one foot in the grave. Only the infirmary and a different cell could save him, but the new agent wasn't about to show any leniency either.

'Later on,' Nikodim recalled, 'when we were doing time together, I often asked Yefimov why he let them get away with those beatings and humiliations: he himself had said how strong he'd become since meeting Pike. Noan gave various answers, never with much confidence. He'd say for example, that previously he would never have managed to endure all the bullying and forgive his tormentors, and mentioned one day that during his time in Pike's Cell, as he called it, not one *zek* had died: the spirits were scared of having anything to do with the shaman and made themselves scarce. On the other hand, it was Noan who told me that Pike had worked at a logging camp for two years and was brought back to prison when he was suspected of plotting an escape. Well, in the cutting area that had been assigned to his group, there was an old birch draped with multi-coloured ribbons and rags. Its hollows, it turned out, were used to bury the bones of shamans. Once Pike chopped it down, he was condemned by the spirits of the dead, who then turned against Yefimov as well.

'But either those shamans eventually eased off, or else he just got lucky – in any case, Yefimov was suddenly given a reprieve. Two things had come together. Volkov, who had become a laughing-stock among both his colleagues and the *zeks* after the episode with the amulets, was dismissed from the Services; at the same time, the city's OGPU officers, who had long dreamed of some spectacular case that might compare with the trials taking place in Moscow, had gathered all the material and all the people they needed. The three of us – Father Nikolai, Yefimov and I – were lumped together as perpetrators in the same religious plot and the case was entrusted to one Captain Izbin, a recent graduate of the law faculty at the Communist University of Tomsk, for whom this was meant to serve as a kind of public defence of his thesis.

'In the view of the OGPU, Noan Yefimov was ideally suited to the Counter-Revolutionary Organisation of Clerics (CROC): as a shaman, he was the perfect complement and foil to the Russian Orthodox Church, and brought a Siberian flavour to the whole affair. It goes without saying that the Chekists needed Noan alive when the trial came round, so a bed was immediately found in the prison infirmary and after his treatment the shaman was taken not to his old cell but to the one shared by Father Nikolai and myself, out of harm's way.

'Izbin, like many children of poor peasants, had been rapidly promoted. His parents had been farmhands all their lives, and he himself had grown up working either for his crust or for a daily wage. He was just in time to catch the end of the Civil War, became a Party member at the front, and then when Blyukher finished off Kolchak,[57] left the army and went to work for the GPU. He was a decent, diligent student at university, but he lacked the imagination and sophistication needed to concoct a trial that you wouldn't be ashamed to show even to guests from the capital. Still, this could be fixed. From his very first day, he was assigned a consultant to assist him, a "bourgeois specialist" if you will, by the name of Kuzmatsky, a former barrister who had been widely considered the best defending advocate in Tomsk before the Revolution.

'Kuzmatsky was a notable figure in the town. A deputy of the State Duma and a friend and comrade of Kerensky in the Socialist-Revolutionary Party, he had even spent a couple of months as Minister for Nationalities, but returned to Tomsk when Kerensky fled Russia. Kuzmatsky was no fool and understood the risks he was taking, but whether the

---

[57] Vasily Blyukher (1889-1938), a legendary Red Army commander during the Civil War, later dubbed 'Red Napoleon'. White leader Admiral Kolchak suffered a series of defeats in 1919 and was executed by a Bolshevik firing squad in January 1920.

town found itself under the Czech Legion or Kolchak or War Communism, he passed up every opportunity to leave. Partly he was counting on his insurance policy – three of the four Bolsheviks he had successfully defended in Tomsk before the Revolution were now members of the Central Committee – but the main thing I suspect, was that he wasn't prepared to start over from scratch.

'For seven years or so, it looked as if Kuzmatsky had made the right decision. He wasn't even forced to share his apartment, and the friends of his who had emigrated, whether to Kharbin or Paris, were having a worse time of it. But after '25, his association with Kerensky once again began to outweigh his revolutionary credentials, the list of his failings grew, and Kuzmatsky could no longer delude himself – he realised he was sinking. Even so, he held on for another fifteen years. He was arrested just before the war and died in the camps.

'In the '20s Kuzmatsky is still considered the best defence lawyer in town, but he's already firmly at the OGPU's beck and call. He's not a scumbag by nature – it's just that the time has come to atone for old sins. By this point defence counsels have completely given up on the idea of putting spokes in the Services' wheels, but even so surprises can happen during political trials, and the Party considers these to be professional failings, unacceptable blunders. Kuzmatsky snitches on his clients, and if necessary, helps break them down, convince them that denying the charges will only harm their cause. With him everything runs smoothly from start to finish. The Procurator's Office returns the favour by trying not to be too brutal towards his defendants.

'When the prison guard left Kuzmatsky alone with us we

assumed he was a comrade in misfortune, but soon realised our error. After introducing himself and shaking everyone by the hand, he immediately got down to business. Essentially he was offering us a typical plea bargain. By way of preliminaries, he explained that nothing could be done about the sentence itself. Only the Lord could help with that, and even then, only by helping us accept it. The OGPU had various priorities; one way or another, it would get its way. Everyone else – be it the court, be it Kuzmatsky – had to let the Services "win". So if we listened to him, we stood to lose nothing in terms of the sentence itself, and we would come out on top in every other way. Play goody two-shoes and it would mean, first of all, that Kuzmatsky could retain the transcript's mention of extenuating circumstance, which he would then rely on during appeal. The Tomsk stage was cut and dried, no hope of any change there, but he might be able to help with what came next. Aside from that, we would not be beaten or abused and no way would we end up in another Pike Cell – we'd stay where we were until the trial was over.

'What Kuzmatsky said sounded perfectly reasonable, and I had no trouble accepting the rules of the game. Things were simpler for me in prison than for others: unlike Father Nikolai, for example, I wasn't responsible for anyone except myself. In the end Nikolai also agreed to go along with it, while still weeping for his wife and children, praying then weeping. Only Noan showed any mettle and categorically refused to sign a single statement against me or Father Nikolai. All three of us – myself, Father Nikolai and Kuzmatsky – spent forty-eight hours straight trying to convince him that it was just a formality: the court would be in closed session in any case, his statements would end up in the file whatever he did and nobody would think of checking whether it was Yefimov's signature beneath them or someone else's – but the shaman held his ground.

'It wasn't his refusal to testify against us though that did for Noan – that really was neither here nor there – but the fact that a month later, under interrogation by Izbin, he suddenly gave his word not only that he would not sign anything, but that if this lawlessness did not immediately cease, he would go straight to the "conscience of the Party" in Moscow – the head of the Central Control Commission Aaron Aleksandrovich Soltz – and tell him personally what the Chekists of Tomsk were up to on behalf of the Russian Communist Party. Then, three days later, in the presence of ourselves and Kuzmatsky, he showed Izbin, who had stopped by for a brief visit, proof that he really had flown to Moscow and back on a tambourine: a beautiful fountain pen with a gold nib and the surname Soltz neatly engraved on its cap, along with his initials and the inscription "To a Delegate of the Third Congress of the Communist International". Damned if we knew how he'd got hold of that in prison. In other words, we seemed to be watching a carbon copy of the episode that led to Volkov being thrown out of the Services. Izbin could hardly let Yefimov's stunt go unpunished. He was far from timid – no Moscow bigwig could put the wind up him – and he wasn't about to forgive the shaman for trying to scare him.

'Kuzmatsky went over every detail of the trial with us – which didn't surprise us in the least. He spoke about what would happen when and how, and was glad to know what Yefimov and I thought of it. Father Nikolai had other things to worry about, although he was promised that if he cooperated in good faith, he would get the chance to see his wife. I have to say that Kuzmatsky was pretty straight with us. In particular, he didn't bother hiding just how pessimistic he felt about it all, though the reason he gave for this was not any malicious intent on Izbin's part, just the cruelty of the times in general.

'At first our lawyer would bring only a rough outline with him, but at a certain point these sketches suddenly began to merge all by themselves into a libretto, the first approximation of a script. Entering the cell soon after reveille and leaving just before lights out, Kuzmatsky must have worked at home during the night as well, because the next morning he would bring a polished version of what we had only discussed the previous day. It was obvious that he had both an excellent ear and literary flair; he immediately caught our words, expressions, phrasing – Father Nikolai's, Yefimov's, my own – and fine-tuned them like musical instruments, licking the speech of his defendants into shape. Nothing was lost. He asked us all sorts of concerned questions about our past lives, and he was particularly fond of the olden days, of times that had no connection with what was happening now, but here too, Kuzmatsky must have had a follow-up system at home where he sieved through everything we'd said, thanks to which a few more details crept into our statements. As a result, the case was transformed before our eyes into something that I myself, were I not in the dock, would have believed only too willingly.

'Literature stitched together with the casuistry of legalese seems to have considerable power. From the point of view of a secular, not to mention Soviet-socialist government, the substance of this trial looked completely insane, but that didn't bother anyone. We were accused of the following: no sooner had the Red Army demolished the Whites and forced them out of the country than clerics of various faiths and religions joined forces in Siberia to take up Kolchak's cause. Putting old enmities and hatred aside, they decided to use their prayers, charms and trances to summon the aid of the angels, devils, good and evil spirits that were under their control, and then in their vast motley horde, march once more on revolutionary Moscow in the name of the Tsar. Under Kuzmatsky's pen, all this was strangely persuasive. The Church, it turned out, really was the sworn and perfidious enemy of the Revolution and every persecution of it was justified.

'CROC – the big Siberian trial of churchmen – was meant to be Izbin's great moment, crowning his appointment as a state prosecutor. But the scale of the affair was such that without Kuzmatsky's help Izbin would never have kept to schedule. In advance of the court hearings, our advocate wrote the statements of all the defendants, witnesses and experts, those of the accomplices and victims, the speech to be given by the prosecutor, i.e. Izbin, and by the counsel for the defence, and their closing arguments, as well as the speeches of the social prosecutors and the social counsels for the defence, whose participation was also foreseen in the draft scenario for the trial.[58] Kuzmatsky even added remarks from the gallery, in fact he wrote every single word right up to the verdict, which on his own initiative, he supplied in two versions – one harsh, the other slightly milder.

---

[58] A distinctive feature of Soviet law was the permission granted to representatives of social organisations (eg the Komsomol, collective farms, cultural institutions) to take part in court hearings.

'Kuzmatsky's task however, was not just to prepare and assemble all the elements of the trial into some kind of unity and to do so as harmoniously and seamlessly as any conductor; it was also, just as importantly, to persuade us not to interfere with any part of his creation, and instead to go along with it and actively cooperate. As far as I can see, the script, or at least its skeleton, didn't take Kuzmatsky all that long to write; he had vast experience and by this point there was already a kind of industry standard in place: all political trials, whether occurring in Vladivostok or Leningrad, were more or less indistinguishable. Nevertheless, from the day that CROC received the sanction of the CP City Committee and we found ourselves in a single cell, Kuzmatsky worked nonstop to meet his deadlines. Which by the way, did not prevent him from showing sympathy towards all three of us. He clearly pitied us: whenever we had a disagreement with the prison staff and he was in a position, thanks to Izbin, to help us, he would always take our side.

'At the same time Kuzmatsky did not conceal the fact that, as a convinced atheist, he found his current defendants somewhat ridiculous. He was fond of implying that in his view we had simply fallen behind the times, we had failed to develop. He was sure that, whatever the fate of the Bolsheviks themselves, God – and not only in Russia – would soon be a thing of the past, that the Almighty was a kind of atavistic holdover. He found my background in the natural sciences particularly hard to come to terms with. Once, he would explain, faith really had been indispensable, people had wanted to understand how the world worked, they needed protection and support, so they went and invented God. But now there

BE AS CHILDREN

was science for the first bit and the state for the second, yet we, like little children, were determined to have it our own way. In our folly we'd stumbled into a deadly game and we weren't prepared to yield an inch. None of us was spared Kuzmatsky's criticism, though Yefimov was certainly given an easier ride. And not because he was suffering more. It was just that Father Nikolai and myself were, in his eyes, adults for whom childhood was a game that they had been playing for far too long, whereas the shaman really was a child. He had been fated not to grow up, and could remain little.

'Kuzmatsky was hardly impartial here. His work was gently leading us to a bullet in the head, or at best to long years in the camps. A man knows when he is guilty before another, and he rarely forgives the person he has harmed. Kuzmatsky was an advocate to his bones and blamed us for his current powerlessness: unlike him, we hadn't found a way of getting along with the Bolsheviks. The shaman was a different matter. Seven years earlier, under the same Soviet authorities, Kuzmatsky wouldn't have had the slightest difficulty securing Noan's freedom right there in the courtroom, and even now he was initially convinced that saving the shaman from the death penalty was the very least he would achieve.

'Yefimov was a goldmine for any defence. His ancestry, first of all. His grandfather and father were both socialists, not to mention that grandpa was a member of Black Repartition, along with Lenin's teacher Plekhanov.[59] Then there was the

---

[59] Black Repartition was formed in 1880 after the revolutionary organisation Land and Freedom split into two branches, one (People's Will) continuing to support terrorism, the other, smaller group (Black Repartition) favouring gradualism and revolution from below. Georgy Plekhanov (1856-1918) was among its leaders.

splendid story of the Buryat shaman and his white filly. By annihilating the entire clan of the feudal lord of the steppes – the evil *bai* – Yefimov's ancestor had confirmed the ancient revolutionary traditions of this family once and for all. Even so, Kuzmatsky hesitated. All these stories – from the *bai* to the amulets, the tambourine and Soltz – could easily be passed off as schizophrenia, permitting a request for clemency on those very grounds: Noan, whatever his alleged crimes, simply did not know what he was doing. In the end though, Kuzmatsky decided that for this court revolutionary credentials would be a safer bet.

'Then when relations between Izbin and Yefimov began visibly deteriorating and Kuzmatsky suddenly understood that the prosecutor would demand the highest penalty, he swung back to schizophrenia again, but it was too late. As a result, Yefimov's death sentence came as a heavy blow to the defending advocate. Even heavier perhaps than he had expected.

'For six weeks Kuzmatsky did everything except sleep in our cell. But then he faded into the background and we were left on our own. He still dropped in every now and again of course, but never for long. Just a quick, cursory visit to see how we were getting on with our roles and to make a few refinements and adjustments here and there. The more suspects were pulled into the CROC Affair, the more contradictions and cracks began to appear – they needed to be smoothed out and filled in.

'I found the lead-up to the trial and the trial itself very hard. A believer always has something to fall back on of course, but even so, the awareness that you will be dead before the month is out would be a struggle for anyone. But it wasn't just the trial. There was another punishment now – Yefimov. Unlike Kuzmatsky, he never doubted he would die, and he told Father Nikolai and myself that he was ready to do so. Thanks yet again to Pike, he now had enough strength to save his Enets prophet and teacher through his own suffering, to pay with his own blood for the blood shed by Peregudov.

'Soon though, even Peregudov was not enough for the shaman. He suddenly announced that he would save not only him, but others too. Not through force, not through power, but by giving away his own life he would deliver human beings from sin. As Christ had taken upon Himself the sins of the world, so he, Yefimov, would redeem the Earth from evil demons; by leading them away, he would liberate it for all time. With him it always seemed the only direction was up. As if in cahoots with Izbin, he brought the passion of a neophyte to the task of joining our faiths, of tying them into one. He terrorised me day and night with his defence of Kuzmatsky's argument: Christ, Turom – it was all the same thing. He adduced hundreds of proofs.

'Trying to entice me into the new Samoyed-Christian faith, Yefimov laid out before me, in terms that anyone could understand, the entire edifice of his naïve, childlike and – for all its deaths, grief and blood – hope-filled Gospel. He began by saying that on Middle Earth sins and crimes have multiplied to calamitous proportions. A thick gloom reigns all the way down to the lowest, ninth *olokh*, and through it, however much you strain your sight, no good is visible. The Middle Earth is deformed and decayed beyond recognition and yet, he assured us in the next breath, they, the shamans, would drive the evil spell from the Earth with prayers and cures, they would cleanse it of filth. The primordial destiny of the Earth has been destroyed, he would explain in raptures, the sun and the moon no longer rise above it, but it can be renewed through prayer and returned to life.

'Initially, if Yefimov mentioned himself at all, then only as a precursor and only through allegory. He spoke about receiving baptism from Elijah and initiation from an old shaman, told the story of a relative, who rather like the Elijah of Slavic myth, had flown across the sky after his death on a hollowed-out log, beating out a muffled, uneven rhythm on his tambourine. Then Noan began homing in. But even now his path was not straight, and his words reverberated with jumbled echoes of Old and New Testament miracles. He told of a shaman who had nine wives and not a single child. Who just before his death, when the spirits of the Lower World had already come for him, had said to his oldest wife (she, almost like Sarah, was ninety years old): "Come closer, my beloved. If I die without leaving issue, weeds will grow over my hearth. Come – I will breathe on you." And he continued: "Soon you will conceive from the life that I have blown into you, and in nine months' time you shall bear a son who will become a great shaman. Then life will take its course and one generation will replace another, until the day comes when I appear again and we will be together once more." He would say that great shamans are conceived either by virgins from spirits descending from the sky, or by old women from their dying husbands, and explained that when shamans come down to Earth they assume the shape of a cross.

'He would say that before a shaman is called, before his

three-day death and resurrection, he has to know, live and take upon himself all the calamities and misfortunes that fell to the lot of his ancestors. This is his inescapable fate. The shaman glorifies them, as it were, with his ordeals. And he would ask me: did not Christ, who was conceived by Mary according to the will of the Lord, did not Christ, with His birth, with the death of the children amongst whom He was sought, with His flight to Egypt and His return, with His own death and resurrection, repeat the fate of Sarah and Abraham, the resettlement in Egypt, the slaughter of all the firstborn and the exodus from the land that had been cursed by God? So too did He repeat the death of the nation, the destruction of the First, then Second Temple and its resurrection after exile and captivity.

'He would say that before the birth of a great shaman the river of deaths and misfortunes is blocked with a high dam, and the sticks used to build the dam are human corpses, in order to delay and intensify the calamities, which years later, when he comes into the world, will sweep the world like a flood. And once again he recalled Christ and the Jewish-Roman War that began soon after His coming, the deaths of hundreds of thousands of people, the ruin of Israel.

'Sometimes Yefimov would go back on himself, all the while continuing his sly, methodical, tireless probing, to see if there was anything we could agree on. He was even ready to make significant concessions. In particular, he said more than once that shamanism could cede its territory to Christ but live on as a kind of younger brother. The clearer it became that Kuzmatsky had no chance – Izbin would never forgive Yefimov – the more confidently Yefimov asserted, as if we had already shaken hands on it, how happy he was that he would suffer, that together with us he would lay down his life for the faith of Christ. Exultation was literally bursting out of him. Unable to calm down, he would give one example after another, almost until lights out, to prove how impossible it was to tell our faiths apart.

'As a rule he would begin quite innocuously – with the Pentateuch. He told strange, not entirely comprehensible stories: they echoed the Old Testament in their details, but without any moral lessons, without guilt and sin, they seemed no more than faded prints. One legend was reminiscent of the story of Cain and Abel, only in sterilised form. On the eve of winter two brothers are hunting a bear in the taiga. After tracking the beast down, the younger begins grappling with it one to one, while the elder, wishing to help his brother, shoots an arrow from behind a pine tree that ends up hitting them both. As soon as he sees that he has killed his father's most beloved child, he takes fright. When he gets home and his father asks him, "And your brother – why did he stay behind in the forest?", he lies that his brother was crushed by a bear and that he has buried the poor boy's body under a fir tree in the taiga. His father does not believe him. After praying, he calls out to his dead son and asks him directly, "Where are you, my boy? Why do I not see you now by our hearth?" A voice answers him from the ground: "My respected elder brother Myy-Kara killed me along with a dweller of the gloomy taiga, pierced my black liver with an arrow." On hearing the truth, the father's face darkens and he even reaches for his sword, but after weighing everything up, he decides not to punish the murderer, so as not to lose his second son as well.

'Another story echoed that of Jacob, who as we know, set peeled willow rods by the watering troughs of Laban's flocks, so that the sheep's offspring would be streaked and fall to him.[60] The same rods reappear here: a shaman, desiring to lure and seize someone else's stallion, cuts out stripes on willow rods, after which he commands a spirit to bring him the horse. But this order proves too hard for the spirit, the stallion is not yielded, and the shaman, it seems, is left with nothing. But that night the stallion breaks his own tether, plunges into a lake and swims over to the shaman.

'After limbering up with the patriarchs, Yefimov would turn once more to the New Testament. To pique our interest he might begin by informing us that when the Magi returned from Palestine, they preserved their knowledge of the Christ Child just as Moses's father-in-law, the priest of Midian, had preserved the faith in the true God, and that here in the North, this knowledge had survived intact from generation to generation. The next moment he would bring in Peregudov, explaining that since knowing Pike, he had a better understanding of the hell that their teacher must have carried in his soul before his conversion. Then it was the Son of God's turn once more. In Yefimov's telling, Christ, in memory of His infant self, granted the Magi the gift of working miracles.

'As to the truth of all this, well, there were no witnesses, at least not in our cell, but the shamanic miracles that followed were a calque of the Gospel ones. Yefimov spoke about voices

---

[60] A reference to a story in Genesis (30: 27-43) where striped rods encourage flocks to conceive and are associated with the increase in speckled goats and streaked sheep sought by Jacob as he tries to breed stronger animals for himself and feebler ones for his uncle Laban.

from the sky, about some great shaman born to a virgin in a manger, with the one difference, that unlike Mary, she was so ashamed that she hid him in manure and fled. But the baby survived, screamed at the top of his voice, and was found and raised by a childless neighbour. Later, once the ice had broken downstream from Yakutsk, her adopted child crossed the Lena without wetting his feet in full view of hundreds of people. Then at the wedding of a poor Tungus girl, when the supplies ran out at the height of the festivities and the bride was weeping from the shame of it, he smacked his lips and three bottles of vodka immediately appeared on the table, along with five reindeer ribs.

'Yefimov would talk of entire tribes being healed of the plague and of a possessed shaman, who after filling his mouth with water and bespattering twenty-five other demoniacs, instantly healed them. He would say that just as in Luke, the twelve-year-old Christ astounds the teachers in the temple with His learning, so do shamans, with the knowledge of hidden ways granted to them since infancy, surpass even old men in their wisdom. He recalled a verse where the Holy Ghost descends on the apostles and they begin speaking in different tongues and informed us, not without pride, that when a Siberian shaman enters a trance he always prophesies in the language of the tribe that has summoned him, whoever they may be. After which, having boxed Father Nikolai and myself into the tightest of corners, he switched to the high biblical language of the Orthodox Church. There was a shaman by the name of Kaunanka, he said, who "trampling down Death by Death, bestoweth Life on those in graves".[61]

---

[61] Verses from the Paschal Troparion, sung on Easter Sunday in the Orthodox Church.

BE AS CHILDREN

'Only once,' Nikodim went on with his story, 'when his endless blasphemies became too much to bear, did I say: all right, let's assume that what you are saying is true and that after a few incantations you are able to come to terms with demons or bribe them, still, how can you not see that there is no path here, no redemption? It's simply a concession, from which not a single person becomes any better. The demons go away, but evil remains. But I succeeded only in annoying him.

'With desperation in his voice, he started yelling that no sooner would a bullet enter the back of his head than the basement would fill with a sweet scent. Pure, unblemished virgins and youths would appear from Heaven and wash his wounds with their tears; he would be resurrected and become the first shaman in the universe to ascend to Heaven while still alive. He said many more such things and finished off with the comment that at the Eucharist his body and blood would be shared among all the paths of misfortune, disaster, sickness – and like pieces of alum, would staunch human grief.

'He was of course a perfect child, a kid like any other, having his fun with whatever he could find, even faith. But in prison,' Nikodim continued, 'company like that was no cause for joy. Staring at him, I became quite certain that we no longer had any need of handouts from God. No need of new miracles. Whenever anything pure and unblemished is born from us filthy, wicked sinners, it only confuses us and trips us up. Let the children go back to the Lord, like angels, let Him gather them unto Himself in Heaven – that is their country. We on the other hand, must deal with our sins ourselves, must slowly and gradually atone for them, must finally choose good and renounce evil. This was a fairly drastic shift inside me, as drastic as any other change in my adult life, even the taking of vows. It started with my conversations with your brother, Dusya, and ended with Yefimov's death.

'At Izbin's request,' Nikodim went on, 'I signed the testimony that Kuzmatsky had prepared about the shaman, but I saw, and still see, nothing particularly wrong here. In the end, this statement played no role at all. But there is something else I do regret. On the eve of the verdict, when it was already clear that Yefimov would be given the death sentence, he asked to be confessed. But after everything I had heard from him over the previous month, I found it hard to oblige him. To cut a long story short, I said no, told him that his request was just another ruse, that he was no less a pagan now than he had ever been. Confessing a non-Christian was a sin I wasn't prepared to take upon myself. I did add though, that he had the right, if he so wished, to ask Father Nikolai. But the priest had heard my rebuff, and scared of committing a sin, was also reluctant, even if normally he might have agreed – he was a kind, tolerant man. A day later I regretted all this, but it was too late. Immediately after the verdict Yefimov tried to say something to the judge – perhaps he wanted to utter a spell – but as soon as he stood up a fit took hold of him. He was taken straight from the court to the prison infirmary and that was the last we saw of him. Three days later, as far as I know, Noan was shot.'

The end of the shaman's life was also the end of Nikodim's confession. All that remained was the epilogue, which both Dusya and I already knew. 'Yefimov's fate had been decided,' Nikodim finished off in a voice faint from weariness and breathlessness, 'and when the OGPU considered which of us – myself or Father Nikolai – to spare, it was me they chose.

Be as Children

Why? Well, I expect my Moscow acquaintances put in a word for me once more.'

***

We were already on the train back to Moscow when Dusya remarked that Father Nikodim hadn't even mentioned Irina and Vanya Zvyagintsev on our visit that day, and yet, if not for Nikodim, Sashenka would have still been alive. And she told me something very similar to the stories about Lenin that I heard years later during Ishchenko's lessons in Ulyanovsk.

She had taken her vow of obedience to Nikodim, her spiritual father, in 1920, and on the eve of the little girl's illness he suddenly brought it up again. At the christening, the child was given the name Aleksandra. Perhaps Nikodim simply didn't want to call the girl by name, perhaps he wanted to keep everything secret – either way, during those days not a single mention was made of Aleksandra, or as she was usually called, Sashenka. Literally twisting Dusya's arm, he demanded again and again: beg God for her death, beg Him, after all the Lord always responds, He cannot say no to you. Beg the little girl's death for her own sake, before she ruins her soul.

Unable to agree, Dusya said nothing, so he mustered all his strength and began shouting that the purer this child was, the more evil she would bring. So many had perished during the first children's crusade – and if this girl really was an angel incarnate, thousands would follow her too. Just like then, nobody would reach the Holy Land. And even if one or two did get there, the Lord would not save the human race solely for them. Sin cannot be redeemed like that.

Like a madman, he kept telling her over and over that

Irina's daughter was the last children's crusade, the 'last and the littlest', after which, God willing, everything would settle down for twenty years or so and we would draw breath again, we wouldn't drown in blood. Two thousand years ago, he said, the infants of Bethlehem had joyfully given their lives in sacrifice, offered themselves like calves to slaughter by the felonious Herod, so that the Saviour might live. But it was with those same infants of Judea that the terrible Bethlehem heresy had started. The children that by divine miracle emerge year after year from the female womb – that second Sodom and Gomorrah, that receptacle of lust and sin, of every abomination and impurity – tempt Man with their chasteness, their loveliness and comeliness, their innocent helplessness. And the son of Adam, Nikodim insisted to her, came to believe that if sanctity was born from his own root, then like shoots on a tree trunk in spring, the Grace that had saved the Son of God Himself would also be born, so neither the child's father nor mother had any need of another Saviour. And then the Lord said, 'Be as children, for theirs is the Kingdom of Heaven.' And Man turned his back on Christ.

Gasping for breath, Nikodim tried to explain to her that since the times of Herod every generation had contained no lack of people similar to the children massacred in Bethlehem. Like infants who live only a paltry portion of the span usually granted us by the Almighty, they teach that on Earth there are only extremes: death and salvation, good and evil. They believe that growing up is always a retreat from the Lord and that all who have left childhood are traitors and double-dealers, sinners and destroyers. That even Christ should not have lived his thirty-three years, that neither His miracles nor

His temptations were needed, neither sermons nor disciples, no need even for death on the cross and resurrection. Had He died an infant, His sacrifice would have been fuller and the world would have been saved long ago. Not knowing or understanding life, incapable of valuing it however long they live, these people spill more and more blood in the name of this simple truth and are unable to stop.

'And then,' Dusya went on, 'he suddenly says to me, out of nowhere: do you remember how Klasha prayed for your soul and buried you for this world? You must do the same for the girl. I object, try to explain that in my case there is nothing stopping me becoming a nun, a bride of Christ, but Sashenka's far too young to be tonsured. I realise that, whatever he might say, there's only one thing he wants from me – her death – and I duck and dive. So then he raises his voice again: how dare I contradict him, my Elder? For fifty years he's kept me on a long leash, fool that he is, but he won't let me wriggle out of it this time. Willingly or not, I'll have to do what he demands. On and on he goes, but then, as if coming back to Klasha, he snaps at me, "Your job is to recite prayers for her soul. The Lord will see to the rest."'

After that conversation, Dusya continued, she didn't see Nikodim for almost a week: either there wasn't a good time, or else she would find an excuse not to meet. Then at the end of August, he had his first heart attack. An ambulance came for him, as she learned once she was already in Tomilino,[62] where she was living at the home of one of his parishioners. She went straight to the hospital. It was serious, that much was clear, and

---

[62] An industrial settlement (originally a princely estate known for its dachas) about 25km south-east of Moscow.

if he were ever to get back on his feet again, then it would not be for some time. Needless to say, the possibility of Sashenka being mentioned again on the ward never entered Dusya's mind. True, there was one time, during a conversation in the staff room with a doctor from the resuscitation unit, when she suddenly thought that now, as he stood on the brink of death himself, Nikodim's attitude towards the little girl might soften.

The moment Nikodim's condition improved and he was moved to the rehabilitation ward, Dusya practically took up residence in the hospital. Occasionally somebody would cover for her for a few hours, but generally she was always by his side. Then towards the end of the first week – they were alone on the ward – Nikodim brought up Sashenka all over again, as if there had been no heart attack, no resuscitation. He took Dusya's hand and didn't release it until she promised to do his will.

***

I don't think I can really call what I had with Irina a love affair, but we did start seeing each other, that much is true. A whole month before that happened, she told me that she had to know why Dusya had begged God for Sashenka's death. It may be that Irina wasn't in her right mind even then, but I wasn't thinking about that, in fact I promised to do all I could for her, and now I suppose, I feel ashamed of the things I discovered, of the excitement with which I searched for them. That ancient story, when an increase in knowledge brings nothing but sorrow. Be that as it may, I now have most of the answers. As for the conversation about Nikodim, I thought better of telling Irina about it – I was scared. I kept it to myself for three decades, and now with Irina dead for almost a year, laid out in her grave like the others, there's no one left to judge whether I did the right thing. My help in any case, has not been needed for a good long time but still, in memory of Sashenka, let me repeat something that would I'm sure, have comforted Irina: her daughter is not to blame for anything.

Formally speaking, Irina and I lived together for a year, but take away the four months I spent in Naryan-Mar and it was a good deal less than that. I loved Irina, but I soon realised I had no chance of keeping her; my trip to the Barents Sea was a way out for us both. For a long time afterwards, I could see no justification for what we had together – sex, framed by conversations about Sashenka. Only twenty-five years later, at the residential school in Ulyanovsk, when I heard Ishchenko tell his class about Lenin walking on his index and middle fingers over Krupskaya in an attempt to speak to her, did it occur to me that maybe I too had wanted something similar.

There were no words, nor could there have been, but caressing her, calming her, if only temporarily, was essential. Sex held little appeal for Irina, what she appreciated far more was when I scratched her back, as you would a child. She would melt beneath my hand, clinging not just to my fingers but to my whole palm, before suddenly recoiling from my touch, her whole body twisting. Then unable to endure the languor, she would fall still.

She also loved to be kissed. Whether with my hand or my lips, I never hurried; I went cautiously, slowly, perhaps because I was afraid. For all her endless admissions and confessions, I was a long way from being able to call her mine and I knew that just as chance had brought us together, so she would leave me without a second thought.

Before our first kiss, with lips that were almost dry, I would take her ear lobe and draw it in, lick it gently, breathe it in and out. Then I would move down a little and kiss her neck with the faintest of touches. I wasn't expecting her to respond right away. I wasn't even looking for a reaction, I didn't want anything from her yet. It was as though we were in a crowded place and I was trying to say something that only she could hear. Her neck was her sacred territory. Tracing rings within rings, I kissed her there with shallow, fluttery kisses, and she would begin to moan a little. With her back turned to me from the very beginning, she would keep her eyes closed, as if she wanted no part in anything, didn't want to see anyone; only now would she soften.

For the time being that was enough for me. Playing, I would pull back my lips, move them away, wait a second and watch as she, unsure, undecided, became scared that that fleeting brush against her vein was the last. But I had no need of her fear, and coming back to her, I again started drawing light, quick circles with my lips. Irina's neck had many nice places, and I paid special attention to the little hollow where the clavicle meets the throat. This was my bivouac, my halting-place, from there the descent began and I had to choose where I was going next: along the shoulder and down the arm to the hand, or straight to the bosom.

My ancestors were serfs in the service of Count Sheremetyev. They sold their own handiwork and managed to buy their freedom several years before the abolition of serfdom.[63] During the Crimean War my great-grandfather made

---

[63] The serfs were emancipated in 1861, the most important of a series of reforms in the reign of Alexander II.

his fortune supplying goods to the State, and just as soon as Alexander II brought the landowners to their knees, he began buying up land in his native district of Arzamas. Acting on his own or through others, he acquired woodland, meadows, fields, and by 1880 had become the owner of a considerable estate, after which he gave up business and lived the life of a proper lord, hunted, received guests and leased his ploughland to peasants from neighbouring villages. He was, by all appearances, quite satisfied with his life, and to catch every drop of the happiness that had fallen his way, he would do a tour of his property straight after his morning coffee, taking just a dog and a double-barrelled gun. He would walk along the boundary of the estate, and like any wild animal, mark out and separate off what was his from what was not, so as to be sure that what lay inside was his and what lay outside was of no concern to him. He was sure that the earth should be able to recognise its master, that the nobles had lost it precisely because they had run off to Moscow and St Petersburg, and eventually the earth had forgotten them, left them.

Irina had smooth, faintly oily skin. Kissing it, I tried to protect her, to fence her off from the world. I knew her well and could advance without any prompting, just by feeling my way like a blind man. Of course I could never restore what she had lost, but her body was rich, fertile soil, and like my great-grandfather's lands, should not lie fallow for so long. Everything about her had been made for motherhood, everything had been prepared for it, and all that remained was to till and sow it once more. But here too I dallied. There are artists who so overflow with passion that they have no need of outlines and sketches, who paint with sudden, sweeping strokes, sometimes even laying on the paint with their fingers. There was no rightness in what I was doing.

Lying with one arm tucked behind her head, Irina was still almost motionless, her left leg bent at the knee as usual. She never interfered, never forbade me, never stopped me. Then, advancing with those same shallow, light kisses, I took the shortest route from her underarm to her big pink nipple, still exposed, untensed. Her breasts were large. They sprawled beneath their own weight, became gentle slopes with neat round domes. I felt as if I were moulding them anew. Pressing and smoothing, I went along the perimeter again and again. Eventually, I took the nipple in my lips, now nudging it away with my tongue, now drawing it back in, as I had with the ear lobe. Sometimes seeing I had arrived too early, that no one was quite ready to receive me, I retreated.

Even though now, with her arm tucked behind her head, the terrain lay open, old memories still led me to my hiding place. I would lay my head and listen to Irina's breathing, to a vein pulsing beneath her ear to the rhythm of her heart. I loved all her hollows and small gullies, all her quiet and secluded spots, and although it was not I but she who needed defending, I imagined settling there and living out my days calmly and serenely, without a single sorrow. For Irina of course, I and everyone else were part of the world that she feared, she was waiting, counting the days until it finally ended and a different life began, in which she would be with Sashenka once more, but as I passed along her border with my kisses, I tried to convince myself, fool myself, that I was erecting a barrier, that like my great-grandfather with his boundary, I was separating her from the past.

In bed with Irina, it was as if she were there by chance, as if for her it wasn't quite for real. A woman-girl, she would become aroused in the most innocent places, the ones where you would normally kiss a child – the cheeks, the brow, the top of her head. She had passed through many hands but she hadn't grown up. The lust and desire she provoked were mixed with tenderness and pity, so strong was the urge to comfort her, to warm her.

Sometimes, while we were still lying next to each other, Irina would talk about her daughter. She would describe the pregnancy and the birth, how Sashenka would smile and get upset, how fond Dusya was of her. Dusya would always bring the little girl treats, entertain her for hours, and at Easter she would give her beautiful eggs that she had painted herself. I, in my turn, would repeat Dusya's own words to Irina, that growing up is the path of sin, of retreat from God: so it had always been and so it would always be. Those whom the Lord does not wish to release into evil, He gathers to Himself well before time. I tried to persuade her that Dusya had begged death for Sashenka only in order to spare the girl agony and suffering, that she was convinced she was doing the right thing. But there was something else that Irina needed far more than my consolations. She would describe with a kind of ecstasy, and never tire of hearing, how depraved and sinful she was, how many lives – including my own of course – she had shattered and ruined.

I have few doubts now that whomever Irina happened to find herself alone with, she always had one and the same thing in mind: the salvation and justification of her daughter. The case she was bringing against the Lord was constructed no less skilfully than Kuzmatsky's script in Tomsk. Sashenka was to be washed clean by Irina's own sin. She multiplied it many times over, and with Sashenka gone this was the only way things could be. At the same time, she was taking upon herself all the evil she saw around her, and like the Pied Piper of Hamelin, leading it away from her daughter.

Dusya's son Seryozha almost never came round to my place on Solyanka Street, but we would occasionally walk around Moscow together. We would usually do the entire Boulevard Ring – from Yauza Gates to Gogol Boulevard and Prechistenka Street. One day Seryozha called to ask if I was free and felt like stretching my legs. We met at Taganskaya metro station, and as we walked down Goncharnaya Street to the Yauza he told me he wouldn't be making any more trips north, that he'd made up his mind and settled his most urgent debts: just the previous day he'd submitted his last drawings and sketches for an academic study by a friend of his about the settling of the Arctic regions of Eastern Siberia. I'd heard that he had other kinds of obligations as well – he must have been referring to those too.

We would always bring a tidy sum back from our six-month stints in the North. Our salary was modest but thanks to all the add-ons – for fieldwork, for being in the Arctic Circle, for being so far away – we would end the season with a decent surplus. Aside from the materials he required as an artist, Seryozha had barely any needs of his own, and I knew that every year many of the Enets, Selkups and Nganasans huddling in their makeshift shelters around the port in Dudinka benefited from his help. On every trip he would spend a month and a half drawing them individually or in groups, working almost around the clock – fortunately the sun never set. Some of this money came from the official budget of course, but to ensure that his models received no less than professional sitters in Moscow he would add three times more from his own pocket.

Even so, most of Seryozha's funds went elsewhere. One day I called on him at home and discovered almost three dozen ancient, pre-Schism icons. Some of them had been hung any old how, the others were simply lined up on a shelf. The ones on the wall were all Novgorod School, and the quality of both painting and preservation was museum standard. I'd already heard about the history of this collection, but I was seeing the icons for the first time. Their owners were exiled Old Believers who lived a couple of versts downriver from Salekhard, by a backwater. When the port in Salekhard started running out of workers during the war, a large community of 'Priestless' Old Believers was sentenced and brought all the way over from their homes in the Altai region, near Barnaul. Only at the end of the 1950s, when mechanisation came to Salekhard, were they no longer needed and their sentences lifted. Now the few who survived – just thirty or thirty-five out of an original two hundred – were free to go wherever they wanted, but bad as the North was, these beggars, poorly shod and clothed, had no hope of returning to the Altai without external help.

Seryozha had long been on good terms with them, and some had become his close friends. In fact, several years previously, seeing that the community was dying out, he had begun transferring one family after another to Khakassia. He gave them enough money for the journey, a cow and wood for their homes. During discussions about the move, the elders in the community had asked Seryozha to take the icons to Moscow until they had settled, just as a precaution. I was astonished to hear that the icons had been in his care for three years already, but he had pledged to keep them secret and hadn't wanted to break his word. Now though he'd decided there was no harm in showing these sacred objects to a few artists. They'd be gone in a week's time in any case: a group of geologists were flying to Khakassia and their boss, an old friend of his, had promised to deliver the panels to their owners without a single scratch.

The North has its own particular life and once you've been there it's hard to adapt to any other. I wanted to say this, but bit my tongue. Seryozha after all, was an adult who took his own decisions as far as his own fate was concerned. It seems to me now that this change of direction had been brewing for some time, because he went on to explain that a promising young artist – a graduate like himself of the Stroganov Institute – would also be on the plane to the River Ob. This successor had already been introduced to everyone and was already on the staff. There were no other clouds on the horizon either: Seryozha had signed two big contracts with Children's Literature, which was putting out successive volumes of Chukchi and Tungus fairy tales with his illustrations. The two books were ready to be sent to the printers, meaning his work on both the fairy tales and the monograph had been completed and accepted.

Plenty of news then, and on the whole it was good news. Seryozha's career was clearly on the up. I already knew he was no ordinary artist, but the North was a kind of sump: it kept you well fed, but that was as much as you should hope for. Three books in a row was a great coup, but I didn't have time to congratulate him: the conversation took another turn. Dropping that topic, Seryozha asked whether there was any chance he could meet up with my friend Alyosha Saburov.

Alyosha was a geobotanist, a man who lived for the forest. He'd been married three times, but never for long. His wives had all believed they could get him to settle down and finish his dissertation – he had enough material for ten theses – after which an ordinary academic career beckoned. I suspect this was his hope too, but he could never resist. As soon as March came round he'd be off like a shot to Siberia or the Far East. It would still be deep winter there, with the field season almost two months away, but he would prepare all the equipment himself, plot the routes and hire workers. He was a leader by nature, while in Moscow he became just a cog in an enormous, preposterous machine in which nothing ever made any sense to him. In the city he would be miserable, muddled, forever falling out with people, and by the end he would have little choice but to leave. Eventually Saburov's wives got tired of life as grass widows and left him. There were no hard feelings though – nobody had a bad word to say about Alyosha.

Seryozha knew that Alyosha was working in Nelidovo,[64] in the Central Forest Reserve, and said he would be glad to go out there. I replied that we'd be sure to miss him if we did. I'd spoken to Alyosha on the phone two days earlier, and he'd told me he'd be in Moscow in four days' time, on January 7th.[65]

---

[64] A town in the Valdai Hills in Tver (formally Kalinin) region, about 300 km north-west of Moscow.
[65] Christmas Day according to the Gregorian calendar still followed by the Russian Orthodox Church.

Alyosha and I went to see Seryozha on January 9th, having well and truly broken the fast and slept our fill. After opening the door and embracing us three times, Seryozha led us to his room and began making tea. The Old Believer icons were gone, and you could smell the damp from a recent leak in the ceiling and the peeling wallpaper. Domestic skills had never been Seryozha's strong point, but now the place looked like the inside of a prison barracks. Compared to our surroundings, the conversation seemed almost refined.

In the main we discussed what most interested Alyosha – the forest land in Western Siberia that urgently needed to be turned into national parks and game reserves. It was already clear how well the two men understood each other, though you could see that for Seryozha this topic was just a pretext. Essentially he only had one question for Alyosha: did he happen to know of any place in Moscow's neighbouring regions with a large swamp, a proper impassable bog, where it would be hard for anyone to find you, however much they tried? He added that it would be good if, amidst the moss, there was an expanse of open water – it didn't have to be a lake exactly – with a high hill not far away on which to settle.

Saburov instantly replied that some seventy kilometres north of their reserve there was a peat bog known as Bear's Moss. He had not been there yet himself but to judge from aerial photographs and descriptions it was exactly what Seryozha was after: it was well away from any roads and measured approximately nine hundred square kilometres, so from the edge to the centre, wherever you entered, was no less than fifteen kilometres. In the middle of Bear's Moss, exactly as per Seryozha's brief, was a hollow, and in the middle of the hollow – an oval lake stretching north to south. It was certainly more than six or seven metres deep, though no one had ever measured it; perhaps even as much as thirty metres, which would explain why the lake was never overgrown. Next to the water was a granitic rock – the entire hollow smelled of it. One of the largest such rocks in Kalininskaya region, it had been left by a Karelian glacier as it travelled north. As far as Alyosha could recall, this rock rose some fifteen or even seventeen metres above the water.

Over the course of twenty thousand years the rock had become covered with deposits and a genuine forest had sprung up. 'The choicest pines and firs,' Alyosha added, 'all native to the region. In Valdai you can count plots as well preserved as this on the fingers of one hand.' He went on: 'The previous manager of the nature reserve was an ordinary worker promoted under Stalin. A big fan of tree planting in Kalinin region, he wanted to drain every single swamp. So he took a good look at Bear's Moss too. Eight years or so ago a dozen tractors were brought there and the order was given to build drainage canals along the perimeter. But nothing came of it. The workers sank tonnes of machinery in the peat bog and gave up.'

Seryozha: 'So you can only reach the rock in winter?' Alyosha: 'Yes. By mid-December in the Valdai, the lakes freeze up completely, even where there are vigorous springs beneath them. Then up until March, the ice is thick and sturdy – it'll even hold a one-and-a-half-ton truck, so long as you don't overload it.' He added that if we decided to go there in mid-March, he'd gladly join us: he was curious to see Bear's Moss as well. Alyosha gave us another tip, too. Walking fifteen or twenty kilometres with a backpack was no problem of course, but if Seryozha had more ambitious plans then he wouldn't recommend going on foot. If we had lots of gear to take, it would be far easier to find ourselves a horse in one of the villages on the edge of the bog. We took Alyosha's advice, and a week later, after he sent us a millimetric map of Bear's Moss from Nelidovo, we set off in my Zaporozhets to explore the area.

There were eight suitable villages, by which I mean ones that could be reached by a dirt road if nothing else, and in the second village, Anikeyevka, we met Akimych, a kindly, trustworthy old man who had both a horse – a gelding called Dolya – and a sledge. We took him with us for our first tour of Bear's Moss. Sadly I can't say much about the lake, as it's hard to see anything under ice covered by a metre of snow, but when the jolts came to an end we realised that we'd passed all the hummocks and that the water table was right beneath us. I liked the island itself very much: a small, round brow of a hill measuring only thirty hectares or so, and just as Alyosha had promised, entirely covered with strong, healthy trees.

The days are short in January and we didn't manage to turn back while it was still light. The moon was out, but we didn't want to risk the horse, so we pitched camp beneath an old fir in a clearing. It was only a little below zero. A warm wind had been blowing from the Baltic, and when we left the village there were even signs of thaw. Having decided to stay, we put some hay out for the gelding, started a fire and prepared a meal. I had two bottles of vodka with me, we began drinking, and sitting side by side on the sledge like hens on a perch, we listened till dawn to Akimych's stories. The old man had plenty. In the winter of '42 his unit was encircled and he spent three years in German captivity, two of them in Bergen-Belsen. On returning to Russia, he was sentenced for betraying the motherland and spent another eight years in one of our camps near Karaganda. He recalled the events of his life without hatred, even boasting at one point that he was the only man in the village to have got back alive and uncrippled.

The following day we returned to Anikeyevka without any trouble and from there, declining Akimych's offer of his bathhouse, we reached Moscow just five hours later. Seryozha was in good spirits and said that everything was working out perfectly; I was also happy enough, although I had only the haziest idea of what lay ahead. I could guess what Seryozha was planning of course, but I didn't take it seriously and saw it as a kind of game. It never even occurred to me that things would start moving so fast.

In the same flat as Seryozha, in a seven-square-metre boxroom with a stubby little window beneath the ceiling, there lived a family of four. Recent arrivals I think from Armenia. After returning from Bear's Moss, Seryozha took just two weeks to arrange the paperwork and swap rooms with them, then spent the profits from the exchange on discarded field gear. He now had a heated tent, an eiderdown sleeping bag, a neat little stove and an inflatable boat – all in working order and reasonable condition. He was also taking tools and foodstuffs to the island, along with supplies of paint and canvas.

I ferried all the goods to Anikeyevka in my Zaporozhets in three goes, and by March 1 they were all safely stored in Akimych's shed, which had become our base. Thanks to these preliminary trips, Seryozha and I returned to the village together on March 15th in a half-empty car. We picked up

Alyosha on the way at a small station in Konyukhovo, and without once getting stuck on the snow road, which had just been cleared by a tractor, we were sitting around Akimych's table that same evening.

However actively I was helping Seryozha, I didn't like his scheme. My mother had taught me to steer clear of things that can't be undone, and Seryozha's room-swap struck me as a big mistake. Alyosha by contrast, was bubbling with enthusiasm. In the car he explained that, but for us, he wouldn't have got to see Bear's Moss any time soon. There were few bogs as remote as it in central Russia; for a wetlands specialist, places like that were priceless. Eventually I got a bit tired of Alyosha's elation and asked whether anything much could actually be seen beneath one and a half metres of snow and ice, but he brushed my doubts aside and resumed his paean to the bog.

It took Dolya the horse several days to carry Seryozha's goods to our destination. On this first trip, when the sledge was particularly heavy, we travelled slowly: Alyosha walked ahead with a stick, testing the ice, followed by myself, Seryozha and Akimych, who was leading the horse by the bridle to reassure it. As soon as we reached the island, we unloaded the tent, stove and tools right there on the shore – we wanted to pitch camp before dark and let Akimych go.

I had the impression that Seryozha was already finding our presence a burden. He kept telling us, appositely or otherwise, how grateful he was to me and Alyosha and Akimych, how brilliantly we'd done all he'd asked of us, but it was obvious that he was tired and desperate to be alone. All the same, when Alyosha said after the first night that he wouldn't survive the winter in a tent like that – better to build a dugout – he didn't object. I agreed with Alyosha about the tent, though I'd been thinking of a log cabin instead. Away from the shore, the island was all rock and we had nothing to break it with. But Alyosha walked all the way round and found a wide cleft filled with sand on the south side, where patches of snow had already melted. Digging was easy there, and the work didn't even take us five days.

It wasn't until April 1976 that Dusya and I restored contact, for the saddest of reasons. That year I got ready to visit Seryozha at the very end of March, as usual. We were both people of the North, accustomed to having our grub and gear dropped from helicopters, to weighing everything to the gram. So whenever I set out for Bear's Moss I would stick rigidly, aside from a few bottles of vodka, to a list of items that had been fixed once and for all: salt, sugar, matchsticks, vegetable oil, pasta, groats, two boxes of tinned meat, another two of condensed milk, paints, canvases, brushes and paper, a few other odds and ends. Once you threw in the potatoes and green herbs that he grew himself, along with the fish and the abundant cloudberries, blueberries, cranberries all around him, a single delivery was enough to last Seryozha a year. I would buy the food in the shop next door to me in Moscow, and the paints and canvases at the stall of the Artists' Union, just as requested, then drive off in my Zaporozhets to Anikeyevka, where Akimych's shed still served as our depot.

From Anikeyevka I made one trip to Konyukhovo – the railway settlement thirty kilometres to the west – where I met Alyosha; we had agreed back in February that we would go together, just like the previous time. Alyosha, who had identified this island amidst the swamp – a real skete, a little hermitage, which you couldn't walk to, sail to, drive to – had been firm friends with Seryozha for some time. In Konyukhovo I also made my final purchases: nails, a new saw and axe, and lastly, a well-made, practical fishing net sold to me by a local craftsman. You wouldn't find one like it in Moscow. Although Alyosha and I didn't stay long, our six hands made quick work of it. We'd realised this on our very first visit, in March '74, when the three of us had dug a spacious shelter in the sand in less than a week, strengthened the walls with timber and covered it with two layers of logs. To keep it warm, we also heaped almost a metre of dry peat onto the roof.

And that wasn't the last thing we built for Seryozha. The following spring, thirty metres out from the shore, we built a small log raft next to a deep pit that had fish all year round. It was easier to fish from that than from the battered inflatable. The jobs never took us very long though, so Alyosha would have a day or two just to roam around the bog. We usually arrived on the island between March 22nd and 25th, when the temperature hovers around or even above freezing but the ice is still firm and only just beginning to thaw.

In '74 and '75 Seryozha had waited for us on a boulder at the very edge of the ice. He rarely took off his old tarpaulin jacket, which was stained with many shades of oil paint from top to bottom, and from a distance made him resemble a colourful carnival flag, but this time the boulder was bare, and Alyosha and I, and even Akimych, were disappointed. None of us were especially worried though. Seryozha might be working or collecting firewood, or just fishing. So there was nothing to alarm us yet and it was only in the dugout, where a thick layer of ice had formed in the corners and on the walls, that we realised something serious had happened.

Now, as I write these notes, it's obvious to me that there was no chance of us finding him alive, but I suppose that some time needed to pass between the missing carnival jacket and the fact that Seryozha himself was no more, because we spent two long days traipsing all over the island. Walking together at first, as if holding on to each other, we covered every inch of the damned hill, which whether up and over or all the way round, didn't even measure a couple of kilometres. Then we divided up the forest between us, and in voices hoarse from shouting, called out Seryozha's name from our respective patches. Catching the sound of another voice nearby, our hopes would blaze up every time, in the belief that Seryozha, thank God, had finally answered.

As might have been expected, Akimych was first to resign himself to the situation. Lighting the iron stove that evening, he said, to neither of us in particular, that wolves showed up around their village every winter. Two or three packs of them. They'd kill a few sheep and leave. Summer was fine, but in winter everyone tried to avoid entering the forest alone. He chose his words carefully, making no direct link with Seryozha, then added that it could also have been a bear roused too early from its den by hunters. But Alyosha and I pretended not to have understood and at dawn we started out again, almost mechanically, only now, unlike the previous day, we were scouring the bog.

Both of us were terrified of drawing a line under the search. Whether or not Akimych was right, it seemed to us that to accept Seryozha's death was to betray him. But time was running out. Alyosha had already told me back in Moscow, when we spoke on the phone, that he could only spend four days in Bear's Moss before he had to return to Nelidovo and then on to Leningrad, to fly with a research group to Yakutsk. So this was the last day – tomorrow, no later than noon, Akimych and Dolya would take Alyosha back to the village.

As I dodged between the hummocks on the ice, I was filled with despair at the prospect of their departure: there was a big difference between searching for Seryozha in a team, pepping each other up and reassuring each other, and roaming this death trap on my own. As if rehearsing how the three of us would soon be leaving Seryozha, the others were preparing to abandon me first. Naturally I wasn't too thrilled by this turn of events, which may be why I suddenly wondered – what if Seryozha had simply scarpered? Got tired of his skete, of the life of a hermit, of a monk without vows or tonsure, without prayers or blessings. Had lost sight of why, for what possible purpose, he had to lie down every day in an icy dugout, as if in a crypt, and when he could no longer remember, had upped and left.

As I turned all this over in my mind, Alyosha must have picked up on my thoughts himself or else he felt a sudden urge to apologise, to explain his departure – either way, he walked over and said that once he got to Nelidovo he would call our mutual acquaintances and see what he could find out. Perhaps we were getting worked up over nothing. Maybe Seryozha wasn't here because he wasn't meant to be here. He could have left earlier in the winter but something had prevented him from telling us. This didn't sound like Seryozha of course, but anything can happen. What if he'd been sure he'd be back by mid-March, before our arrival, only to be held up by something – maybe even a stint in hospital for all we knew. In any case, the main thing was that he was alive, that it was too early to bury him. I listened to him in silence, neither agreeing nor disagreeing, then changed the topic. As soon as it got dark that evening, we went straight to sleep, and at first light Akimych harnessed Dolya and said he'd be back for me in four days – he had to pick up his pension and couldn't come any sooner.

The following day I continued the search: Alyosha was gone and without him it didn't feel right to carry on pretending that Seryozha was alive, that he was hiding somewhere. I knew he was dead and I was only after one thing: to find his remains and give him a fitting burial. I had even identified a place for his grave: a sun-lit glade surrounded by pines, a hundred metres or so east of Seryozha's dugout. I didn't waste any more time on the island – we'd combed through every metre of it – and turned all my attention to the bog. Using the shadows of the larger trees, I divided it up into sections, and straying ever further from the shore, methodically searched every one. I was out all day; in the evening I carried a kerosene lamp around the dugout and studied what Seryozha had left behind.

In the days before the war, Nikodim, eager to see what Dusya's son had learned at the Stroganov Institute, proposed that Seryozha make some sketches for frescoes to decorate the small Church of Christ's Nativity in the village of Solodovo, twenty kilometres from Pskov. It had been built back in 1913, but the war meant there was no chance to paint it before the Bolsheviks took over. It had remained a cold, unwelcoming church, unloved by locals. Perhaps that was why it hadn't been closed. By the end of the '30s it was the only church in the entire district, attendance grew and services were held on a regular basis. Some money even materialised to make the church presentable.

The priest at the Church of the Nativity, Father Innokenty, had been Nikodim's classmate at the seminary, and when he wrote to Nikodim in Moscow, asking him to find him a God-fearing artist to do the frescoes, Nikodim immediately put him on to Seryozha. There was a good deal of wall space to be covered, and Seryozha only managed to finish sketches for the sanctuary and the lower tier of the bell tower before he was called up. According to his mother he carried on drawing at the front, bringing back some eight or nine notebooks filled with sketches.

Returning to Moscow in the autumn of '45, Seryozha learned that all through the war the bell tower of the Solodovo church had been used by both our own and German artillery-men as an observation post, and as a result of these joint efforts the church had been flattened. But he kept on with his drawings all the same. The first time I saw his sketches was in '62, and that viewing led to a serious falling out. We didn't meet or talk for several months and it wasn't until the beginning of Lent that we begged each other's forgiveness.

I was barely out of hospital when all this happened, and I was in an uncompromising mood. I'd been told about Seryozha's drawings by both Dusya and my parents, and I was firmly set on seeing them. I kept nagging Seryozha, until still hesitating, he gave in and invited me over. For all my pestering, I was disappointed by what I found. There was something soppy about both the fresco sketches and the icons, in fact they reminded me of the pictures that in recent times have started to adorn our creches and kindergartens. The reason for this was simple enough. Seryozha drew the Son of God only as a child: even for the Saviour to have grown up would have been a retreat from the Lord. Waiting for Christ the innocent babe, the infant who does not know or stop to think about His calling, Seryozha threw out the Last Supper, the Crucifixion, the Resurrection. The church was to have no temptation of Christ in the wilderness, no Christ Pantocrator. Christ the prophet, Christ the teacher were gone. In Seryozha's frescoes the Son of God neither worked miracles nor healed, neither argued with the Pharisees nor preached to His disciples. He was an infant, tied in every possible way to the Virgin Mary, inseparable from her; and Seryozha, it seems to me thought that this was how everything should remain.

Unable to stop, to look from the outside at what he was doing, he kept drawing and drawing the Mother of God suckling Christ, and Christ just lying there peacefully in her arms. Or Christ in the manger welcoming the exhausted Magi, their feet battered from their long journey, or Our Lady saving her child, fleeing to Egypt to escape the wrath of Herod.

The psychiatric hospital had an excellent library, where among other things, I started reading early Christian literature and Gnostic texts. In one of these books I came across a legend about the Christ Child, a very early one according to the commentary, dating from the second or even first century. Depressed by this child obsession, I told Seryozha that in one of the Apocrypha Christ is different. Refusing to bear insults meekly, He calls down one death after another on the heads of His offenders, all exactly the same age as Christ, until Joseph, after yet another funeral at a neighbour's home, says through his tears, 'We have become loathsome unto these people.' There was no malice in Seryozha, but it could take him a while to get over things. I don't know whether he'd ever come across such texts, but it was a long time before he forgave me for citing these words.

In the dugout, right there in the sand, several dozen canvases stood facing the wall, some finished, some already stretched over a frame. But both these and the rolled-up paintings had grown damp over the winter, with patches of mould here and there. The works varied. The ones at the head of Seryozha's bed though were mainly the usual infants. I would return home from the bog after sunset, when it was already too dark to take the paintings outside. The kerosene lamp burned like a candle in church, with a yellow, darting light, and as I took it from canvas to canvas, never leaving the dugout, I tried to understand without prejudice all these attempts to paint Christ lying in the arms of the Mother of God, or fleeing with her to Egypt. I thought I might finally discover why it was that in Bear's Moss, just as in Moscow, Seryozha had only depicted Christ as a child. I can't say I made great progress, although I did notice that the faces painted on the island were less gentle, their features more angular and tense. Each of these images of the Son of God was still the image of a child, no doubt about that, but now it seemed to me, you could also make out what awaited Christ in the future.

Resting against the adjacent wall was a row of northern landscapes, although there was the occasional infant here as well. Almost three dozen large canvases in oil and tempera, the sketches for which probably dated back to the field trips. Arctic beauty spots were few and far between; instead, Seryozha had mainly painted the outskirts of dirt-poor northern towns. A lichen bog, a corner of which had become a rubbish dump, encroaching on a shack. Another bog, ploughed up every which way by the wheels of a truck. Deep furrows, the turf ripped out all the way down, just scattered here and there with broken planks, old tyres and concrete blocks wrapped in tendrils of rusty steel reinforcing bars. A tractor drowned between two sheds, its exhaust pipe sticking out like the periscope of a submarine. In the foreground a sickly fir grove, to the side a pair of reindeer-hide tents by a shallow creek. A filthy village. In a yard, next to a sandpit, a pack of stray dogs. A woman walking past with a string bag. Poking out of its holes, as from a flower bed – a bottle of milk, a bottle of ethanol, a jar of pickled cucumber. Outside the entrance to the town hospital, patients side by side in their beds on the sterile white snow. Their faces calm and at peace.

Like Seryozha, I knew my way quite well around the slums of Tiksi, Naryan Mar, Dudinka, Salekhard. There were plenty of Enets and Nganasans, Selkups, Nenets, Evens and Dolgans huddled in shacks and movable sheds, barns and trailers that all looked alike. Left without their deer, they lived on a diet of fish and charity, for both of which the nearness of the river and the port was a great boon.

Several makeshift shelters overhang the water at the old wharf. The one on the edge has neither a porch nor a ladder. By the door a pole has been driven into the seabed; a boat has been moored to it. There's a net and two large fish. A sandy spit. Three tramps sleep around a campfire; a woman bends over the pot, stirring slop with a little branch. Specks of sunlight bounce from one bottle shard to another.

These pictures of course appealed to me more than his icons. But the infant faces were also an integral part of Seryozha's life; they had started earlier and almost certainly mattered more to him than the North. Although I understood this, I still could not get away from the thought that, if he'd carried on with the field trips, fate would have been gentler on him. As I gazed at Seryozha's paintings, it sometimes occurred to me that maybe he himself had wanted to go back, but couldn't bring himself to change tack yet again.

Almost as soon as I began heating the dugout regularly, the ice thawed in the corners and the air became as close and damp as a bathhouse. In this tropical climate, the mould on the canvases spread with a vengeance, gobbling up the paint. As if hurrying after Seryozha, the artworks were rotting before my eyes. Desperate to air and dry the canvases, at least a little, I moved the ones already stretched over the frames well away from the walls and arranged them along the perimeter of the dry heat emanating from the stove. Then, whenever I was in the dugout, I would move them around, making sure that none of the canvases lost out, that they each received their due of warmth.

I spent every evening almost until bedtime engaged in this slow dance around the red-hot iron stove, and at first it seemed only natural that I name each of Seryozha's paintings after one Samoyed or another, those down-and-outs who had tagged along on our field trips, and for almost a quarter of a century now, had been telling us the legends of their tribes. What pitiful scraps they knew. I was surprised only when I realised that for some unknown reason I was unable to detach the name from the painting. However much I tried, the drowned tractor, in my mind, was always Saktyr the Enets. The hospital with its beds on the snow was Egusan the Selkup, while the tramps and the pack of dogs were Tusna the Evenk, may she rest in peace. Among all the Samoyeds I had met in the North, she alone could trace her line back seven generations. What was more, I had recorded almost one hundred folk tales from her. I'm a sober-minded person by nature, and mysticism, unless it concerns God, leaves me cold, so this on top of everything else felt like sheer delirium.

In the end though I did find Seryozha. In Siberia, corpses discovered in spring after the thaw, are called 'snowflakes', and this was the case with Seryozha too. The day after Akimych left, a warm front from Central Asia melted what was left of the snow, and I was still some way off when I caught sight of a piece of the tarpaulin jacket. Coming closer, I saw a cheek and a forehead with frozen, icy hair.

I thought I would manage to bring Seryozha's body back on my own. I fetched the handsaw from the dugout, and after putting a couple of planks beneath me, began sawing through the ice, trying to cut a circle around the body. Sawing, I thought how much this reminded me of a bird. You begin by tracing wide circles, by wandering all around the island, all around the bog, then the circles become narrower and narrower. For the first hour I worked without a hitch, the ice here was thin – there was a powerful spring beneath it at this exact point – and the saw went through easily. But when, having completed a semi-circle, I tried to start from the other side, the ice cracked and began disappearing beneath the water. If it wasn't for the planks, I would have sunk, but by clinging on to them I was able to crawl away just in time. Only once I got out onto the shore did I realise there was really no point courting danger: I could no longer help anyone by hurrying. Better to wait for Akimych and to spend the time until he arrived on Seryozha's paintings. The next morning, when I already knew I'd be taking the canvases back with me to Moscow, I decided that before setting out it would be worth trying to dry them not by the stove, but outside in the sun – luckily, it was beating down as if it were summer.

I spent a couple of hours or so carrying one painting after another out into the light of day, then after moving them all some two hundred metres to the south side of the island, I propped them up against trees and warm stones. The sand was already dry here. The result was that by midday I found myself attending a kind of solo exhibition of the artist Sergei Igrenyev. Many of the paintings had genuine power, and everything together – the canvases, the big ancient pines, firs, sun, sand, stones – combined so well that I knew it would all stay with me for good.

I studied Seryozha's works one by one, sometimes going back for a second look before carrying on. In the late afternoon, the sun which had been at my back, moved round to the side. It hadn't bothered me until then, but in front of Seryozha's 'Woman with Broth' – which to myself I called Itte – I just couldn't settle, couldn't find the right spot to view it from. I kept stepping away from the canvas, then moving back in, tilting my head this way and that, until the light, reflecting off the varnish as if from a mirror, hit me square in the eyes.

I squinted in surprise, and there and then everything in the picture – the campfire, the woman, the tramps slumped on the ground – vanished, and Itte himself appeared. A superb oil portrait of the old Selkup, whose stories I had spent almost a week writing down the previous summer while sitting in his hut. It immediately dawned on me that the rest of Seryozha's other works were also portraits of people whose memory each of us had been trying to preserve in our own way. I had been writing down legends and songs, folk tales and life stories, while Seryozha had been hiding the people themselves, wrapping them up in the cocoons of innocuous urban landscapes.

He hid them in dumps and vacant lots near the shacks and slums where they were born and died, which they had come to consider home. Their true homeland, the boundless lichen bogs, was not far off. There the Samoyeds' ancestors, generation after generation, had grazed their thousand-head herds of reindeer. Now they called barns and trailers, movable sheds and makeshift shelters their homes; and however awful this life may have looked, it gave them a roof and a refuge, it fed them and kept them out of the cold.

The people Seryozha painted most frequently were the Nenets, whom the group he travelled with had been studying since 1950. By now he was friends, even close friends with many of them. But he also painted Selkups and Dolgans and Mansi – all of these peoples, unable to adapt to the rules and customs of others, drank themselves to death year after year and left the world without blaming anyone for anything. It was beyond Seryozha's power of course to repay our debts: until his own time came to leave the world, he sought simply to understand them. His art was natural, it was at peace, and the people he painted rested inside it like foetuses in the womb, disturbing nothing around themselves.

It seems to me now that the northern paintings were also intended for the church that Seryozha was meant to paint. That church was small and squat, but just beyond the crib, as if parting space, there began the country of the child nation, the homeland of those who had been the first to know about the Saviour, an infant just like them, and had sent their Magi thousands of miles to worship Him. Several of his pictures showed a bog spreading over the canvas with a couple of tents and reindeer grazing nearby. A slow broad river curved round a promontory topped by a pallid birch grove; a snowy road weaved between shacks.

The huts and makeshift shelters bothered no one, they made the land no less empty and vast, and the people, as innocent as at the beginning of time, were yet to separate themselves from it. Meek and quiet, they seemed to be concealing themselves almost intentionally, merging with the landscape, and it was only when the flame of the kerosene lamp or the light of the sun fell on their faces that they emerged embarrassed and hesitant from the shadows. Seryozha painted them drunk and placid. Either they would be nestled up to each other sleeping, or they would be trudging along, not knowing where they were going. Sinless, they needed only a glass of vodka to be granted heaven. Heaven was wherever they were: it had after all been made for children.

On the paintings with Christ, the Promised Land was harsh and stony, having despaired of ever absorbing the blood of endless wars and strife. But here the heavenly pastures were swaddled in downy snow in winter, while in summer, warmed by the sun, they were covered in soft moss and herbs, even in town. The soil was fluid and leisurely, there were no barriers, no borders, and the land, the people, the beasts – all were kin to all, flowing easily into one another until each was filled. In Seryozha's portraits an arm bent at the elbow could become a nose, as could the protruding backside of a woman bent over a campfire, a tree twisted by the wind, or a lorry's uneven tracks in the distance. The eyes could be a pair of heads sticking out of blankets on hospital beds (inside the hospital, fleas, bedbugs and cockroaches were being frozen to death, and in the meantime the patients had been taken out and placed in the snow beneath a streetlamp), trailers poking out of a forest on either side of the road, or the lighted windows of a brick barracks.

Alongside these, the same eyes, nose, lips were sketched by dogs casually sprawled out in the sand or a parrot with a towel thrown over its cage, forgotten on an uncleared table. From these paltry, insignificant fragments Seryozha had assembled and moulded human faces, just as the Lord had once moulded us from clay, but he hadn't separated anything from anything else. Like gophers poking out of their holes, the people in his canvases never moved an inch from the dust from which they had been born; meek and poor in spirit, they shrank back at the slightest danger.

The next day towards evening Akimych arrived in a foul mood. Dolya the gelding was scared out of his wits and shaking. The journey had been a difficult one – at one point they'd even fallen through. Thankfully it was a shallow spot and they had managed to climb back out. But the horse had hurt himself and couldn't settle. Retrieving Seryozha that same day was out of the question. Dolya needed food and rest; Akimych was exhausted too.

A night's sleep did him good. The next morning we got

up, had a mug of tea and walked over to the bog. The wind had changed direction the previous evening, it was cold and clear, and the small cracks out of which water had trickled the day before had iced over again. But Akimych still feared for the horse, so we left Dolya on the shore. We were going to do the job the old way: we laid out ten boards as a precaution and once again I started sawing the ice around Seryozha. Now though we were working in turns, looking out for each other. It was easier like this of course, and three hours or so was enough for the two of us to complete the task I'd begun on my own two days earlier. Once the sawing was done and we'd got our breath back, we paused over a cigarette. Then we ran wooden beams under the hacked-out chunk of ice and caught it in the net I'd brought as a gift for Seryozha.

Now it was Dolya's turn. After closing the net up like a wicker bag, we stretched a strong hempen hawser to a safe spot halfway between the island and the ice hole. Akimych had already brought the horse over. All we had to do now was fasten the hawser to the harness and make sure that the net didn't catch on anything as it was pulled by the horse. That was my job. I cleared away driftwood, used an axe, boat hook, oar – whatever worked – to chip away ice. But as soon as Dolya pulled the net out of the water, both I and Akimych, who had just walked over, immediately noticed something tied to Seryozha's shin – a string bag with a heavy cobble inside it. But it was a cheap, cotton rope, over the winter it had gone soggy and started to rot, and one tug from the gelding, who had sniffed the shore, was enough for the edges of the ice hole to cut right through it like a knife. Only a half-metre scrap of cord was left; as for the string bag, it had sunk back down to the bottom with the stone. Without a word, we both pretended there had been no bag. I freed the last bit of rope and threw it into the water where the stone had vanished.

Just behind Seryozha's dugout, past a line of old firs, there was a glade stretching almost to the top of the hill. I'd already made a note of the spot, and it was there that Akimych and I decided to bury Seryozha. We dug a grave in the sand, knocked together a cross, and carefully trimmed the chunk of ice to fit its coffin. Not that there was anything much to lay in the earth: a cheek, a jacket – everything else had been picked to the bone by fish and crayfish. Once we'd finished digging, placed the cross and levelled off the earth, I recited the appropriate prayers and we had the customary drink. Back in the dugout, after heating the stove and warming ourselves up, we each opened a tin of stewed meat, and without hurrying, drank to Seryozha once more.

After finishing off the bottle, Akimych crashed out, while I started going through Seryozha's papers: thought I might find a diary or perhaps a letter. But there was nothing and I went to sleep too. We'd agreed to get up while it was still dark and complete at least part of the journey in the frost. Akimych feared for Dolya and even wanted to leave the sledge on the island. I had a hard job talking him out of it, but money settled the issue. Unable to resist fifty roubles – a huge sum for any villager – he agreed to fix a light wooden crate to the runners instead of the sledge: we would take the paintings, if nothing else.

It didn't take long to load up and at about half past six our column moved off. The cargo still weighed plenty and both of us, not to mention Dolya, were jittery. We walked slowly, me probing the path in front with the boat hook and Akimych at a little distance behind, leading Dolya by the bridle. There were lots of holes in the ice and places where it had become very thin; we'd walk straight for a hundred metres then veer off to avoid danger. In the end it took us three times as long as usual to reach the village, and we did the last bit of the forest when it was already night. There was a full moon, thank goodness, so at least we didn't get lost. Then, just as I had done three years earlier, when I'd driven Seryozha to Bear's Moss, I made a few runs back and forth between Anikeyevka and Moscow, carrying his canvases on my roof rack.

As I was doing this, I was already aware, that whether I wanted to or not, the first person I had to call on in Moscow was Dusya. Of course I had no intention of telling either her or anyone else I knew about Seryozha's suicide. Nor did I plan to say anything about its causes. Seryozha was a closed book – he didn't confide in me or anyone else – but the real reason why he had left Moscow was no mystery to me.

Four years before this, in the spring of '72, it had become clear to me that Irina was beginning to tire of our relationship. For a month or two I carried on hoping – for what, I'm not sure – and it wasn't until a week before I was due to fly out on a research expedition to Yamal that I accepted the situation and stepped aside. Breaking up with Irina hit me hard. I'd believed right until the end that I could find a way of dealing with her despair, that I could put a stop to her endless flight from one bed to another, but I never got very far. To cope with all that had fallen upon her, Irina needed help, but she found a crutch neither in me nor in any of those who'd come before me. In the end she had only one choice – to keep looking.

BE AS CHILDREN

Thanks to my mother, who found the right way of talking to me about it, I've never blamed Irina for anything, I've only pitied her, and relations between us remained warm until the last days of her life. If we were both in Moscow, we'd see each other once or even twice a month. We'd walk down Gogol Boulevard or stop at the Squirrel Café in the Arbat. Irina had a sweet tooth and she loved the eclairs and apple pastries which the Squirrel was famous for. Whenever we met, we would talk almost nonstop about Sashenka, just as we always had, but we occasionally touched on other things too. Irina didn't conceal that she was now living with Seryozha and how much he was doing for her. Or that before Seryozha, when I'd gone off to Tiksi, she'd had two brief liaisons with people I didn't know. They had also made her all sorts of promises, but they'd let her down, hadn't helped her at all.

Seryozha was an extremely attractive man, but preparing to be a monk since childhood, he had I'd been told, steered clear of women. At any rate, I knew of no other relationships before Irina. She got together with him without thinking it through: she'd just decided that surely Dusya's own son knew the truth about Sashenka's death. Her hopes were in vain: in him, as in me, the little girl's death elicited nothing but horror, and anyway, he had become estranged from his mother a long time ago. A year and a half with Seryozha was enough to rid Irina of any illusion that he could help her, and her old boredom and indifference soon returned. The moment she gave up on someone, she didn't tread softly, didn't spare their feelings. Irina's departure sent Seryozha into freefall.

Irina it seems, could hardly tell us all apart, or only vaguely; she wasn't interested in anyone and was in no rush to show any sympathy. At the root of every liaison lay the fate of her girl. It was in her daughter that she found the sole aim and justification of her love affairs. If she picked up a new partner, then she did so for Sashenka, for Sashenka's sake: it meant there was somebody out there who could help her save her daughter, could deliver her from her torments beyond the grave, or like me, could investigate who exactly had convinced Dusya to beg Sashenka's death, when and why. Various people fell under suspicion, including Father Nikodim, but the lack of certainty was driving Irina out of her mind. A single suggestion was enough for her to damn an entirely innocent person.

She'd staked a great deal on Seryozha. She'd been hearing all her life about the hopes Dusya had pinned on her son, and had decided that nothing had changed, that things were still as they were. This being so, Seryozha surely knew or could at least find out whether what Dusya had said was really true – that Sashenka was now in Heaven, among the righteous – or whether she, Irina, had been lied to and the Lord had not and would not forgive her daughter the evil she had been capable of committing.

A union whose foundation is the death of a child can hardly be expected to develop like any other. Small wonder then that both I and Seryozha often acted unacceptably towards Irina. As if someone had forgotten to tell us that it is wrong, when you're trying to hold on to a woman, to make a leash or a net, out of God. It's scant justification of either of us to say that we were caught, or rather trapped, between Irina and Dusya – after all the more evil Dusya caused, the more ecstatically she was venerated.

Seryozha spent a long time looking for the words Irina

needed. Tried to persuade her that his mother was no saint, even if she had taken her vows forty years ago. All that stuff about her begging death for Sashenka was rubbish, he told her, repeating again and again that Dusya could never have done that even if she had wanted to. But he walked into a wall of tears before he had barely begun. Because there was nothing in the child's death except delirium and madness.

Irina had conceived with enormous difficulty, after trying many times and having been told by the doctors that she would never have children of her own. As a precaution she spent seven months of her pregnancy in hospital, terrified of even moving, and gave birth to a girl who in her beauty, sweetness and intelligence was a genuine miracle, only for everything to be taken from her in the space of a single day. People can say what they like, but without Dusya's words at the cemetery, the little girl's death would have appeared even more monstrous. Their meaning was terrible, but at least there was a meaning, and Irina was desperate to cling on to it.

It took Seryozha a while to realise how far things had gone, and when he did, he was forced into a retreat. By giving in, he eventually assumed the role that Irina was prepared to grant him. Started telling her stories about monks, priests, laypeople, who without doubt, were close to God, loved by Him, and could therefore intercede for Sashenka. Many of those whom Seryozha had known since childhood had died a martyr's death in the '30s. The circumstances of the time meant that they couldn't be canonised of course, but they had led saintly lives and in Seryozha's stories they always turned out to be praying for Sashenka right at that moment. The Lord would have to answer their prayers. Whether or not Dusya had been right to say that if the Lord had not taken the girl, she would have become the Devil incarnate, they would save her. All Irina had to do was not get in their way – enough sinning, enough lechery, infidelity.

It's not hard for me to picture her listening to him, her hands clasped on her knees, her fingers now extending to form a roof, now locking tight. Sometimes she would weep, almost as bitterly and hopelessly as when she herself spoke about Sashenka's death, sometimes she would give a long sigh, but she was also capable of joy if she saw that today, thanks to the person Seryozha was talking about, Sashenka would be given a reprieve. Heeding the prayers of a saint, the Lord would soften towards this guiltless soul and receive it.

The idea that Seryozha was doing all this to get Irina into bed is shameful. He just loved her very much and was desperate to make her life at least marginally easier. Of course he also asked God to help her put an end to it, stop sleeping around, especially because Irina was no whore by nature. Her own sexual experiences passed her by; she'd got through dozens of men and yet in the end, it was as if she hadn't even noticed.

All through the year they spent living together, Seryozha would tell her his stories about saints almost every day. She could no longer manage without them, and he'd also got used to them. True, just before Irina left him he suddenly noticed with bewilderment, even fear, that the death and salvation of Sashenka were gradually taking the shape virtually of a new apocalypse, a universal picture of destruction and retribution for sins, with exoneration and forgiveness to follow.

I know for a fact that Seryozha's stories reconciled Irina to a great many things and a great many people, but for Seryozha himself nothing about the girl's death became any less painful. His situation I suppose was even harder than mine. After all, the daughter of the person he loved – and I've never heard of anyone being closer to him than Irina – was taken away by his own mother. His cross was a heavy one and now with Seryozha long dead, it's easier for me, as I recall his life on the island, to understand why all this proved too much for him than it is to grasp how he could have borne it at all.

Well, I didn't go to see Dusya. I put it off and put it off until there was a ring in the middle of the night a week or so later, and I grabbed my dressing gown, opened the door and saw her on the threshold. Half-asleep and unsure what to do, I started fawning on her: even though there was neither a chair nor a stool in the corridor, I tried sitting her down and making her comfortable. Dusya in her turn, began sobbing with shallow, old-womanish gasps the moment she entered the kitchen. She was convinced that Seryozha had killed himself and she was just waiting to hear me confirm it. But I kept silent and it was clear that I wouldn't speak first no matter what, I'd just carry on playing dumb.

Out of despair perhaps, she didn't even cry. Instead after a few sniffles, she suddenly plucked up courage and asked while my back was turned, 'Dima, please tell me how Seryozha died', and added: 'I need to know the truth.' Before this point, when she, fingering and crumpling the hem of her apron, was waiting for me to come out with it all without being asked, and I, turning away from her, was boiling up some water, taking biscuits and bread rings from the cupboard, putting everything on a plate – all this time I wasn't trying to mock her, it was just that I was no longer used to her after so many years and I felt terrified of looking Dusya in the eyes.

By the time she asked about Seryozha, I had calmed down and set about explaining, perfectly coherently, that his death had been an accident. No doubt about it, an accident. Seryozha had been in the boat at the time, fishing with a net, had got caught up in it and fallen overboard. But she didn't stop her interrogation there, trying one angle after another and even asking one and the same question three, five times, just in case I contradicted myself. Luckily any such slips were trivial. For example, instead of 'fishing net' I said 'string net' at one point, but she didn't notice.

On her way over, Dusya was quite certain that Seryozha had taken his own life, but now I could see her wavering. Essentially, the one thing she needed to know that night was whether he was or was not a suicide, everything else – how I'd found him, who'd been with me, where I'd buried him – was just to test my story. But I didn't trip up here either. I gave a lengthy, detailed account of the five days I spent looking blindly for Seryozha. First with Alyosha, then after Alyosha left, with Akimych. For the first few days we had just walked around the island with no plan and to no real end, then we divided it up into squares, numbered them, and prodding the snow with sticks, checked each of them thoroughly. We knew Seryozha wasn't the kind of person to go away without first telling someone, or at least leaving a note in the dugout, yet that was what we hoped and prayed for, as if for a miracle.

Seryozha had no gun, and Alyosha and Akimych thought a bear must have mauled him or else a stray pack of wolves; it wasn't even a body we were looking for so much as a few scraps of clothes – but there was nothing anywhere. Then

BE AS CHILDREN

Alyosha and I split. I carried on searching the island, while he decided to inspect the lake and the parts of the bog closest to the shore. But Alyosha found nothing either on the lake or in the gaps in the bog where powerful springs bubbled up amidst the moss. Where the ice was covered with snow you couldn't see anything beneath it at all.

The day before Alyosha left, a south-easterly brought warmth from Central Asia. The snow on the ice melted and disappeared in just two days. When the sun was high, the ice shone so brightly you couldn't even look at it, but for two hours or so at a time – at sunset and sunrise – it became entirely transparent and you could see every little root and leaf as if sealed in glass. By that time I was already looking for Seryozha on the lake, walking round and round as if I were tied to it, tracing ever broader circles.

I found him on the fifth day at dawn, three hundred metres or so from shore. The body, like an air bubble, was completely frozen into the lake. Perhaps he'd been fishing shortly before everything iced up, around the start of November. In summer he might have managed to wriggle out of the nets, but by the end of autumn the water's too cold and Seryozha must have had less than five minutes to free himself. Or else the current pulled him under some driftwood, in which case he would have had no chance at all. The lake, I continued, had probably iced over already. The body had bumped against the ice as it floated up. Over the winter Bear's Moss freezes all the way down in some places, but even where the water is deep the ice is rarely less than a metre thick. By spring Seryozha, unprayed-for, unburied, had grown into it as if into a crystal font.

Twenty-four hours later, I went on, our friend from

Anikeyevka, Akimych, arrived in a sledge, and we decided that taking care not to damage the body, we would try to saw or hack out the *kukol'* of ice containing Seryozha.[66] We worked until nightfall, the ice crackled and sagged beneath us, but in the end we managed and under moonlight, with the help of the horse, we dragged Seryozha ashore. In the morning I went off to dig the grave, while Akimych started fashioning a coffin from boards that had been set aside for a shed. He didn't make it to size, but bigger, so that Seryozha could be placed in it as he was, in the lump of ice. We buried Seryozha at midday sharp, twenty or so metres above his dugout, in a beautiful forest glade surrounded by ancient firs. I recited several prayers for the soul of the deceased, and after planting a cross at the head of the grave, we lowered Seryozha into the earth. Then we sat on the little mound above the tomb and drank to his memory in the usual way.

After that night, doing our best to avoid all sensitive topics, Dusya and I began meeting up regularly – two or three times a month. She would drop by without needing a reason, just to remember him. She no longer wept and made no reproaches, as if with Seryozha's death everything had been forgiven and exonerated. In a quiet, colourless voice she talked about the Revolution, the Civil War, Amvrosy and Nikodim, about herself and her ecstatic, exalted state of mind after giving birth

---

[66] The *kukol'*, worn by Orthodox monks who have attained the highest degree of holiness, is a small pointed hood accompanied by two long flaps hanging down over the monk's mantle in front and behind, usually decorated with crosses (Mikhail Nesterov's painting, *Evening Bells*, depicts one such monk). According to the website of one Orthodox monastery (Novo-Tikhvinsky), the shape of the hood, reminiscent of baby hats, is thought to serve as a reminder of the call to 'become as little children'.

to her second child not long before those events. One day she confessed to cursing Seryozha angrily when he was five years old, then without making any connection, she said many tender things about her brother Pasha, and how for all her love towards him, she had brought him, too, nothing but evil.

I already knew from Nikodim that in 1920 she had foolishly begged Pasha to put off his vows for a while and that several months later he had gone missing somewhere in Siberia, vanished into thin air right at the end of the Civil War. Then she returned once more to Seryozha, whose resemblance to her brother – his face, his figure, his ways – had always startled her; on more than one occasion she had even got them mixed up, especially from the back, and had called her son Pasha. Such a likeness she kept telling me could not have been an accident: the Lord in His mercy wanted to give her an opportunity, as it were, to repent, to correct her mistake. Seryozha wasn't yet ten when she began to think ever more insistently that his calling in life was to be a hermit monk. Taking the tonsure would relieve, would free Seryozha of the curse she had placed on her son. By taking Seryozha's hand and leading him to the Lord, she would also atone for her guilt towards her brother.

Seryozha was three when Dusya started taking him with her to church. Standing through a full service almost every day, he knew the entire canon by the age of five and was in the habit of confessing and taking Communion at least once a week. For Seryozha, Dusya explained to me, church was home. What was more, in preparing her son for monastic service, aware of how tough that life would be, she hardened his will and his body as best she could. Seryozha grew up strong, and above all, resilient.

There were days when Dusya spoke with a kind of detachment, as if she were not speaking about herself at all, frequently hopping from one topic to another. She might go back to the '20s again, and then without the slightest connection, tell me that Seryozha had not visited her for a whole year even before he went to Bear's Moss. Nothing would make him agree to see her. 'That was probably why he went off to that bog of his,' she explained, 'just so I wouldn't pester him.' She couldn't even recall when they had spoken on the phone for the last time. Maybe her pain really had gone numb by then, or maybe she wanted to reassure me, lull me, because during our strange conversations she would still set the occasional trap.

Once for example, Dusya asked, as if randomly about the little icon Seryozha had received for his christening and always kept with him. I'd found it on a stool next to the camp bed, but I had the sense to tell her that I had seen it through the ice as we were placing Seryozha in his coffin. That it was hanging from his neck. I realised that from the day she learned of Seryozha's death Dusya had been reciting one and the same prayer, making one and the same request to the Lord – for her son to have drowned on Bear's Moss while fishing, for him not to have taken his own life – and I tried to tread very carefully.

It was probably because of this, the fact that I still had to be on my guard at all times, or because almost half the names Dusya mentioned meant nothing to me, that I listened to her with only half an ear and didn't even try to piece things together. She was complaining about Nikodim, who in '33, during a break between two spells in the camps, had destroyed in one day what she had spent ten years constructing. Just as she had once done with Pasha, so he persuaded Seryozha that he knew too little of life, that it was too soon for him to leave the world and take the tonsure. She spoke about the vow which Seryozha made before the war, when he promised the Virgin Mary, that if she helped him get through it, he would take himself straight to a monastery when he returned from the front. Then she added that Seryozha was badly wounded on three occasions, but survived. He didn't make good on his promise, though.

True, I did have the impression that she was finally prepared to forgive her son for not taking his vows. At any rate, when I told her that Seryozha had lived on Bear's Moss like a true anchorite for a whole two years, that aside from the visits from Alyosha, Akimych and myself he hadn't seen a single human being, she seemed to agree with me. Now she accepted everything, forgave him everything, just so long as Seryozha hadn't killed himself, hadn't committed the sin that nobody had ever managed to redeem.

***

For Dusya herself, Nikodim's confession changed little, but for me it was different. I'm speaking above all of her relationship with Seryozha. It was only after hearing Nikodim that I managed to put two and two together, but the upshot was a sad one, and I felt even sorrier for her, and Seryozha, and Pasha. By then I'd stopped trying to avoid Dusya. She was old and weak and she was fading, as if Nikodim had passed on the baton. It seemed to me that she would have gladly gone a long time ago, but the Lord was in no hurry to take her. This, and the fact that she was no longer bursting in on me at night, allowed me to make my peace with her. I even began visiting her without needing to be begged, especially as I now had time on my hands. I bought food for her, did whatever she asked me to do, and just as I had with Nikodim, talked with her for hours. It was the talking I think that mattered most to Dusya. Like any of us she needed to get everything off her chest as the end drew near. She talked a great deal about Pasha, with far more detail than before, and never tried to dodge my questions, in fact she went out of her way, almost eagerly so, to fill in what I'd heard from Nikodim.

In Dusya's telling, Pasha's death in Tomsk added nothing to her memory of her brother. When in 1920 she had begged Pasha to take his time, not to hurry with his vows, she already felt that she was destroying him, but egged on by her mother, she was unable to stop. She kept on at him day in, day out, insisting that it makes no difference whether you are a monk or a layman, the only terror is spiritual death – everything else, even the grave, is a lesser evil. Then Pasha went to Siberia and disappeared. Although she took herself off to Khabarovsk a year later to search for him, she had few hopes of success. Her mother once again was the reason she went; in her own mind she understood that, amidst a sea of evil, Pasha had by some miraculous instinct found the causeway by which he could be saved, only for her to push him off it.

Now that she knew about Pasha's last days, she could agree with Nikodim, that in all likelihood, her brother's Procession of the Cross had not been blessed: the Lord had not even let him finish what he had begun. However you choose to call his venture, the outcome would have been fresh and even greater bloodshed. This second path was a false path, but it was because of her that Pasha had taken it. Pasha loved his mother, he respected her, but he had long been free of her influence when it came to anything serious. His sister was a different matter – his trust in Dusya, her intuition, was at times almost blind. It was from this, his faith in her, his love for her, that evil was born. By impeding Pasha's tonsure, she had single-handedly condemned her brother to death. As with her husband, knowing or not knowing where and when he died could not change a thing.

There was something else too. Her remorse towards Pasha was more than matched by the guilt she felt before the Lord. She had deprived the Almighty of a sacrifice that had already been promised, had already been placed on the altar. A calf without a single blemish, as befits an offering to God. She had started calling Pasha a calf by the way, on the day that her mother first showed him to her after giving birth. All her life she had been trying to pay back her debt to the Lord. Whether this was even possible was a question she had put to each of her confessors, but receiving no clear answer, she had decided that the damage could not be repaired. This didn't mean that the only thing left to do was twiddle her thumbs. Recompensing the Lord for at least some of His losses was within her capabilities.

There were several reasons why she took the veil – the need to atone for cursing her son, her falling out with her Elders, and thirdly, perhaps most crucially, to give up her own soul to God in place of Pasha's. But the measure of one was not the measure of the other. Pasha was as pure as a child, while evil was tugging and dragging her soul into the pit of Hell. Aside from Pasha, she was guilty before God, to whom she had lied in her confessions year after year, before her husband, to whom she had been unfaithful and whom she had sent to the Caucasian Front, where he had been duly killed in 1918, and before her son, whom she had given away just like that to the unclean spirit.

Her awareness that the exchange was inadequate, that her soul was scant consolation to the Lord, tormented her more acutely with each passing year, sometimes driving her literally out of her mind. Incapable of stopping herself, she searched almost hysterically for someone she could give up in Pasha's place, so that it would be an honest swap, no short-changing, like for like. This haunted her and haunted her. You could see now, from the occasional slip of her tongue, that even Sashenka's death was part and parcel of this quest. Nikodim really was terrified of a new children's crusade, and he was prepared to do anything to prevent it, working on his novice day after day, switching between carrots and sticks to win her help. But Dusya's own desire to save the little girl from sin, to return her to the Lord just as pure and innocent as she had entered the world, was also strong.

Sashenka was born in '66, but back then, in the mid-1920s, Dusya's endless searching turned up nobody worthier than her son. No wonder that just as soon as Seryozha started school she began thinking about his vows, that from the age of nine she raised her son, whom she loved so passionately, with the monastery in mind. But here too there was something else that came out even during her confessions. She would explain, and herself believed, that there was no other way of lifting the curse which she had placed on him in her fit of anger. Growing up Seryozha resembled Pasha to a staggering degree, not just in his appearance but also in his rare inner tact, his fear of offending another person, and Dusya was unable to resist the temptation.

Still, she did once tell me that every now and again something would snap inside her and she would no longer understand whether she was doing the right thing for Seryozha. Maybe it was still too early, maybe there was no need to push him so hard at all – why not let him grow up and decide for himself whether the monk's path suited him? But there was no one to turn to for advice: Amvrosy had died and was lying in the cemetery of some obscure sub-unit of the Gulag, Nikodim was in prison and her correspondence with him had dried up. However often she wrote, she never received a single reply. In short, there was no help on the horizon, and after wavering a little, she would generally fall back into her old habits.

What reassured her more than anything was the joy Seryozha took in preparing to serve God. He felt no envy towards his peers, how they lived or what they did. He was happy to spend all day reading the Old and New Testaments, the Church Fathers and the Lives of the Saints, and enjoyed learning Latin, Greek and Old Church Slavonic. He found just as much as pleasure in physical exercises that train the body, that teach it to endure pain by subjugating flesh to spirit, to ignore hunger and cold. Sometimes she would suggest to him that maybe it was wrong of her to deprive him of his childhood, bad that he didn't have even an hour to play with his peers, if only to kick a ball about outside. But no sooner would she tell Seryozha that he needed a break from his studies than her son would immediately assume he was being punished, start asking what he'd done wrong, how he'd managed to upset her, disappoint her. Frowning and sniffling, he'd say that she probably thought he was too weak, that he would duck the first obstacles on his path – and the Lord had no need of cowards. But he wasn't a weakling, on the contrary he'd shown manliness and unusual staunchness ever since childhood, and she, feeling very confused would eventually give in. After hugs and tears on both sides everything would go back to how it was before.

Dusya told me that she didn't know why Seryozha hadn't become a monk. There was a time when she had blamed herself: for cursing Seryozha when he was a child. The Lord hadn't wanted to accept a sacrifice that had once been dedicated to the unclean spirit. Or maybe it was the fault of the times, which were themselves thoroughly demonic. I wouldn't object to either argument – both sounded reasonable – but the list of causes, it seems to me, should be lengthened.

I could see from Dusya's stories that Seryozha really had resembled Pasha very closely, and at first he had found it easy and joyful to follow the example he had been set. At the age of ten, having borrowed a few phrases from the oath of the Young Pioneers, he took an entirely voluntary vow, in the presence of his mother, that he would enter a monastery just as soon as he came of age, and he did this with great gladness and with a pure heart. But Pasha had grown up on his own terms, two steps forward, one step back, while Seryozha had been moulded by others, his edges smoothed according to a given template. And it wasn't just Dusya: his grandma was also keen to remind him at every opportunity that he wasn't free, that in such-and-such a situation his uncle would have acted differently.

Besides, he was living two lives. At school to avoid drawing attention to himself and getting his family into trouble, he would say the same things as everyone else. He too, joined the Little Octobrists, then the Pioneers. In short, the Antichrist and his minions were advancing on him from one flank, Pasha from the other, and the territory on which Seryozha did not have to hide or look over his shoulder was shrinking year by year. He was, whatever anyone thought, being brought up to dissemble, and the fact that one of the masks happened to appeal and make sense to him made little difference. It saddened him of course to know that he would always remain a copy, but even so, Seryozha's desire to please his mother, whom he loved madly, would have been enough to make a monk of him, had Nikodim not intervened.

In '33, during a one-year gap between his prison stints, Nikodim returned from Abakanlag and settled a hundred kilometres outside Moscow, in Savyelovo. Dusya visited him regularly there – once or even twice a week. Their relationship gradually started to recover. She set about purging herself all over again, as though she hadn't confessed or received Communion for several years, as though she were not a nun herself. Learning as before to open up to him and fuse with him as one, she cleared away obstacles and barriers, tore down railings and fences, and saw with joy that her efforts were rewarded: what had bound them in the past was still alive. For her this time was as radiant as the very beginning of their relationship. Fourteen years earlier, young, naïve, ardent beyond measure, she would prepare for confession by diligently recording her every sin in an exercise book; now she did the same before setting out to Savyelovo. Just like then, if the confession went well, she would feel light, almost happy. Especially because Nikodim found little fault with her now and absolved her with visible joy.

For the first few months, she made do with her own experience during confession, and if she did touch on her loved ones, then only in passing. Above all, as if sensing something in advance, she found various pretexts not to bring Seryozha with her, even though Nikodim frequently asked about him and said how glad he would be to see what he was like now. She did of course tell him that her son was finishing high school in the summer, that she was bringing him up strictly and that he was nothing like most of his peers: she understood that he had a hard life ahead of him and she was toughening him up as best she could, teaching him resilience and endurance. Dusya mentioned neither the seminary nor the fact that Seryozha was planning to take his vows after he graduated from there, yet she herself did not know what she was waiting for or why she was dragging things out.

It wasn't until June 2nd that she brought Seryozha to Savyelovo, once he had already received his school-leaving certificate. His childhood was officially over, and as they looked to the future both she and he felt that the Elder's blessing was essential. It took Dusya almost a month to prepare for the pilgrimage to Savyelovo. She wanted Nikodim to see that Seryozha was a mature, serious man, that he had intelligence, responsibility, strength of will – qualities that you don't come by just like that. She understood that it would be best if Seryozha himself told the Elder that he had no illusions about how hard things were for the Church at this time, but that having thought it all through, he could see no other path for himself than the path of the spirit, and before setting out on this road, he would like to receive Father Nikodim's blessing.

She was sure that Nikodim, however hesitantly, would approve Seryozha's choice, that he couldn't do otherwise. Sometimes she could even see the entire dialogue unfolding before her eyes, knew who would say what and when, and the conversation she imagined was always long and detailed; they might even have to spend the night in Savyelovo, but in the end everything would turn out well. Dusya was already a famous seer, her visions rarely deceived her, but this time she was badly mistaken. Nikodim listened to her with a sullen expression and obvious displeasure, and in reply he announced, without mincing his words, that as her spiritual father he could not give her his blessing for her son's tonsure. On the contrary, he was convinced that such a step would be wrongful and not pleasing to the Lord.

It was clear that he had no wish to continue the conversation, that for him it was as good as over, but at this point, according to Dusya, it was not she but Seryozha who decided to ask what he had done to deserve this rebuke, and Nikodim changed his mind and agreed to explain. After telling them that he hadn't meant to upset anybody, he repeated almost word for word what Father Amvrosy had once said about Nikodim. Such unanimity among her Elders was something new, and Dusya was deeply struck by it, even though Nikodim himself was not hiding the fact that he had changed.

He told them both that after his time in prison and the camps he now saw many things differently, and this had a direct bearing on the conversation they were having now. Both she and Seryozha had to understand that, first of all, an oath taken by a ten-year-old boy whose only dream is to please his beloved mama counts for nothing. God has no need of vows like that, He deems them worthless. There is no freedom in such words, because the love of a child for his mother, his dependence on her, is itself a kind of bondage, and what goes on between them is not the Lord's concern. In short, if Seryozha, despite his childish oath, chose not to enter the monastery, his soul would incur neither sin nor loss; on this score Dusya had nothing to worry about.

Secondly: he, Nikodim, was firmly set against the early taking of vows. There's no rule without exceptions of course, but in this particular case he was convinced that the time for Dusya's son to withdraw from the world had not yet come. Seryozha did not know life, his mother had raised him in desperate fear of sin, had watched his every step, lest he went somewhere, saw something, heard something he wasn't meant to. He, Nikodim, could understand Dusya: she had raised her son with the dream of handing him over to the Lord pure and innocent. But it is no feat of faith to reject a world of which you know nothing. A person should come to God only after enduring and overcoming every temptation. What was needed was the long labour of the soul, only then would Seryozha be able to help those who came to him, and the Church would benefit from him too. 'For now,' Nikodim continued, turning to Seryozha, 'you are travelling too light: your mother has built a wall between you and the world and you're just walking along it from one end to the other. Never mind climbing over the wall, you're scared even to see what's on the other side.'

Dusya herself could not disobey Nikodim, but she was in

no doubt, she told me, that Seryozha would find the strength of character to hold his ground. Two months later however, he suddenly announced that he was entering the Stroganov Institute of Art, and Nikodim, whom he had visited just the day before in Savyelovo, approved his choice. Thoughts of bohemians, drinking bouts and female life models flashed through her mind, but even so Seryozha's decision, following his rejection of the tonsure, did not alarm her. She even listened sympathetically to what he had to say, confusing though she found it. All she understood was that the persecution of the Church was about to end, the regime would come to its senses very soon, and when it did they would need to start building and doing up thousands of churches, restoring frescos and icons – there could be no better service for a monk. Seryozha spoke fervently, breathlessly, and she could see there would be no retreat.

Aside from the canvases, I brought some ten jotters and notebooks back to Moscow from Seryozha's dugout, all filled with sketches from the front. The pages were densely covered, and judging by the fact that one page contained drawings in pencil, charcoal and pen, the notebooks must have been used at different times haphazardly. Seryozha must have taken whichever notebook lay closest to hand, and finding a blank space, started drawing. As a result, the usual sketches of the Christ Child gazed unreproachfully, even compassionately at the port of Dudinka and scenes from Samoyed life.

This swirl of life contained only one refrain – long, usually spiral-shaped processions of people with only a few fully drawn figures and the faintest of outlines for the rest.

From these notebooks you could guess that the human chain ascending to Heaven tier by tier was meant to resemble the Tower of Babylon. I often thought of asking Dusya whether she knew anything about the notebooks, but for obvious reasons I was wary of touching on the last days of Seryozha's life unless I really had to. Only once did she mention the drawings herself. She described how, at Nikodim's request, Seryozha had sketched out frescos for a church in Pskov region while still studying at the Stroganov. The church had just been restored, or else it was one that the regime was planning to return to the Patriarchate. Either way the walls needed to be painted from scratch. And although all of this would later sink into oblivion, the work had absorbed Seryozha completely and it was only when he started travelling to the North on field trips that it took a back seat. But Seryozha came back to these sketches later on as well, touching up here, filling in there.

In Dusya's telling, this artwork, had things ever reached that stage, would probably have been deemed insufficiently canonical for church walls, despite its traditional techniques (two years spent restoring frescos in Yaroslavl had left Seryozha with an appreciation and love of that town's particular style). And the main reason for this was the recurring topic that Father Nikodim had suggested: the history, in essence, of the human race, conceived from start to finish as the return of the Prodigal Son.

The idea was that the lower tier would be painted as if the wall were merely a support for the figures trudging wearily over the earth and over the stone slabs of the church floor that served as its continuation – Adam and Eve, followed by Cain, Abel, Seth, all walking across the country given to Man after his expulsion from Paradise. The first steps of people reeling from the catastrophe that has befallen them. The people cast out by the Lord, who had said to Adam, '...cursed is the ground because of you'. At the same time, it is from this very place that the few whose faith in the Saviour still glimmers begin their path back to the Lord.

It's a long, agonising journey, only a handful keep the memory of God alive, and the thread is thin, it could snap any day. Only after the Exodus does this terror gradually abate and recede. From Sinai, the chain of Adam's descendants, stretched out all along the perimeter of the church's interior, begins to climb step by step, tier by tier. Higher and higher, to the throne of the Lord.

To judge by Seryozha's sketches, he intended to paint hundreds upon hundreds of people from the Old and New Testaments, who, no matter what, walked doggedly towards the Lord; next, Christendom's most revered saints and martyrs; and finally, beneath the dome, all around the Lord's radiant, sun-like throne in Heaven, their seed, their spiritual children. There, up high, no faces can be discerned, only the outlines of bodies and the light emanating from those who have been saved and cleansed of sin. A sea of light from exultant throngs that have returned to their Maker.

Dusya brought up the topic of Seryozha's monastic vows on one other occasion, but no good came of the second attempt either. In '39 Seryozha graduated with distinction from the Stroganov, and in '41 the war began. He was working in Uglich at the time, in restoration workshops, and when he returned to Moscow in September he went straight from the railway station to the recruitment office and signed up as a volunteer for the People's Militia. The city was already in chaos. He was sent from the office to one unit, from there to another, and so on all around Moscow until he was finally told to go home for the night. The next day the same thing happened. Eventually the enlistment officer, sick of the sight of him, ordered Seryozha home with a few choice insults. He was to wait for his call-up papers and keep out of their way.

It wasn't until mid-October that Seryozha, along with many other new recruits, all as untrained and unseasoned as he, most of them students, was sent out to fight. The Germans had just broken through the front line near Vyazma and were threatening Moscow, advancing at the rate of almost twenty kilometres a day. In essence there were no regular forces to speak of. Almost all the armies shielding Moscow from the west had been trapped on every side, while those units that had managed to escape encirclement had been left without artillery and tanks, any means of communication or ammunition, and were retreating in disarray, cold and hungry. Trying to plug the gaps and win time for the transfer of fresh divisions from Siberia, the General Staff was sending tens of thousands of volunteers to Rzhev, Zubtsov and Volokolamsk. With one rifle for every three soldiers, plus a handful of cartridges, these men were standard cannon fodder and had no illusions about what was awaiting them. On the eve of their departure, the company commander, who had taken a liking to Seryozha, gave him a night's leave.

At home he didn't bother going to bed and sat up all night with Dusya, drinking tea and talking. Seryozha was all meekness and acceptance, as befits a person who has made a choice and knows it to be the right one. At dawn he got his kitbag together and put on his greatcoat. They sat down for good luck in the customary way, and then, Dusya explained, she, without knowing why, just couldn't resist asking him yet again to vow that if he made it through the war, and God willing got back home, he would finally take the tonsure. Seryozha agreed instantly and willingly: perhaps he was convinced that he would never emerge alive from the slaughterhouse to which he was being sent, perhaps he didn't want to upset her just as he was about to say goodbye. One way or the other, and despite being seriously wounded on three occasions, he did survive, only to give the monastery the slip for a second time. After his return though, Dusya never returned to the subject.

Three quarters of the sketches, Dusya continued, were done by Seryozha during the war, when their unit was withdrawn from the front line for a breather or reorganisation; she'd even heard that he would sometimes draw in the trenches as well, but only if it was a quiet day and there was no need to shoot at anyone. The rule of the 'non-shedding of blood', as Dusya called it, was rigorously observed. Although Seryozha never had the opportunity to paint a single church, the Lord, she went on, rewarded him handsomely. In October '44, outside Kraków, a burst from a submachine gun smashed the wrist of his right hand. It was a hard-fought skirmish, dozens were wounded, and after one look at his hand the surgeon told the medical assistant that it had been blown to bits and would have to be amputated – gangrene could set in at any moment.

He was saved by a nurse. Sorting through Seryozha's kitbag, she found the notebooks with the drawings inside. Repeating over and over that to remove an artist's hand is to offer him a noose, she convinced the doctor to take a risk.

Abscesses formed in the wound for several years afterwards and as winter approached he would always experience terrible pain as little fragments of bone came out with the pus, but he returned home uncrippled.

Ever since she had taken her own vows, the thought that every person needed to have a full burial service sung for them while they were still alive, or else they would not be saved, had clearly captivated Dusya. She came back to it time and again, but words, thank God, were as far as it went. Dusya was worn out and weak, and I was convinced that this was how things would remain – her doctrine would no longer cause anyone much trouble.

In April 1980, I noted in my diary that Dusya seemed to have finally accepted that Seryozha's death really was an accident; she had calmed down, stopped setting traps, and whole weeks would pass without Bear's Moss even being mentioned in our conversations. Now though, I think that it wasn't until the second half of June that for her the topic was finally closed. The possibility that her son had committed suicide was a dreadful burden for Dusya, and once she managed to lift it she regained a strength of which her frail body had seemed hardly capable.

I have few doubts now that Seryozha's initial consent and then refusal to take the tonsure, were for Dusya, the master-key by which to understand the destiny of the entire human race. The first was clear evidence of the possibility, even proximity of salvation; the second was the sign of inescapable ruin. I had barely managed to convince her that Seryozha had not taken his own life, when she, after scrupulous comparison of his life on the island in the bog with the lives of hermits venerated by Orthodox believers, evidently reached the conclusion that her son's retreat from the world conformed with Church prescriptions. Consequently he had fulfilled that for which she had asked God after Pasha's death.

Seryozha's voluntary seclusion in the skete of his dugout, combined with burial services for the repose of the living, instantly completed her mental picture of Salvation. More than that, it seemed to sanction Dusya, in fact it encouraged and blessed her personally, as a matter of urgency, to lead every person she knew to God. This work which was taking place inside her only gradually came to the surface.

On June 23rd, when I was already on my way out, Dusya suddenly announced that in ten days or so she was planning to travel to Bear's Moss – she wanted to spend some time by Seryozha's grave. I didn't start telling her that she was in no fit state to wander around a mire, that only yesterday she'd struggled to walk as far as the toilet; I just brushed the idea aside with the listless comment, as if it were too obvious to mention, that you couldn't cross Bear's Moss in summer. Thirty kilometres of impassable bogland would defeat even a special ops commando. But I achieved very little. The only upshot was a new round of interrogations as to whether Seryozha really had died a natural death.

Then for three days straight, from morning till night, the phone never stopped ringing as she demanded, pleaded, sobbed – in a maudlin voice that was so unlike her – that I lead her over Bear's Moss. She would call me at home, at work, in other people's flats, stop her ears to all my attempts to explain that the bog could not be crossed in summer, that the only season when you could reach the island on which Seryozha lived was winter – it was absurd to even consider walking fifteen kilometres there and fifteen kilometres back, over bottomless mire, at this time of the year – and would simply repeat over and over again that there was no alternative. Dusya was literally laying siege to me, and in the end I caved in and said fine, I'd see what I could do. Apparently this was all she needed for the time being, and the phone went silent.

The moment the calls suddenly ceased, I realised that I'd been digging my heels in for nothing. I'd already sold my Zaporozhets by this point, so we would have to travel to Anikeyevka in stages. Five hours in a basic compartment to Rzhev, then six hours by work train to the passing loop at Konyukhovo, and unless we could hitch a lift, another ten kilometres on foot to Akimych's village. But right now, this suited me perfectly. The quicker Dusya wore herself out, the better it would be for her and for me. Meanwhile I told her what to pack and we agreed to meet on August 8th in the waiting room of Rizhsky station an hour before the departure of the evening train to Rzhev.

This gave me a week's breathing space. It was only on August 7th that she called to check that our agreement still stood, and while she was at it, to inform me exultantly that she had tried to speak to about fifty people and all those who happened to be in Moscow had declared, without a single exception, that they also wanted to travel with us. Some said they would even take their children so she guessed we might end up with seventy-odd souls, or even eighty. I reacted calmly to this news, what worried me first and foremost was Dusya herself, and I calculated that if my plan worked out well as far as she was concerned, then her flock would pose no special difficulties.

Both of them – Nikodim and Dusya – had grown weaker before my eyes, visibly flagging as they prepared to leave this life. The main thing of course took place in their souls, when they remained alone with themselves and the Lord, but much was open to view and not hidden from anyone. They were repenting, they were waiting for words of forgiveness and exoneration not only from their confessor, but also from the people before whom they were guilty, to whom they had brought evil and pain. Their own life seemed right to them only in patches, in scattered bits and pieces. The fact that they had, despite everything, managed to steer a true course through parts of it, was due they explained, to their monastic vows, which they had taken voluntarily, consciously, and to the torments which they had had to endure. They spoke of these as ordeals sent from above.

In the final months of his life Nikodim frequently repeated the words of one of his cellmates, Yevstratov, that those who had been on the front line and survived the two world wars, as well as those who had survived the camps without selling out to the authorities – all were marked with the stamp of divine miracle. They should have been dead and buried dozens of times, but the Lord had preserved them tirelessly. It was only this belief, it seems to me, that allowed Nikodim to make any sense of things. Getting carried away, he would claim that there are hundreds, thousands, even millions of such people, that they constitute a genuine Divine Host and are invincible for that reason. As with ancient Israel, the Lord Himself is on their side. The horrific meat grinder that Russia had passed through in the twentieth century – trials by fire and water – was where the cleansing and saving of the human race had begun.

Still, Nikodim's exultation rarely lasted for long, and overall, as he prepared to give up his soul to God, he viewed the world with considerable indifference. Calmly and without regret, he would say that it was a long time since he had been able to discern anything in it except futility and cruelty. Trying to rouse him, I would tell him about friends and acquaintances, but he found all these relationships confusing. In old age, without models or rules, he had lost all confidence; appraising people, he tried to hew close to his own experience in the monastery and the camps, and when this could not help him he became timid and muddled.

Godmother resembled him strongly before she died, yet she retained more trust in Divine Providence. Klasha's burial service for her, still a young, energetic woman, and the tonsure that followed, had made Dusya's path from ordinary life to the veil, to the service of God, direct and short, but though there is strength in simplicity, there is also enormous temptation. She called me to explain that on Bear's Moss the Lord would indicate the place where our burial services were to be sung, and assured me that these ceremonies were salvific for each living person who agreed to them. In this way, such a person enters the possession of God before even leaving this life.

With these services for the dead in mind, Dusya, as a rule, would speak only about us, her close circle, but her instinct would sometimes lead her to erase every boundary with a single stroke and then I would hear things that sounded like outright heresy. In particular she insisted, again and again, that the real Apocalypse will not resemble the one we know from John the Apostle.

Be as Children

In Dusya's telling, no earthquakes, no terrible beasts, no all-consuming flame will precede the end of the world. In the final hour every human soul without exception will be treated in the same way as Dusya herself was in 1926, when Klasha sang for her repose. A solemn service will begin for each of them, in accordance with the full rite. Long, sad, unhurried, so that not a single, even involuntary sin will be forgotten and unabsolved.

These obsequies will happen in churches, in open fields, forests, steppes – wherever the Lord had determined that the person in question should live. The songs and prayers will merge into a vast, truly universal ceremony for the repose of the dead, slow and attentive, filled with tenderness and sympathy towards the people, who after thousands of years of wandering, are returning to their Father's house. A calm, kind ceremony, during which the tribe of Adam will weep and forgive all offences, soften and repent. Consoling and cherishing one another as brothers, all will embrace and kiss.

While the ceremony takes place, the springs and wells from which human beings have drawn evil will run dry: as a snake sheds its old skin, so we will cast off our past life, a terrible life, sinful through and through. Our souls will be cleansed and with them the Earth itself. The infertile, thorny desert will be transformed into a fragrant paradise in which the human race will, as before the Fall, be alone once again with its Maker.

***

I should say that whether in Moscow, when Dusya was still talking me through the expedition to Bear's Moss, or on the train, or when we were already in Anikeyevka, I always knew I would never bring her to Seryozha's island. That would have been madness in every possible way, and I wasn't even considering it. My role, since Dusya had chosen me as her guide, was to become a sort of Ivan Susanin for her, only with kinder intentions.[67] I would lead her round and round the bog until she finally waved the white flag; then if all went well I would bring her back in one piece to Moscow.

I've already mentioned that in the '60s there were plans to drain Bear's Moss and plant it with pine. Massive steel shovels were welded to the rear of caterpillar tractors, and the machines, as if ploughing the land, followed each other around the perimeter of the bog. The result was a series of regular deep trenches, all flanked by two high banks of peat, like parapets. With time, foresters fashioned little bridges for their own use out of the slender, stick-like butts of birch, fir and pine, and laid them over the water-filled ditches. After years of neglect though, the crossings had become rotten and flimsy, and the weight of even a single adult was enough to break them.

In fact, now that the enthusiasm had faded and everyone had gone away, the part of the bog where the land reclamation specialists had once worked resembled not so much a young forest as a well laid-out cemetery. After sprouting, the pine saplings had quickly grown to a height of five or six metres, but the roots, failing to find firm soil, were unable to sustain the trunk any longer, and the tree withered amid the water like a scraggy little girl. Still, there were occasional healthy specimens. They must have had the good fortune to find a spot where the floor of the bog was raised or stony; as for the

---

[67] *On Susanin*, p.23, n.1.

others, a year or two was enough for rain and snow to strip the bark and break off the branches, and the trees, bleached bone-white by the sun, became monuments to themselves.

Of the dozens promised by Dusya, the only people I found at the station at the agreed hour, aside from her, were Irina and Vanya, who had recently got back together. Everyone else had made their excuses the previous day. Both Irina and Vanya looked older and greyer, and you could see that Irina had calmed down and made up her mind to live out the rest of her life as she had begun it – by guarding with Vanya the memory of Sashenka. She had taken no further interest in any of the men she had left; for her we were just a means of helping her daughter. As far as I can tell she never even suspected that Seryozha had killed himself and she certainly never linked his death to the fact that she had once walked out on him.

During our journey to Konyukhovo, whether we were in a railway carriage or waiting three or four hours at a station with our eyes peeled for the local train we needed (few were sticking to the timetable), I was constantly expecting godmother's legs to buckle and for her to start expiring in our arms. I was so sure of this that only after the ten-kilometre forced march to Anikeyevka, as we trudged through the rain-sodden village, did it finally occur to me that the last thing Dusya resembled at this point was a woman at death's door. Irina and Vanya could barely put one foot in front of the other, but she was sprightly, cheerful and very much the indefatigable Dusya of old who had played hide-and-seek with us all and chased us around. She kept this up for almost twenty-four hours, which even now I can explain only as a miracle. In Anikeyevka, we stayed overnight at Akimych's place, and in the cool of first light we took the path that led through the forest to the bog.

To begin with, and before godmother began to suspect anything, I led my brigade confidently along the crest of one of the peat banks, explaining every now and again that there was no shorter way to Seryozha's island. Unlike the mire the baked peat was dry and springy underfoot, but even so, now that we were on Bear's Moss we could barely walk. We were a feeble group: Dusya's high spirits were ebbing – she was over eighty after all, plus she'd been bedbound for several months with a heart complaint; Irina, Vanya and I were also no longer young, and crucially, no longer used to hikes of this kind, so it was no surprise that by the time we reached Anikeyevka we were already tired. And now, after endless hours in an uncomfortable, packed compartment, surrounded by filth and cigarette smoke, and only a short night at Akimych's, we'd got up at dawn to walk over this damned bog.

The forest was fine – nothing to complain about there – but by eleven o'clock the sun was right over our heads, with not a hint of shade anywhere, and as we walked along a ditch we were literally melting. The temperature had been touching thirty by lunchtime for several days already, but now it seemed even hotter. Steam was coming off the bog in waves, and with all the vegetation rotting in the heated water and the scent of the stupefying, soporific Labrador tea – there seemed to be fields of it all around us – our stomachs were churning and our heads aching. The lack of air was especially hard to deal with: if you got knocked off your stride climbing over a fallen tree or clambering up a peat bank, you had to stop to allow your heart to settle. You'd just sit on the ground for several minutes, wheezing and whistling like an asthmatic.

Seryozha's island. I would explain that there was no better route, that even the odd little detour would pay off handsomely in the end. After all, it was one thing to cross a quagmire that could suck you in at any moment and quite another to walk along a dry, well-trodden path. But at a certain point I could no longer convince her. After hearing me out, Dusya insisted that from now on we make straight for the depths of the bog. It was clear though that neither Dusya nor I would get our way, and the arc we'd been following would be replaced by a kind of L-shape, a knight's move. For six or seven hundred metres we would walk along a peat bank as before, but on finding a bridge we'd cross to the other side, and from there we would advance to the next ditch over genuine bogland, watching out for each other all the way.

This outcome suited me too – we were still unlikely to get very far from the forest. Especially since the crossings were all rotten and couldn't support an adult's weight. Vanya, who was thickset, had the hardest time of it. The wood snapped beneath him with barely a sound or just gave way, after which there would be a lot of dismal fussing as we tried to pull the poor man out of the water and put him to rights. All such episodes ended the same way – with me taking out my hiking axe, chopping up two or three dry young pines and laying down a new crossing.

Although my plan seemed to be working, by the evening I didn't know what to think. Irina and Vanya were in an even worse state than before, only godmother still looked eager, but she had grown weaker too. About an hour before sunset, a hundred or so metres away from the path on our side of the ditch, Dusya noticed a pine that was twice as big as its companions. She perked up and wanted me to climb it to check whether Seryozha's island could, at long last, be seen.

All around me, as if in a desert, I see one and the same thing, and deep down I don't really care whether I'm walking or climbing... conveniently enough, the pine tree she's chosen has branches all the way up, like steps. Once I'm on the lowest, godmother holds something out to me – to help me, I suppose. It's a pair of theatre binoculars, the same ones her mother-in-law used during the Civil War to tell fortunes with porridge. I'd heard more than once about Igrenyeva's binoculars – the family heirloom – but the thought that Dusya could have taken them with her to Bear's Moss had, I must admit, never occurred to me. With the talisman in my pocket and Dusya urging me on – 'Higher, higher!' – I climb without complaint to the very top.

The tree sways and shakes beneath me, it just can't settle in this soft runny earth. But then I seem to find my balance. I hold my breath and wait a minute or two, then, keeping dead still, I slowly raise the binoculars to my swollen, pus-filled eyes. For all my squinting though, I can only see watery streaks. Godmother is down below, trying to explain something to me, but she's lost her voice and it's hard to make anything out. Then Irina gets involved, followed by Vanya, and the two of them keep waving their arms like windmills until I finally realise that it's not my eyes that are the problem – the binoculars aren't in focus. Sure enough, once I turn the ring in the middle, the picture becomes sharper, but even now I can hardly claim to have spotted anything significant.

The day is fading and it's as if the sun-warmed bog has been swathed in cotton wool; patches of clear water are few and far between, and the moss is covered by dense whitish vapours that become thinner as they rise, turning into a light haze. The sun has still not set, everything's quiet. If occasional gusts of wind do disturb this magnificence, then not for long. They are just too weak to disperse the shroud, which gathers and puckers as it catches in swirls on bushes and pine branches, hanging on them like crumpled laundry and calling to mind Dusya's stories about her mother-in-law – those plays of hers in Pskov. That's all the binoculars are good for, I think to myself sadly: they've been specially trained to show smoke and mists.

I'm trying not to move of course, so as not to break the tree, but still, I'm not just swivelling my head left and right: to please Dusya, I try to cover every inch of the horizon. No great discoveries though; everywhere it's the same viscous, uneven layer of vapours. But my diligence is rewarded. I've almost finished my survey and I'm running my eyes cursorily over the last section for the second time when in the north-west, where the sun should be setting, straight ahead of us on our current trajectory, I see something resembling a human chain.

A long, long procession of people in absurd baggy garments stretches from the forest to the depths of the bog, perhaps even, as godmother hopes, to Seryozha's island. I can't see that far of course, but even though I had been quite certain that there was only mire ahead of us, I'm not surprised; in fact I'm glad Dusya was right all along. She'd told me hundreds of times in Moscow that it wouldn't be just us walking to the lake, there would be many, many others, but I hadn't wanted to follow her, I'd been a doubting Thomas.

Fortunately, I still possess some remnant of common

sense. Ignoring what Dusya, Irina and Vanya are yelling at me from the ground, as they crane their heads back, I decide to check everything one more time. Especially as the day is on its way out and the air is becoming more transparent. I readjust the focus and study this ungainly pageant centimetre by centimetre. And once more I no longer feel sure of anything. As before, I can't understand what it is I'm looking at – human beings or tall healthy pines. Perhaps there's a ridge of sand beneath the water and the trees have struck root there. The theatre binoculars weren't made for this, and now I think that what I took to be clothes is actually the fog catching on branches: the steam seems to be breathing, with a rise and fall, and when the wind gets up, the pines, swaying with tiredness just like us, trudge slowly away.

Deceiving godmother would be shameful, but it seems that the truth will deceive her even more. Caught in two minds, I cautiously explain to her, from my perch in the tree, that in a few hours' time, if nothing else happens, we will walk into something closely resembling a human chain. Only the people in it haven't reached the bog from the Anikeyevka side, but ten kilometres further north, through a different section of forest – I don't know its name. But then I backpedal, adding that I can't see much through the fog and the dusk, and I can't guarantee that ahead of us are the people we're looking for, not a strip of healthy forest. In any case, I tell her, we don't stand to lose anything – wherever trees have taken root, there can be no mire or bog, so the path is quite safe.

None of this bothers Dusya. She is sure, from my very first words, that there are people there, hundreds, maybe thousands of people, the ones she told us about back in Moscow. And they are also walking to Seryozha's island. It's just that they set off earlier and got ahead of us. We'll catch up with them soon, says godmother, and then, fearing nothing, we'll walk with everyone else. I've made my own calculations. I can see a row of pines leading into a forest, so sooner or later, God willing, we'll get out of this bog. Meanwhile it's getting dark. It's August already, which means proper nights. In the dusk we keep losing the trail, stumbling, falling to the ground or sinking into bog holes, and in the end even Dusya realises that we've walked as far as we can. We're in luck: right ahead of us is a high, bare patch of dry ground – a tractor must have got caught on a snag and turned up an entire mound of peat. There could be no better place to spend the night, and although we haven't caught up with the column, godmother accepts the situation and allows us to pitch camp.

We have food with us, but by this point in the day we're so worn out that we've forgotten all about it. As soon as we get the okay, we collapse on the spot. My last thought is to thank Providence – today at least seems to be over. But I soon realise that I've been too hasty. I've told myself so many times that godmother's an old woman, no longer capable of anything much, yet she keeps making a fool of me. The same thing now. There's still no sign of light when I'm suddenly shaken out of my broken, nightmare-filled sleep by Vanya. Fending him off as best I can, I eventually open my eyes. I can barely think straight, as if the Labrador tea and everything else have left me with a dreadful hangover. The sky is overcast, there's no moon, but it's not pitch dark either; all around there's a soft, barely discernible light, as if from a shaded night-lamp. I ask Vanya why he's not sleeping and what it is that he wants. He's also in a bad way and struggles to get his words out. Nevertheless, I understand that Dusya and Irina have disappeared. They can't have got far of course, but that's no consolation. In a bog, a few metres are enough to perish without trace.

I get up and try to work out which way they could have gone. Nothing much occurs to me. Vague shadows flicker here and there, and occasionally I seem to hear godmother's voice, only I'm hearing it from different sides. In any case, Vanya and I can't agree where to look for her, and we almost come to blows. It's obvious we can't carry on like this. Whether he's right or wrong, I need to agree with Vanya and go wherever he wants. Luckily my meekness pays off – after a hundred metres we walk straight into Dusya and Irina. I was already picturing two drowned bodies, feared I wouldn't see either of them alive again, and now the one thing that matters to me is getting both of them home.

For now though, Irina and Dusya aren't interested in us or in Moscow. Will-o'-the-wisps are flickering around us, as in a game of hide-and-seek. There's a sea of them, and ever-patient Dusya carefully gathers all the ones she finds in her palm. She looks for them on the ground as if they were cranberries or wild strawberries, picks them off the bushes like raspberries, and doesn't seem to notice that her palm is still empty. Still gathering, she explains to Irina that the will-o'-the-wisps are godly souls, which like candles, have been lit by the flame of Grace. All around us – she shows Irina – are the souls of the sinless and those killed through no fault of their own: they have come to meet us, to lead us to Seryozha's island.

She tells Irina that they have nothing to fear now, they can walk for as long as they wish over the unsteady, shaky earth with which Dima – that's me – tried to scare them off in Moscow and on the train. Dima, godmother repeats loudly, wasn't trying to trick anybody: to walk over the weak, fickle soil beneath our feet and not die really is just as hard as to live one's life from beginning to end without allowing sin to enter. She also tells Irina that one will-o'-the-wisp is the soul of her daughter and that Sashenka feels joyful and merry to have her mother with her once more. And the main reason she's joyful is that salvation is so very close, it's right there.

Irina must have heard about Sashenka already because I can see her rushing from one firefly to another and every time, just like at the cemetery, she calls her daughter in a wild, ugly voice. But the will-o'-the-wisp flashes, then disappears, and Irina is left with nothing. At least Dusya is there to soothe her, to explain that the wisps are just children – they're happy, that's why they're playing. Never letting themselves get caught, always running around like there's no tomorrow.

This all seems like madness to me. Godmother and Irina are tearing around the bog as if they have lost their minds, and maybe the Lord is preserving them for now, but how long will His patience last? I walk over to Vanya and tell him we have to stop them. We can't just stand idly by and wait to see whether the quagmire sucks Irina in. He agrees, but neither of us has any idea what to do about it. One thing's clear: we'll never make godmother see sense so, without saying anything to each other, we go over to Irina.

Vanya takes his wife by the hand while I explain to her, as gently as I know how, that these aren't the souls of children she and Dusya are seeing, they're just flashes in the bog. Will-o'-the-wisps are a bit like ordinary electric light. In Siberia, in winter, whenever they have to walk home in the dark, shamans use willow twigs to strike exactly the same kind of sparks out of snow. But I'm not sure Irina's even listening. Worse, Vanya is no longer helping. I didn't even notice when it was that he joined Irina. Now they're working as a pair – Irina is trying to catch will-o'-the-wisps again, and to make it easier for her, Vanya is chasing them in her direction.

Even so, none of my fears come true that night. Right up until dawn, Providence watches over all three of them. The sun has not yet risen over the eastern edge of Bear's Moss, but the last will-o'-the-wisps have melted away. Dusya and Irina seem to have been waiting for just this moment: they instantly slump to the ground and fall asleep on the moss.

I realise that unless I give them a few hours' rest, Dusya for one won't manage to get back up. Wordlessly Vanya and I divide up the tasks – he sits next to his wife while I'm with godmother, both of us waving sticks to keep the horseflies away from the sleepers. Irina sleeps calmly and quietly, and sometimes a smile flickers over her face, as if Sashenka really were with her once more. Dusya is worse off. She's agitated, her arms and neck keep twitching, she gasps for air in her sleep and makes hoarse sounds, as if trying to say something.

From this point on, nothing went well. Irina woke up some time around midday, the worse for wear though still lively, while godmother, for all our attempts to rouse her, just wouldn't come round. Later, back in Moscow, the doctor treating her said that she must have had a stroke during her sleep, in which case there was little we could have done other than get out of Bear's Moss as quickly as possible, for both our sake and hers. Dusya could barely stand or speak, and with one thing and another it took us five days to reach Moscow.

The bog alone accounted for two of them. Waist-deep in water, Vanya and I lifted Dusya over ditches, then took turns carrying her on our backs all the way to the clearing. From there I went ahead on my own to Anikeyevka, reached the village by nightfall, and went back the next morning with Akimych and Dolya to fetch them. That was day three.

In Anikeyevka, Vanya and I decided that travelling by train, with all the endless waiting at stations, would be the death of godmother. I had to leave them again, although at least now they were in a village, with food and a roof over their heads, and I set off for Rzhev. There, in the town hospital, a hundred and fifty roubles were enough to persuade a doctor to fetch Dusya from Anikeyevka in an ambulance, then drive her and me straight to Moscow. And that pretty much is the whole story of our trip to Bear's Moss. As I see clearly now, if it differs from the trip I made with Akimych to bury Seryozha, then its not by much.

The return to Moscow was the beginning of the final and shortest bit of Dusya's life. It lasted less than three months. She was treated by Aleksei Ivanovich Karagodov, a famous neurologist who also happened to be the son of her friend from the gymnasium. He'd never been part of our circle, but he agreed to help just as soon as he was asked and never refused to come out to see her when we needed him. While Vanya and I were still dragging godmother over the bog, I'd asked the Lord to give both her and us the strength to reach Moscow. I wanted her to die not like Seryozha, but in her own bed, so that before she left us a priest could administer the last sacraments, even in her current state, and see her to her final rest in accordance with the rites.

Every now and again Karagodov would say, when visiting Dusya, that remissions could still occur in such cases. A stroke's a stroke, and it leaves plenty of destruction in its wake, but you should wait a month or two before giving up. Dusya needed rest – the strain and stress she'd been through were extreme for someone her age, not to mention all the toxins that were still in her bloodstream from the bites. Most importantly, her brain had to be given the chance to heal the damage. All this would take at least four weeks – only then would it be clear if there was any hope.

The same group that went to Bear's Moss with Dusya – Irina, Vanya and I – now took turns by godmother's bedside. But although we all requested prayer services for her recovery and lit candles, no one believed they would ever have a conversation with her again. But Karagodov was proven right. Exactly as he had predicted, godmother ate nothing at first, sleeping day and night, but then her appetite began to return. Her skin, bloated with fluid from her blood, livid in colour, grew paler as the swelling subsided. Her face recovered first, her legs a little later. It was as if, in the course of a week, godmother herself had shrunk and begun to look almost like the Dusya of old.

The improvements though were only to her body; the soul as we know is a different matter. I wasn't the only one thinking along these lines, so it's no surprise that when after the Apple Feast,[68] amid delirious ravings, mutterings and cries,

---

[68] The Apple Feast of our Saviour is the folk name for the Feast of the Transfiguration (August 19th); the day has pre-Christian origins in East Slavic cultures, coinciding with the beginning of autumn and the harvesting of fruit.

she suddenly began to recognise us and consciously utter a few meaningful words, we took this to be a genuine miracle. Then over the course of a week we watched the delirium evaporate completely and, rejoicing like children, we refused to believe that she might succumb to it ever again.

We were being too hopeful: the reprieve did not last long – less than a month – and came at a considerable cost. For as long as she remained conscious, Dusya made every effort not to drop her guard, as if she were expecting a stab in the back at any moment. She knew she wasn't well, but tried not to talk about her illness. Nor did godmother mention Bear's Moss. As a result, I still don't know whether she even remembered the four of us struggling over the mire to catch up with the column walking towards Seryozha's island, or gathering will-o'-the-wisps with Irina.

Karagodov told us day in, day out, that the main thing was not to upset Dusya, and we were as scared of bringing up the recent trip as she was. We often discussed how we would change the topic if Dusya started asking what happened and when, what we'd say if she insisted, and what we'd be sure not to mention.

Godmother was a meek patient, affectionate and thankful for the smallest kindness, but even so I could see how oppressed she felt by her lack of independence and the constant presence of strangers in her home; there was nothing she wanted more than to be left alone. Alas, Dusya was in no condition to be left alone. All we could do was spend most of our time on duty sitting in the kitchen. Three weeks later, when a second stroke was followed by a deterioration – Dusya started getting confused again, she would call me Irina, and Irina Vanya, and then usually towards evening when she was tired, she would start babbling away again incomprehensibly – I suddenly sensed that it was actually easier for her like this. That she was pleased that she no longer needed to police her every word, didn't have to watch herself, fear herself.

I now understand that this retreat into childhood, this manoeuvre, was essential: she knew there was no other way of skirting the abyss, of saving herself, and besides, this was the only means of gathering strength for the final push. I can't speak for others, but this all seemed fair to me: she was going, leaving our world, a world whose consciousness she no longer needed. We were under no illusions; we understood that the end was near, that there was no point hoping for a fresh miracle. Not that Karagodov was holding out any such hope. Inevitability is its own consolation, and I remember how as her speech and movements become ever more incoherent and chaotic, I observed this with a sense of acceptance.

The task of deciding what she was bidding farewell to and why, and what she was planning to take with her, took Dusya eleven days. Freed of so much ballast, she lived another whole week. We'd stopped doing shifts, and barely ever stepping out of the flat, sat rooted to her bedside. We knew we couldn't leave.

Although godmother still did not recognise us or react to our words, it was clear that she wasn't delirious, and certainly not senile. Karagodov briefly mentioned autism, but here too this was hardly a typical case. The point, it seems to me, is that Dusya had somehow managed to tie up the last three months of her life like a sack, the better to trap her illness, and now that it was no longer anyone's beginning or end, it was no longer needed.

Having dealt with her sickness and laid it to rest, Dusya led us once more to Bear's Moss. As she described us walking into the depths of the mire towards Seryozha's island, godmother didn't turn to anyone in particular but we understood that she was not the only one who had to go back there: the middle of the bog was where Irina's, Vanya's and my own salvation would also begin. Now that Dusya had overcome and conquered her infirmity, she spoke with a clear, at times even solemn voice.

***

Walking the path by the ditch that we had walked before, crossing the same bridges, she explains to us that the lake we are trying to find our way to and which between ourselves we call Seryozha's lake is in fact Lake Svetloyar. And Seryozha's island is nothing other than the hidden City of God, the famed Kitezh. Alluding I expect, to me and to Alyosha, godmother adds that only a few have been granted the opportunity to see the city with their own eyes – not for nothing was it built amid impassable, untrodden bogs – but even those who have happened to wander into the depths of Bear's Moss have mistaken the bell towers and fortress turrets for a forest, for age-old firs. The centuries came and went, until human woe overwhelmed the Holy City; it plunged underwater like the Earth during the flood, and sank to the bottom of the lake.

Even then the Lord did not abandon the righteous: the bells of Kitezh have not ceased their tolling. As before, their chimes continue to summon and gather from every corner of the world those, who through no fault of their own, have been murdered, killed, tortured to death. Rising from their trenches and mass graves, they walk and walk, seeking their peace in Kitezh, their refuge within its salvific walls from evil and sin.

It follows from Dusya's words that the town sank into the waters of Svetloyar only recently, but whether Seryozha's death had anything to do with this is unclear. The people walking, just like us, towards Svetloyar are still a long way off, at best we'll need half the day to catch up with them, so the conversation is, as it were, a preliminary one. We've spent the night on the peat mound, not the worst bed in the world, and we've slept our fill, so the walking is easier now than yesterday. Seems we've got used to having mire beneath our feet, and the temperature's dropped a little, too. There's also less of the vermin that were eating us alive only yesterday. Of course, if you forget to keep waving the insects away, then you'll certainly get bitten, but this is no Egyptian plague.

The sun is at its peak when both I and the others clearly discern a long human column winding between the stunted little pines towards Kitezh. The air is pure, transparent, and there's no need for either a tall tree or a pair of binoculars to understand that what we have before us is not bog vapours resembling baggy, formless garments, but ordinary flesh-and-blood human beings wending their way towards Svetloyar. Even from here you can see that the column is not moving in a straight line but in smooth curves, like a river. Those heading straight for the lake immediately turn after crossing a ditch: now they're looking for the next bridge.

Later, when we are close to one such bridge, godmother won't forget to show us that the crossings are made of exactly the same rotten pine trunks, but whereas before they'd snapped under Vanya's weight, and even under her own, here each bridge is crossed without fear by thousands upon thousands of people. The Lord has reinforced the flimsy wood, and it's become firmer than rock.

From the side, the column resembles a vast Procession of the Cross: some people pray loudly, others chant psalms in chorus. Against all expectation, we don't go over to them, nor do we join the rear of the column, as we had planned to; instead, we stride off at a fast clip straight for the Holy Lake. Sometimes we are almost running, which makes it hard for Dusya to speak. Nevertheless, we've already been told that ahead of us are people we have known or could have known in our lifetimes. Having chanced to live at the same time, we would be saved together, too. Those who lived before us have already gone ahead and are already safe from harm within the walls of the Sacred City. Those who have come after us are still in the forest.

Meanwhile there appears on the horizon the edge of Lake Svetloyar, in whose waters all those called by the Lord are to be cleansed of sin and baptised anew. We walk along an endless line of maimed, ragged soldiers of the First World War. Trying with their last ounce of strength to keep their shape, they march past us company by company. Many are on crutches, and the kitbags over their shoulders are filled with blown-off, amputated limbs.

Dusya is frightened: she was looking for somebody, but now she's scared that she's late, she's missed him. Still hoping, she stands on tiptoes, even makes a few little jumps, and suddenly sees from behind, the tall ungainly figure of an armless officer. A little boy is tagging along at his feet. Her face is transformed. Yelling and shoving her way through the line, she rushes towards them. Only now do we understand that it's her husband, Captain Igrenyev, and their younger son. Then, with tears and lamentations, she hugs and kisses them for a long long time, while people curve around them like a river around an island.

When Igrenyev catches up with his comrades and carries on towards Svetloyar, godmother comes back to us. She's found the man she was so scared of missing and now we walk back without haste, against the flow of the column. Along the way, she, Irina, Vanya and I meet many people we know. Dusya exchanges greetings with them, or if they are far away, she bows. We do the same. Usually she only gives us their names, but there are some she tells us about in much more detail. While godmother was still pushing her way through the line of soldiers to run to her husband, I noticed that some three hundred metres ahead of him the two Processions of the Cross that once collided in Chukhloma were crossing a bridge over a ditch. With candles, icons and banners, they were walking side by side together, and as they approached the Holy Lake I doubt that any of them stopped to ask themselves whether they were walking with or against the course of the sun through the sky.

Troops keep filing past us and there seems no end to the columns of crippled men. But now the last unfortunate has walked past, and almost immediately Dusya spots her beloved mother-in-law, old Princess Igrenyeva. More tears and embraces; then at godmother's prompting, I return the theatre binoculars to the princess and Igrenyeva claps her hands with joy.

More soldiers. We draw up alongside those who died in

the Civil War. Entire hecatombs of victims. Whites, Reds, Greens. Only some died in battle. The rest were killed when they trusted words of mercy and forgiveness, they were chopped up, drowned, had bullets planted in the back of their heads. The number of those who never bore arms at all – old men, women, children – is beyond all reckoning. They died of typhus, cholera, Spanish flu, starvation. They weren't even buried – they were thrown into ditches like carrion.

Next, a couple of kilometres later, godmother is approached from the column by a decrepit monk leaning on a stick. Sinking to her knees, she kisses the side of his faded, tattered cassock. He tenderly strokes her hair and asks her to stand. The old man is visibly moved. Slowly, solicitously, he makes the sign of the cross over Dusya and blesses her, at which point Irina tells us that this must be Dusya's beloved confessor who died in prison, Bishop Amvrosy.

After Amvrosy, as neverendingly as the soldiers from the First World War and the Civil War, come the orphans and the untended. A commanding officer walks out in front bearing a sign with the name of a children's home, then come the children themselves, commune by commune, in the same order in which they once set out to liberate Jerusalem. Realising that we are unable to tell most of them apart, Dusya fills us in whenever she has the chance. Fifteen years later, I will encounter the names of some of the children in the local newspapers of Black Sea towns.

I see Ivan Kostandinov who was buried not far from Novorossiisk; I recognise the blind artist who sculpted Lenin's head. The communards placed the head in the same spot where Kostandinov died, on a rock by the grave of their comrade. I remember the entire Taganrog brigade that tried to cross the Black Sea along a path of moonlight. One meeting is especially moving. Godmother is surrounded by the children of the commune named after the *babushka* of the Russian Revolution, Yekaterina Konstantinovna Breshko-Breshkovskaya, in which Dusya worked for almost a year on the recommendation of Father Nikodim. The youngest come snuggling up to her, they stroke her, tell her that never again did they have such a good and kind German teacher, and just to please her they vie with each other to shout 'Guten Morgen!' the loudest, even though it's already evening. Then they are gradually pushed aside by older children: standing in a semi-circle and singing in unison, they chant the counting rhymes and ditties which Dusya didn't manage to record in Khabarovsk. I notice that once more godmother's eyes are wet.

The next encounter will relieve her soul of a burden almost as great as the untimely death of her husband at the Caucasian Front. Yet another vast Procession of the Cross, an avalanche of different classes, ranks and ages. As if Russia herself is bearing down on you with all her mass, while out in front, like a shepherd, walks a man as similar to the living Seryozha as one drop of water to another. This is Pasha, no doubt about it, and his journey to Siberia in 1921 must have succeeded after all. The Lord had come to his aid – the people had risen. So both she and her mother had been right to talk him out of his vows back then in Moscow, right to repeat over and over again that he hadn't yet done what he was meant to do in the world. Pasha is also very glad to see his sister. He cranes his neck towards her and sends kisses.

Pasha's procession is followed by an almost kilometre-long column of Samoyeds. Family by family, many of them with reindeer, come Enets, Selkups, Dolgans, Evens. There are several old men out in front, some evidently of very different stock. I'm almost certain I can see Peregudov, but godmother keeps silent, and I don't feel comfortable asking. Actually, there aren't so many northerners, it's just that they aren't tightly packed and there are quite a few gaps between them. Then just before a bridge over a ditch, where everybody, like it or not, has to slow down, the reindeer nibble some lichen on the sly with their soft lips. Unfortunately there isn't much lichen on Bear's Moss.

In the '20s, life separated and scattered the Enets in all directions. But now they are together again. Those who never left, who carried on herding as they always had done in the Lena delta – Seryozha and I knew many of them well – mix with those who guarded Lenin, and then as they tried to force their way to the Holy Land, to the lush pastures around Lake Hula in the upper reaches of the Jordan, fell in battle with the Polacks and died on the banks of a quite different river, the Pripet. I think I can also see the Enets whom the captain of an American schooner agreed to take to the other end of the Earth, to the French Kerguelen Islands near Antarctica. The horns of one of the reindeer at any rate are wound with a ribbon in the colours of the French flag.

Next come two different columns, and in both the main role belongs to Lenin. In contrast to the weakly organised, undisciplined peoples of the North, the combined brigade of the Gorki children's home and the Glukhov textile mill that marches directly behind the Enets exhibits an excellent military bearing. True, the thin rickety hands of the children drown in the mighty palms of the workers, but as they sing the Internationale all their voices merge. The commissar in this brigade is Ilyich himself, newly healthy, strong and energetic, assisted by the members of the soviet that were chosen by the collective. There are six of them. From the Bolshevik Party: Nadezhda Krupskaya, Lev Trotsky and Felix Dzerzhinsky. From the workers: Glasha, a cook, and Ivan Zubov, a metal caster; from the communards: Lenin's nephew, Kolya Yelizarov.

The residents of the children's home are followed by a very different procession. Out in front, almost right on the heels of the Gorki children, strides Katya Maslennikova, wailing wildly. The Latvian Riflemen proceed at a stately pace to the accompaniment of her remarkable commemorative lament, bowing their heads and bearing on their shoulders a little coffin covered in black crape.

Next – fresh kilometres of unfortunates: women and children, men old and young, soldiers, *zeks*, ordinary peasants. Life has ground them all up and mixed them together, and it's hard to pick anyone out. Ragged, hungry, covered in wounds, they are all terribly sick, all exhausted to the bone. For these wasting bodies, every step is a struggle, and I understand that without God's help they will never cross the bog. But for now they keep filing past, and we watch these Babylonian rivers of grief and suffering, and even though there are few people we know, or rather recognise, we stand there and howl.

When Irina caught sight of her daughter, she did not shout, did not rush towards Sashenka, did not cry, but became as still as a pillar of salt. The girl came over to her instead, and they literally grabbed each other. Their fingers became white from the strain, and nothing could have prised mother and daughter apart. They stood like that for a long time, neither seeing nor hearing anyone, then Vanya walked over to them and embraced them both. Dusya did not want to disturb the Zvyagintsevs, so she and I sat on a hummock fifteen metres away and talked. Then, finally believing her own happiness, Irina turned her head and looked at us imploringly, and although the tail of the column was still a good kilometre away, godmother gave in. Now it was only the two of us walking towards the forest.

2001-2007

BE AS CHILDREN

Even worse than the heat were the blood-sucking insects – the midges, mosquitoes and especially horseflies. Before leaving the forest, we put on hooded tarpaulin jackets to give ourselves at least some protection, but there was no stopping the disgusting things. Covered in thick, sticky sweat from head to toe, we were a tempting prize, and the horseflies ran riot. As soon as your jacket clung to any part of your body for even a second, a couple of them would be right there, biting through the thick material to get at your blood, to say nothing of our bare faces. With our swollen, livid skin and bog muck up to our ears, we resembled a bunch of homeless drunks feebly traipsing God knows where or why.

Each of us had our own personal swarm. Hundreds upon hundreds of the beasts, crazed by the sun and the blood, swirled around with such malice and fury that the air rang with a continuous mournful whine. There was no point even trying to pick out an individual specimen, but sometimes, if I looked over my shoulder, I could see that the swarms were forming beautiful dazzling spheres in which the four of us – Dusya, Irina, and usually bringing up the rear, Vanya – were tauntingly framed in all our ugliness. Exhausted beyond every conceivable limit, I looked at these silver globes, these cocoons, and thought despairingly that we would never be rid of them.

By midday godmother began fretting about the fact that we were still walking along the edge of the forest, just as we had been all day. Evidently she had begun to suspect that she was being misled and she kept trying to tease out the truth. She would ask cautiously whether I was quite sure that we hadn't taken a wrong turning, that we were still headed towards

Afterword

by Caryl Emerson

The leitmotif of *Be as Children* is the human procession. Pilgrimage, forced march, trek of exiles, crusade: these are journeys undertaken if possible on foot, often with flawed maps but always with a strong moral dimension. In Russian folk belief and in Orthodox Christian utopias, space is not abstractly metaphysical, but realistic. The physical matter that fills our life now will be perfected, not abolished, in the world beyond. Heaven is a place one can *walk* to. The trial of moving one's mortal body through Russian space, across Mother Damp Earth and against all odds, is a venerated cultural constant – and the further one wanders, the holier one becomes. We recall that the murderer turned preacher Yevlampy Peregudov feels joyous and light, purified of his sins, only while wandering. Even our souls occupy space: they retain feet to climb with and a craving for physical embrace. Godmother Dusya plays a desperate game of hide-and-seek with her own errant soul. Russian folklorists have called this picture of the cosmos, which clings so lovingly to embodiment, 'mystical materialism'.[1] Atheist Marxist materialism tapped into it eagerly. Sharov, who trained as a historian of pre-modern Russia before he began writing novels that culminate in the Soviet era, had a perfect feel for these continuities of medieval geography.

Those who set out on processions in this novel are wounded. Some are homeless war orphans (the 'untended', of whom there were several million in Russia by 1922); others are 'special children' born deaf or blind; all have suffered irreversible shock and loss. To reach the end of the journey is to be healed. But the goal is often only a glimmer embedded in legend, sacred writ, the lessons of an eccentric schoolteacher or holy fool. It is very far off. As usual, Sharov works with a vast pan-Eurasian expanse. Those who know his second novel, *The Rehearsals* (completed in 1988) will not be surprised at the presence of Siberia, but in this novel, his seventh (2007), the wilderness extends to peat bogs north of Moscow, the Caucasus, and the sub-Arctic tundra. This immense space is criss-crossed by so many separately narrated life-stories – some historical, others quasi-historical, fictive, or utterly fantastic – that they scarcely seem capable of being coordinated. The absence of chapter divisions (little author-crafted 'rooms' where the reader can pause and take stock) further increases our sense that these stories, told by wounded narrators, have

---

[1] Andrei Sinyavsky, *Ivan the Fool. Russian Folk Belief.* Trans. Joanne Turnbull with Nikolai Formozov. Moscow: Glas, 2007, p. 136.

Afterword

no boundaries or fixed direction. But when the reader sees at last where the procession is headed, as we do with Dusya's final vision, the parts begin to come together. Looking back, we see that the abstract template for procession governing all the smaller trajectories has been a choice between the Marxist-Leninist March of History, and 'God's Path'. That second option applies to various worldviews in this novel, the most tenacious of which is the belief of Sharov's Lenin that a path of sacrificial atonement is now required of Russia, a nation otherwise beyond redemption. Neither route is easy, logical, self-evident, or just. Sharov called his novels 'parables' and expected his reader to put in serious interpretive work. To keep us from losing heart, he adds tantalising political particulars, musical subtexts, the exotic ethnography of Russia's Far North, and hilariously comic moments, deadpan as well as fiercely satirical. Lenin devises a secret syllabic language out of a Rabelaisian list of native Russian soups. An Enets brigade mounts machine guns on the antlers of its reindeer and routs the Polish army. Competing with this antic comedy, and often back-to-back with it, are scenes of unexpected lyric tenderness, including one of the most haunting processions in the novel: an aged female body, Krupskaya's, becomes an entire country as Lenin's fingers move wearily, inconclusively over it. The novel is a rebus, and this Afterward provides some clues.

Consider the novel's operatic frame. The first-person narrator Dmitry begins his story in 1970, but Sharov prefaces it with an evocation of the Great War (1914-1918) through the prism of three Russian operas. They become the novel's mythopoetic substrate. Human agency in them is dependent upon bodies of water edged by dense forest: lakes, bogs, swamps, rivers. Rimsky-Korsakov's *Sadko* (1898), a folk epic, tells of a gusli player from Novgorod, who after years of wandering, weds a sea-princess. Saint Nicholas descends to put an end to this pagan underwater realm – but since the marriage is not consummated, the bride can become a river connecting Novgorod to the sea. The other two operas draw on real military invasions during desperate periods in Russian history. Both plots turn on treachery: one to save the nation, the other to betray it. By Sharov's time the first opera, Glinka's *A Life for the Tsar* (1836), had long been patriotic cliché. Its peasant hero Ivan Susanin, tortured to death in the winter of 1613 by the invading Polish troops he had led astray, saves the life of the teenaged Tsar-elect-in-hiding, Mikhail Romanov. In Act IV Susanin, about to be commandeered as a guide, confides to his adopted son Vanya: 'I'll lead them into the swamp, the wilderness, the quagmire, the bog!' During this original *Smuta* or 'Time of Trouble' that separates Russia's two dynasties, northern wetlands under ice and snow are already a national asset. (Sharov's Dmitry humours Dusya on her final expedition to Bear's Moss by agreeing to become 'a sort of Ivan Susanin' to her.) Glinka's opera became the House of Romanov's most famous musical ornament. Yet its message of voluntary martyrdom for the state was so irresistible to the subsequent regime that it could not be abandoned: the monarchist libretto was rewritten in 1939 to better accord with Bolshevik ideology.

Far less politically correct is Rimsky-Korsakov's 1905 opera *The Tale of the Invisible City of Kitezh and the Maiden*

Afterword

Fevroniya.[2] In the year 1238, a great city sinks under a lake to protect it from the invading Mongol armies of Batu Khan. The invasion was real, as was the disappearance – or obliteration – of the city, called Greater Kitezh; the miraculous part of *The Tale* concerns the salvific resources of the lake that received the city, Lake Svetloyar, a crystal clear, almost perfectly oval body of water in the Nizhny Novgorod region of central Russia. Russian schismatics believed that their sunken Kitezh was modelled literally on a miraculous New Jerusalem, and therefore 'nothing unclean shall enter it'.[3] Legend has it that the city would remain under water until the end of the world and the Second Coming. A cult developed around the site, inspiring *fin-de-siècle* poets, artists, and religious thinkers, fascinated by pre-Petrine folk culture and a possible Russian Apocalypse, to make pilgrimages and conduct litanies on the lake's shore.

This same illusive Kitezh, Russia's final refuge, material-

---

[2] For fascinating socio-cultural background on this deeply Christian and pantheistic *Kitezh* opera (including the fact that personally, Rimsky-Korsakov was a non-religious skeptic), see Simon Morrison, *Russian Opera and the Symbolist Movement*, University of California Press, 2019, ch. 2, 'Syncretism', pp. 79-130. Sharov would have appreciated the tension between maker and theme.

[3] Ksana Blank notes that Russian spiritual culture knew two competing sacred spaces, the first official, sanctioned by the state, and constructed solidly of stone (the New Jerusalem monastic complex outside Moscow); the second unofficial and aesthetic, symbolised by Kitezh, 'a dream-like vision of a mystical, intangible, and purely Russian version of the heavenly Jerusalem', as fluid and ephemeral as water. Sharov's *The Rehearsals* opens on the official sacred space; *Be as Children,* on the unofficial. See Blank's article, in Russian and abridged in English, in *Novye Ierusalimy. Ierotopiya i ikonografiya sakral'nykh prostranstv* [New Jerusalems. The hierotopies and iconography of Sacred Spaces]. Indrik, Moscow, 2009, pp. 1-13 (12).

ises at the end of Sharov's novel. But now the column of war casualties, victims, and untimely dead streaming toward the bog contains all the slaughter of the twentieth century, not only the carnage of the thirteenth. Dusya's son Seryozha, icon-painter and drowned martyr, has somehow enabled this crusade. There Irina will find at last her beloved four-year-old daughter Sashenka and fuse with her again. There, finally, forgiveness will repair the tragedy of Chukhloma, in which Orthodox and Old-Believer processions collided and crushed each other on Christmas Day. That fictional event in the novel is Sharov's allegory for the abiding trauma of the seventeenth-century Schism. Lenin's dreamt-of crusade of the untended never makes it to Jerusalem. But the radiant procession to Seryozha's island has reason to hope that it will find a New Jerusalem beneath its own sacred lake – for the catch in the Kitezh legend is that those submerged domes and tolling bells can be seen and heard only by the pure in spirit. Sharov's seekers, like Dostoevsky's, spend their lives qualifying for the quest.

Sadko is an ecological folk legend; *A Life for the Tsar*, patriotic boilerplate. Sharov needs them both. But it is *Kitezh* that hovers over the novel as its moral topography – softening distinctions between resistance and acceptance, and between this world and the next. For the novel, transition to another world begins with Seryozha's disappearance in the northern bog. For the opera, it begins with Act Four. Only two of its heroes are still alive after the Mongol onslaught: the maiden Fevroniya (spirit of forgiveness) and the weak, corrupt drunkard Grishka, who betrayed his city to the Mongols. His guilt, which drives him mad, permeates the last Act, just as Father Nikodim's confession of collaboration with the Services

AFTERWORD

and the martyrdom of the Christianised shaman Noan Yefimov darken the final parts of the novel. As Fevroniya prepares for death, two heavenly creatures appear to her. The first is Alkonost, Bird of Mercy, who points out her bridegroom, fallen in battle but now walking toward her across the bog. The second is Sirin, Bird of Joy, who brings immortality. The people of Kitezh, heavy human matter that has sunk to its salvation rather than risen to it, celebrate the delayed marriage procession to a refrain of pealing bells. Recall the Paris Opéra scene described in the novel's opening pages, that 'endless column' of underwater officers tethered, like Seryozha, to the bottom of the lake with stones. Gazing at the stage, Sharov assures us: 'These figures are alive'. In the final scene of the novel, when narration moves into the blazing present tense of eternal time, we are aware that everyone can now see, recognise, and rejoice. *Be as Children* becomes a progression of musical genres, or transformational performances: from patriotic mythological opera during a world war to Lenin's death wail (a comic bit of commissioned folk art at the novel's epicentre) to Dusya's final passage and Irina's deliverance. We are returned to those opening operatic sites, but now reworked as a liturgy.

Thus can one tease out a musical infrastructure. Even more complexly choreographed however is the interweave of life-stories, the novel's biographical inside. *Be as Children* is woven of three main strands, each with its own hero. The first is Yevlampy Peregudov, outlaw and Christian seeker turned apostle to the Enets nation. The second is Vladimir Lenin, founding Bolshevik, increasingly paralysed by strokes in his final two years, whom (in Sharov's fantasia) the Lord summons to renounce Party and Revolution and redeem Russia with a children's crusade. The third is the narrator's godmother Yevdokiya Mukhanova, known as Dusya, a protectress, seer, and holy fool. Dusya opens and closes the novel, as if enclosing the other two strands in her womb. At first the strands seem to intersect by accident. The Enets nation contributes a brigade to Lenin's Jerusalem campaign, although for its own reasons. Father Nikodim, Dusya's confessor, happens to be teaching geography in the Taganrog children's home at the time of its spectacular breakout. The same Nikodim turns up in Khabarovsk, rescuing Dusya and hiring her to gather street languages for Lenin's data-bank on the untended. By the time we learn that Nikodim has spent several months in Tomsk with an Enets housemate, a descendant of the shaman killed by Peregudov, we can no longer trust in coincidence. All three strands share certain *Kitezh* themes: Orthodox faith battling heathens (be they shamanist or Marxist-atheist), a 'Grishka' figure consumed by guilt, and collective salvation attainable by moving across water toward blessedness. Taken together, these strands instruct us in the wisdom, and helpless horror, of being 'as a child'.

Two transcendent images of the child bookend the novel. The first is Irina's Sashenka, dead at age four and thus forever immaculate; the last is Seryozha's series of icons of Jesus, who is always portrayed as a child, without sin but already all-knowing. The children in Orthodox icons look backward as well as forward, immune to both seduction and surprise. In Sharov's novels, this sort of wisdom can accrue not only to 'displaced persons' but also to whole displaced peoples, as it does in the work of Andrei Platonov, which Sharov so admired; but indigenous 'childlike' nations like the Enets are safe only as long as they live innocently in their own space and time. Once colonised by the mainland, they grow up, are corrupted, and lost. In between the little girl Sashenka and the icon-painter Seryozha – both parts of Dusya's all-embracing strand – are Ishchenko's twelve lectures on Lenin to the pupils of Ulyanovsk Special School No. 3.

In this central narrative, children come down to earth and are instrumentalised, first gently and progressively, then with accelerating ferocity. Lenin never liked babies (bourgeois family life is the death knell for revolution), and he and Krupskaya, for whatever reason, have none of their own. But Lenin's two strokes and encroaching second childhood combine to persuade him that children, orphaned or 'special', would be more reliable participants in the communist project than the polluted adults of the proletariat. The historical prototype for Lenin's project is the semi-apocryphal Children's Crusade of 1212, from the same century as the Mongol attack on the city of Kitezh but in more southern parts of Europe. Two charismatic teenagers, inspired by visions, recruit thousands of children for a campaign to convert Muslims in the Holy Land to Christianity. It was to be peaceful; the seas were expected to part so the crusaders could walk to Jerusalem. Most of these children, it appears, perished in shipwrecks or were sold into slavery.

There is also a more contemporary source, wholly non-fictive, for Lenin's vision of an underage army mobilised to a sacred cause: the flourishing of a biopsychosocial 'science of the child' during the first decade of Bolshevik power.[4] This

---

[4] Andy Byford, *Science of the Child in Late Imperial and Early Soviet Russia.* Oxford University Press, 2020, ch. 5.

Afterword

revolutionary paedology combined rehabilitation for trauma (an urgent social need) with the utopian intent to create, out of abandoned human material, new Marxist norms for health and intelligence that would govern the New Soviet Person. Holistic therapies adjusted to the individual child were practised alongside ideological conditioning of a most aggressive sort. Minors with a criminal past were not to be incarcerated but sent to special school-sanatoriums staffed with nutritionists, psychiatrists and master teachers. Pupils were referred to not as juvenile offenders but as 'morally defective' or 'ethically backward'. According to Marxist sociology, external material conditions had caused the defect, thus a change of condition could heal it.

The 'defects' of deaf and blind children were of another order, of course – but the same policy held sway. The best-known educator in this area is the developmental psychologist Lev Vygotsky (1896-1934), who insisted that 'handicap' is a concept thrust on a 'special' child by the social environment. Every child is whole to itself from birth. Children cannot regret the absence of a sensory organ they never knew, but they will always sense when value is bestowed on them by others. Revere the blind child as a prophet, a seer, and there will be no sense of inferiority or disablement. Doctor Demidov, who brings his deaf-blind twelve-year-old ward to meet Lenin in Ishchenko's Lesson Two, is a participant in this robust pedagogical initiative. Lenin, with each successive stroke, is growing downward to be worthy of it.

A more militarised, less sentimental version of child reclamation was put into practice in Ukraine by the educational reformer Anton Makarenko (1888-1939). Although criticised

AFTERWORD

for its authoritarian methods, this model too was partially adopted in Bolshevik policy. In the 1920s, Makarenko directed first the Gorky Colony and later the Dzerzhinsky Commune for orphaned and homeless children. The strongest among these children were skilled at stealing, begging, and prostitution; they had neither talent nor interest in any other work. Organising these delinquents with iron discipline into brigades led by their own commanders, Makarenko took hundreds of young, blasted lives and 're-forged' them, often with spectacular success, to serve the technological and behavioural ideals of the Revolution. By the end of Ishchenko's Lesson Seven it is clear that Lenin too is offering his crusade of the untended, with its own security agency (Cheka) and personal language of touch, smell, and vibration, as a type of re-forging. But the goal this time is not to realise the Revolution but to do penance for it, by dissolving in anarchy and sacrificing itself utterly.

Sharov's attitude toward these odd twists of his fictional plot (Lenin, a principled atheist, turning toward God, or cultivating the company of 'special' children) is not easy to decipher. Irony is surely present, given Sharov's oft-repeated conviction that simplification, whether through revolution or by refusing to grow up (or both), is a temptation that we must resist. But in this novel, irony is more often lyrical than bitter. A madcap imagination is applied to the historical record, but so subtly does Sharov respect certain documented details and so inscrutable are his subjects that we usually come out of these altered episodes feeling that we've learned something true. A favourite site for Sharov is the psychiatric ward, a catch-all meeting ground for epileptics, amnesiacs, the disabled and politically suspect. These inmates have ample time to tell

AFTERWORD

stories, as well as legitimate reasons for mixing them up. It is striking though, how often the transition points between story-strands (the novel's informational hub, as it were) relies on a sober-minded academic setting or device: ethnographic fieldwork, a dissertation, the public defence of a legal thesis, classroom lectures where the narrator, now turned district school inspector, is listening in. Here Sharov shows his hand as a scholar, lovingly working through bits of the certified past. Some facts need a nudge, others a new angle (supplied by the invention of 'Krupskaya's diary'), but a great deal corroborates the published record. Sharov's accounts of ritual practices in Far North shamanism (spells, ecstatic fits, clothing, musical instruments), all components of their 'cosmic-materialistic' worldview, can be traced to ethnographic studies published in the 1920s.[5] The thieves' song used by Sharov's serial murderer Sergei Paranyanov in his leniency plea from a Tomsk prison to the Moscow authorities is an actual document published in Irkutsk in 1926.[6] The first V. P. Kashchenko School-Sanatorium for Defective Children opened in Moscow in 1908, and from

---

[5] Accounts from 1925 of possession by shamanistic spirits may be found in G. V. Ksenofontov, *Shamanizm. Izbrannye trudy (Publikatsii 1928-1929 gg.)*, repr. 'Sever-Yug', 1992, p. 169 ff., which also contains documents on the blend of shamanism and Christianity professed by the Enets Noan Yefimov to his cellmates in Tomsk. For a prescient overlap of novelist with his translator on these indigenous Arctic peoples, once aggressively Russianised and now resisting, see Oliver Ready's account of his visit to the Russian Far North (long before Sharov published his novel), 'Sledge ride to seven heavens of Nenets', *New Statesman,* 4th December 2000 (https://www.newstatesman.com/node/193802). Ready quotes the view of his guide, the Nenets writer Anna Nerkagi, that her small reindeer-herding nation viewed foreign visitors 'as children with nothing better to do'.

[6] Khandzinskii, N. 'Blatnaya poeziya', in *Sibirskaya zhivaya starina*. Irkutsk, 1926. Vyp. 1 (5), p. 26.

Afterword

1920 to 1924 Kashchenko (brother of psychiatrist Pyotr) served as rector for its successor, the Pedagogical Institute of Child Defectiveness (Krupskaya was their ardent patron). The historian Christopher Read, drawing on post-Soviet revelations about Lenin's piteous physical condition from 1922 on, notes that the Central Committee, alert to their leader's erratic behaviour, was 'at pains to control Lenin politically', fearful that 'he still retained sufficient prestige to embarrass them' yet denying him access to the cyanide capsule he kept in reserve.[7] Humiliating sickroom scenes, laced with rage, define the texture of the Lenin strand. In his biography, Read remarks that the final disabled months at Gorky did offer Lenin some of his old pleasures: excursions into the forest (albeit now by wheelchair), mushroom hunting, sleigh rides. And 'the presence of children delighted him'.

The Lenin wail, commissioned by the Latvian Brigade in Ishchenko's Lesson Twelve, is also based on an authentic text. A ritualistic 'funeral lament for Lenin' was recorded in Irkutsk in November 1924, a scarce half-year after Lenin's death, composed by a sixteen-year-old peasant girl at the suggestion of local Komsomol authorities.[8] The Revolution that had begun as a Western ideological import in the capitals was mythologised as it moved East, becoming ever more colourful, malleable, childlike, folklore-like, shamanistic. Does this migration (and the fact that this lament for the deceased Bolshevik leader was encouraged by local party officials) make it 'fakelore'? The question is complex. The folklorist Alexander Panchenko, who

---

[7] Christopher Read, *Lenin.* Routledge, 2005, pp. 280-81.
[8] Alexander A. Panchenko, 'The Cult of Lenin and "Soviet Folklore",' *Folklorica*, 10.1 (2005): especially 22-23.

has studied the Lenin Cult, distinguishes between authentic Lenin myths assimilated to traditional Eurasian archetypes of popular leaders (predominantly the sly, charismatic rebel or trickster), and the more pious, heroic, sanitized tales centrally distributed from Moscow. Most researchers agree that the mummification of Lenin in a Mausoleum on Red Square was not only to preserve him 'as he really looked', a visual aid in the coming world revolution, but also reflected the widely held conviction that Lenin was omniscient, potentially immortal, and with the help of science might be raised from the dead. This faith was not faked.

So finally, the Dusya strand. It mingles holy Kitezh and unholy collaboration, thirst for belief and repression of religious practice. Dusya is the person closest to the narrator, who is her godson. Like the other two focal narratives, hers contains humour in unexpected places. Her highborn mother-in-law engages in divination by porridge throughout the chaos and famine of the Civil War. Dusya's virtuosic manipulation of her two rival confessors Amvrosy and Nikodim (both of them voyeurs on her sensual life) is comically predictable. Remember that Dusya is a natural-born actress. The reader never learns the precise nature, depth, or cause of her guilt, compounded of sexual appetite, maternal neglect, spousal indifference, and what can only be called an addiction to the idea of original sin. No amount of confession releases her from it, not even her tonsure in 1927, because her habits of self-torment and erotic teasing are so exquisitely harmonised. The pathos in these sections belongs not so much to Dusya herself as to the tribulations of her men – husband, surviving son, and the duo of jealous 'shepherds' of her soul, Amvrosy

AFTERWORD

and Nikodim. Although a mediocre seeker, Dusya proves to be a hard worker, loyal listener and good reader. At Nikodim's in Khabarovsk she is directed to the memoirs of Viktor Shklovsky (the Russian Formalist critic who fought on various fronts and sides in the Great War); she finds there, surely by design, a description of her husband's death by detonation. Dusya is not only an actress, she is also a seer. The inner structure of her strand is already tilting, like Dostoevsky's *Crime and Punishment,* toward a detective novel that can be resolved only by epiphany and otherworldly reconciliation. If the ideological struggle in the Peregudov strand is shamanism versus Christianity, and in the Lenin strand is a humanistic 'science of the child' co-opted to redeem Russia, then Dusya's story unfolds against the fate of the Russian Orthodox Church.

Sharov was a close student of Russian schismatics and sectarians. The Great Church Schism of 1667 under Tsar Alexis, which split Orthodox Christian believers into two mutually anathematising populations, is a foundational event in his novel *The Rehearsals*. For Sharov as historian, that seventeenth-century cataclysm was a defining factor in the Bolshevik victory over three centuries later and has never been healed. Like the Great Schism, the twentieth-century reform movement, called 'Renovationism' or the 'Living Church', began as an attempt to modernise canonised Church practices. Some argued for the right of bishops to marry (although parish priests, the so-called 'white clergy', were expected to marry, the 'black clergy' of hieromonks and bishops was celibate); others called for the translation of the liturgy from Old Church Slavonic into modern Russian, and almost all reformers sought more autonomy from the state. Recall Dusya during the Civil

AFTERWORD

War, in provincial Gustinino with two small children, trying to maintain contact with her confessor Father Amvrosy, already thrice arrested. She despairs of knowing whether Tikhon, who has been serving as Patriarch since 1917, or the breakaway Renovationist movement is the true faith. In fact, all churchmen will soon be compromised, for the Bolshevik reaction to this confusion in its enemy's ranks was the rational one of divide and conquer. The government's response was threefold: carrot-and-stick promises to both sides (rarely honoured), a campaign of random but unrelenting terror against clerics, and immediate infiltration of both rival hierarchies by the secret police.

As an historian, Sharov had a keen sense of the background tensions motivating political action – and as a novelist, he chose his focal years with care. In 1922, after the Bolsheviks won the Civil War, Patriarch Tikhon was placed under house arrest. Left-leaning reformist clerics staged an insiderly coup in May of that year, seizing Church property and preaching cooperation with the new regime in the spirit of 'Christian socialism'. The Renovationist schism was at its peak then, as Lenin began dying and the untended were being mobilised. The imprisoned Tikhon, with two years left to live, denounced the rebel organisation as 'without grace'. Well into the 1930s, these two parallel churches continued to declare each other heretical, with Soviet power bribing, spying on, and selectively liquidating both. In 1927, the year Dusya takes the veil, the official Church pledged absolute loyalty to the Soviet Union, hoping in return for a cessation of persecution. That did not happen of course – although the Renovationists lost their bargaining power and soon dwindled away. This Church backstory is the third random slaughter we need to grasp, after

AFTERWORD

the disintegration of the Enets nation and the disappeared crusade of the untended, in order to experience these three strands as a single texture. The participants are growing old and exhausted, their stories have lost momentum. The revelations of the dying Father Nikodim – Chekist, priest, and now an intimate of the narrator – are the final solvent. Events that earlier had seemed like coincidence, predestination, or twists of fate, turn out to be simply the omnipresent workings of state power, the Services beneath everything.

The strands then, become gradually translucent. Sharov arranges his novels so that successive layers of story emerge through narrators linked less by shared action than by earlier tellings. But these tellings are not simple flashbacks. Readers of Sharov's third novel, *Before & During*, might remember Semyon Kochin, the narrator's childhood neighbour, who pasted scraps of his novel-in-progress to the window-pane because a novel, he insisted, was a living thing, 'photosynthetic, no less than a plant', and each time the scraps were deciphered they came out differently: 'no two explanations were ever the same, nor did one ever contradict another'.[9] The same could be said of this 400-page parable that every reader will hold up differently to the light. For all the killing fields and human waste of the larger picture, the separate filaments in a Sharov novel end up illuminating one another in incongruously tender ways.

Consider the fate of Dusya's brother Pasha. The Bolsheviks feared a counter-revolution, the reader expected a political murder along the lines of Dostoevsky's *Demons*, but nothing of the kind, says Nikodim: this gentle young man had been

---

[9] Vladimir Sharov, *Before & During*. Trans. Oliver Ready. Dedalus, 2014, p. 58.

organising officers and Cossacks for a Holy Cross procession (the novel's penultimate one) from Siberia to Moscow, to beg the Lord's forgiveness for all the shooting. Pasha could not be saved from typhus. Nikodim could not be saved from further punishment. But he has given up trying to save anything but a bit of his own self-respect. Nikodim now takes his truth from a captain he met in a transit prison: 'Faith pushes its way up through human weakness'.

***

In an afterword to a collection of essays by Sharov published in Moscow during the year of his death, 2018, his nine novels are thus described by the Russian-American cultural theorist Mikhail Epstein: 'A mix of history and phantasmagoria, of God-seeking and psychopathy, an experiment in penetrating the collective unconscious of Russian history [...] Sharov 'felt history organically, as an extension of his own "I"'.[10] Two years earlier, in 2016, Epstein's insight had been confirmed by Sharov himself. During one long summer afternoon, he had been interviewed by the journalist Olga Andreyeva.[11] She asked him: 'Who is the historian? A scholar or an artist?' Sharov answered elliptically that scholars and artists had entirely

---

[10] Mikhail Epstein, 'Letopis' Svyashchennoi istorii (vmesto poslesloviya)' [A chronicle of Sacred history (in place of an afterword)], Vladimir Sharov, *Perekrestnoe opylenie (vremya, mesto, liudi)* [Cross-pollination (time, place, people)]. Sbornik esse. Arsis Books, Moscow, 2018, p. 278.

[11] Olga Andreyeva, 'Zhizn' – eto tol'ko ispytatel'nyi srok'. Pisatel' Vladimir Sharov o literature i smysle russkoi istorii ['All life long we're on probation'. The writer Vladimir Sharov on literature and the meaning of Russian history]. https://gorky.media/context/zhizn-eto-tolko-ispytatelnyj-srok/ 20th August 2018.

different languages. History 'terribly wanted to become a science', to 'turn all words into terms'. But everything in reality was so endlessly complicated, so constantly in motion. Only literary words were suitable to this complexity, since they are 'infinitely imprecise, with infinitely multiple meanings'. He then remarked that he had two basic ideas about life. 'There's no doubt that the world is a sort of madhouse. For my whole life I have been escaping this madhouse, and it is catching up with me. There's nowhere to hide. That's the first idea. And the second: that a huge part of our life and culture has been entirely lost, its roots chopped out. But it's possible to restore it somewhat. Not fully, but at least a bit of it. If one doesn't take this task on, if one restores nothing and leaves everything as it is, then history turns into complete delirium, understood by no one and explained by nothing'. Here the novelist would appear to imitate his own Dusya, wandering sinner and seeker of roots. By practising prose fiction, Sharov assured Andreyeva, he could at least figure some things out for himself. 'I would not have taken upon myself, as a historian, to set out all that mobility. [...] History is uncovered only in pieces, bit by bit. Before each new novel, I have very depressed periods when I'm empty. I sustain myself by occasionally writing historical essays. And then life begins again in a novel'.

Caryl Emerson is A. Watson Armour III University Professor of Slavic Languages and Literatures, Emeritus, at Princeton University.